Also by Norman Bogner from Tom Doherty Associates

To Die in Provence

NORMAN BOGNER

7th AVENUE

A TOM DOHERTY ASSOCIATES BOOK
NEW YORK

This is a work of fiction. All the characters and events portrayed in this book are either products of the author's imagination or are used fictitiously.

SEVENTH AVENUE

Copyright © 1966 by Norman Bogner

A Forge Book
Published by Tom Doherty Associates, Inc.
175 Fifth Avenue
New York, NY 10010

Forge® is a registered trademark of Tom Doherty Associates, Inc.

ISBN: 0-812-57570-9

First Forge edition: October 1998

Printed in the United States of America

0 9 8 7 6 5 4 3 2 1

For my
MOTHER, FATHER, LEAH,
and
GERALD MASSEY

Contents

The harvest is past, the summer is ended, and we are not saved.

JEREMIAH

I

SPRING
BLOOD
WATER

1

The sound of cars coming off the Williamsburg Bridge was deafening in the late, icy December night, even though Jay lived several streets away from the main arterial road. The wind from the East River, which had ice blocks roaming about unpredictably like fugitives on the move, blew a hollow, raucous note when it collided against the damp splintery wooden structure that he lived in with his family. The walls of the apartment, painted a variation of what once might have been sea-green by a still unrepentant landlord forced into this diabolical act of folly by a housing inspector, concealed latent bubbles of condensation which created a sense of illusory movement if you stared at it for any length of time. To counteract the gloom of the interior, Jay glared out at the slate black, moonless sky, full of swarming, snow-bearing clouds which moved relentlessly lower before releasing their burden on the millions of already frozen, unprepared New Yorkers who were making do with what woolens they had preserved from the late twenties. As Jay had been raised on the torments of a Lvov-incarcerated winter, somehow lived through without adequate food or clothing, the prospect of New York feebly imitating the tundra did not daunt him completely.

Restaurants and movie houses provided enough heat if you had the nerve to exchange angry sneers with waiters who tried to get you to order more than toast and coffee by flapping the menu in your face and continually changing clean ashtrays, or the ushers, that hopeless tribe of casual labor who in government statistics were not even designated as "unskilled" but for official purposes occupied some nether region of nonexistence, who flashed their lights in your face when it became too familiar, and it would after five performances; they carried on a wordless, outraged inquisition into your activities: pervert or vagrant? Fame carries its own form of danger, and Jay, handsome enough to implant his face in the memory of most people, was something of a celebrity on the East Side, inasmuch as ushers and lame waiters recognized him immediately and put out sudden alerts for the owner when he slumped down on a chair or dangled his legs on an armrest. For all of them he represented some unclassifiable hybrid being: a cross between a thug and a gigolo. He was tall with broadish shoulders, large fisted, severe in expression, and he always had some money on him. What he did, if one can describe total passivity as doing, was not illegal or immoral. He became part of the furnishings of every establishment within a square mile of the bridge, but unfortunately no one was permitted to claim him as a permanent fixture and therefore enter him on tax returns under the heading of depreciation of machinery. He was unclaimable because he was a condition rather than an object.

He got up from his seat by the window, nodded to his father, who was going through the employment section of the evening paper with his magnifying glass in search of a position that was less tiring than waiting and required less skill than ushering, and draped three scarves round his neck, before entering an old army jacket which his grandfather had cast off when Jay was still an infant and was one of the possessions he had brought with him from Poland on the long haul via Rotterdam to New York, six years previously.

Jay walked down Rivington Street, studying the long line of brick-fronted houses which, like arthritic old men, leaned forward in a line that had never been straight. Gnarled wood and crumbling gray brick surrounded him; also there were cooking smells that hung on the frosted air, emanating from kitchens where women tried all of the permutations that potatoes, cabbage, turnips, and soup greens allowed. As the streets were almost warmer than the houses, many of the front doors stood ajar, flapping against wall cavities whenever a gust of wind came up from the river. The mile of the East Side that Jay roamed resembled nothing so much as a peculiarly recurring nightmare which he was forever trying to banish from his mind. Several thousand schemes occurred to him daily, but they all required a certain amount of capital, and as his salary, what there was of it, went on helping to keep his parents, his one brother, and his sisters, the very concept of capital, money in the bank, belonged to fantasy.

Jay's trade, if it could be called that, came under the heading of electrician. What he had learned, he had learned badly in Vienna under the tutelage of a half-demented stepcousin of his father's brother-in-law who gave his days to dodging creditors, and his nights to drinking slivovitz smuggled in from Yugoslavia, and to the inspection of new faces in all of Vienna's eighty-seven brothels. One day Uncle Klotz, as he was called, paused in front of a vellum-skinned freckled redhead, a recent arrival, aged sixteen, from an unidentified Hanseatic city, and attempted to effect her escape. Amid the chaos of the ensuing scramble, Uncle Klotz succeeded to a heroism which even as a man of action he had not been aware of and wounded the owner of the enterprise in the right buttock with a letter-opener. His gallantry was rewarded, however, and he fled with the unnamed inmate—they had not yet been introduced—to the lofty heights of Kalenberg, leaving a poorly outfitted work-shop, thirty-one disgruntled workmen who had not been paid for weeks, and invoices and receipts that might have stymied a computer; to Jay, Klotz's unwitting heir apparent, thrice re-moved on his brother's side, gangling, confused, inexperi-enced, with no aptitude whatever for electricals, fell the task of reorganization. In a broken scribble, whose characters were markedly oriental, Jay wrote off to Lvov, attempting to explain the situation. As his father had paid his apprentice fees for one year, he glanced briefly at Jay's illegible hen tracks and de-cided that they embodied a demand for money, he wrote back immediately, and with astonishing concision, "No money available."

Left to his own devices, Jay managed, by what sleight of hand it is difficult to describe, to procure a contract to service the electricals in a group of Vienna's brothels. Not unlike a dying man, the business gave signs of a mysterious resurgence of glowing health before the final gasp whisked it into the hands of screaming creditors, befuddled tax officials, and semistarved workmen, blaming its demise on the outlaw electrician who was taking his pleasures in a remote *Gasthof* on the fringe of a wood beyond Kalenberg, and was armed with an American flintlock and hidden under a honey-colored growth of hair which with his snarling high-pitched laugh revealed a marked similarity to a hunted wolf. The end of Klotz's Electricals can be directly traced to the wiring contract Jay fulfilled for a band of gypsies who were running a fair on the outskirts of Vienna; a short-circuit left half of the city in total darkness for nine hours, interrupted an international chess tournament, and provided virtually military assistance to a band of thieves who systematically looted all but a stationer's shop in the district of Floridsdorf. In the midst of this squalling confusion, Jay, disguised as a son of a Turkish Army General, hurriedly departed for Lvov on a coal train, carrying with him several hundred thousand schillings' worth of counterfeit securities which Klotz in his own flight to safety had abandoned, and two hundred schillings in currency which the gypsies had advanced him. Upon his arrival in Lvov, his father, a man of few but direct words, after a great deal of arm-flailing and half-swallowed oaths which fell like snakes' heads from a mouth whose lips barely moved, demanded by way of compensation and for demi-pension in the family homestead Jay's entire capital. With great reluctance Jay handed the money over because it was pointless to argue with the Veteran, a nickname given to his father by the townspeople in remembrance of the two fingers he had blown off in order to avoid conscription in the last Russian-Polish velitation.

All this seemed very remote now, as Jay wandered the streets wide-eyed, gazing into warm, well-lit restaurants where diners pushed away half-finished steaks, chicken legs, nibbled duck breasts. He gasped at the windows, his heart beating at an abnormal speed, palpitations in his temples—the legacy of hunger pangs, and the knowledge that physical relief lay behind two inches of plate glass. The food was a bare thirty feet away and was not an optical illusion but something immediate and tangible. He had been removed by force no less than eleven times from Gluckstern's restaurant, which represented to him the crazy pinnacle of gastronomic delight. He moved swiftly away when the headwaiter returned his stare with a threatening gesture; the memory of his last expulsion still rankled. The headwaiter, catching sight of him, had furtively whispered to an over-sized busboy who had then approached Jay menacingly, seized him by the collar and hurled him through the open door into the gutter, all this at the moment when Jay's visit was just bearing fruit. For Jay had been caught redhanded with a half-gnawed lamb chop which he had slipped into his shirt pocket just as the man whose dinner it was, in fact, returned to the table, and mistaking Jay's guilty manner for a theft of a different kind, shouted to the headwaiter that his cigarettes were missing and pointed a finger at Jay.

There were two hours to go before Jay's shift began at the Washington Market, and he wondered how to kill the time, how best to improvise some activity that would take his mind off food. The insistent, nagging pain in his stomach was fertilized by the biting cold and the slow but steady gray jigsaw snowflakes which had already started to stick on the sidewalks. The shift would be more difficult than usual this evening because there would be the danger of slipping, and when a man fell with a hundredweight sack of onions on his shoulders he might be out of work for as long as a month. He entered a small diner on Delancey Street and sat down at the counter. A thin man with gnarled protruding veins and fiery red hands walked, or rather drifted, over to him. The man wore a white apron and a white starched topless crown which, when he bent over, revealed an area of hairless scalp. His tired, drawn face, a face that had almost never come into contact with the sun, was mute testimony to the fact that he belonged to that antlike army of night-shift workers whose meaningless existence never leaves a mark on time, and who are discharged by the body of society like some noxious product.

"Hi, Jay," the man said.

"The usual."

"One white draw and a pair down," the man said to himself

in the jargon of the professional counterman, as he slipped
some bread in the toaster.

"Christ, it's so goddamned cold," Jay snapped.

"Like the heart of my mother-in-law," the man said without smiling. "You working tonight?"

"Do I have a choice, Immie? So long as I don't break a
leg or get a killer, I work."

"You're a smart boy. It's stupid to knock your brains out."

"It's stupid to eat too, but I have to."

Conspiratorially Immie moved over to Jay. His breath was
bitter, compounded of cigarettes and an acidic stomach, and
Jay drew away slowly.

"I know a guy who wants a runner," Immie said.

"Bookie or numbers?"

"Numbers in Chinatown." Jay lifted his eyes skeptically.
"So, what're you scared or something? A big guy like you
can handle himself."

"I saw what they did to that Mick. Ran into him at the pool
room. He's got a career as Frankenstein with his face now."

"If you want to make money you gotta take chances. And
anyway he was a welsher."

"That's their story, not his."

"Well, think it over, huh? When you're dragging potatoes
and freezing your ass off for a sawbuck a week, you might
change your mind. The bread's not bad—half a yard a week,
plus commission . . ."

"Plus what you can steal?"

"Unhealthy . . . unhealthy thought," Immie said, his eyes
brightening angrily. "That's a one-way ticket to Canarsie.
They give Lepke a contract when a runner makes himself a
partner."

"Thanks for thinking of me," Jay said.

"Sure. I just thought—"

"Yeah, fine."

Jay watched the minutes on the clock tick by. He still had
an hour to go and weighed Immie's proposition in his mind.
An active criminal career offended his commercial instincts.
A number of young men who lived on his street had found

security and respectability in petty crime—protection, collecting, thuggery, fencing, drug-peddling—for respectability was
directly related to the amount of money a man brought home,
and by these standards Jay could only be called an outcast.
The visions he cultivated for himself centered on an undefined
activity that came under the heading of big business. A chubby
hand touched his shoulder and Jay looked up into the face of
Barney Green.

"Dangerous to sit alone counting your money," Barney
said, whisking the snow from the collar of his camel's hair
coat. "After a while you start to talk to yourself, and then
you're certified one hundred percent crazy and they take you
away and you live happily ever after in Rockland State. But
you eat regular. Not one dissatisfied customer."

"What've you got to feel good about?" Jay said sullenly.

"I'm working. Some idiot wants me to emcee his wedding
and I get a Finski for making a public nuisance of myself.
Want to come?"

"I'm working."

"So? Go sick for tonight. I got a waiter's jacket and a tie
you can wear and you can eat till it's coming out of your
ears."

Jay's stomach began to perform a silent ballet.

"Yeah, great. It's a deal."

"Ever see such a boy, Immie? Two things he can't say no
to, food and gash, but I love 'im."

A cheerless hall, in which dankness, the effluvium of an un-
ventilated kitchen, and the stomping of hundreds of pairs of
feet reconstructing the steps of an off-key foxtrot, provided
the scene for the first hot meal Jay was about to have in three
weeks. The hall was above Moszynski's restaurant on Second
Avenue, the cuisine was "exquisitely and exclusively Moszynski's own."

"Here's the men's room," Barney said, handing Jay a tan
linen jacket, four sizes too large for him, and a black bow tie
which had recently come into contact with green-pea soup. A
minute later Jay emerged from the improvised changing room

transformed; when he moved he resembled a man fighting a choppy sea.

"Beautiful." Barney beamed at him. "Who designs your clothes?"

"Omar, the tentmaker."

"Don't get caught in a draught, or you'll fly away."

Jay extended his arms: "Look, I'm floating. Do you think anyone'll say anything?"

"Course not. They'll be stunned into silence. If the bride's father gives you a funny look, grab a few glasses." He picked up a napkin from a table and handed it to Jay. "Here, carry this over your arm. Christ, it really suits you. You've got a career . . . a future, my boy."

Jay disappeared into the crowd around the hors d'oeuvres table. He picked up a plate, wiped a speck of dust off it with his napkin, and then seizing a serving utensil, began to heap everything within a radius of six feet onto his plate. No one in the buoyant crowd of eating, talking, dancing guests noticed him, until the bride, inadvertently reeling from a rather fiercely administered Kazatski whirl, crashed into him. Four minutes had elapsed since Jay had served himself, and fortunately for the bride, a double-chinned satin-bedizened slug of a woman with the prospect of a mustache before long, Jay's plate had been wiped clean.

"Gee, careful," Jay said.

"Oh, sorry. Hy gets all excited when he dances."

"Never mind. It's your night," Jay said with magnanimity, planting a resounding kiss on her sweaty forehead. "Congrats . . . success and long life—and to you too," he added, returning her to a tall, thin man, beardless and bespectacled, who gave him a Bugs Bunny smile. "You're a lucky man, Hy."

"Telling me!"

The stamp of approval having been given him by the bride and groom, Jay noticed the atmosphere of the guests warm considerably towards him as he approached the hors d'oeuvres table for a second encounter. Just as he was about to launch into the attack, a waiter, a real one, sharply tilted the serving dish away from him.

"Closed, Mister. No more eating till we serve dinner."

"When?"

"Few minutes . . . they're setting up the tables."

"But there's still some liver on—"

"Sorry, boss's orders."

The bastard's going to eat it himself, Jay thought.

"I'm the bride's cousin," Jay said.

"I don't care if you're the groom," the waiter said.

Can't bluff him, Jay decided.

"I'll have a word with Mr. M," Jay replied, using Moszynski's name in vain.

"It's M's orders I'm obeying."

Careful . . . careful.

"I have the pleasure in making the acquaintance of Mister—?" a white-haired man with two carnations stuffed into his lapel, wearing a double-breasted tuxedo that had been the rage of the Congress of Vienna and was a living advertisement for mothballs, addressed Jay.

"Er . . ."

Steel-rimmed spectacles were placed over watery blue eyes which blinked until they became accustomed to sight.

"Forgive me. How could I mistake a Ratkin? Pity your father couldn't come, but believe me I understand. I couldn't expect anybody, especially a relative on my wife's side, to get out of a sick bed."

Must've seen me eating and mentally added up the bill, Jay reflected.

"Grippe it was?"

"And bronchitis," Jay ventured. "He'll be in bed at least another week."

"Beautiful couple, no? He hasn't got too much class, but with a wife like my daughter . . . my little Esther, he'll learn, eh?"

"Can't miss—"

"I'm paying for the honeymoon. He's a student yet with the bar exam to take. Hasn't got a pot to piss in . . . but still a lovely boy, Hy. What's the good of talking . . . money can't buy everything . . ."

"Definitely."

"Oh, the honeymoon? They're driving over—I lent him my car—to my bungalow in Mount Freedom. Mountain air . . . s'wonderful. C'mon over and say hello to your Aunt Hennie," he said, indicating a berouged, besequined balloon at the end of the room.

Controlling his panic with an iron nerve that might even have impressed Hitler at Munich, Jay pulled his ears, stuck his tongue out, then clicked his teeth violently, hoping by this demonstration to simulate the symptoms of instant grippe.

"You're not well?"

"Grippe."

"Oh . . . well go over to the bar and tell him to give you a rock and rye. That'll kill those lousy germs."

Jay sidled over to the bar and glanced around apprehensively. Then, with sudden decision, he walked behind the bar.

"Okay, I'll take over," he told the barman.

"Yeah? On whose orders?"

"Mr. M's."

"Fine. There's another six bottles of Carstairs over there and remember what Mr. M says"—he pointed a long solemn finger at a brown bottle—"that no one and I mean no one can have any Canadian Club unless he's got a note from the bride's father." The bartender gave him a final scowl as if to enforce this point and was swallowed up in the crowd.

In order to test the efficacy of the mythical M's instructions, Jay immediately seized a glass, swished it around in some clean water—poverty had made him crankily fastidious—and poured himself a four-inch shot of the forbidden elixir which he mixed with ginger ale. He took a sip of the drink, fingered a lonely meatball; hummed in time to the music, which took a bit of doing, as the musicians were in the midst of a polyphonic conflict, and smiled glowingly at the guests. As he was about to repeat his previous action—the bottle in his right hand, perpendicular to the glass—a voice froze his arm, giving him the aspect of one of those timeless urchins trapped in a Hellenic frieze which depicted Dionysus at his pleasures.

"What are you doing?" asked a rather plump girl with a

moon-shaped face, long wavy hair with a hint of red, a warm naïve smile, and cat-green eyes. Under fire, Jay quickly assessed the situation: an easy hump.

"Ummmmmmm . . . pouring a drink."

"You don't work here."

That should have been a question, Jay reasoned.

"What makes you think—?"

"I've followed you since you came in."

Very definitely an easy hump, but where?

"You're not a relative . . ."

"Not a close one."

"And you *don't* work here," she said again.

"I'm an assistant."

"Relative or bartender?"

"Both . . . have a drink."

She nodded . . . thank God. Jay lifted the bottle of Carstairs.

"C.C., please."

"Got a note from Mister—?"

"Berkowitz, that's the bride's father for your information. Neither have you."

He placed the bottle of whiskey recklessly on the top of the bar and chucked the girl under the chin. Then suddenly he spied Berkowitz wagging a threatening fist at him from across the room—he was trapped between Aunt Hennie and some ancient matriarch. He performed a strange little mime, his fist jerkily moving to his mouth, until it occurred to Jay that he had been using the wrong bottle.

"You better have the other rye, or he'll be over in a minute with the sheriff."

"Okay . . . but when he's not looking switch bottles."

"Sold."

"My name's Rhoda Gold."

"Congratulations."

"No, no kidding."

"I believe you. You've had your drink so—"

"What's your name? Honest, I won't tell anybody."

"Jay Blackman. And you can shout it from the rooftops."

"I live in Borough Park."

"I'll pin a medal on you."

"Gee, you're really a smart aleck, aren't you?"

"Are you asking me, or telling me?"

"Aw, c'mon, be nice. You've got a nice face."

"I wish I could say the same about you."

"Why are you this way? Actually I'm sure you're very kind. Do I scare you?"

"I came for a free meal. So far I've had only hors d'oeuvres, two drinks, a kiss from the bride, which I could've lived without, a discussion with Mr. Berkowitz about the fact that the groom, Hy Schmuck, is a nothing law student, and *no* hot food. Conversation I get, but roast chicken I'd prefer. Answer your question?"

"They'll serve dinner after the emcee does his act."

"So I've been promised . . . by millions."

"Do you have a job?"

"Why?"

"I just wondered . . . that jacket isn't yours."

"That's the nicest thing anybody ever said to me." Jay laughed.

"So I broke the ice? You're human," Rhoda said, placing her hand on top of Jay's. "You can't be married, with that mouth."

"My mother tells me the same story."

"I'd like to meet her, she sounds like a clever woman."

The lights darkened in the hall, giving it the atmosphere of a cavern where a Black Mass was about to begin. A feeble spotlight, pregnant with dust motes, illuminated the stocky figure of Barney Green.

"Evening folks . . . it's a pleasure to be . . ."—he removed a card from his breast pocket and glanced at it—"to be at Maison Moszynski."

A heckler shouted:"Shaddup."

"If that gentleman would be good enough to take a bow." The man stood. "Sir, if I were you I'd lance that pimple growing between your shoulders." The crowd laughed. "Thank you, thank you, ladies and germs. Any more comedians in the audience without a license are welcome to try their hands. No takers? Good. Y'know, I don't have to do this for a living, but I'm too nervous to steal. Please don't applaud, you'll interrupt the bride and groom . . . Ha-Ha. Haven't had so many laughs since my mother-in-law got her tittie caught in the car door."

A swarthy dark little man, just above five feet with piercing angry eyes, and elevated shoes, appeared at the doorway—the legendary M.

"Evening, Mr. M," Barney said. "Taking five minutes off from your chopped liver?"

Even Jay laughed. Most of Barney's persiflage was vintage East Side—heard in every bar, poolroom, and candy store from Delancey Street to Williamsburg.

". . . So this Mr. Ginsberg and his wife decided to go to Monticello for their twenty-fifth wedding anniversary. Ginsberg gave her a few dollars to buy herself a new dress and to get rid of her for a few hours so that he could *operate*." Squelched titters from some pseudo Ginsbergs in the audience. "I mean, after six hours on the Derma Road, listening to his wife's stories about operations—not to mention her face, how much can a man take? He strolled down the street and a gorgeous redhead comes up to him, looks him up and down and says: 'Five dollars.' Ginsberg looks her up and down and says: 'Not a penny over two dollars.' He's a dress manufacturer. The girl turns up her nose and walks away. The same evening Ginsberg gives the Missus an airing. They walk down the main street, look in all the shops and the Missus has a new dress on, a new bag she's carrying. Frankly she looks fifty. Suddenly out of the shadows comes this gorgeous redhead and pointing a finger at Ginsberg's Missus says: 'That's what you get for two dollars.' "

"He's pretty cute," Rhoda said to Jay who had moved in front of the bar when he spied M.

"I've heard it before. Not bad."

Barney was winding up his act with a song, and now it was the musicians' turn. The trio of men on stage with him, to judge by their instruments, rather than the soporific, practically unconscious expressions on their faces, were an accordionist, drummer, and clarinetist, and called themselves the Murray Meltzer Minstrels. Meltzer, the clarinetist, also sang, when not in a coma. Barney, realizing that he was an obvious foil, woke him from his customary stupor, and pulled him into the spotlight. Six thousand weddings and bar mitzvahs were written, like the tail end of a stillborn epic, on his face.

"Do you play requests?" Barney asked.

Astonished by the stupidity of the question, Meltzer raised a swollen lip and said:

"Course we do. What're you, a crazy?"

"Then do me a favor, take the other two zombies and play poker."

Meltzer sniggered: "What do you think we been doing all night?"

"Okay, Benny Goodman, then show me that thing you been licking all night isn't a licorice stick."

Barney then went into his own unique rendition of "Smoke Gets in Your Eyes," which brought a gurgling sob from the expectant bride; it was apparently her song.

When the lights went back on, the crowd once again began to dance to the lazy uncertain melodies of the Minstrels, and Jay looked about him a bit awkwardly, fearing that he might have been recognized by the hawkeyed M.

"Don't worry, will you?" Rhoda said, taking about three inches of sleeve before she reached his arm. "You can eat at my table. There's someone who didn't come."

She and Jay glided over to a corner table already occupied by six hungry relatives. She examined the place card next to hers, and Jay was instantly transmogrified into MR. ISIDORE GOLDFARB, an expatriate tailor from Bosnia, lately settled in the Bronx and unable to make the pilgrimage to Second Avenue because of an ailing mother. Jay settled down to eat with a silent, methodical, pythonic rapacity which resembled some obscure manufacturing process in which yarn is fed into a machine that swallows it whole and fails to disgorge it.

Conversation? If Rhoda had expected any, she had engaged the wrong supper partner, for Jay was *committed* to a policy of single-minded consumption of everything served within an arm span. A certain Plotnik, seated along his right diagonal, "a surveyor of situations," followed his trail right up to the fish course before making a cautious appraisal.

"You're not Goldfarb—he limps."

Sensing danger through his mouthful of boiled carp, Jay replied.

"I never said I was."

"Then who . . . ? May one ask?"

Fingering his seventh roll and with flowing sleeve, Jay said: "I'm a Ratkin, but there wasn't room at the family table."

"Aha, that explains it," Plotnik said.

If only the chicken would come, then I can go, Jay thought.

"From where originally?"

"Well, yes . . . certainly."

"Pardon?"

"Essen . . ."

"Essen? I thought you people come from Pinsk . . ." Plotnik turned to a woman who was obviously the chronicler of the Ratkin dynasty.

"Pinsk," she pronounced with ethnic certainty, "all from Pinsk."

Reinforced, Plotnik continued: "Sophie says Pinsk!"

"Maybe she's made a mistake," Rhoda said.

"Sophie?" Plotnik was already writing out the order to certify Rhoda. "How can she make a mistake when she's a third cousin on Ratkin's—God rest her soul—mother's side."

"I'm not really my father's son," Jay said, confounding even Sophie, who glared at Rhoda.

"Enjoying?" a whispering voice behind Jay asked; M himself doing a poll of the guests before retiring to his lair.

Get rid of him quickly before *they* start asking him questions.

"Mr. M, how can you of *all* people ask such a question? We're eating food prepared in your kitchen, Kischka stuffed by your own hand. How could it be less than magnificent?"

Mr. M took a step back, patted Jay's shoulder affectionately,

. bowed his head like a king before the pope, and his facial
muscles tensed, approximating a smile.

"Good . . . so long as you're enjoying," he said, backing
away.

"Not your father's son? What a thing to say! Sophie?"
Plotnik demanded justice.

"What a thing to say!" Sophie rejoined.

"I'm the son of my father's sister-in-law, who lived in Essen, and when my father came to Essen from Pinsk for my
mother's funeral, he adopted me."

Plotnik drummed the table for several minutes, and then
with a nod from Sophie said: "That explains."

"That explains," Sophie seconded him. "But from Pinsk
they come."

Having performed major surgery on half a chicken that
would have done a jackal proud, Jay saw Barney coming towards him and got up from the table.

"Stuffed your guts, huh?"

"There's still dessert."

"Well, I'm cutting out."

"Oh, okay. I'll come too."

"Hey, what about me?" Rhoda said indignantly.

"Who's your friend?" Barney asked.

"Miss Borough Park, 1934."

"I want to come too."

"I'll kill the first one who stops you," Jay said.

"With you, I mean."

"Look, honey. I'm a man of few words: yes or no? If yes,
have you got a room, and are your parents sleeping?"

"The answer's no, but I'm still coming with you."

"Suit yourself. But I'm not interested."

"But a wedding's a . . ."

"A wedding."

"It's an omen."

"Yeah, like the electric chair."

As they passed the cloakroom, Rhoda took out her coat
check.

"It's got a black fur collar," she said to the attendant. "Have you got a nickel, Jay?"

"A dime . . . my last one."

"Well, give it to me and I'll get change. What're you waiting for? Give it to me. Be a *gentleman*. It's not so much to pay for the meal you've just had. The people who work the checkroom don't get any money. They live on tips."

Reluctantly Jay handed her a dime and held out his hand for the change that never came.

"It'll pay for the carfare back to Borough Park."

"But I'll need a nickel to get me back."

"It's okay, sport, I'll treat you," she said, handing him her coat to hold.

2

Borough Park was neither a borough nor a park. The borough was Brooklyn and the only park of note or size that supported anything remotely verdurous was called Prospect, and this was located in a precinct—so fanciful is the Brooklyn gift for place-name fabrication—known as Grand Army Plaza. These names must have been devised by an illiterate madman given unlimited access to an unabridged version of General Cornwallis's Brooklyn telephone directory. Undaunted and unburdened by anything resembling a sense of history, Jay padded down Rhoda's street on Twelfth Avenue, a prisoner of her self-deluded ecstasy. His shoes were wet through to the newspapers that lined them. The street was tree-lined and the heavy snow that fell caused a vellication of bare, lifeless limbs which made him think he was on his way to a funeral.

"Much further . . . ?"

"It's the house after the lamppost. You'll have to take your shoes off because they're all probably sleeping.'' She stopped in front of a largish, siamese-joined structure which had its chimney over the roof of one house, its water pipe narrowly missing the bay window of another, and its doorway in peripheral alignment with the place they were actually entering; a perfect example of the architectural mutations ably produced at the turn of the century by a firm of cement contractors. Unaccustomed to this type of grandeur, Jay thought he was on to a good thing.

"You can't go home now," Rhoda said.

Jay agreed without pressing the point.

She led him into a darkened room that had the aroma of a year's sleep bottled, endemic to people who despise fresh air and conduct most of their activities in bed. Rhoda pointed at a sleeping figure in a bed by the door.

"My kid sister, Miriam," who at that precise moment passed some wind. "It's her tonsils and adenoids . . . that's why we can't open the window."

"Uh, I see," replied Jay, not seeing and least of all understanding.

Rhoda picked up her nightdress and opened the door.

"Where you going?"

"To change."

"What? You kidding? I *schlep* all the way to Oshkosh . . ."

"Borough Park—"

"—To have you change in another room?"

"Shush, you'll wake Miriam."

"What is this? I could've stayed home if I wanted to go to bed with the papers."

Charmed by the directness of his approach, Rhoda still, however, refused to yield.

"It's only the first date. We've got to get to know each other."

"Get to know?" Jay was incredulous. "What're you talking about?"

"You can't get blood from a stone."

"Who ever said anything about blood from a stone? I think

maybe you don't understand me. I'm not here for conversation—''

"Isn't the snow beautiful?"

"Or weather reports. I want to know about the weather I listen to a radio."

"Calm." Rhoda's voice was firm.

"I am calm."

"You're losing control."

"Look, give me a nickel and let me go home."

"It's a blizzard."

"Honestly, I don't know where I am. I've never been to this part of Brooklyn."

"I'll make you breakfast in the morning. I've got the day off work."

"You've got a job?" She was definitely a catch.

"I'm the manageress of Modes Dress Shoppe."

A flash of insight revealed to Jay that she was like a set meal that he had to eat in sequence—without jumping courses.

He wanted his fears confirmed.

"Aren't we going to sleep in the same room?"

"Course not."

"I might grab your sister."

"She's only nine and she bites people."

"Second thought, forget it."

Rhoda came up close to him and gave him a lingering kiss on the mouth; when she felt Jay about to grab her in a headlock, she gently moved away. Her breasts on his chest felt marvelous; her body was heavy and warm and it excited him. By way of a compliment he said:

"You weren't made with a finger, sister."

"Oh, gee, what a dirty mouth you have. You should get yourself a job in a burlesque house in Jersey, they can use your kind of talent."

"I say something wrong?"

"No, it's all right. You're just a pig, a good-looking pig." A terrible fear infected Rhoda. "You are Jewish . . . ? I mean with your dark hair and dark skin you could be . . ."

"Want proof?"

"Sleep well."

Jay's concupiscent sleep was interrupted right in the middle of a defloration ceremony he was performing with thirty-seven nubile women in the middle of Yankee Stadium with a roaring crowd cheering him on. A hand shook his shoulder firmly.

"You a murderer on the run?" Miriam asked, tightening the knotted belt on her bathrobe.

"Ever been punched in the mouth by a grown man?"

"All cons on the lam sleep in their clothes."

"Why don't you take a walk if you can't sleep?"

"But it's still snowing."

"Smart girl. Where's your sister?"

"Myrna or Rhoda?"

"Rhoda."

"She's sleeping in the living room."

"What time is it, anyway?"

"Dunno. Maybe seven or eight."

"What time's everybody get up?"

"Pretty soon. Poppa goes to work half past eight."

"Oh . . ." Jay hadn't thought of male authority on the premises.

Miriam opened the door and was about to leave:

"Just a minute. Where you going?"

"To pee . . ."

A few minutes later Jay detected an angry voice booming through the frangible walls.

"I'll give him. Don't worry. I'll give him a bullet up the ass."

Jay jumped out of bed, and then the door was savagely flung open and a short, gray-haired man—with a fine bristled mustache and tufts of hair peering out of his ears like frightened mice, resplendent in a double-breasted serge that glowed faintly in the early morning light—addressed him:.

"Explain!" Jay noticed that he was carrying a hammer. "Explanations!"

"My name is Jay Blackman—"

"What kinda name is thet? Arab?"

"Jacob Blaukonski."

Mr. Gold weighed up this new information for a moment, and shifted the hammer to his right hand. It looked heavy, and Jay hoped he had gained ground in the discussion.

"So? Where's my Rhoda, murderer?"

"Blaukonski!" Jay reiterated. "In the—"

"Liar. In the old country, you know what we do to men like you? From a tree we hang them and then—"

"What's all the screaming?" Rhoda appeared on the scene, wearing a fluffy, pink, woolly nightdress. Jay hoped he would survive to do her proper justice.

"Shame you-self. Walking in front a grown man—a strenger—undressed."

"Poppa, you should be very grateful. He took me home from the wedding in the middle of the snowstorm. If not for him—"

Unpacified, but somehow relenting, Mr. Gold thoughtfully assessed this additional testimony. With the gravity of Solomon, Sidney Gold handed the hammer to Miriam, a born perjurer.

"Put it beck in the closet."

"Okay, Poppa?" Rhoda ventured.

"Okay," he replied, throwing his hands in the air.

When they were all robed, and this meant for Jay a quick wash and brushing his teeth with tooth powder and his index finger, they gathered in the kitchen where Rhoda was frying eggs and making toast and coffee while Miriam laid the table. Myrna had already gone off to the shop where she worked, and which did a thriving business in sheet music. Despite the Depression, people still sang at home. Although neither theology nor ontology were his *métier*, Mr. Gold made a brave attempt at playing the Grand Inquisitor; after considerable persistence he learned that Jay was not an Iberian, and, to his relief, not Sephardic, a sect of Jew he regarded as distinctly Islamic and whose ethnic make-up was as remote and suspect as the Mongolians. He received only tidbits of information and he watched with growing dismay as Jay consumed a five-egg omelet which, with a mental acuity that was indeed surprising,

especially in the era of pre-Trachtenberg arithmetic, he sub-
tracted from the slender dowry that was Rhoda's birthright.

Breakfast ended and a future vague date was made with
Rhoda at which time he would meet the rest of the family—
her invalid mother who was still sleeping, the musical Myrna,
and her married brother. Jay departed with a sweet kiss tingling on his mouth and fifteen cents of Rhoda's money. The
undertaking had revealed a profit, and he could now pass
Gluckstern's restaurant with impunity.

Affairs at Rivington Street, Jay discovered after a long, invig-
orating walk across the Williamsburg Bridge to save the three-
cent trolley fare, the frost billowing from his mouth like
chimney smoke, were in a state of turmoil.

"Aha, you're home. I said the bum would come home,"
his father growled, emerging from his usual sullen pandicu-
lation which alternated between taciturn inertia and, at its most
active after a two-hour spell of keeping his legs on the windowsill, stomping about the apartment to "wake up" his numb
feet. "A whole night your momma is walking around, crying,
praying that you're still alive. Did I say he would come home
when he got hungry?"

"You said," Jay's brother Al affirmed.

"You shut up before I shut you up," Jay retorted.

"Fighting?" Morris Blackman interposed.

"Where's Momma?"

"Sleeping and no thanks to you," Al said.

"Your Uncle Sol called why you didn't go to work last
night."

"He's very annoyed," Al added.

"A two-dollar-a-week pretzel salesman doesn't have to tell
me who's annoyed," Jay shouted. "I'm keeping everybody
on my ten dollars."

"But Al can't work in the market with his bad back," Morris complained. A reference to the strain Al incurred during
his first and only night's work in the Washington Market and
which resulted in nine medical examinations by the labor compensation doctor, confirming what Jay had said in the first

place: that Al was too heavy for light work, and too light for
heavy work.

"Why can't he work? He's older than I am."

"But you're stronger," his father said.

"I wouldn't bet on that. The two of you ought to get jobs."

"Jobs!" Al laughed.

"Jobs? Where is there jobs? They grow on trees?"

"He's got imaginitis," Al said, giving Jay a fishy look.

"If you look, you find. There's a job as a dishwasher going
at Immie's."

"A dishwasher? That's the way you talk to your father?"
Al was scandalized.

"I suppose *you* can't afford to work, now that you're collecting Relief."

"I go down to the unemployment office every day, smart
guy."

"Yeah, and wait for someone to buy you coffee."

"I go to union meetings."

"I know! I know! You're much too busy to work."

Morris Blackman had digested Jay's suggestion.

"A dishwasher!"

"There are no jobs, I repeat jobs, for bookkeepers," Al
said.

"Who ever said you were a bookkeeper?"

"What did I go to night school for for a year then?"

"Don't ask me! I think you were playing with yourself."

"To learn bookkeeping and now that I know it and passed
tests there's nobody hiring."

"Dishwashing!" Morris snarled.

"Some day when I'm making big money, you'll come on
your hands and knees begging for a job," Al said.

"Meanwhile, you're sitting on your ass and eating food that
I pay for."

"Out! Out! Out!" Morris screamed, pointing a finger at Jay.
"Language like that in mine house."

"The lease is in your name ... nothing else. If I get out I
take all the furniture and Momma too."

"She'd never come," Al said.

"Well, she can't stand *him*, so she'd have nothing to lose. I'd probably get the lease put in my name if I asked the land-lord."

"Cause you hump his daughter, that's why," Al said, mor-ally outraged. "There's more to life than humping *shiksas*."

"Get married and we'll be rid of you," Morris said.

Celia Blackman emerged from the bedroom. She was a smallish, stout woman, with close-cropped gray hair, wearing a dressing gown patterned with bright sunflowers that matched the drapes in the room. She smiled at Jay, revealing a mouth full of gold teeth, which her father had invested in when she was fourteen, fearing that his small capital would be seized by creditors during imminent bankruptcy proceedings, and she would be denied a proper start in life. Eleven teeth had been removed from an unprotesting Celia, and her father had gone to his grave a happy man. Everyone to whom he owed money denounced the unwitting accomplice of his scheme. Until a magistrate declared that teeth, even by the loosest interpreta-tion of Polish law, could not be termed assets, several plans were afoot to kidnap Celia, but they came to nothing. The remainder of her teens was spent trying to disengage herself from the label "Gold Mouth" which greeted her every public appearance. Morris Blaukonski's appearance on the scene stilled wagging tongues, and gave her a respectability which she had not dreamed possible, and which she was grateful for, even after she came to despise him. The period of her disen-chantment with him began when in a fit of temper he set fire to the textile shop that had employed him for five years, after an altercation with the owner who had proved incontestably that he was colorblind. The flight from Lublin to Lvov with two small children had all but killed her. A career as a grain salesman augured well for the reformed pyromaniac and they prospered until Morris came under the spell of a Russian mill owner, by name Alexis Pyotr Markevitch, who had formed a syndicate to grow wheat in Russia's uncharted Taiga region. Enthusiastically enrolled as Markevitch's principal agent, Morris squeezed what he could from Lvov's businessmen to finance the venture. The enterprise came to an abrupt end two months after Jay's Viennese expedition, when Markevitch strangled his wife with a leather bootlace and absconded with the investors' money, leaving his agent to face an enraged mob, bent on drawing and quartering him. Morris's first impulse was to burn Lvov to the ground, but the town had grown too large for a single incendiary to deal with it. Flinging curses at Lvov that would last an eternity, he despatched his wife and four children to Rotterdam with his last two hundred thousand zlotys, instructing Celia to book a passage to America. Half-crazed, he set off with two drums of paraffin to the deserted Markevitch mill, narrowly missing a squad of Russian police, and proceeded with great energy to remove the symbol of his humiliation; the conflagration would have got him an immediate commission with General Sherman's raiders had his destiny taken him to Georgia. His arrival in New York coincided with the height of the Depression, and added fuel to his already iron resolve to abandon work forever and live off his children whose respective births were in his view designated to secure this end.

Jay went over to his mother, put an arm round her shoulder, and hugged her.

"I was so worried about you that something happened."

"He's a loud mouth," Al said.

"When he gets married it'll straighten him out."

"Or he should join the army," Al added, confident that he himself could never pass the medical examination.

"Plenty time for marriage," Celia said.

"He's twenty-three and strong as a horse," Morris replied in one of his infrequent verbal exchanges with his wife.

Celia kissed Jay on the cheek and he held her tightly in his arms; his father and brother looked away angrily.

"It's a disgusting way a grown man carries on with his mother."

Al nodded and stretched his legs on the windowsill, beating Morris to his familiar retreat by a second; Morris scowled at him and Al removed his legs.

"You always picking on him," Celia said. "If not for Jake we'd be on the street."

"And you defending him?" Morris spiritedly shook a fist at his wife. "Against me all the time. No respect . . . in Poland he would have respect. Honor thy father and mother it says."

"And thy brother," Al added.

"That's right . . . for an older brother respect too. The way that boy talks it shames me. And that's what I kill myself to bring to America."

"Poppa, you never killed yourself for nothing, not even yourself."

"It's not a mouth he's got but a garbage can."

"Garbage can."

"One more word out of you, Al, and it'll be lights out."

"See the way he threatens your own son," Morris groaned.

"A career he's got as a murderer. Why don't you join your friends in Brooklyn, they get paid for killing people."

Celia touched Jay's hand affectionately.

"You had breakfast?"

"Yeah. I met this girl at a wedding that Barney took me to."

"Whose wedding?"

"Dunno. And I took her home."

"And you stayed all night? What kind of a girl—?"

"A nice one. It was snowing too hard to come home and I slept in her sister's room."

"A filthy boy—"

"She was nine years old, Poppa."

"Nothing do I put past you, brother."

"Honest, Momma, don't listen . . . she's a nice girl and her father's a *businessman*."

Morris sprang to his feet, the bones in his legs cracking, seized his newspaper, rolled it up truncheon fashion and slammed it on the table so hard that a cup and saucer, as though on a trampoline, flew off and smashed on the floor. As a prelude to a morose spell of impotent, silent rage that could last as long as three days and which curtailed his activities so that he would leave his bed only to go to the toilet, he would always grind his teeth with such rancor—his jaw white and terrifying from the exertion—that blood would appear on his gums and he would rush to the bathroom and gargle salt water for an hour before taking to his bed, his post at the window ceremoniously guarded by Al.

"Insults! Insults ..." he raged. In his haste to leave the room, one of his slippers fell off and he flung it against the wall. Celia followed him to the bathroom.

"Always have to upset him, don't you? A man who does no harm," Al said.

"He has no feelings for anything or anybody," Jay said.

"Someday when you're a father, just remember how you treated him."

"He's never been a father to me."

"You've never allowed him to be one."

"Look, let's stop the bullshit. Sylvia told me what he did to Momma when she was pregnant with me."

"I wouldn't believe anything Sylvia told me if she swore on a stack of Bibles."

"Well, she's your sister too, and she's got no reason to lie. She was twelve years old at the time. Don't look at me as though I was nuts. Why do you think she married Harry when she was fifteen—a man she hardly knew? Because she wanted to get away from Poppa."

"Honest, Jay, what's the point of all this old crap?"

"Because it was *me* not you that Momma was pregnant with when the old man pushed her down the stairs, that's why. Why do you think she hates him?"

"Momma doesn't hate him ... she just loves you more— that's what's caused the trouble. That's what's made him bitter."

"I may as well talk to the wall. Momma loves all of us and if not for her we'd be dead and buried somewhere in Poland."

"I don't know why Sylvia tells you these stories. Rosalee hasn't got any bad feelings against him. She never mentioned—"

"How the hell could she? She was four, you were two, and Momma was pregnant with me, so how could she know a goddamned thing?"

Celia came back into the room and sat down heavily on a chair at the kitchen table.

"Please boys, no more arguing. Poppa's not well." She handed Al and Jay glasses of tea and they sat for some moments in uneasy silence.

"Jake, I don't like to ask—"

"All I've got's a dime."

"The Relief don't come till next Wednesday."

"I get paid tonight and I'll bring home some vegetables."

"I'll make a soup. A nice thick one like you like with marrow bones."

"Oh, Momma. Don't worry, you'll be all right as long as I'm alive."

It snowed again that night, a thin, powdery, sugar-fine snow that concealed the heavy glazed underseal of ice on the sidewalk and which glinted under the street lamps. The streets were dark and deserted, except for the drone of a lonely car skidding on the road. Jay tried not to think of the cold and walked slowly. He flexed his toes with every step he took to keep the circulation going, and he felt tired and hungry. A long night of unloading fruit crates and sacks of onions and potatoes awaited him and the thought of it almost defeated him. He passed row upon row of darkened shops of all kinds: delicatessen, butcher, jewelry, clothing, and he wondered if he ought to risk a robbery. A jewelry shop, with a mound of zircons parading as diamonds caught his eye; a sign in the window announced: BEST PRICES FOR OLD GOLD, ALL PAWN TICKETS MUST BE REDEEMED IN THIRTY DAYS. Then in the corner of the window a statement of policy: CREDIT MAKES ENEMIES, LET'S BE FRIENDS. He had to have a car with a driver if he smashed the window; there was probably an alarm in the shop and there were police patrolling every few minutes. It was too icy to try to make a run for it.

The snow suddenly changed to hailstones and he moved his muffler up to his face, but the hailstones got through and cut into his skin. He reached the market about half an hour later than usual, and saw that the night shift had begun. He entered an office where a checker was busily comparing invoices against the goods the men unloaded. A slow, joyful smile irradiated the checker's face whenever he came upon a shortage and he would shout for the boss's son to report the discovery. A mutated scutcheon in embossed brass revealed a hand holding a scimitar over some amorphous melonlike object; a legend written in the style of a penmanship textbook proclaimed the firm's motto: "Buy from Solomon Bell, the man who knows his onions."

"Late tonight, aren't you?" the checker said without looking up.

"No money for carfare, so I had to walk."

"Yeah, well the boss's sure to be understanding. Here"— he handed Jay a stained brown envelope—"your pay."

Jay opened the envelope and counted the money three times. "There's a mistake. I've been shorted two dollars."

"Shorted?" A voice rang out from the backroom. It belonged to a tall broad-shouldered man, wearing a torn green sweater, who was Jay's cousin.

"That's right, Artie," Jay said to the man who came towards him. "There's a mistake."

"Here, let's see that," he said, taking the pay slip out of Jay's hand. "Mistakes are possible, but we don't short people." He studied the slip of paper for a moment. "No mistake. Eight dollars and twelve cents."

"But it should be ten dollars and twelve cents."

"Lookit, it says right here, that you worked Monday through Saturday."

"What about Sunday?"

"You didn't work, and you don't get paid."

"I was out sick."

"Glad to see you recovered."

"C'mon cut it out. I haven't ever been paid for overtime and I haven't been out sick one day in a year."

"You got a beef. Put it in the hands of a lawyer."

"I'll take it up with the union."

"You're really a smart guy, aren't you, Jay?"

"I just want what's coming to me."

"A rap in the mouth's coming to you. That's what's coming to you."

"Don't threaten me, Artie, okay."

Artie turned to the checker who pretended not to hear.

"Did you ever hear such shit, Harry? I mean if my father hadn't given him a job as a favor to his mother, would we ever've taken him on?" He glared at Jay. "You got complaints, you can fuck off right now. I don't have to stand here listening to a schmuck like you asking for pay he didn't earn. You wanta work"—he peered at his watch—"you start right now, docked an hour on next week's pay,'cause you're an hour late."

"I still want my two dollars."

"Want all you want. But what you get's another story."

"Two dollars!" Jay put out his hand. Artie stared at his hand for a moment then spat on it. Jay wiped his hand on his trouser leg. "Give me my two dollars and I'll forget what you've done."

"Look, shitass, outa here, right this minute," he said, pushing Jay out through the open door and following him out. He had the collar of Jay's sweater in his hand and shoved him into the gutter. A number of men with sacks on their shoulders stood watching. Gray shafts of frost came out of Artie's mouth. "If I catch you around here again I'll personally break your head and you can forget about working in the market altogether because I'll shitlist you with everybody. You're a troublemaker."

He was about to release his hold on Jay's sweater when Jay swung out. He hit Artie right below the armpit above the rib-cage and he fell back slightly, more surprised than hurt. Jay came towards him slowly and feinted slightly to his left, letting Artie throw a punch which glanced off the top of his head. Jay had allowed for this and it enabled him to throw a short left which caught Artie in the pit of the stomach and straightened him up, but he did not follow up.

"Finish him," one of the men shouted.

Jay refused the advice and waited for Artie to get set. For a moment he forgot what they were fighting about and then he was hit on the bridge of the nose and his nose began to bleed. Artie came in close and his arms moved like pistons into Jay's stomach. Jay took a short, quick step back and swung out a looping left which caught Artie on the side of the jaw and dropped him. He got up quickly and rushed Jay. When they were close he lifted up his knee to kick Jay in the groin, but Jay turned his body to the side and blocked it with his hip. He crouched low, weaving from side to side, Artie over him punching him on the ears and the back of the neck. Jay bobbed his head suddenly to the left, then swung a sharp right which caught Artie between the eyes and sent him reeling back. Jay came after him patiently and just as Artie had pulled up his guard, Jay caught him with a left to the right eye which closed it almost immediately. Artie retreated into the gutter and Jay followed. They were between dozens of sacks of onions and potatoes, and Jay was satisfied that Artie had to go through him to escape. Artie rubbed his eye in terror, trying to force it open. When he realized that it was closed, he ducked his head low and rushed Jay again. Jay waited. When Artie was on top of him, he leveled a left to his stomach, opening his guard, then dropped him with a right hand that went to the point of his jaw. Artie lay quietly in the gutter and Jay walked up to him, put his hand in his pocket, peeled off two dollar bills, and returned the rest of the money to Artie's pocket. Then, almost as if it were an afterthought, he cradled Artie's head in his arm and Artie opened his left eye. Jay stared at him for a moment, then spat into his face.

For some hours, Jay drifted through the market streets; dazed and uneasy, several times he lost his way. His hands were numb and he could not clench his fists without causing a long grinding pain that traveled from his elbow to his spine. A clock in the meat market, some miles away from where he had started, showed him it was now three in the morning. He watched from a doorway a butcher's helper unload a great side of beef with a thin layer of frost on it. Gelid and blood-red by turns, as though the colors and shape were created by the man's struggling rhythm, the beef was carried to a shed where it was hitched onto a long swaying hook. At the front of the

stall, boxes of trussed chickens lay unattended. Jay moved out
of the shadows quickly, seized a chicken, and ran down the
street. He increased his speed when he heard the sound of
clattering feet pursuing him. Finally, almost half a mile away,
he stopped, fell heavily against a lamppost, and waited stoically for his pursuers. There were no sounds apart from the
thumping of his heart and the groan of the unrelenting wind
coming from the north side of the embankment; he peered
across the river which was black and tumid with ice blocks,
and he knew that the only hope he had existed beyond the
lights, beyond the swaying, dank dock tenements which lay
across the waterfront like a festering sore. The hope was
Rhoda.

Somehow he found his way back to Rivington Street,
crawled into bed with his clothes on. The chicken squirmed
out of his jacket and fell with a thud on the floor. Jay struggled
out of bed and took the chicken into the kitchen and placed it
on the wooden draining board. A dead, idiotic eye, glazed and
passive, stared back at him. He picked its wobbly neck up
from the board and shook it.

3

The living room in Rhoda's house was warm and furnished
in a medley of periods that came under the general heading of fire auction sale. It bore all the marks of pilgrim taste:
from its chintz drapery, its dog-eared love seat—which if
taken at its word, çould at best only accommodate half-grown
pygmies and would have been a Procrustean bed to anyone
suffering from even incipient steatopygia—to its veined fuchsia sofa, and its beige stippled walls. It was, in short, a room
that any lunatic asylum might be proud of. In a chair that was

in conflict with the natural arch of his spine, Jay's eye level was in perfect line with Rhoda's kneecaps.

"You seem surprised . . ."

"Do I? Well, to be honest, I was afraid my father scared you off," she said.

"Me scared? No, nothing like that."

"It couldn't've been you wanted to see me again. After all, I made it clear I wasn't what you boys call a hot number."

Not much, Jay thought, taking a nibble from a piece of cake before it dispersed on his lap.

"Hot number? Where'd you get that idea?"

"I mean, I'm human too, but nothing more than necking. And when you had me by the throat, I said to myself: 'This guy's a crazy.' What with Poppa two doors away, Miriam in the same room, and Momma liable to use the bedpan any time at night? You were panting."

"No, I was cold. Chills."

"Some chills. They probably have to lock you up when you get a cold . . . with chills like that."

Jay finished his cake, did a quick inventory of the room for more cake, and finding none, slumped deeper into the innards of the chair.

"Still hungry?"

"No, I'll just have something simple like a steak."

"No weddings this week?"

"I'm wanted dead or alive in every catering hall from Eastern Parkway to Tremont Avenue. They've got posters up with my aliases."

"You're not kidding. If food gave you brains, you'd be a genius."

"The fire's going out." He got up and looked in the coal scuttle.

"There's some more down in the basement. First door on your right," Rhoda said.

Bemused, Jay opened the second door on the right and came upon Myrna posing in front of a mirror, her naked breasts uplifted in her palms, in an attempt to defy the natural gravity of her body.

"Hey, you some kind of nut or something? Don't you knock?"

Jay covered his eyes with his free hand and backed away slowly.

"Sorry . . ."

"You know this isn't a boardinghouse."

". . . Said I was sorry. I thought it was the basement."

"I'm sure. It says Basement in big black letters on my door, doesn't it?"

"What? Where?"

She had covered herself up with a pink chenille bedspread, a study in the variations of nobbles any fabric could ever be subjected to. She turned around. She had blackish-brown hair, parted on the right side—a homemade bob, he'd seen a million of them—liver-brown eyes surprisingly limpid, sleek pubescent calves, thinnish arms, a small almond-shaped face, and a fleshy nose that hooked slightly. A born spinster, Jay thought, and probably a fabulous lay going to waste. He made a mental note to get around to her in due course.

"You Miriam's boyfriend?"

Snotty and embittered, but good teeth.

"Not exactly. More like Rhoda's friend."

"Oh, love without sex, that kinda friend?"

"Can I put my hand down?"

"Where's Rhoda?"

"In the living room."

"She shouldn't let you roam about by yourself," she said smiling.

An offer?

"You must be musical Myrna."

"Go to the head of the class."

"You play instruments or just sell them?"

"I'm the Garbo of the guitar."

"Oh, a comedian, huh? I've met a few."

"You're Jay?"

He paused and surveyed her figure: "Yeah, I'm Jay."

"Are you a boxer, Jay?"

"When I have to be."

She came towards him, the bedspread blowing in the stiff breeze from an unplastered crack, and stopped when she was very close to him. Her face almost touched his, and she kissed him on the tip of the nose.

"Hello, Jay, the boxer. You roll yourself into a little ball when you sleep. Like a baby."

"Errrrrrrr . . ."

"I covered you the other morning."

Not enough time, not even for a quickie.

"Thoughtful."

"I loved you from afar." She giggled and he realized that she was amusing herself.

"Uh . . . we'll be friends, Myrna."

"You can rely—"

"—Rhoda'll be wondering . . ."

His hands were grimy when he returned to the living room—no shovel—and his face was flushed.

"Where've you been, down a mine?"

"Getting the coal."

"I was going to ring the alarm for a cave-in."

"Met your sister on the way . . ."

"And you were nearly attacked?"

"No, nothing like that." Rhoda had her number. "I just said hello and she said hello."

"Interesting conversation. Didn't she tell you about her music?"

"Not much."

"Oh, well, she'll get around to it." Rhoda laughed maliciously. "She plays the clarinet. She played in the school band for four years and then she tried out for Paul Whiteman's. Wanted to be the only female clarinetist in America."

"Sounds like she's a talent."

"They told her to get a job in a music shop. Never got over it."

Myrna, fully clothed, even coated in the community black fur affair that Rhoda had worn, poked her head through the doorway.

"I'm off."

"Home late?"

"No, when the concert's over. Nice to have met you, Jay."

"Feeling's mutual."

When she had gone, a little bell tinkled from a room above, and Jay wondered if another family occupied the top floor.

"It's Momma. I'm on duty tonight. Won't be a sec."

Minutes later Rhoda returned, informed him that Momma wanted to meet him, and showed him into the upstairs bathroom so that he could wash his hands.

"Said she heard your voice and liked it. She's got chronic arthritis."

"Oh, sorry about that."

"Nothing to be sorry about. She's been bedridden for about nine years and nothing can be done. It happened after Miriam was born."

"Hard on your father . . ."

"He doesn't make demands, know what I mean? As long as he's got soup and chicken on Friday night he's happy."

"Um, yeah, I can understand that. Soup and chicken . . ."

In a room of heroic proportions, Jay stood, his mouth agape. Mrs. Gold peered at him over pince-nez, a vestigial remnant of the Tsarina's court. She wore a lace cap, which looked like a converted doily, her pallid face was rouged on both cheeks in perfect circles; it was evident that she had taken the rouge pot, wet it, and impressed it on her face without bothering to spread it out. A magenta line around her mouth created the illusion of lips, contrasting violently with her limestone complexion. It was a face capable of a variety of expressions, none of them human, and it was clear to Jay why her husband lived for chicken soup.

"Your name?"

"Jay Blackman."

"Formerly?" Her voice had the metallic timbre of clock chimes.

"Jacob Blaukonski."

"You will stand up straight when you talk to me."

"Momma doesn't have many visitors."

"Yeah, I can see."

"Speak up."

"Nothing."

"What kind of talk is nothing?"

"That's a pretty bedjacket," Jay said.

"Momma knits them herself."

"You like it?"

Jay was afraid she might offer it to him.

"Yes . . . nice colors," he replied cautiously.

"Occupation?"

"Momma, I thought you just wanted to meet Jay? He's not applying for a job."

She considered this for some moments, then waved Jay to a chair by her bedside. A host of home remedies from witch hazel to Geritol stood like minions on her table; silent witnesses of her battle with failing health.

"At Court we always asked these questions, you will understand," she said, pointing a reedlike finger at him.

"I'm not sure . . . ? Isn't this Borough Park?"

"When an Officer asked for a Lady's hand, interviews were held."

Protestingly, he turned to Rhoda:

"She thinks I'm a cop. I'm in fruit and vegetables, Mrs. Gold. At least I was."

"A man without a job is like a soldier with no gun. That's why interviews—"

"Momma, you're tired. You're not well," Rhoda said.

"Interviews, you will understand me . . ."

"I had my interview yesterday and they said I could go on Relief."

"C'mon, Jay, Momma's exhausting herself," Rhoda said, yanking him out of the chair.

"Nice to have met you, Mrs. G. Hope you feel better."

"Tchekov himself attended my mother and myself. Today they send a general practitioner who writes notes to himself in Latin. I don't call that literature. He was a poet, that one. *Bongkiss*, he prescribed in those days, and he cured people. The general practitioner laughs when I tell him about it. If I had my Hussar here, I wouldn't be in bed. He'd take me riding across the steppes and we'd have the *season* . . .''

"It's only the season for carrots and potatoes: You don't get greens till the spring."

"What? He's mad—your young man, Rhoda—but I'm sure you know what you're doing."

Outside, Rhoda whispered: "She liked you, Jay. Oooh, I'm so glad." She squeezed his arm affectionately. He turned her towards him and kissed her on the neck.

"Oooh, you better stop. Wait till Poppa's in bed."

"Clever woman, your mother."

"Oh, she's read, and read, and read."

"Yeah, I can tell." Intellectually above him, he'd better watch his step.

Rhoda took the love seat when they got back to the living room, and Jay was assigned the comfy club chair, favored by her father. Definitely a bird's nest, he thought, sliding into it. She stretched out an arm that revealed nice pink, healthy, hairless skin, and touched his hand.

"We've come into each other's lives."

Jay agreed that they had indeed come into each other's lives. He kissed her fingertips to prove the point.

"It's like history, well, two different countries, you Poland and me Russia, coming together. I think it's absolutely marvelous."

"Yeah, I see what you mean." The conversation was taking a serious turn.

"You like me? I mean really?"

"Would I be here?"

"I guess that proves something," she said coyly.

"Haven't I shown that I like you very much?"

"You've made a few grabs at me."

"That's not normal?"

"If you do like me, then tell me what happened—to your face."

"Fight. Someone tried to steal money from me. My boss—"

"So that's why you told Momma you were on Relief. And he fired you?"

"He didn't get around to it."

"Then what are you gonna do?" Her face expressed concern and he was curiously moved. "It's important what you do. Work for yourself and be your own boss."

"I never thought of it. I haven't got any money. If I did, I'd get myself a pushcart . . . fruit, I know."

"How much would you need?"

He grew pensive. Economic problems always fascinated him. Working for himself would make him independent.

"About fifty dollars. But where would I get it? Tell me that?"

Her brow ruckled and his momentary elation vanished. Hopeless situation. For someone on Relief the idea of starting up a business was preposterous. He couldn't buy himself a cup of coffee.

"Funny, I'm twenty years old and I've worked for seven years," she said with a faint hint of despondency. "Seven years . . . not much fun when you're a kid. Yeah, we've all got sad stories. Must've been tougher on you than me. We've always had what to eat and decent clothes, but not much else. Everything goes on paying doctor bills. And in all that time I've only saved seventy-five dollars."

He grew more uncomfortable and decided to say good night. Awkward position to put her in—a comparative stranger. Either a sense of decency or something that might be described as principle constrained him; it was rather a sense of depriving himself of his manhood that made him get up and put on his jacket. He coiled the scarf around his neck and rolled a cigarette before leaving: too windy outside.

"I'll give it to you," Rhoda said.

He dropped the tobacco on the carpet and in a dream swept it under the sofa with his shoe, then he bent down to scoop it up, stopped, not remembering what he intended to do in the first place. She handed him a cigarette, lit it for him, and he stood in the center of the room puffing. He picked up a knit-

ting magazine and leafed through it, then began reading an
article which he did not understand on crocheting tablecloths.
After a minute he put the magazine down, strode to the mantelpiece, shook the cuckoo clock, and smelled some wax tu-
lips.

"Good night," he said.

"You're going?"

Halfway out of the door, he stopped again, and remembered
that he had not rolled a cigarette and he stood in the darkened
hallway with his pouch of Bull Durham.

"It's ridiculous," Rhoda said. "I've saved for the dowry
that Poppa can't afford to give me. And it's seventy-five dollars. It's no money. Either you come to a man with a proper
dowry or you go to him with just the clothes on your back.
Seventy-five dollars is so stupid. I've been kidding myself for
seven years. It's yours . . ."

"You're not making sense," he said.

"I think I've fallen for you."

"And . . ." he faltered . . . "I'm crazy about you."

"You didn't have to say that. I'll give you the money without that."

"How could I take it?"

"Easy. You don't love me now, but maybe someday."

An unemployed carpenter, temporarily employed by an unsuccessful trio of thieves, came to make Jay's pushcart. The
wood was purchased from a lumberyard overstocked with unsalable varieties, and Jay was assured that it was the best mahogany. That the wood was not even a distant cousin to
mahogany—the closest it ever got to mahogany was when it
lay some fifty yards away from it in the lumberyard—mattered
little to Jay. The wheels of this failed rickshaw—had Jay but
known—could have made him fifty dollars from the Smith-
sonian Institution, for they had crossed America in the 1849
Gold Rush.

Christmas and the New Year had come and gone, and all
Jay and Rhoda had to show for it was the memory of an
unpleasant party at which both food and drink were absent.

The new year—1936—they decided would be their year. Like two hungry children listening to a fairy tale in which a mountain of chocolate figured prominently, they stretched out their hands trying to gather in the elusive luck which they sensed was the reward they were both entitled to. During the winter months, Jay just managed, by handling few perishables, to stay alive. The profit was in fruit and he sold vegetables—they were safer. He lived from week to week, mainly on Rhoda's confidence—her capital had already been depleted.

The month of scallions, cucumbers, hymenic radishes, and grapes (green gold, he called them) brought with it the thaw he had worked for in his relations with Borough Park's matriarchy, many of whom, during his first months' business, mistook him for an impostor, thief, or pimp. March, however, also brought his emotional relationship with Rhoda to a dramatic head. Were they "keeping company," or was he living off her? As he had not yet done the deed, he came to regard his relationship with her as that of a priest's with a nun. For him, the whole stillborn affair was something of an ordeal. Although he still had the occasional Saturday night in Scranton with Barney, and a twice-a-week exchange with the landlord's resilient daughter, he began to feel that, as far as Rhoda was concerned, apart from some innocent necking and his intimate knowledge of the trunk section of her anatomy, he would never gain the precious ground needed to secure entrance to the darker mysteries. Outrage gave way to silent melancholy, and he devised a plan of seduction, by arithmetic progression—slip, followed by bra, followed by panty-girdle—which failed miserably during February. His physical lust for her became so great that he feared he would do violence to gain his objective, which as he well perceived, once gained, would commit him irretrievably to precisely what he was trying to avoid: marriage.

Every evening, with unfailing regularity, he met her at the entrance of Modes Dress Shoppe; his appearance was too disreputable to allow him to enter without raising questions and jeopardizing Rhoda's position.

"Want to go to a movie?" he asked her one evening, outside the shop. Lately he had gone to the movies whenever he could, regarding it with pragmatic certainty as the key to higher things and experiences he had never had. It had improved his manners and Rhoda encouraged him to go, even on his own; his conversation, formerly a compound of sex and vegetables, was now broadened to include glittering references to stars. The plots of every film he had seen he bandied with anyone who would tolerate such a discussion, and the intimate details of the stars' personal lives he announced with the confidence of a paid informer.

"Can't, I've got to sit," she answered.

"What's the matter with Myrna?"

"She's got tickets to a concert and Poppa's going with her. Takes him out of himself."

"A new music lover. So we've gotta sit in?"

"You can go on your own, if you like."

"Have a heart, Rho, I've been three times without you."

Reluctantly he accompanied her home, waited till she had given her mother dinner and put Miriam to bed, before he could eat with her.

"You can have a bath if you want," Rhoda said. "I've got clean things for you that you forgot to take last week."

He accepted her offer although with some suspicion. He had wanted to ask her countless times but she had never given any sign of noticing his condition. He looked and smelt like a garbage collector. A short while later, morbidly clean, he appeared at the table, tunelessly trilling "Melancholy Baby." He allowed Rhoda to begin first—one of Robert Taylor's tricks—before annihilating his dinner. She sat moodily and silently picking at her food.

"Something wrong? I've done something?"

"No, just not hungry, I guess. I'm a little down in the dumps."

The emotional state of women meant virtually nothing to him, and he could only relate unhappiness to physical deprivation. Trying hard to overcome his total lack of curiosity and the apathy that set in when he had eaten he said:

"Weighing you down at home, huh?" He waited for confirmation and when she did not answer he got up from the table and ambled into the living room. "C'mon in, we'll listen to the radio." Patiently, he waited for her to join him and after an hour he went back to the kitchen.

"You're still sitting there moping. Maybe I oughta go home?" There was a ghost of a chance that he might catch Barney.

"No, don't go yet."

"What's the good of me staying if you don't want me to?"

"Of course I want you to stay. It's just . . . I don't know myself."

"You do, but you're not telling."

"You've had the pushcart three and a half months."

"Yeah, so?"

"Oh, we don't seem to be getting anywhere."

"I've made twenty-five dollars this week. I wouldn't call that standing still, would you? I've got a future, thanks to you and I'm not forgetting."

"You don't know what I'm talking about, do you?"

His eyes lit up angrily, and when she turned to him, she thought that she had never loved anyone so deeply in her life.

"I'm not stupid. Maybe I didn't go to school, but I'm not stupid."

"Who ever said you were?"

"I'm struggling to make a living, to make something of myself."

"Don't be angry with me, Jay. It's just—I feel all mixed up, deep inside."

"Everyone's mixed up too, if that makes you feel any better." A remarkable statement from someone who apart from catering to his basic drives had never given evidence of confusion, she thought.

"The better we get to know each other, the less we seem to know about each other."

It took him a moment to digest this oracular generalization; he was not at all fond of rebuses and he attempted to devise an answer that would put the burden on her.

"That's according to Hoyle?"

"I'm not explaining myself well."

"That's a fact. You aren't explaining at all."

"You make it so hard."

"Hard? I haven't said a word."

"I've got to talk to you, make you understand."

"Who's stopping you? I'm interested to know myself. More I can't say."

"Three and a half months we've been seeing each other."

"That's not a lifetime."

"Oh, Christ!"

"What are you picking on?"

"I think you're purposely playing dumb. You don't want to know."

Couldn't be him, he hadn't put a hand on her. Immaculate Conception or something like that.

"Have you gone to a doctor?"

"A doctor . . . what for?"

"To be examined."

"What are you talking about? I don't need a doctor, I need you."

Marriage, better keep his mouth shut.

"Let's listen to the radio."

"I'm sick of the goddamned radio."

"I'll catch a movie, maybe. Sylvia Sydney's on at the Loew's Delancey."

"Just walking out on me like that? Pick yourself up and walk out."

"Go to bed early . . . you'll feel better in the morning. And we'll go for a walk to Prospect Park."

"I don't want to go for a walk."

"Coney Island then? That'll make you happy?"

"One thing'll make me happy and you know what it is. Do you love me, or don't you?"

Good question, he thought, no dodging it.

"Of course."

"What kind of answer is of course? Don't say anything you don't mean, I really couldn't bear it."

Definitely dropped in the shit, no doubt about it.

"I told you I loved you."

"Well, it's your move, isn't it?"

"My move, huh?"

"What are you gonna do about it?"

A good systematic bang, that's what.

"I'm waiting . . ."

"Look, let's go to Scranton next week. Your father makes me nervous."

"What's he got to do with it? I'm talking about marriage."

"Marriage?" He snapped his fingers in her face. "Just like that? For marriage you need money."

"Between us we're earning."

"Oh, sure. I banked a million dollars last week. You're forgetting I've got a mother that needs . . . and a father that hasn't worked from the day he arrived here. I'm his meal ticket. And a brother that's a bum that sits all day on his fat ass in front of the window, and only gets laid when I slip him a buck."

"Excuses I can live without. I'm not gonna sit around waiting for them all to drop dead."

"God forgive you," Jay said, wringing his hands like Guildenstern, trying to extricate himself by theatrical gestures. He worked himself into a rage, his face plum red, his hands shaking in anger, his balls in a proper uproar. "Cursing my family! You like putting people on the spot!"

"Good night, Jay. Hope you enjoy the movie."

"Russian roulette, that it? Playing with fire?"

"I haven't got anything to lose. It's one way or the other. The not knowing is what kills people." She started to cry soundlessly. He made a move to leave, and when she bit her lip to prevent herself from making an outcry, he knew she had him, and he cursed her for possessing stronger weapons than he had. The tears he could cope with, her forbearance defeated him. He wondered if a good beating, a beating carried out in cold blood without mercy or love, would release him from her. It would probably bind them even closer, the Gordian knot of the blows, the shared violence, in which the beater is even more subtly victimized than the victim, would make their union indivisible.

"Okay, what do you want from my life?"

"Just be a man. Have some guts for once in your life and stop moaning and complaining about what you had and didn't have, that's all I want. And I don't want it for me, but for you. You could have done what you wanted to me three and a half months ago on the night we met, but you didn't have it in you. It had to be a cinch. Well, I'm not an easy lay. And not because I think that what I've got's so goddamned precious or any crap about never being the same afterwards. It's because I want a man to lay me and to know when he does he's laying a woman and not some piece that's been handed around by everyone who's got a prick. A beauty I'll never be, but I'm not sorry about that because I'm not so bad. But someone to give me a bang I won't have trouble getting. That answer your question?"

She was speaking his language and fighting him on his ground. She terrified him and he hated her for it. She got up from the table, pushed him out of her way and went into the living room. He heard the radio. Astonished that his body was responding, he found himself standing over her in a threatening position. She was smoking a cigarette and he stared with fascination at the lighted end. She held out the cigarette to him.

"Here burn me with it, beat me up. Just do something . . . don't threaten to do something and then not do anything." He sank down on his knees before her, and she wiped her eyes with the frayed sleeve of her dress. Then he sprang up almost in a trance and kissed her. Her mouth was open and her tongue flicked out at his.

Without moving away he started to undo the buttons of her dress. He stopped, waiting for her to raise an objection, to move his hand away. Her mouth pulled at his and he felt as though she were swallowing him up and he tried to break away, but she tightened her grip around his neck. He could hardly breathe. She was all over him at once, taking, taking,

taking, and he continued unbuttoning the front of her dress. She looked at him, still on his knees, with resigned affection, then she slipped her arms out of the dress.

She was about to undo her brassiere strap, her arms were spread-eagled behind her, and then as though remembering that Jay was cast in the major role, she brought her arms back and clasped his neck, waiting. He slid his head on her breasts and kissed her for what seemed to be a long time in the hollow of her breasts. She lost her breath and he took this as a signal to go further. He eased off her panties and stroked her gently between her thighs and she sat back deeper in the sofa, her eyes glazed, moaning.

"I won't hurt you, promise."

"I don't care."

He continued to stroke her and when she looked up she saw that he had undressed himself down to his socks and she wondered vaguely when he had done it. Except for infant boys, she never remembered seeing a man's organ and she stared at it with interest. She stretched out her hand until she had it and she held it tightly in her fist, and it excited her to feel it alive in her hand. Without releasing him, she slipped down to the floor and they sat facing each other like conspirators without a plan. Slowly he guided her head to him and before she reached him she kissed him anxiously on the mouth, moving quickly, then allowing him to guide her again. She rested her head on his lap and like a child he fed it slowly into her mouth. She held it tightly in her mouth as she had with her hand, and then he put his hands on both her cheeks and she moved her head up and down slowly, then quickly, when she sensed his excitement. He watched her and she knew he was watching her and he stroked her lips, exciting her, and making her want to please him even more. His body became suddenly rigid and she felt it oozing into her mouth. Almost in pain, he forced her head off with a sharp push at her forehead. He looked at her fearfully and his face was white with shock.

"Spit it out!"

"That what whores do?"

"Spit it out!"

"Dew. Your dew."

She pressed her head against his chest and his warm flesh reassured her.

"Why did you . . . ?"

"Why? I love you, silly. It's yours . . . it belongs to you." She paused, lifted her head up. "Now . . . ?"

"Have to wait a few minutes."

She moved her head passively back to his chest and for the first time since they had met, she felt stronger than him. She looked at him and now it was small and there was sperm gathered at the head of the opening. She held him for a long time, until it seemed to her that her excitement had subsided. She forgot where she was and what they were doing, only that she was warm and secure. He opened the hook of her brassiere strap and then she remembered what they were doing. He cupped her breasts in his hands and slowly licked the nipples of her breasts. It gave her an uncomfortable tingling sensation and she felt vulnerable. Then he moved himself between her legs and began rubbing against them. She bent her head and kissed it again and it was hard and throbbing. She spread her legs and he pushed his fingers inside her, rhythmically from side to side, forcing the lips to open. She felt wet inside and she became embarrassed, but she did not remove his fingers. Her back was slowly edging to the floor and then she was lying flat. He moved on top of her, but his finger still held her lips and she sensed that he was slowly moving inside her. The movement was slow and easy as though he were frightened of injuring her, and then she felt a sharp, stinging pain as if she had cut herself with a piece of jagged glass and he was pushing harder and the pain subsided but it began to irritate her flesh. He swayed from side to side and she felt something uncontrollable, like a fever, come over her and she moved with him to increase the feeling of fever. The fever was reaching its height and she worked under him like a slave given a task by his master. They came together, and he rolled off her. He lay by her side gasping. When he could catch his breath, he took her face in his hands and kissed her.

"I do love you," he said.

"Do you?"

"I said—"

"It's easy to say now. Wait ..."

"For what?"

"Till you're sure that you mean it. Till you're sure that I'm not forcing it out of you."

"I am sure," he protested.

"Then it's all right. We'll be okay."

"Good to feel you."

"I've done the right thing. I've done right by myself. Waiting for you. I'm sorry for what I said before, but I had to for your own good."

4

August, and the heat was more oppressive than ever. Jay, like Metternich before him, to whom he bore an unconscious likeness, defended the policy of the status quo. Rhoda, to her unutterable dismay, had been correct in her surmise: a lover's troth plighted in the zeal of preconnubial ecstasy had the same validity as a confession extracted by the police after rubber hose treatment. Her influence decreased proportionately with the degree of intimacy she permitted Jay. But now that she had given herself to him, she was caught in the ineluctable trap she had set: her hunger for him surpassed his for her, and she found herself making time schedules of her family's daily movements so that she and Jay could be in the house alone. Matinees and matutinal visits allowed them the greatest privacy, but somehow they left her listless and dissatisfied. Her lunch hour, a period of her day which formerly had been neutral, now took on a ritual significance. The mere mention by her boss of: "Lunch, Rho ... ?" brought her out in a cold sweat, red flushes, and a fit of stammering which made the simple "yes" or "no" reply a trial of anguished and tortuous explanation. After a while, she began to wonder if the word *lunch* itself contained any hidden double entendre that she had not been aware of. As a consequence, she dropped it from her vocabulary and whenever anyone used it in her presence she attempted to find in the tone of voice, the facial expression, a clue to the meaning intended by the inquisitor.

But despite the surface guilt she displayed, or thought she displayed, over her meetings with Jay, she was without real guilt and she thought that she had never been happier in her life. Her luminous hazel eyes possessed a warmth and a sun-flecked crystalline brightness which sang with joy, and her body, now that she and Jay had both discovered it, emerged as though from a long period of narcoleptic sleep as a vessel of manifest beauty. It became for her, like Myrna's clarinet, an instrument capable of exquisite melodies and harmonies. She had always been a big girl, supple, full-breasted, with marvelous heavy hips, strong limbed and agile, although with a tendency to fat. Her body, almost without her realizing it, even though she was more profoundly conscious of it, took on a new firmness, a tensile thickness. It was as if she were holding a printed page too close to her eyes and excluding peripheral vision, so that she lost sight of the expanding contours of her body.

On a Saturday morning when she knew the bathroom would not be in continual use, she took a long leisurely bath. She had just stepped out of the bath, reached for a towel when Myrna walked in.

"Sorry, didn't know you were still here," Myrna said, handing Rhoda a towel.

"You're home early."

"I worked overtime on Wednesday and the boss gave me off the rest of the day. Want to do some shopping and I thought I'd take Miriam with me, and after we'd go to the park." She watched Rhoda drying herself. "Like to come? Or are you seeing Jay?"

"Not till tonight. Saturday's his busy day."

"Why aren't you working?"

"I wasn't feeling well and . . ."

"Really, what's the matter?"

"Don't know . . . I just feel rotten."

"Go to the doctor for a checkup."

"Maybe I will."

"Hey, just a minute," Myrna said anxiously, "look at your stomach!" Rhoda peered down at herself. "You've got a pot-belly."

"What are you talking about?" she said fearfully. "I haven't got my girdle on."

"Girdle? He's . . . Jay . . . ! You're pregnant. He's knocked you up, the bastard."

"What're you talking about?"

"Oh, honestly, Rho, do you think I'm an idiot or something? Don't you think I know what's been going on?"

Rhoda tried to ignore her.

"About a week ago, I called for you lunchtime at work and they said you'd left already. So I looked for you at The Fountain and then I went home to get a sweater. When I came in I walked by the living room and there you were . . . with him."

"You never said—"

"What was there to say? Was I supposed to warn you? A little late for that. Should I have embarrassed you by saying I saw you? Nothing for me to do, except keep my mouth shut and forget . . ."

"Does Poppa . . . ?"

"Don't think so. Better if you don't say a word. Jay know?"

"I doubt it." She was excited and yet disconsolate.

"He'll marry you, won't he? I mean even if you weren't . . . you're keeping company. Everybody knows that, even Momma and Poppa. I ran into Howie the other day, and he's heard from Poppa that you're spoken for. Wants to meet Jay . . . usual older brother business. I think he hopes to make a touch on Jay. Oh, maybe that's not fair to Howie, he was excited really."

Fully dressed, Rhoda examined herself in the mirror.

"You really can't tell when I'm dressed."

"But how long'll that last . . . another month or so? You'll tell Jay."

"Guess I'll have to . . ."

"Well, if he tries any tricks, Poppa'll have to speak to him."

"Oh, no, I wouldn't want him to . . ."

"Somebody's got to fight for you. You want the same thing that happened to me to happen to you? Spoiled my life. Can't have children. God, I hate Jay."

"You don't," Rhoda said.

"I do and I don't. I hate him because he gets away with murder with everybody, and at the same time I don't hate him because he's too good-looking to hate, and the trouble is he knows it and uses it."

"He's got a good heart and he's good to his mother."

"So was Dillinger."

They both laughed half-heartedly.

"I'll see him this afternoon," Rhoda said.

"Oh, Christ, no, this is the end," Jay said, throwing his hands helplessly in the air. "As soon as I stand on my feet, *this*. Well, you can't have it, so forget it."

"Oh, of course, I'll just forget about it. Sorry I bothered you."

They were standing in the gutter, behind his pushcart, and the street was rank with the smell of garbage and putrefying food. Broken wooden boxes lined the curbside, and flies were conducting a hallelujah dance on spoiled fruit. Rhoda could barely stand the odor.

"It should come to this," Jay groaned.

"Whose fault is it? Mine or yours . . . ? You're supposed to be the expert."

"The question is, am I the one?"

She slapped him hard across the side of the face and he almost lost his balance.

"Okay, I'm sorry. I can't stand here talking. I'll see you tonight and we'll work something out." He kissed her on the cheek. "Bear with me . . . it's such a shock that I don't know what I'm saying."

At seven o'clock in the evening she was surprised to see him pull up in front of her house in an old black Model T Ford. He did not come inside, but blew the horn twice, and she went out. She opened the car door and he flicked his index at the seat.

"You shy or something?" she said indignantly. "Since when don't you come into the house? And where'd you get the car?"

"Barney loaned it to me." He started up the engine and they drove across Brooklyn, towards the Manhattan Bridge, in silence.

The summer evening was warm and sultry and people sat in front of their houses on bridge chairs, gasping for a breath of air. Two-family houses and overcrowded apartment houses rolled by Rhoda's eyes in an unchanging montage of poverty.

"Where we going?" she asked finally.

When they came out of the Holland Tunnel on the Jersey side, he replied. "Scranton."

"What for?"

"What do you think?" he said harshly.

"Don't you even ask me how I feel?"

"What's to ask?"

"Is this the only thing that you can think of? Nothing else?"

He turned off at the exit marked Union City and proceeded slowly to the center of town. At a light, he fished out a piece of paper from his pocket and studied it. He drove for another five minutes and they found themselves in front of a theater which was a riot of dancing neon lights. Several hundred men stood in line outside, waiting for the darkened box office to open. Rhoda read the sign outside: ALL NIGHT BURLESQUE—THIRTY LOVELIES EXPOSE THEMSELVES TO A NIGHT IN A MOROCCAN HAREM.

The door on Rhoda's side was suddenly opened and Barney Green gave her a pat on the arm.

"Shove over, huh. I'll get in the back."

"No, it's okay, Rhoda'll go in the back."

"I will not," she said angrily.

"Jay, use your *kopf*. What're you arguing over nothing?"
Rhoda moved forward and Barney climbed in behind them.

"So Rhoda, what's new? Long time no see."

"You know what's new, or you wouldn't be here."

"He's doing us a favor," Jay interposed.

"You can die from such favors."

"Glad to see you got a sense of humor, Rhoda. But believe
me, it's for the best. You're both too young to get saddled
with a kid. You got your lives to live."

"Can I quote you on that?"

"Shut up," Jay said.

"Don't tell me to shut up. You think you're talking to one
of your whores? I'm pregnant with your child."

"Calm. Calm. Let's have some calmness, kids. No point in
losing your head."

"You know, don't you, that this ride is costing Barney ten
dollars that he gets for the act he's supposed to be doing tonight . . . plus gas and wear and tear on the car."

"That what it's costing, Barney? Gee, you're really a
sport."

"One more crack and—"

"Yeah, go on."

Jay got back onto the main highway and the car picked up
speed. He kept it at a steady forty. Rhoda looked out of the
window. It was still light. She had never been to this part of
New Jersey and she was curious to get to Pennsylvania, for
she had never been there either. She wondered if it would be
much different from upstate New York, or if the people spoke
with different accents. Jay turned sharply; the air that blew
into Rhoda's face became foul. She had never before smelled
anything like it, and she fought to contain the nausea that
welled up in the back of her throat.

"Close the window, will you!" Jay voice was filled with
irritation.

"What is it?"

"What is it, the little lady wants to know? It's Secaucus," Barney said. "Never heard of it?"

"Never."

"It's where they kill all them pigs," Barney explained. "Like the Chicago stockyards, only here it's pigs. The pigs from all over the country are sent here for slaughter. Once when I was working a club in Trenton, I pick up a little Polack piece, and before I can make with the thing, she insists on me taking her back here. So we drive and drive and finally get to Secaucus and she says she's only got an hour 'cause she's gotta get to work in the slaughterhouse at four. So right outside the joint with the pigs squealing like mad we make it. She was a packer there. Afterwards I walk her in, and she asks if I want to watch for a while—you know, the pigs being killed. I figure, what've I got to lose—it's an experience I never had and maybe it'll be interesting? Funny thing was that after a while I didn't mind the smell. I got used to it. So we go to a room on top, like a barn, and there are about ten guys all with big meat cleavers in their hands—the biggest ones I ever saw—and what happens is this: they get the pigs all jammed up, so they got no room and there's a terrific noise of them squealing and moaning and pushing each other 'cause they can't help it. And about one a second is like forced into a small wooden opening and one of these butchers pins the head on a block and whams it off. Then he yanks it out and hands it still squirming to one of these packers who skins and guts it. Never seen anything like it. It was fascinating and I'll tell you something—amazing. It makes you sexy. I mean I had the urge come over me like I never felt it before, so I grab the Polack and she says it makes her sexy too. So she cuts out and I follow at a slow trot and there's like no place to make it in except in the empty pig pen, and that's where we went. Honest, it was fabulous. What was her name? Jeannie Something, one of the best, no kidding."

"Sounds sensational," Jay said.

"We're making good time. Ought to be in Scranton pretty soon."

It had grown dark and Rhoda stared out of the car window as they reached the outskirts. Black factories, with huge cylindrical smoking chimneys set back from the road, glowered on what had once in the distant past been countryside; like the dead risen, they stood thundering black smoke which drifted into her face and made her eyes smart. It was a strange, foreign country, a country in which she feared she might die. She became dizzy and breathless.

"You're very quiet all of a sudden," Barney said to her, hoping for a reaction to his story, and when none came he continued. "You're taking this in the right way, Rhoda. To be honest, I didn't expect you to take it any other way. Smart girl. You and Jay are going to make it in a big way. I got loads of confidence in you."

"Things are better now than they've ever been," Jay affirmed. "We've got a future, don't we, Rhoda?"

She did not answer and now they were driving along the main street which contained scores of brightly lit clubs. Wherever she looked there were bars, and girls leaning against walls. They're both frightened, terrified, she thought, and they want me on their side because they need me. They can't stand up to me, but they don't know yet that I know that. She made a vague attempt to examine her motives: had she got herself pregnant to trap Jay? If this was the case, then she had an obligation to herself, not to him, to go through with it, because nothing could be gained by holding him. If they married because she was pregnant, the cornerstone of their relationship would be reduced to sand and the whole structure would totter the moment the scaffolding was withdrawn. She probed her mind, and discovered that there had not been any plan—at least any plan that she herself had devised. She had given herself to him in the muddled and ambiguous hope that she could make something of him: provide him with a character and identity that he did not possess and never would, unless it was shaped by love.

Jay parked next to a noisy bar, overflowing onto the sidewalk with loud drunken men talking Polish and shoving each other to make more elbow room. Jay opened the car door and she waited for Barney to get out. Like a general on an inspection tour, he moved through the pack of men with Rhoda and Jay trailing him. She could see from the smiles he got that he was well-known to them, and that they approved of him. At the bar, they made room for him, and a woman wiped the chipped, scratched wooden surface in front of him with a sopping rag.

"Usual, Barney?"

"Er. Yeah, two rye boilermakers. Doubles. Rhoda, what would you like?"

She ignored him. The room was stiflingly hot and the men, with their sleeves rolled up, collars open, revealing tattered, dirty undershirts, sweated and drank. She had never seen a bar so crowded and with so many drunken men pushing each other without breaking into open fights. A man with two beer mugs was propelled out of the mob, all fighting for service. He was dead drunk and his head hit the top of the bar with a dull thud. The woman who had served them took the two mugs out of his hands, filled them with beer, then lifted his head up. He took some money out and was almost pushed to the ground as others fought to squeeze in his place.

"Sally here yet?" Barney said, all business.

"Upstairs, waiting for you."

"Sure you won't have a drink, Rhoda?"

"C'mon"—Jay put his arm around her shoulder—"have one. Good for the nerves."

"My nerves are okay. But you have another drink."

"Same again," Jay said.

They had three more rounds of drinks before Barney made a move.

"She's waiting . . . better go upstairs or she'll think it's a stand-up."

"One more," Jay said. He turned angrily to a man behind him. "Cut out the shoving, buddy. Can't you see I'm waiting to be served." The man threw out his arms helplessly, and indicated the men behind him who had shoved him into Jay. Jay swallowed his drink in one gulp, took a quick sip of beer and pushed after Barney and Rhoda who were slowly making their way to a staircase at the back of the room.

On the first floor Barney took a right turn, and she followed him down a long badly lit corridor.

"It's a hotel. They got rooms here for people that want to stay the night."

He opened a door, held it for her, and waited for Jay.

A woman sat knitting in an old red leather chair. She was about fifty, thick-set, with graying black hair and she studied a magazine pattern. She made a final stitch before putting down a shapeless slab of wool that was part of a sweater.

"For my nephew," she said. "Can't follow this goddamned pattern—everything you gotta do piecemeal. Back first, then the front."

"Want a drink, Sal?" Barney asked.

"Afterwards. Don't drink on the job."

"Doesn't that give you confidence?" Barney said, hoping to make Rhoda smile. He waved a hand and said: "My friends."

"No names, okay, so long as they're friends of yours is enough." She pointed to the door, and the men walked towards it.

Jay held Rhoda's hand and kissed her softly on the mouth. His mouth tasted of beer and cigarettes.

"Nothing to be afraid of," he said.

"We better get started," Sally said.

When they had gone she locked the door and motioned Rhoda into another room. It was a bare room, with bottle green drapes that had faded patches. In the center of the room was a long wooden scrub table with a thin mat placed down the middle, and just by the table was a black metal stand containing bottles, a hypodermic needle and instruments that Rhoda knew were the kind surgeons used. She had seen similar ones in a hospital showcase when Myrna had had her appendix removed.

"First time?" Sally asked. She waited for an answer. "Don't want to talk? That it? I understand. There's nothing to be frightened of. I've done this a couple hundred times and nothing's ever happened."

"I'm not afraid," Rhoda said. She watched with interest as Sally screwed two metal clamps to the sides of the scrub table.

"Foot rests." She sniggered. "You know those straps they got in the backs of cars for people to hold on to when they're getting in or in case of short stops. Well, some people use those for foot rests too." She finished tightening the clamps and sighed. "There we are, honey. Now you just undress and it'll be over before you know."

Rhoda walked into the other room, opened her bag, and saw that she had four dollars. She closed her bag, and stared at the knitting which was folded up neatly on the leather chair. Sally came into the room.

"It's for my nephew's birthday. Outgrows everything in a week." She chuckled. "At least it seems like a week. Well, I'm all ready, so you better undress and I'll give you a little massage that'll relax you."

"No, I don't think I want a massage," Rhoda said. "I think we'd better forget about it."

"Forget it? Why?"

"I've changed my mind."

"It's for your own good. I've had a lot of experience in this and you may be sorry after that you missed the chance."

"That's my worry."

"You know I've been paid already; twenty bucks and this isn't a department store. I don't give refunds."

"Keep it."

"I intend to. I'm taking a big risk, you know. I can get ten years for something like this. And your boyfriend isn't going to like throwing twenty down the drain, with nothing to show for it."

"Well, he'll have to live with it. I'd like to go now."

Sally unlocked the door.

"It's your life you're playing with."

"I'd thought of that."

"Better explain to your boyfriend, 'cause I don't want trouble."

Rhoda walked quietly down the stairs. There were a group of men at the bottom and she saw that Jay and Barney were

not among them. As she descended she spotted them at the
bar with two women all holding drinks and about to clink
glasses. She pushed her way through the crowd of men, rank
with beer and sweat. Outside, she took a deep breath and
started to walk down the street which was lined with women
in doorways, under lampposts, and against the walls of buildings.

"Know how I get to the station?" she asked a woman.

The woman pointed a finger and said:

"Straight ahead . . . just follow your nose."

"No, thenks, oh, maybe, all right, yes. A little, little, piece.
No thet's too big. I only got a small mouth." The reluctant
eater was Maurice Dobrinski, licensed matchmaker, Talmudic
Sophist, and tort expert of the vagaries of premarital difficul-
ties. Sidney Gold had decided to consult him. In Borough
Park, men removed their hats when they passed Dobrinski on
the street, and women performed a curtsey. A scholar, a sa-
vant, the pillar of the temple, a man whose eyes burned with
an otherworldly fire and whose mustache was embalmed with
the wax of a thousand days, so that it held a hypnotic fascination for all who peered at its sebaceous sheen. This paid
meddler into the disputes of his betters supported his arguments with spurious precedents which he barely understood
and, if this failed, could summon up a host of irrelevant, obscure logomachies which by their weight, total pointlessness,
and the utterly confused manner in which they were delivered
destroyed any attempt at sane communication.

"Sit by the window," Mr. Gold said to Dobrinski. "You'll
get a better view."

Dobrinski pointed to the top part of his skull and said:

"The view's in here."

"They should be here soon. I told them two o'clock."

"They're all coming?"

"I hope so."

"The boy's mother and father are very important. They'll
make him do the right thing by Rhoda."

"After you've spoken to them."

Dobrinski ruffled some papers in his briefcase.

"All the authority I need, I got in here."

"And if thet doesn't work?"

"You let me worry . . . I have never lost yet," Dobrinski said with a smile.

Several minutes later they heard a dull thud, as though the door was being rammed, and the house's delicate foundations seemed to sway. Mr. Gold stormed to the door.

"Missus Bleckman?" he asked.

"Mistah Gold?" Celia replied.

"Why don't you dense?" Morris Blackman said furiously. "Not funny. Where is . . . ?"

"The murderer? Hiding behind his mother," Morris shouted.

"Come in and welcome to mine home." He ushered them into the living room where Dobrinski had commandeered a table, stacked his papers neatly, and was giving the impression of meticulous officialdom at work. He was busily changing nibs on all of his pens, and he had set out two inkwells.

"Would you please sign?" he said to the Blackmans, pushing a ledger in front of Morris.

"Sign what? I didn't come here to vote and thet's the only time I sign. But I don't vote. When they put up a Jewish president I'll vote."

"It's not to vote," Dobrinski hastily explained, "but for mine records. Nine thousand signatures I got already."

"Nu, so what you need mine for?" Morris replied contentiously.

Dobrinski dealt him one of his seraphic smiles, opened his arms as though to embrace him, flicked a paper out which Morris took, tried to read, then in despair handed back.

"You see who has signed it?"

"I see it's signed. But I don't understand . . . ?"

"It is a document giving me certain powers . . . signed by the Chief Rabbi of Palestine." Actually it was a receipt for clothes received which a Jewish orphanage had issued to the donor, namely Dobrinski, who had spent three months collecting them in order to peddle the best of them to a secondhand dealer with whom he had a working arrangement. When he was satisfied that Blackman was impressed, he went on to add: "So far in thirty years I have solved four thousand disputes and this book is mine record."

"What is all this about?" Morris turned to Gold who was smiling and rubbing his hands together. Dobrinski was costing him ten dollars and he wanted his money's worth. "A telegram you sent me. I never got before a telegram."

"I never sent one before," Gold said. "I gave good directions?"

"I'm here, no?"

"We're here," Celia said. She turned to Jay and squeezed his hand reassuringly. "A mother's love you've got." He held her tightly and looked morosely at the ceiling. It needed a paint job.

Gold felt it was time to get down to business.

"May I present mine adviser, Mistah Maurice Dobrinski."

"At your service." Dobrinski extended a hand to Blackman. He loved him already.

"What for adviser?" Morris growled.

"Your boy didn't explain you?"

Jay received three sets of surprised glances which he carefully avoided. Rhoda would pay for this, he'd make her pay!

"Nothing about mine Rhoda?"

"No, not a word." Celia shook Jay's arm.

"Per-epps, I should explain," Dobrinski interceded.

"They been going together for now"—Gold counted on his fingers—"seven months . . . kippink company."

"Never a word to me," Morris said. "Who knows where he goes? He's a bum."

"Thet we know," Gold said, shooting a dagger look at Jay.

Dobrinski flapped a quire of foolscap paper at Gold, indicating that he was prepared to commence.

"His cousin, he beat up and he had to go into hospital," Morris said. Dobrinski made a quick note of this and shook his head sagaciously at Jay, then wagged a finger. "But he brings home money now. How's thet possible? His momma and me is afraid to ask, because we think he goes with a gun."

"Not a word about mine Rhoda?"

"Where's your wife, Mr. Gold?" Celia asked.

"Nine years an invalid. It would kill her if she knew."

"Tch, tch, tch," Celia pursed her lips.

"And she's a good girl, Rhoda. But when she brought *him* home, I became worried."

"In Poland they know how to treat boys like him," Morris said.

"And in Russia, too. You give a cossack fifty kopecks . . ."

"Please, please"—Dobrinski got to his feet—"nothing can be settled in this way."

"His uncle sent over the police looking for him."

"Genug, Moishe," Celia said.

Dobrinski, his notes set on a music stand, his dental plate revolving at fifty r.p.m., launched into the fray. He began with a short history of Judaism. The travails of its people under Pharaoh, the glories of Joseph, Abraham, the hairy brother, and the unhairy brother, David and Goliath, all were recounted in his most confidential raconteur style occasionally enlivened by fist-waving to enforce his points. After this there followed a request for old clothes for the starving children of Palestine and an injunction to donate generously to Borough Park's Synagogue. He collected twenty-nine cents from Morris Blackman under protest. It was when he suggested that they should adjourn for tea that Morris rose to his feet and in a thunderous voice demanded to know why the conclave had been assembled in the first place.

"Two hours' traveling for a murderer and I'm here an hour and I don't even know why I've come," he protested. "Now we're drinking tea? I could have stayed home and drank tea there."

"Not a thing am I mentioning," Gold countered, his face the color of horseradish. "Rhoda . . . Rhoda . . . in here," he shrieked. Rhoda appeared, her eyes bloodshot and circled with black lines. She stood to Dobrinski's right, averting her eyes, and he patted her affectionately on the behind. "Not a thing am I mentioning . . ." Gold continued. "But look at that girl, a beautiful girl, a wonderful sister and daughter. You see

her?'' Morris shook his head in some confusion. ''Thet's not
a gas belly she's got. From chopped liver she didn't get such
a belly. She's not a big eater at home. So I ask you, from who
did she get such a belly?''

At this Dobrinski approached the Blackmans with his papers.

''Statements by people who know what *he* did and have
sworn to God to me personal, that he's the one.'' He handed
the documents to Morris who examined them carefully.

''That's truth,'' Gold averred.

''Please explain me what this means?'' Morris said. ''You
are cordially invited on the 6th of August 1936 to attend the
Bar Mitzvah of Mordecai Bernstein at the Minorah Temple,
3 P.M. How does he know to invite me?''

''A mistake,'' Dobrinski replied, snatching the paper from
Blackman.

''She's pregnant?'' Celia asked rhetorically.

''Who the hell started all this?'' Jay said.

''I swear I didn't say a word,'' Rhoda cried. ''I wanted to
go away and have it on my own.''

''Then who told them?''

''Myrna.''

''Myrna! None of her goddamned business.''

''No swearing in this house,'' Gold said. He shook Dobrinski's lapel. ''We have a man of God here.''

''In the year 1906 in the case of Esther Meltzer and Hymie
Tenser—the very same situation—it was decided that the man
was responsible and under the Latvian Convention of 1840,
he had to marry the aforesaid Esther. Here''—he handed Jay
some tattered onionskins—''read for yourself what it says.
And even more recent, the case of Selma Horowitz and Jacob
Petzel, the very same thing.''

''You're welcome to him,'' Morris said to Rhoda. ''I never
had nothing but trouble from him. Maybe you'll make a
mensch outa him.''

''And in the Bible, not to mention the Torah, it says—''

''But he's mine baby,'' Celia cried.

''Such a son-in-law. God's punishing me.''

"I wish him good luck and good-bye," Morris said.

". . . that a man of the Levy Tribe who did the same thing and upon refusing to marry was stoned to death in Mesopotamia—"

Jay realized that the situation was hopeless, and he was condemned to marry Rhoda. Sneeringly he asked her: "What do you want?"

"I just want us to be happy."

"Will you be happy if we get married?"

"Only if you want to."

There was a sudden hush, even Dobrinski stopped.

"All right," Jay said, and he felt lifted high in the air, dizzy, frightened, and somehow delivered.

"We're good for each other," she said.

"Better you than me," Morris said. "Have him with mine compliments."

Dobrinski, prepared for any eventuality, now began a sermon dealing with the nature of marriage, what was expected of the partners, how the children should be raised. When he had finished he handed them about twenty address cards of firms that would give them special discounts if they mentioned his name, and for whom he acted as unofficial agent. He said a prayer for them and for the child and urged them to call on him if it was a boy, as he was licensed to perform circumcisions and he would undercut everyone else's prices because of the unusual circumstances of their meeting.

"You see, I told you, let me worry," he said to Gold as he counted the money he had been handed. "God smiles on such marriages."

5

Jay knew with a certainty as deep and unchanging as a geometric axiom of Euclid that his love for Rhoda—if indeed it had ever existed and he wondered about this—was stillborn. Neither money, nor social position, neither time nor place, neither blood ties, nor the prospect of paradise, would alter this. If he had ever felt anything towards her, apart from a rampant urge to sleep with her, he could not remember it, and he thought this peculiar because he possessed to an uncanny degree the power of memory, of minute mental reconstruction of face, feeling, situation, place, moment, time. He could not only remember how he had come to get a scrape on his knee when he was four years old, but he could also recall the exact street of the occurrence, the time of day, who his companions had been, the color of the brick on the wall, the smell of burning wood fires and the arc of the smoke tailing up in the air like a bird without a body, something felt, elusive, evanescent. His first sexual encounter he could reconstruct down to the last detail of shape, position, emotion, and movement, both his own and those of his thirteen-year-old accomplice, an indentured Slovak domestic with hair like a flaxen wheat sheaf, long muscular legs, yellowish eyes tinted with gamboge, fists as raw as a hambone, and a body odor like something which had been hung in a smokehouse for a decade. He could still see how she wiped the almost endless spume that continued to shoot forth from him on her striped blue apron. But of his dealings with Rhoda he could remember virtually nothing, except that she was for him an abstract principle in a determinist universe, which, by force of circumstance, final and immutable, had deprived him of his freedom and altered the course of his destiny.

At her suggestion he retired from the ranks of food peddlers. Her value to her employer, the chief of Modes Dress Shoppe, was similar to that of a Prime Minister's to his Sovereign. In fact, Rhoda *was* Modes Dress Shoppe; she sold dresses, bought them, hired staff, and did all the fittings. Her chief, a Mr. Finkelstein, who had spent nearly thirty years as a wholesaler in burlap sacks, did not even trust himself with the bookkeeping, a duty which, with a sigh of relief, he had delegated to Rhoda after her second week in the store. What precisely Mr. Finkelstein did in the shop would be almost impossible to say, for it would involve a form of scientific speculation better left to physicists. He occupied a place in the store adjacent to the cash register and perched on a three-foot-high stool, nodded to whoever came in. He was incapable of composing a coherent sentence, and so had developed a type of truncated verbal shorthand that was comprehensible—so complete was their communion—only to Rhoda, who translated these signals into action. So total was Mr. Finkelstein's reliance on Rhoda that he would even have let her shave him if she had been willing; for with the exception of gray wiry hair which seemed to be fitted to his skull by some kind of cilia-producing machine, and trousers that were all creases, bearing the impression of every chair he had ever sat in, the only distinguishing characteristic Mr. Finkelstein possessed was a face permanently bleeding from razor wounds. Like decorations for valor he wore four or five toilet-paper plasters every morning. On the particular morning that Rhoda brought Jay to the store to meet him, Mr. Finkelstein had stumbled in, ashen-faced and bleeding—so truculent had the combat been that he had nearly slashed his throat—resembling a volunteer at a barber's college, run by madmen, and specializing in a new and sinister type of assassination.

"My fiancé, Jay Blackman, Mr. Finkelstein."

Jay held out his hand, which Finkelstein held for some minutes and forgot to return. Finally Jay had to yank his hand away.

"I've hired him," Rhoda said. "He'll be a big help to me,

specially when I go buying. I won't have to carry those heavy bags on the subway."

"And leaving . . . ?" Finkelstein, with some confusion, asked.

"Oh, he'll work the same hours as me," Rhoda translated for Jay.

"Paper forms . . . ?"

"Yes, I'll get him to fill out a tax form, and we'll start him at twelve dollars a week."

Jay waited with some apprehension for Finkelstein to reply. He had closed his eyes, supporting his chin in a manner at once pensive and profound.

"Well, what's happening?" Jay said with a hint of irritation.

"He's asleep."

"Asleep? Just like that?"

"It's all right, you're hired," Rhoda said.

"How do you know it's all right by him?"

"If it wasn't he would have stamped his feet."

"Oh, great. Stamped his feet."

"The only time he stamps his feet is when a woman wants to return or exchange a dress, or if she wants a refund."

"What are you getting me into?"

"Jay, honey, in a few months, you'll know the whole business inside out and we'll open our shop, and we'll also manage to save some money."

"Then we can shit on old Finkelstein."

"Don't talk that way."

"Why not, it's a goddamned good idea. It's better to learn a decent business than wheeling a pushcart. I'm glad I listened to you."

"Come into the back with me. First thing you've got to learn is where the stock's kept."

In the back room he saw a jungle of hanging dresses, which without women to fill them reminded him of unripe fruit. He waited for Rhoda to give him his instructions. It all looked simple enough: a woman would pick out a dress and he'd get it from the back—you didn't have to be a genius to tell a 38 black from a kelly green 34. He noticed two little rooms off to the side with dusky maroon velveteen drapes where the doors should have been.

"What are they for?"

"Changing rooms."

"The women change dresses in there?" he asked with interest.

"Well, they don't go on the street."

The job suddenly fired his imagination: better than freezing his ass off on a street corner. Decidedly.

"And I—?"

"Once you know the stock, you can approach a customer."

"Not before?"

"No! You see the whole point is to sell. If a woman comes in for a 36 beige wool dress and we haven't got the size or color, you switch her to something that we do have. If you don't, she walks. Or if you're having trouble getting her to switch, you T.O. her. Turn her over to me or one of the other girls. Mr. F hates they should walk."

"How can he stop them?"

"You got to make sure that they don't walk because you haven't tried. Whoever comes in, buys. That's the sort of thinking that makes a shop successful."

Jay agreed.

He spent the next few days studying styles, color, sizes, the types of approach that women liked, and those that failed. He proved to have an intuitive knowledge of how to persuade women to like something, and also the added authority of being a man in a vanity business, for women would accept his opinion more readily than a shop-girl's. What particularly attracted his attention was the accounting procedure that Rhoda employed every evening and which was called checking off. She would tear out the paper roll of the register at the last sale each day and check it against the tickets on the spike, and the two had to tally. She would then count the receipts and enter the figure in a ledger which showed the previous year's sales for the day. At the end of the week and month they would know how much they were up or down over the former year.

*   *   *

Jay's master plan did not take shape until he had been in the shop for a month. He had made astonishing progress and could sell a woman just about anything he had in stock. Even Finkelstein, who was not given to anything as energetic as enthusiasm, purred when he watched Jay. Dresses that had been packed away in camphor two years previously as unsalable were sold at almost twice the price they had originally been marked at. He had never seen anything like it in his life. Women waited in line to be served by Mr. Jay, his new appellation. If he didn't have the right size, he sold them a larger dress and had it altered. Modes Dress Shoppe had never had such a season; they were almost always out of stock. On the fourth pay day, Finkelstein handed Jay a little note scribbled on the back of his newspaper which said "up two dollars." This represented for Jay a new beginning, for he had never before had a rise in salary, but despite this additional remuneration, he felt restive and dissatisfied. He was beginning to love the business with a passion which choked him when he spoke about it, but he hated making profits for Finkelstein. In his fifth week he overcharged a woman fifty cents on a dress and pocketed the difference. This, over the week, netted him an extra eight dollars, but he knew that this policy would work only a short time. What he needed was something that would enable him to create capital, and for this he had to have Rhoda's complete cooperation. The first month also confirmed that he could never be satisfied with Rhoda and he had two affairs with women he had picked up in the shop.

On his third buying visit to Manhattan with Rhoda he decided to put to her the proposition which had been forming in his mind. They were on their way to see the dress jobber they did most of their business with and had first stopped for coffee in a luncheonette on 38th Street.

"We're up three hundred dollars over last month and five hundred over last year," Rhoda said proudly.

"Yeah, and it's in that *putz's* pocket."

"It's his business, isn't it? We only work there."

"Why do you think we're making more money?" Jay demanded.

"Because of you. Isn't that what you want to hear?"

"I want to know if it's true."

"Of course it's true. The women love you. They can't say no to you."

"The point is we're getting nowhere fast and the *nebishe* is on the gravy train."

"The point is we're still not married."

"The point is we're getting married on October tenth and that gives us six weeks to make money so that we can get an apartment."

"Okay," she mused, "what do you want us to do?"

"Go into partnership."

"With who? The bank?"

"Finkelstein!"

"What? He'd never allow it, so don't bother to ask."

"Who the hell wants to ask him. He mustn't know a thing about it."

"I'm not going to start stealing from him, if that's what you're hinting at."

Jay finished his coffee slowly, gazed at Rhoda patronizingly, and realized at that moment that she could no longer teach him anything about business.

"Rhoda, you're wonderful in a shop, but a head for business you haven't got."

"Why? 'Cause I won't become a thief?"

"Do you think I'm such a fool as to suggest beating the till?"

"Then what?"

"We average a hundred and fifty dresses a week. There's no reason why we can't sell two hundred."

"None."

"But the other fifty dresses should be our dresses."

He waited several minutes for this to register, but she gave him a blank look.

"You pay cash for everything, right?" She nodded and felt

for the two hundred dollars in her bag. "Well, most retailers do business on credit and settle in thirty days. So we buy dresses on credit from a jobber that's looking for business and settle with him when the bill falls due. We sell Finkelstein's stuff and also our own, and give him a bit of ours so that his sales are going up."

"But what about ringing up and making change?"

"You do all that in any case. We do our business in cash. It's so simple it's disgusting. What do you do with the register paper after you've checked it against the tickets?"

"Enter it in the ledger."

"But with the paper?"

"I throw it away."

"Does he see it?"

"No, he doesn't understand how it works. He just looks in the ledger and compares the receipts."

"Fine. Then every time we sell one of our own, you ring up a nickel or a dime and he gets it, and that way everything looks all right to the customer 'cause she can't see what you're ringing up. His profits increase and we make money without overhead."

"What if we can't get rid of our stuff?"

"But we will."

"What if we can't and then there's a bill to settle?"

"I go to jail. They don't put pregnant women away."

"Oh, Jay, I'm scared. It's a terrible chance to take."

"Of course it is, but we've got to take it. It's a cinch, and Finkelstein's not losing on the deal. The other important thing is that we establish credit, so that when we open up our own shop, people will know us already. And we've got to settle our bills earlier than the limit so that we get a reputation for being good business people and then everyone'll have confidence in us. You've got to get the jobbers and manufacturers to *think* you're respectable, then everything's possible."

When they got up from the table, Jay picked up Rhoda's bag.

"What're you doing?"

"I want to hold onto the money so that I can flash it when we make our order."

"We can't use it." Her voice was panicky.

"I just want to inspire confidence."

New York was in the midst of a prolonged Indian summer that had set back most of the dress people a month in selling their merchandise. Only Modes had gone against the trend and was doing business in fall dresses. They had made the same mistake as all the other retail stores, but because of Jay's dynamism, they were selling dresses that women could not wear for at least two months.

"Should we place the order with Benny?" Rhoda asked.

"No, absolutely not. He'd be suspicious if suddenly you wanted credit. We've got to find our own guy and then educate him."

Rhoda considered Jay's suggestion.

"Hey, wait a minute. About two months ago, I met a new jobber, a small one, that was looking for customers."

"What's his name?"

"Marty—?"

"Think, will you!"

"He's on Thirty-ninth Street just off Seventh Avenue. Cass, that's it."

After considerable difficulty, and with the assistance of three people who worked in the district, they found Marty Cass's showroom, which was the top loft in what had formerly been the headquarters of a camphor supplier. They took the service elevator to the eighth floor, and Rhoda watched with interest as Jay tested various expressions of bonhomie on a face which seemed designed by nature for nothing less than total motility: puckers, grimaces, scowls, risive extensions, condescension, certainty—in short the *mise-en-scène* of his every emotion, which in a curious way revealed that he was almost incapable of any strong emotion. In the showroom Jay decided on a flagrantly bored expression with the hint of a smile.

Marty Cass was a man in his middle twenties, with a long

cigar protruding at a rakish angle from his mouth, a Leo Car-
illo mustache—which Jay admired, and made a mental note
to copy—soft gray eyes, and wavy black hair done up in a
style similar to the whipped cream pompadours used by soda
jerks to decorate a banana split. He wore a powder blue suit
and a hand-painted tie of a horse—also painted blue—and Jay
immediately realized that the man, a few years his senior, was
destined for success.

"Hello . . . hello . . . hello, children. I'm Marty Cass. Now
what can I do for you?"

"Mr. Cass, you may not remember, but we met once a few
months ago at Benny Herbert's showroom."

"Remember, of course, I remember. You're Saks Fifth Avenue's dress buyer." He handed Jay a cigar.

"What is it, a blackjack?" Jay asked. "They can book you
on a Sullivan charge for smoking one of these."

"Glad to see you've got a sense of humor."

"I wouldn't be here if I didn't have one!"

"I'm not from Saks Fifth Avenue," Rhoda protested.

"I know, my child, just openers. You've probably been sent
by my father-in-law to see if I'm doing any stealing."

Jay lit the cigar.

"It's a miracle if you don't get a lip hernia from these."

"Just stub it out. I'll rewrap it and sell it as a second,"
Marty said. "Seriously though, I do remember meeting you.
The question is, was I standing at the time? I mean in an
upright position? I didn't promise to pay you ten thousand
dollars for your body?"

"No, nothing like that, and in any case I'm spoken for"—
she gave Jay's sleeve a little yank—"and we're here to do
some buying."

"Where's the showroom?" Jay asked.

"You're in it. Actually, it's not exactly a showroom . . . sort
of a closet that made good. But don't let that bother you. I've
got goods . . . goods, the likes of which you've never seen.
Now I'll show you what no human eyes have ever before
beheld." He wheeled out a rack of dresses, removed a dust
sheet.

"These look like they've given birth to hundreds."

"The latest Paris knock-offs."

"These were knocked off two years ago. I've been selling them for the last three weeks."

"You must be a genius."

"He is," Rhoda agreed.

"Now look, Mr. Cass—"

"—Marty."

"Fine, Marty, *I'm* Jay Blackman. Now listen, if we want to see ancient clothing that was worn by the Romans, they got museums for it. We want some hot numbers"—he fished in his pocket, took out a wad of notes, the outside one was a fifty and the others were singles—"not this old *dreck*."

Marty studied the roll of notes.

"I got a better idea. Want to come in with me as a partner?" He wheeled another rack out and showed Jay his new line. "Here, my dear, the blood of my heart."

"That's better," Jay said. "The other crap's good to use in a fire. The insurance company'd give you fifty percent on them."

"We're from Modes Dress Shoppe," Rhoda said.

"Where?"

"Modes! From Borough Park. Fourteenth Avenue."

"Sorry, we don't ship goods overseas."

"Didn't you ever meet my boss, Mr. Finkelstein?" Rhoda asked.

Marty thought for a few minutes, and tugged his mustache gently.

"How long've you been with him?"

"Seven years. I started with him after he'd been open a month."

"I'm just trying to remember. Let's see . . . did he ever have a dog?"

"That's right, he did. But it died, oh, about a year ago," Rhoda said.

"Yeah, I do recall. This *mashugunah* came up to my father-in-law's showroom with this dog. Yeah, that's way before I got married. How could I forget? He let the dog pick out all the dresses. Whatever the dog smelled, he bought. Oh, my God. What a day that was. He was barred from the showroom after that. In the middle of placing the order, he asks to go to the bathroom, and vanishes for the rest of the day. And this dog, big sonovabitch, collie or something like that with long hair, was racing all over the building looking for him. We had to call the A.S.P.C.A. to get rid of it. Then the next morning, the janitor found Finkelstein in the toilet. He'd locked himself in and couldn't get out and said he didn't want to make any noise because he was afraid it would disturb us. And *you* work for him?''

"We both do," Jay said. "I'm about to start up my own business in a couple of months and we don't want to leave him high and dry."

"I'm amazed that he's still in business."

"Yeah, well, Rhoda's running it for him."

"And you thought of me. Well, every new account's like money in the bank. I try not to run my business on one-shot deals. Long-term thinking. And as this is our first transaction, it has to be a successful one so I won't stick you with any garbage. All our future business is based on the first order. Now, would you like me to tell you what I think you ought to buy?"

"Oh, c'mon Marty. We're both cute. Rhoda and me didn't bring our seeing-eye dog with us 'cause we don't need one. Save the buildups for the Finkelsteins. We're gonna go into business in a—''

"—Little shop," Rhoda interjected.

"—Big way. No half-assed operation."

"Big way . . . small shop? You lie and she swears for you, that the arrangement? You got your signals crossed, children."

"Small at first, then as big as the biggest."

"Jay, my dear, you can't tell me stories. I invented the game. How do you think I married my wife? How do you think I became a—''

"Unsuccessful jobber? First you had to be an unsuccessful shipping clerk."

"Is he always a million laughs? My dear boy, I love you.

I can't help not loving you, because I can see in your heart that you're a crook of the first order. And because we're both crooks, we're gonna make it. Now first of all, put away the phony bankroll. What've you got under the fifty, toilet paper?''

"No, singles." Jay smiled, and for the first time felt genuinely at ease.

"I'll give you a hundred dollars' credit, and you pay me promptly on the tenth or I put it out for collection, *capisce?*''

"Make it two hundred," Jay insisted.

"Doesn't this boy know when he's on to a good thing, my dear?''

"Leave Rhoda out of it. I'll split the difference with you—a hundred and fifty.''

"Split the difference? Now he's doing me favors. People go bankrupt from such favors. A hundred and a quarter and that's it.''

"We'll get rich together," Jay countered.

"I can't live on promises. Take a hundred and thirty-five in assorted sizes, and colors.''

"Black and navy only. And we want sixteens to forty-fours.''

"What's wrong with the colors?''

"Nothing, except that we can't sell them. And we'll buy only winter goods.''

"It's a heat wave. What's the matter with you? You've only been in this country a long distance? We have an Indian summer that lasts till the end of October every year.''

"It'll turn cold. I'm getting married, so we're bound to have snow.''

"Rhoda, my child, tell him about the weather man.''

"He's right, Jay.''

"I'm taking the risk. If I'm right I want first priority on reorders and you'll get an order for five hundred dollars, provided you guarantee delivery.''

"I think you ought to listen to me 'cause you're going wrong on sizes and colors.''

"I think you don't know Borough Park," Jay said sharply.

"The women we deal with buy dresses for three occasions: weddings, funerals, and bar mitzvahs." He picked at the dresses. "Kelly green, red, powder blue, beige, you can't wear for more than a season."

"Then what about sizes? We don't sell furniture covers."

"A slim flat-chested woman has never been seen in Borough Park. All our customers are double-breasted Mrs. Americas who've had a few kids and eat potatoes all year round to prevent colds and they've got plenty of hanging bits. When I go into the corset business I'll buy small sizes. But now, sixteen to forty-four. Big sizes you can make smaller, small dresses you can only use as dish rags."

"The man knows what he wants."

Jay and Rhoda spent the next hour selecting dresses; when they had finished, they had ninety-six dresses which came to one hundred and thirty-eight dollars which Jay believed they could turn over with a hundred percent profit in two weeks. By this time Marty himself was persuaded that Jay would be as good as his word.

"You're three bucks over the limit," Marty said as he helped Jay fold the dresses.

"I'm an inexperienced buyer."

"Chop a dress off then."

"Chop your head off first, and that's a fact. I want ninety-six garments, not an odd lot. Remind me to buy you a drink the next time I'm in town." Jay signed the bill, extended his hand to Marty, and pinched him affectionately on the cheek. "Stick with me and you'll be wearing a diamond ring on your *pipik*."

"Gotta love him, don't you? But one word in your ear: the last guy that hung me up, got his head split open. Still in the hospital."

On the way down in the elevator, Rhoda turned fearfully to Jay.

"Think he meant it?"

"He's a bull-shitter. Likes to talk. But a nice guy."

"What if we can't pay?"

"No such word as can't. Won't maybe, but not can't. Before I went up there, you didn't think we'd get dresses. Now that we've got them, you're worried about not being able to pay. Rhoda, catch up with me, will you! Or I'll leave you behind."

She was unable to answer and she was terrified, because she realized that even though his manner had been playful, an attempt to simulate confidence and thereby create it, he had been serious. She was no longer in the position of coaching a sharp-witted but uneducated roughneck, a potential hoodlum; she was being pulled along by a determined man, a man incapable of even rudimentary idealism, a man whose savagery, drive, and antisocial tendencies had been quickly harnessed; an animal built for survival. She studied his face and now that the performance was over she could see that he was nervous and worried, but like a beast of prey who had set a trap, he was ready to spring.

"Jay, I want to ask you a question."

"Who's stopping you?"

"Do you love me?"

For a moment he thought about her question, and then like a snarling, cornered animal said:

"I'm gonna marry you, isn't that enough?"

The cold weather that Jay had so confidently predicted came three weeks later. A combination of feverish salesmanship and promises of secret trysts with the majority of Modes' Amazonian clientele enabled him to pay Marty well within the promised time. A freakish bit of luck convinced Jay that he was one of God's chosen few. Mr. Finkelstein, a winter sportsman of three decades standing, made his annual hegira to Lakewood's frosty climes two months earlier than usual. The cold snap had caught everyone unprepared and Finkelstein, making one of the boldest decisions of his life, decided to take advantage of the absence of sunshine and the lower-than-season rates, which also coincided with the retailer's Thirtieth Pinochle Convention. Garbed in a remodeled Alpaca coat with a fox collar, a legacy of his late wife, and smelling like a man who had been poisoned with some unknown Borgia henbane— the commingled fetor of oil of wintergreen, bay rum, and a recently acquired mustard plaster—he appeared at the shop carrying a suitcase which had spent its existence in the valley of dust under his bed until he rediscovered it. When he entered the shop he fell into a silent reverie, having forgotten the purpose of his visit, and so went to his usual stool. Rhoda tugged his collar.

"What's wrong, Mr. Finkelstein?" She pointed at the suitcase from which the leg of his long underwear was attempting to escape.

"To Lakewood . . . two weeks. Look after—" He gave Jay a wayward smile, rotated the wax in his eardrum with his index finger, and with his morning's lacerations fled into the street. Jay ran after him, caught him a block later at an intersection.

"Your valise, you forgot it," Jay said.

Finkelstein for a moment did not recognize Jay and thought he was under arrest so he raised his hands in the air.

"It's Jay!"

Finkelstein lowered his arms when he realized that the voice was familiar. He took the suitcase from Jay, and to make sure that no pilfering had been done while it was out of his sight he set it down on the curb and opened it. He examined the contents with great attention to detail; having satisfied himself that his eleven packs of pinochle cards and his single pair of long underwear had not been tampered with he shook Jay's shoulder affectionately.

"You wonderful . . . take care—" he uttered with some difficulty, then as the light changed he darted across the street.

Finkelstein's unexpected departure drove Jay to new heights of audacity. As soon as he got back to the shop he told Rhoda that he had to get in touch with Marty and would go to Manhattan. She gave him a helpless shrug, realizing that any comment she made would result in an argument.

"It's meant to be," Jay said exultantly.

"What is?"

"That we're gonna make it, what else? I've got another idea."

"To rob the old man?"

"That's the wrong attitude. We're helping him and ourselves. What's he losing on the deal? If not for us he'd be out on his ass, starving, or in some goddamned home for nut cases. As it is, he's going to Lakewood without a care in the world, and can play pinochle till he's blue in the face. Live and let live."

"All of a sudden you've got so hard."

"Not all of a sudden. I just never had the right chance before. Now listen, when Ruthie and Mary come in, make them wait on the tough customers, the ones who would walk even if we had them, and you sell our stuff to the ones who want to buy."

"We're out of practically everything."

"Do I have to draw you pictures? Sell what we've got, till I get back with more *schmatas*."

"What about tonight?"

"Well, what about it?"

"Howie's wife is making an engagement dinner for us at the house."

"Uch!"

"You don't even know them, so how can you—?"

"I met them once."

"Jay, listen to me. They're gonna be your family, whether you like it or not, so make an effort to get along with them. You never know when you need family."

"I've got my own, and that's enough."

"Howie likes you."

"He doesn't even know me."

"Give him a chance."

"Myrna gonna be there?"

"Naturally."

"Then count me out."

"Jay, I promise you. I swear to God, if you don't come, you can forget about your little scheme here. I'll pack it in. She's my sister, and I love her."

"She can *plotz* in hell for all I care . . . but I'll make an effort."

"You'll be back what time?"

"Late this afternoon . . . I'm off."

"Jay, kiss me."

He went over and gave her a peck on the cheek and then flew out the door, leaving her standing in the middle of the shop, her arms open, like a statue, expectant, hopeful, and grasping nothing. She picked up a broom and started to sweep the floor before opening the door to the morning's trade. Disconsolately, she got out the dustpan and gathered the bits of material, wondering what had happened, what had gone wrong with her and Jay. Never once in all the time that she was pregnant—and she was now entering the fifth month—had he asked how she felt, whether she was tired, what the doctor had said, how the marriage arrangements were going; he had always been difficult to pin down, but she had never before noticed how impersonal their relationship had become. It seemed to have gone from genesis to death without any of the intervening life-action which would have filled it out, and made her sense of loss something tangible, a slice of life with substance and meaning. Loss she was experiencing, for sure, but it was of a kind she could not pinpoint, because they had not created anything that functioned. Since she had assumed the role of confidante and accomplice the intimacy they had possessed for a fleeting moment had vanished like a ghost, so that all she retained was the memory of it. She attempted to reassure herself by examining it every now and then, as one did a school diploma, in an effort to recapture a moment in time which she had lived through and which ultimately belonged to her. She loved him, and she recognized that this was her weakness, for Jay's strength lay in utilizing weakness. He was like an animal which can attack only when it is certain that defense, let alone retaliation, is impossible.

"Oh, *he's* here," Marty said to an attractive redhead whose arm he had taken while they waited for the elevator in the little hallway outside his showroom. "The Rudolph Valentino of Borough Park—the scourge of every happily married man. Just look at that serious, beautiful face, would you believe he'd steal your handbag the moment he had your dress off?"

"Where're you going?"

"To lunch if it's okay by you. I'm interviewing for a show-room girl. Eva Meyers, this is Jay Blackman—an alias if I ever heard one."

"Forget about lunch," Jay said, taking Marty's free hand and ushering him back inside. "I want some dresses and quick."

"Where's the fire? I'm conducting an interview."

"Look, spare me the act and give this young lady a boff some other time."

"Hey just a minute. Who the hell do you think you're talking to? You ought to get your mouth washed with soap," the young woman said.

"I want to buy a thousand dollars' worth of merchandise. If you're too busy to see me, I can go elsewhere."

"Eva, my child, sit down in my office for a minute and have a drink, while I get rich."

"Oh, all right, but I don't like him."

"But I like you," Jay said. "Only I haven't got time now, but I'll get around to you and that's a promise."

Eva gave him the "sign" and he smiled at her.

"Jay, what's wrong with you? I don't mind you wrecking my business but my love life not even my wife interferes with."

"I want five hundred dresses at two bucks a throw."

"This isn't a whorehouse."

"Same difference."

"I said credit up to five hundred dollars. I'm not running a mission here."

"You'll get paid in two weeks' time and I'll give you twenty percent down in cash right now. So you're only going three hundred over your limit."

"What's the excitement? Finkelstein drop dead?"

"He went to Lakewood for two weeks."

"You know, if anyone found out we'd all wind up in the can."

"You're safe. You're just a supplier—a businessman taking a risk—nothing else."

"You're a hard man. Hey, you still looking for a store?"

"Of course I am."

"Well, I heard the other day that a little jewelry shop on Fourteenth Street is going out of business. It's a small place, regular asshole, you got to slide into it sideways. And if a woman's got big tits, you'll have to wait on her in the street."

"You know what rent they're asking?"

"I only like just heard. Why don't you go down there and find out who the landlord is. Good location near the department stores."

"Not interested really, but thanks just the same."

Jay picked out everything he wanted and was about to leave when Marty grabbed his arm.

"You gotta slow down or you'll have a heart attack. Look, why don't you have lunch then come back up and we'll kill a bottle and have a few laughs? We'll interview together."

"Till what time will you be here?"

"About five or so?"

"Maybe I'll see you then, but now I've got to meet someone."

In the street Jay rushed into a taxi waiting at the curb. It was some moments before he realized that this was the first time he had ever been in a taxi.

"Fourteenth Street, Mister," the driver said, pulling up by the square.

Jay walked down the long street, trying to take in everything at once; the number of shoppers, the types of stores, what the competition might be like, whether it would be possible to buck the big chains by combining personal attention with good value. His mind seethed with inchoate ideas—special bargains, sales, and then it occurred to him—the gimmick that would make his business different. The simplicity of it astonished him, but it was something that no one else had thought of. The department stores were too large and had to carry too many different types of dresses—catering to everyone's tastes—to try anything so radical. If he couldn't make a big profit on every dress he sold, and he knew instinctively that this wasn't possible, he had to make a small profit and sell in volume. It would limit the range of dresses he could buy, but that hardly mattered so long as the profit at the end of the year was reasonable. A one-price store: EVERY DRESS TWO DOLLARS! No alterations or fittings because that was a headache and one had to pay dressmakers good money.

He located the jewelry shop. The small window contained hundreds of rings, watches, bracelets, cufflinks, earrings, and clocks of all sizes. It was as though someone had robbed a customs shed, filled up a suitcase with contraband and dumped it into the window. It was all so chaotic that he became dizzy as he tried to take it in. No one in his right mind would possibly buy anything in there, he reasoned, so the owner had to rely on niggling watch repairs in order to keep his head above water; and this had no doubt also failed because people would be reluctant to trust their watches to a man who ran a junkyard.

Jay entered the shop and saw a tall, thin man with a receding hairline and the dandruff of a lifetime on his jacket. The man seemed surprised to see him and looked at him queerly as though the notion of someone who wanted to make a purchase was not only singular but also unnatural. He gasped and came towards Jay, still staring vacantly.

"Er, can I *help* you?"

"I think you can."

"You want to buy something?"

"Not exactly."

The man sighed with relief.

"Then what—?"

"I've heard that you plan to give the shop up."

"Plan to?" The man wondered if Jay were insane. "I already have! Wouldn't have it another minute if it were up to me."

"That's pretty definite."

"It should be. I've sweated it out for three years, and I'll be relieved to get out. Going back to my old job with Ingersoll. I must have been crazy to leave in the first place. Why, are you interested in the shop?"

"I might be," he said cagily.

"Well, I'll tell you something—something for nothing. If

you were to put up a sign in the window that said ONE DOLLAR GIVEN FOR EVERY PENNY you wouldn't have five pennies at the end of the day. You couldn't give money away in this store.''

''Why's that?''

''The location. Wrong end of Fourteenth Street. People go to Hearns, Ohrbach's, or Klein's. They don't want to know about the little guy. Save your money, Mister. Rockefeller couldn't make a go of this.''

''When are you leaving?''

''In exactly ten more days, I wish it was tomorrow. My God, it's been like being trapped underground in a coal mine for three years.''

''I wonder if you can tell me—if I'm not getting too personal—what the rent is here?''

''Fifty a month too much.''

''Fifty a month.''

''That's right. And it's not worth a goddamned penny. The landlord couldn't give it away,'cause it's a jinx store. Nobody's ever made a living here. Two people have gone bust before me and I'm getting out just in time.'' He wrote something down on a piece of paper and handed it to Jay. ''Here's the landlord's address and phone number if you want to get in touch, but do yourself a favor and look elsewhere. You look like a nice boy and it'd be a pity to ruin yourself.''

Jay took the piece of paper and studied it for a moment.

''Thanks for your help.''

''Help? What I've done is a public service.''

Jay went at once to a phone booth in a cigar store on the corner and made an appointment with the landlord. Then he rang Marty to say he could not come back.

''Say, please, I'm begging you to come. I've got three dolls here all waiting to get screwed, and I haven't got three *petzels*. Everybody wants to work for me.''

''You should go into a different business,'' Jay said.

''Yeah, what's that?''

''Ass. Then you don't have to worry about sizes and colors.''

"Listen, comedian. You made a hit with Eva. Amazing . . . she's the only one I haven't banged. I had it all set up, until you loused me up. I think she wants to make it with you."

"I'm thrilled."

"No, no kidding, she's the real thing. Brains and gash, but she's playing hard to get."

"Yeah, I know, *it* wouldn't melt in her mouth. See you, Marty. We'll get together next time I'm in town."

"Don't forget to bring money."

Jay hung up and lit a cigarette to control his excitement. It was going his way—he'd have everything—money, women, good clothes. Then in the midst of his fantasy he saw Rhoda's sad face, pleading with him, her long fingers pulling at him, her mouth on his, the hurt victimized look in her eyes, the whine in her voice, and he understood why his memory broke down—disintegrated into a thousand confused, warring factions—when he tried to think about her. It was so unbelievably crystal clear that he felt himself go chill: he hated her.

The shop was closed when Jay returned, so he went straight to Chez Gold. Supper preparations were in progress: Howie's wife, a matronly twenty-four-year-old blonde with carefully plucked eyebrows and two extra front teeth which crowded all the others, giving her an overbite and emphasizing her evolutionary connection to a lower, less prehensile form of life, greeted Jay with a horsy giggle and wrestler's bearhug.

"Hello, Jay."

"Hello, Janet." Jay sniffed the air. "What are you wearing, onions?"

"Oh,'scuse me, I was just in the middle . . ."

"That's the story of my life."

A potential size forty if ever he saw one: had her breasts never been firm and supple? He didn't envy Howie his love life.

"Where's everybody?"

"Poppa's not home yet; Miriam's in the kitchen; Howie went to the delicatessen; Rhoda's having a bath; Momma's in bed as usual, and Myrna's listening to the radio."

"Fine, I'd like to eat by myself in any case."

"Oh, you—" she gave him a playful shove against the wall—"such a sense of humor. Howie thinks you're a scream."

"Gently with the lapels, the suit's not paid for yet."

"I hear you're taking over the whole dress trade."

"You ought to join the police force with those muscles."

"Oh, you . . . Be back as soon as I've finished with dinner."

"Don't hurry."

He fell into a chair, draped his legs over the side and waited for the others to come home. He was tired, hungry, and wished he had stayed in Manhattan and had a night out with Marty and the redhead. Family dinners bored him, and the prospect of an evening—an entire evening—with them all dancing round him like flies, filled him with particular dread.

"Hi, bigshot."

Jay looked up from the floor—he always looked at the floor when thinking. Myrna. His gaze returned to the floor.

"I said, hi."

"So, what am I supposed to say?"

"You could return the greeting."

"Consider it returned."

"You've really got it in for me, haven't you?"

"What gave you that idea?"

"I didn't bring Dobrinski into this—it was Poppa's idea."

"But you told him, didn't you?"

"I had to. Someone had to stick up for Rhoda."

"Where I come from, people mind their own goddamned business or they get their heads banged in."

"And they take girls to Scranton for A.B.'s."

"I'll tell you something, Myrna. When I didn't know you well I didn't like you and now that I know you I can't stand you."

"So long as you do right by Rhoda, that's all I care about."

He got to his feet angrily and seized her by the shoulders, and she dug her fingernails into his back until he could feel them pressing into his flesh. He held her head firmly between his hands, increasing the pressure on her temples till she almost screamed. Then he bit her lip, like a mad starved animal attacking a piece of meat. She pulled away quickly and uttered a pained, muffled cry, putting her hand to her mouth.

"I'm bleeding, you bastard."

"Tell your father that you cut yourself shaving!"

"What a nice guy you are. I wonder if I've done Rhoda a favor?"

"There's no wondering about it. She'll hate you for it."

"The way you do?"

"You're wrong, I don't hate you. I only think you're stupid. Anyone who gets in my way is stupid and gets paid back."

"I think she's better off without you."

"My very words. You must've been peeping through the keyhole."

"My God, my God, what've I done to her! You're not a man, you're scum. You've come out of some sewer like a rat carrying disease and you're poisoning all of us."

"And you . . . what are you?"—his face was white, his eyes protruded—"a piece of ass that I can knock off any time I want to. And you hate me for knowing that I can. Someday when you're begging for it, I might just let you have it so that you can see what you've been missing. I'll draw it out so that when you think you're enjoying yourself you'll be suffering and when you are enjoying yourself you'll be suffering until the only thing you're sure of is that you enjoy suffering."

"On top you're all smiles, smart answers, and good looks, but inside—wow! There's never been anyone who can match you for pure ugliness, for . . . oh, I don't know . . . you're like a dog with rabies."

Jay laughed, his mood rapidly swinging to one of elation.

"Right now you'd like me to fuck you, but I'm not ready,'cause I'm waiting for my dinner. So go into your room and give us a tune on your clarinet—a Paul Whiteman special . . ." He began to laugh.

The front door slammed and Howard Gold, aged thirty, bearing hot dogs, pastrami, and corned beef, rolled into the room.

"Hey, what's the joke? I must've missed something terrific.'' He took Jay's hand warmly. ''Hello, brother-in-law-to-be.''

A born *schmuck*. On his deathbed he'll wonder what went wrong with his life. He did, that's what.

''Hello, Howie.''

Myrna pressed her finger to her lip; the blood had congealed and it throbbed.

''Whatsa matter, Myrna? I say something wrong?''

''No''—she relieved Howard of his package—''I'd better help Jan.''

''Funny girl, that Myrna.''

Jay agreed.

''Sensitive, deep down, but she's made a mess of her life. I kinda feel sorry for her. Whole life wrapped up in music and having to work in a store. Have you ever heard her play?''

''No, not yet. I'm hoping to.''

''Never heard a sound like it. Really beautiful. It touches your soul. I hear you're doing great in the dress business. Rhoda never stops talking about the way you've improved things. I'm so glad you're coming into the family. It'll be like having a kid brother.''

''Yeah, exactly.''

''I'll tell you something funny, Jay. Even though I'm six years older than you, I sort of feel like I'm the kid brother. Hard to explain. I suppose because you've been struggling since you were a kid in Europe it gives you a kind of authority with people.''

''Is that what it is?'' he said disingenuously. He despised Howard but liked him. ''I've got plans for myself. I'm a nothing, so whatever I become's better than what I started with.''

''I wouldn't say that.''

''No, I don't suppose you would.'' Jay smiled indulgently at Howard's weak face which had already begun to develop the gray unhealthy color of a wage slave, a man born to work for others and who could probably courageously defend someone else, but who was incapable of fighting for himself. What terrified and frustrated Jay was his desire to pick Howard up by the collar, shake him out of his stupor, and make him face up to life. Killers were born, not made, he thought. It occurred to him that perhaps he had been wrong about Howard's refusal to face life, perhaps that's precisely what he did do. Perhaps he recognized that he had more limitations than assets, that his instincts were designed for compliance. If this was the case, Jay would despise him even more, for having given in, accepted his weaknesses, instead of trying to conquer them.

"You'll soon be one of us."

The prospect sickened Jay.

"I'll always be what I am," Jay said.

"No, I mean a married man with responsibilities."

"I've got responsibilities, always had them."

"Well, you'll add to them. Kids are great."

"I can hardly wait."

"No, seriously, it'll be wonderful to have a little person who's just like you—exactly, except in miniature."

"One Jay Blackman's enough."

"Amen," said Mr. Gold, who had entered, carrying six secondhand suits which he had purchased from a woman whose husband had run off, and who, despite this calamity, had exhausted him with a display of bargaining that rivaled his own.

"Hello, Poppa."

Mr. Gold glared at Jay.

"No hello from you?"

"Hello."

"Hello, Mr. Gold. That's what you should say to show respect."

"Poppa, Jay wasn't being disrespectful. You're probably tired."

"Feet all over mine furniture, doesn't get up when I walk into the room. That's showing respect?"

Jay got to his feet. He restrained his natural impulse to knock Mr. Gold down, and smiled warmly.

"Too late," Mr. Gold said. "He had to be reminded."

"Can't do right in this house. I don't know why Rhoda made me come to dinner. We could've gone out."

"I'm going to wash mine hends, then we'll eat."

Mrs. Gold was carried to the dinner table by Howard and

her husband. She descended twice a year—for Passover and when the Yom Kippur fast was over. This evening, for Rhoda's engagement dinner party, she made an exception. She had seen Jay only twice and although she already distrusted him, basing her judgment on several full accounts given by her husband, she wanted to confirm that Rhoda was about to ruin her life.

"Why we eating delicatessen?" she protested as soon as she was seated in her wheelchair.

"Jay likes it," Howard replied.

"I've also made pot roast and a roast chicken," Jan piped up in an effort to placate her.

"So what we need delicatessen? Thrown-out money. There's plenty to eat without it."

Fine start, Jay reflected. He was really going to enjoy dining with the Golds.

"We'll all get to know each other better by having these family get-togethers," Howard said.

Myrna glowered at Jay as he lifted his head up to Howard.

"When Jan first came into the family, she thought we were all very peculiar, didn't you, hon?"

"Very peculiar," Jan agreed.

"What do you think of us, Jay? C'mon, tell us."

Jay waved his fork as though it were a baton and the musicians had strayed from the music, then he began to chuckle to himself as if he had been told a little joke which somehow nullified Howard's question. Smilingly, he returned to his food.

"What's funny?" Mrs. Gold, with admonition in her voice, demanded.

"Howard asked a question that's entitled to an answer," Mr. Gold said, waving his napkin in a manner that was at once seignorial and threatening.

Rhoda, sensing danger, squeezed Jay's kneecap, then patted it.

"Oh, this is silly," Howard, attempting to save the situation, declared. "I was only making conversation. We're all, except for Rhoda, practically strangers to Jay."

"I don't see what's silly?" Mrs. Gold said.

"Your momma's right: a man who sits down at your table and is goink to marry your daughter should know how he feels about pipple who is to be family."

"Am I supposed to make a speech?" Jay asked, pleasantly.

"No, only answer the question."

"Forget I asked it," put in Howie. "Let's talk about the state of the world. Do you think Roosevelt's New Deal really works?"

Ravenously Jay swam through his soup, making loud plashing noises with his spoon. Better to avoid a dispute till he'd got through the main course—then both barrels if necessary.

"I'll have to think about it for a while," Jay said to Mr. Gold, his cutlery flashing like rapiers on the serving dish.

"Jay's doing very well in business. We're gonna open up our own store pretty soon. Right, Jay?" Rhoda was conciliatory.

"I've looked at a location today. On Fourteenth Street."

"He's a real doer, isn't he, Poppa?" Howard said.

"From where you getting financial—?"

"Finance?" Jan suggested.

"Finance then?"

"It's a problem, but I hope to have a bit of my own when the time comes," he answered, chewing a hot dog.

"Well, I hope you got money,'cause from me"—Mr. Gold struck the table with a karate flat-hand blow—"you not getting a penny."

"Millionaires we're not," Mrs. Gold said.

"Four children I raised and there's still little Miriam to look out for."

"Who asked—?" Jay said and was cut off.

"Mine final word on the matter. It's closed. Not another word. I mean you come into mine house, eat mine food, do I say how much you should eat? Fruit, candy, dinners." Mr. Gold's ochre skin took on a scorbutic tinge as he tried to find a continuation. "Everything you're welcome to, but I got no money to throw in the street."

Jay pushed his plate away, not enough time for seconds.

"Money . . . a fortune's been spent on doctor bills in this house. So it's not fair to demand. God knows how long I've got to go," said Mrs. Gold.

They'll have to shoot her, Jay thought.

"You agree, Myrna? Say what's in your mind, you're the eldest," Mr. Gold demanded.

"Not a word has she said," Mrs. Gold added.

"Better leave me out of this," she said with a blood-curdling look at Jay.

"Momma, Poppa, listen!" Rhoda stood up, on the verge of hysterics. "We haven't asked you for a penny. I don't know why you've got it in for Jay, but it's not fair."

"Why we got it in for him?" Mr. Gold moaned, tipping his soup over. "You ask such a question? Not a night's sleep have I hed since you started goink with him. Dobrinski warned me," he hinted at something obscurely horrendous. "In front of a bus he could push you, a boy like thet." Jay laughed, it was funny. "See he laughs. Believe me he thought about it, and now he wants I should give him money. *Bupkiss*, I'll give him."

"*Git gesugt*, Sidney. Not one penny does he get."

"He thinks I find money on the street."

"Eat your chicken, Poppa," Jan insisted. "I cooked it the way you like—*gedempfte*."

"Eat?" Insane suggestion. "How can I eat with so much aggravation?"

"I'll eat it," Jay suggested.

"See from mine mouth the food he'd steal. That's the kind of son-in-law I'm gettink. And to think of the chances that Rhoda hed. She hed a boy who wanted to take her to King's Highway to live, a boy who would've given her the world."

"She can still go, I won't stand in her way," Jay said, all humility.

"In her condition?" Mrs. Gold cried shrilly.

"So, she's slightly irregular," Jay said.

"See . . . see . . . how he talks about her, like she was a *schmata*, not flesh and blood," Mr. Gold shouted, seizing his wife's wrist.

"I think you all owe Jay an apology," Rhoda said.

"Me apologize? On my deathbed I wouldn't apologize."

Jay's fingers were greasy from the chicken and he stuck them in his water glass and bathed them, then he picked up the edge of the tablecloth and wiped his mouth.

"See what manners?" Mrs. Gold said, pointing.

"When you eat with pigs you behave like one or it embarrasses them," Jay replied, coolly, rising from the table. He took out a dollar bill and put it on the table. "It wasn't worth it, but here."

"Jay, that's not nice," Howard said.

"Say you're sorry, please, Jay," Jan pleaded.

"He can drop dead. C'mon, Rhoda, I'll take you to the movies."

As though under a hypnotic spell Rhoda got up, only to find her father bobbing and weaving, his fists looming in the air, in their path. Spittle oozed out of the corners of his mouth and he danced dervishly to the left and right.

"In mine own house, insults!" He sprayed his wife's pince-nez.

"Tell him to sit down, Rhoda,'cause I don't want to put him in the hospital."

"That's not funny, Jay. Say you're sorry to Poppa," Howard begged.

"Not possible, Howie. You wanted to know how I felt about you? Well, it's hard to put into words, but I think I've found a family that's even worse than my own—the three of you excluded"—he pointed to Howard, Miriam, and Jan in turn—"and now I better go."

Mr. Gold returned to his place and brought his fist heavily down on the table.

"I hope he never has a happy day. The rotten bastard!"

II

SUMMER

CHOLER

FIRE

6

There was snow in the wind which swirled dizzily like a corps de ballet out of step with the music. The evenings came early and the days, what there were of them, became intervals in the darkness that the East Side drowned in. Jay had just come in. His mother, singing a medley of complaints brought on by old age, and hardly mitigated by the fact that her life was emptier than it had ever been, missed him now that business and Rhoda had usurped her former claim. She sat at the kitchen table drinking tea, her china blue eyes taking in the image of her universe—Jay.

Confused and miserable she turned to the one source of love that had always remained constant.

"I can hardly walk the stairs any more. It's my varicose veins."

"As soon as I've got some money I'll move you out of here, so don't worry about it."

"Your father will have to come too."

"If you want him to."

"I'm glad you came home early." She picked up his hand and kissed it. "You're such a good boy, but nobody understands you."

"You do."

"I'm only an old woman. And I don't count now."

"Oh, Momma, you'll always count first with me."

She held the palm of his hand against her cheek as though it possessed magical properties and could remove the anguish of a life devoted to scrabbling after food, bearing children whom she held in contempt, and tied to a man whose sense of reality began and ended with himself.

"What do you want to say to me?"

"I made a mess."

"I know you did. You have to clean it up. She's got your child," Celia said with an air of finality which closed off all argument.

Jay had never paid much attention to the furnishings in the apartment, treating it always, with frustration and apathy, as a kind of flophouse, but tonight his attention was caught by a change. There were new drapes, vaguely herbaceous in pattern, a bridge table, secondhand, and something with extended ears—an inanimate spaniel which might be loosely classified by the Salvation Army as a sofa. He waved an arm around the room, his heart filled with dismay.

"What's all this?"

"I've been saving. Nickels and dimes to try to furnish. God knows how long we'll be here. Might even die here."

"Don't talk silly. As soon as I'm on my feet, I'll have you in a decent apartment."

"But in the meantime, we have to live."

"I've got a better idea. You can move in with Rhoda and me. I signed a lease the other day for a place in Williamsburg. What do you say, Momma?"

"She wouldn't like me on top of her—a new bride."

"I couldn't care less what *she'd* like."

"You mustn't feel that way."

"I can't help myself. I don't love her and there's nothing that can change that. If we live to be a hundred, it won't matter. I've got myself into this and I'm drowning. But just because we're getting married doesn't mean I have to kid myself. I lie to other people, not myself."

"She's good for you. You're gonna become something, Jake."

"So she's good for me . . ."

"You've got a start in life."

"Yeah, but the end's also the beginning. I feel like she should be a sister. I want other women, all the time. I can't help myself. It comes over me and I start to think I'm being swallowed up. I can't give her enough of me and she wants everything. Whenever I'm with her, her eyes, her hands, they're all over me. It's as though she'd like to eat my flesh and the only way I can protect myself is to treat her bad—say horrible things. Everything that's bad in me, rotten, comes out like from a sewer. But nothing stops her. She comes back for more with her sad face, and her whining eyes, and all I want to do is vomit. I get sick to my stomach.''

"But she's an attractive girl and she's clean.''

"That's the terrible part of it. I want her and she attracts me, but then I feel as though I'm gonna die. I'd be happy to live with her and also have my own life. Personal. Nothing to make me responsible. Oh, God, I don't know how to explain it, Momma. But there's this awful goodness in her and it moves out to me like a snake and I'm afraid of it, and I hate it, and I want to make her see the world, people, me, the way it all is, and she won't let me. If she would fight me, it would be better, but she gives in all the time, to everything, and when she gives in—this sounds crazy—I know she's won. We do things my way . . . and it turns out to be her way, but without me realizing it.''

Celia Blackman held her head tightly with both hands, tears running down her cheeks, and she shuddered suddenly as though attempting to exorcise Jay's demon.

"The child will make things better.''

"I don't see how. It'll make me worse because then I'll be chained.''

"Oh, Jake, you don't understand anything. It won't make the marriage any better, but it'll give you something to love. You need something to love. What's between you and me won't change, it'll bring us closer. I'll love it, 'cause it's yours, and it'll be part of me, but we'll have something that's ours, that needs us.''

A short time later, Al came home. He had crept in quietly, his gum soles not making a sound, until he was behind Jay—just the corner of the wall separating them—and out of his mother's line of vision. His short squat body seemed to be designed for spying; a voyeur attending a forbidden intimacy.

Celia gasped when she caught sight of him.

"Aha, caught you. Planning a bank robbery," he said with a heavy guffaw.

"You've frightened Momma, idiot."

"One of these days, Jake," he hinted darkly—the avenging angel.

"You'll find a job?"

"I've got one, wise guy."

"Pretzels two cents a throw, or pickling corn beefs. The only thing you could do, and that provided you swam, would be as a lifeguard in a *mikvah*."

"See, Momma, the way he talks to me," Al whined. "The minute I got good news, too."

"You shouldn't sneak up like that, Al. It almost gave me heart failure."

"I wanted to surprise you, but I didn't know he was home."

"You saw your poppa?"

"Yeah, he was outside Katz's Delicatessen."

"Planning a revolution?"

"No, trying to get work!"

"Jake, leave him alone." Celia looked at Al expectantly. "Nu, what's the news?"

Crestfallen he turned away, wishing that he could restart the scene without Jay there, take his mother in his arms, dance her round the room, and exclaim in an exultant voice that he had finally got the job he had been looking for.

"Rosen and Freed have given me a job as a bookkeeper."

"What do they do, manufacture salamis?"

"No, big mouth, they're the eleventh biggest firm of accountants in the whole of New York State. It means that I'll be able to study for my C.P.A. exam at night school. I already signed on at City College."

"*Mazel tov,*" Celia said.

"What are they paying you?"

"Not much to start with. Thirty-five dollars a month."

"In another twenty years you might be making fifty a week at that rate."

"It's not a fortune . . ."

Jay laughed vindictively.

"What's so funny?" Al countered, glaring at him.

"You, that's what. You're small potatoes and you always will be."

Al, both protesting and hoping for approval, regarded his mother, but she remained silent and averted her eyes; he had taken sides with his father too many times against her for the strangulated maternal feeling that struggled within her to come to the surface. She shared Jay's opinion of him: a fool, and a lazy one at that, who was so susceptible to authority, not power, that he would agree to anything so long as his satellite function was reinforced. She enjoyed watching Jay prick holes in him, and because of this she secured additional fuel in the drama of self-immolation she figured in. What feeling she had once possessed for Al had been worn down in the same way as a clerk wears down an eraser, in an attempt to correct mistakes.

"I can't expect to start at the top, can I?" Al said defensively, but his mother had ceased to listen. Her eyes were rivetted on Jay's unhappy face. "But I've got a future. There's no telling, once I'm a full-fledged accountant, how many pies I can get my fingers into. Most of the big business people in industry don't know a thing about the products they sell or make, but they're accountants who know how to make books balance, how to cut losses. It's an age of accountants."

Jay took out a large bankroll, peeled off a five-dollar bill.

"Can you change this?" he said, offering it to Al who stared at it.

"No, sorry, I can't."

"Well, until you can, keep your trap shut about big business. You're your father's son, and the two of you just talk a good game. He's always shooting his mouth off about millions too—that's what he does with the rest of the bums in front of Katz's—but one sensible idea about business he never had. Know what he thinks about when he looks out the window with his feet up? Well, I'll tell you. He sees life passing him by, but he believes it's not, and that down in the street he's a king and everybody asks his advice. He's running the world from that window of his and he sits there counting money that he never made—money that belongs to other people—and when he realizes what he's doing, he hates everybody and since Momma is the easiest target he takes it out on her. He knows she won't stand up to him any more, so she has to pay for his failure. You build him up, make him feel he's something, and that's why you're the only one he can stand, but don't make any mistake about him: he doesn't love you any more than me and if you ever make something of yourself he'll hate you for it because then you won't be able to give him what he wants."

"Jay, honestly, I don't understand you. Nothing about you makes any sense to me. There's something so rotten in your heart that I can't believe we're really brothers. I only hope Rhoda can change you, but boy has she got her work cut out for her, and even though you only thought to introduce me to her once, she seems a nice person, and she doesn't deserve a husband like you. I hope she can change you, 'cause if she can't, you'll kill her."

"That's enough," Celia shouted. "I can't stand any more fighting. All we have is fighting. 'Cause Jay's making a living, everybody is jealous of him."

"Momma, that's not true," Al protested. "We're all happy about it. It's the way he treats people, don't you see? He's got you buffaloed too, and all you do is yes him to death. He doesn't need that, he needs somebody to set him straight. He's using you."

If Jay had had a gun he would've shot him. Instead, he tried to counteract Al's remarks, for he realized that his mother had been terribly upset by them.

"Momma, he resents me for one reason only: you love me. And he wants to take away the only thing we've ever had in our lives that means anything. Our love. And Poppa's put him up to it. In a week I'll be out of here and I hope Momma will be too. So you and the old man can eat each other up without us."

"I'm not going, Jake," Celia said without emotion.

"You think it over."

"She'll never leave him—not for you or anybody—'cause she loves him. And everything you've done to make her feel different works only up to a certain point, but they've had a *life* together and there are some things you can never touch."

Jay took out a ten-dollar bill and put it on the table. He stood up and went over to Celia whose head was being supported by her hands, and kissed her and squeezed her against his body. "Buy what you want, Momma." He picked up a small package that had rested at the foot of the table and opened it on the table. It contained a silk beaded evening gown. "From me to you . . . for the wedding."

She ran her fingers over the silk and then kissed his hand.

"I've got to go now." He picked up the ten-dollar bill and put it in her hand. "I love her"—he addressed Al—"and there's nothing you can do about the way we feel."

Jay had arranged to meet Douglas Fredericks, the landlord of the Fourteenth Street shop, at the office of his real estate broker. It was a small office with four desks, populated by three men who chewed cheap cigars, in between bites of sandwiches that lay spread out on wax paper, and who sipped coffee from cardboard containers. The windows were all tightly closed, and Jay wondered if the three of them slept there as well. Finally a bespectacled man came in wearing a windsor knot the size of a large peach, a white-on-white shirt with a collar that needed turning, and a blue pinstripe double-breasted suit, the shoulders of which moved independently, as though a midget was inside and was operating them for some recondite purpose.

"What can I do for you, buddy?" the man said, biting into an egg-salad sandwich, most of which landed on his lap.

"I've got an appointment to see Mr. Fredericks."

The man examined his desk blotter and then put on another pair of thicker glasses which made him squint.

"You Blackman?" He gargled some coffee.

"That's right, Jay Blackman."

"You're early. Mr. Fredericks said one o'clock."

"I'll be late next time, okay?"

"Joker, huh? Well, I hope you're not wasting my time."

"And who are you?"

"Warner."

"Broker?"

"No, I'm a concert pianist."

"Well, I'll tell you something, Warner. I didn't come here to have a shitassed rent collector ask me if I was a joker. I'm not one of the people in your tenements who's come to ask for a paint job. Clear?" he said politely.

"Now just a second"—Warner was on his feet and the egg salad fell on his shoe—"I don't have to—"

"Sit down and wipe the egg off your shoe. We're just using the office to discuss a lease. We could've discussed it any-where—in the park. You get your commission from him and he rents it at the price I'm prepared to pay, so your contri-bution is exactly nothing. So if I were you, I'd get back on the phone and dun a few old ladies for rent."

At that moment Douglas Fredericks entered. He was a tall spare man wearing a pearl gray suit and navy suede shoes, with a black homburg under his arm.

"Would you be Mr. Blackman?"

Jay stood up and offered his hand.

"Yes, that's right."

"We spoke on the phone."

"Uh-huh."

"Good, then that's settled. Can we pull up some chairs, Warner?"

Warner picked up two chairs and dragged them over. An errand boy, right approach, Jay thought.

"Now, have you seen the store?"

"I had a look through the window. It's in a bad way."

"That's the tenant's concern," Fredericks said, smiling. "The location is excellent for the right type of business. About two hundred thousand people pass by there each day. And as it's a six-day street—well I'll leave the arithmetic to you."

"All they do is pass by," Jay said. "The store's got no frontage. In fact it's almost invisible to the naked eye."

"If you're selling the right thing, people manage to find it."

"You've got all the big department stores fifty yards away," Warner tried to get in his two cents.

Cut his head off first shot, then he'll keep quiet, Jay thought.

"Look, don't tell me what's obvious. The fact is the store's small, difficult to see, and is at the wrong end of Fourteenth Street. People cross the street—they don't pass by the store. They wouldn't look at that store if it had a fire going in it for a week. I'll be honest with you: I had a talk with the present tenant."

"A poor businessman."

"To have taken the store?"

"Hardly that. He just doesn't know how to run his business."

"The shop's a big gamble. Everyone who's had it has gone bust."

"So why do *you* want it?" Fredericks said.

"I'm a gambler. I think I might be able to make a go of it."

"With what?"

"Dresses."

"That's a laugh," Warner interposed. "The big guys'll cut your throat in a month."

"It's a risk I'm prepared to take."

"The price is six hundred dollars per annum," Fredericks said.

"I'll give you four hundred eighty dollars and you paint, and put in a new window. You haven't got the frontage in width so it'll have to be eight feet on both sides in depth. That'll give me sixteen feet for window displays."

"Your offer is out of line," Fredericks said, a bit heatedly. Warner smiled.

"It's not an offer, it's a fair price. The store could be empty for six months. If I have a three-year lease at my price, you break even in terms of actual money, and you increase the value of your property by having it rented. If I build up a successful business the value of the property can increase three or four times. If I go bust, you still haven't lost anything. It's entirely up to you, but remember one thing: we're having a depression, and people are going out of business, not starting new ones. I can get a store anywhere in Manhattan, by just giving two months' security and they won't even ask me to sign a lease. So what I'm offering you is fair.''

''Get us some coffee,'' Fredericks told Warner.

''Black for me, no sugar,'' Jay said.

Warner glared at him, then left the room. The two other brokers eavesdropped on their conversation between phone calls: they looked at Jay with a mixture of anxiety and contempt. He was so young, so able to spot weaknesses in arguments, pouncing like a beast of prey.

''You're pretty tough for such a young man,'' Fredericks said. ''That's a compliment.''

''Depends which side of the desk you're sitting on.'' Jay didn't like the ironic tone, and Fredericks' patronizing manner. ''I'm sure you're a very clever man, Mr. Fredericks, but I don't really think there's much you can tell me about myself.''

''It's a convincing performance''—Fredericks tapped Jay's hand affably—''but it becomes obvious after a while.''

Jay got up.

''Sorry we've wasted each other's time. Good luck.'' He walked to the door.

''Oh, do sit down.''

Jay concealed the smile on his face and when he turned around he appeared surprised and impatient.

''I thought we'd finished,'' he said.

''Want a job?''

''Doing what?''

''Managing my property.''

''I'm not a rent collector.''

''You wouldn't have to be one. Seventy-five a week to start with and after the first six months I'll up you to a hundred if you're satisfactory.''

''I only work for myself. I'm through knocking my brains for other people. If I don't become my own boss right now, I never will.''

"You won't make as much working for yourself."

"Not at first, but if I can't make a hundred a week after a year then I've got no business being my own boss and I'll know I'm just like everyone else—a strictly no-talent zombie. Have we got a deal on the store?"

"For five and a quarter."

"Fifty bucks a year won't make any difference to you."

"It shouldn't to you either if you're going to be such a big man."

"It's a question of principles."

Warner set down the coffee and squinted at Jay.

"What would you know about principles?" he said.

"I'm not talking to you and anyway you're not exactly an expert yourself." Fredericks shooed Warner away as he would a fly. "Five hundred, that's it."

Fredericks extended his hand and Jay shook it warmly. He rather admired his calm easygoing manner, tricky without being obvious. That was the way the successful played at business.

"I'll send you a lease at the end of the week. Have you got a lawyer?"

"No . . ." It hadn't occurred to him that he might need one.

"You can use my man. He'll look out for your interests." Jay nodded and smiled.

After he had left the office, Warner tried to make out a strong case against Jay, but Fredericks remained unmoved.

"He's a bastard, with a real nasty streak," Warner concluded.

"Probably be a millionaire in ten years. He's an operator," Fredericks said, amused. "I think he'll increase the value of the property."

Dobrinski, splayfooted, and whispering to himself, stood in his freshly pressed morning suit in front of the *schul*. It was brisk, and he shivered a bit, as he doffed his top hat to the women who entered. When he saw Myrna, in a green velvet dress, he embraced her warmly and brushed the back of his hands over the exposed part of her bosom.

"It should be you next time, please God. The prettiest maid of honor I've seen," he testified.

Myrna disengaged herself from him.

"He shouldn't happen to a dog."

"You shouldn't say such things." Dobrinski sighed, his belt was too tight. "God looks after his children."

"Rhoda'll need more than God."

"Why shouldn't they be happy?" He quoted some percentages he had worked out: women who had gone into marriage pregnant and had happy lives with their husbands, and he showed Myrna some tables he had entered in a little leather notebook which verified this.

"Better show them to Jay," she said and walked past him.

About fifty people had turned up to witness the spectacle of Jay and Rhoda's wedding. Finkelstein, about one hundred dollars lighter after his foray into Lakewood's pinochle league, had, in Rhoda's honor, kept the store closed to mark the blessed event. Thoroughly discomposed from so much nodding and handshaking, he sat reading a newspaper on one of the back benches. Jay's two sisters, Sylvia the eldest, a slim woman in her early thirties with a beautifully molded face, sharp brown eyes, a firm jawline, and prematurely gray hair, held the hand of her sister Rosalee, six years her junior, whose features did not have the same fineness as Sylvia's and whose face was dominated by a large nose that hooked slightly and gave it a fugitive hunted aspect. Her hair was also speckled with gray but it lay hidden under a henna rinse with too much red in it and seemed to belong to the maroon family under direct light.

"It's hard to believe, little Jay getting married," Sylvia said.

"Best thing that could happen to him. Poppa'll be glad to see the back of him. He's caused him nothing but grief," Rosalee said.

"Two sides to it," Sylvia replied, a bit tartly. She didn't like her sister very much.

"I know whose side you take."

"I don't take any, but it's always been obvious that Poppa prefers Al to Jay and it would make anyone bitter."

"Look"—Rosalee abruptly pulled her hand away from Sylvia—"let's not go into it now." She pointed at the Gold family's representatives. "They look real *dreck*."

"How do you know?"

"I met Rhoda a few times. Jay brought her around."

"I liked her," Sylvia said firmly.

"I guess Jay did as well. He knocked her up."

"Must you be so crude?"

"I'm a crude person."

"You convinced me of that a long time ago."

"And you're a regular lady. You and your husband always so damned snotty."

"We've tried to elevate ourselves. You could do the same thing."

"No thanks, I prefer us as we are. Herman and me don't try to make impressions. He's good enough as he is."

Sylvia was afraid it might turn into an argument.

"Someday the truth'll come out about Jay—that's what Herman says."

Sylvia turned away from her sister and stared straight ahead of her at the panel where the Torah was kept.

"Herman is a butcher, he ought to keep out of things he doesn't understand."

"So it's out at last, your true feelings," Rosalee said. "I always knew how you and Harry felt about us, but I'm glad to find out that I hadn't been imagining it. In my book the both of you are phonies. And your well-educated husband is more of a shit than anybody else in the family. What is he, after all?"

"A fine decent man!"

"A two-bit arithmetic teacher, dearie, not Einstein."

"We're in *schul*, don't you have any respect?"

"Not for you I don't."

Sidney Gold watched the two sisters angrily talking and he was happy that his wife had been unable to come. She'd meet them all at the reception afterwards, and that was, from his point of view, bad enough. He already detested Jay's family, and would be glad once the day was over so that he would be free of them. They were like a pack of wolves who could not find food, so had begun to attack each other. He retired to a little dressing room in the back of the synagogue which was occupied by Rhoda and Myrna.

"Some family!" he groaned. "They heving arguments already and you're not even married." He put his arm around Rhoda affectionately. "You're a good girl. Such a good girl. What am I doing to you?"

"Shush, Poppa, it'll be okay. Everybody gets nerves," Rhoda said, trying to calm him.

"Everybody but the bride," Myrna said. "You should be reassuring her," she turned on her father angrily.

"I don't even know if I'm alive . . . such confusion."

Dobrinski knocked on the door and opened it before waiting for a reply. "The Rabbi's ready." He smiled at Rhoda. "Oh, you're a beauty, *mein kind*. Five minutes, then you come out. I'll tell you when."

He scurried next door to a small drafty room which was used as a classroom for the Hebrew School.

"Ey, you're in *schul*, so put out the cigarette," he admonished Jay.

Jay made a threatening movement and Dobrinski ducked his head as if dodging a tomato. "I'm not joking, I'll make them stop the wedding," he threatened.

"Respect," mused Morris, "he doesn't know what it means."

Jay killed the cigarette and sat down at a desk.

"He's excited," Celia said. "He can't help himself."

"I'll be back in a couple minutes."

Barney Green strode into the room.

"Geez, Jay, I almost didn't find it."

"You wouldn't've missed much."

"I never been a best man. Hello, Mrs. Blackman, Mr. Blackman."

"So he's got a friend," Morris said.

"Oh, sure, plenty of them."

"Like you?"

"Lay off him, Poppa."

"Whatsa matter he couldn't hev his brother Al for a best man? What for he needs you? A gengster."

"Who's your friend?" Barney said.

Celia began to cry, and Morris held her shoulder.

"See, you've made Momma cry."

"Not a happy day has she had from you," Jay cried.

The next half hour was a nightmare for Jay. He went through the rituals, repeated the prayers in Hebrew, drank the wine, put the ring on Rhoda's finger, broke the glass, and at last, and with some reluctance, after three cues, kissed her, thereby sealing the bargain and, he thought grimly, his fate. He had never had a serious illness, but suddenly he felt as though a fever had come over him and was drawing his life away, relentlessly. His mother, tears streaming down her face, moaned like someone bereaved during the entire service, and when he was told to walk down from the small platform, he broke away from Rhoda, dropping her hand the way he would a cigarette in the gutter without thought or interest, and he went to his mother and held her tightly in his arms, shutting his eyes the way he did when he was a child and was trying to imagine what life would be like when he became a man. He had made a mistake, married the wrong woman; he should be leaving the synagogue with his mother by his side—one person now in the eyes of Jews and the law, their destiny recognized, irrevocable. She released her hold on him and pushed him towards Rhoda who stood stock still where she had been abandoned, waiting hopefully to begin her married life.

Like a man without mind or will he followed her into the hired car waiting by the curb to drive the four blocks back to her house. His eyes were glazed and he stared at her without recognition. She held his hands and leaned her head against his chest.

"Jay, darling, I love you. I'm so happy . . . I don't think I'll ever be this happy again."

"I've signed the lease for the store," he said, waking from reverie. "This morning, I signed it."

"Oh, gee, that's marvelous," she said after a moment's hesitation and trying to regain her composure.

"We get possession next week, so that means we've got a lot to do."

She gave him a blank, hopeless look.

"I expect to be open in two weeks."

"That's impossible."

"Why? The painters are starting on Monday as soon as the jeweler's packed up, and I'll have to be there and do the buying as well."

"But we're going on our honeymoon."

"Oh? Well, we can't do both, can we? And the store's more important."

"Is it?" They were nearing her house and she dug her teeth violently into the soft flesh in her cheek to restrain herself from screaming.

"What about Mr. Finkelstein? We've got to give him decent notice."

"He can drop dead. You gave him seven years, isn't that enough?"

"We can't do things that way, Jay."

"I don't want to argue with you, Rhoda."

"And I don't want to either."

"Well, you've got me! After all your planning and scheming, you've got what you wanted, so goddamnit, you'll do as I say or you can go to hell."

He helped her out of the car and smiled at some guests who had arrived before them. She held his hand as they walked up the stone steps, wondering how she could best deal with him; he flared up at everything she said, ignored her point of view, insulted her intelligence, discarded her every suggestion. At that moment she accepted as fact what before had been a brooding uneasy intuition: that she and Jay were unsuited and that their marriage was doomed. Unsystematically, she considered her reasons for wanting him, for courting the disaster that was obvious to everyone. The child she was carrying, *his* child, counted for almost nothing; there was no rapport or sympathetic understanding to attract her; the act of merely sleeping with him was not enough to explain it. She never for a moment believed that fate, or forces within herself or the universe, compelled her to pursue him; the urge for self-destruction was latent in her, as in most healthy human beings, but she desired neither forgetfulness nor anguish. There was only one answer that came close to explaining her need for Jay: she loved him and she had chosen him, realizing that life with him would be hopeless, and insufferable; life without him would have been a living death, a valley of ashes almost inconceivable. She had chosen active suffering rather than passive death.

Reluctantly Jay held the door open for her.

"One thing, Rhoda, and remember it. Just because I married you doesn't mean I'm divorced from the rest of the world."

"You're upset . . . nervous, like me," she said. "You don't know what you're saying."

"That's just the trouble. I do know."

It was late, dark, and cold when they got to the small furnished apartment that Jay had taken for them in Williamsburg, just across the bridge from the East Side. He was drunk and slept on her shoulder in the train that took them there from her house. They walked three blocks south of the river to get to Roebling Street, and the smell from the river was vile, rank with fog and tug fumes. He breathed heavily, and the odor was a compound of cigarettes and cheap rye; he staggered suddenly into the roadway and grasped a fire hydrant to stop himself from falling.

"Jay, let me help you. It's only another block and we'll be home."

He moaned softly and she lifted him up by the shoulders. His eyes were bloodshot and the lids kept dropping like window shades with a broken spring.

"Ach," was the sound, deep and guttural, that burst forth from his lips. "Agh . . . I'm gonna . . ." He began to vomit into the gutter. He moved his head from side to side, as a nervous cat would, then spewed forth again, on his shoes and trousers. She held his head firmly and he brought up some more and hit her dress with it.

He tried to say something but was unable to and waved her away.

"It's all right, get it out of your system."

"I should have listened to you and eaten," he said, wiping the tears rolling down his cheeks. "I don't know what happens to me, Rhoda." He wanted to apologize, but he couldn't bring himself to do it.

"Don't worry, baby. S'long as you're feeling better. I'll make you some lemon tea when we get home."

He put his arm round her neck and leaned on her as they walked down the block. Roebling Street, where the apartment house was located, was a gray, dreary street, treeless and almost totally characterless. A few food shops and a delicatessen were spotted like mud patches amid the large number of apartment houses which lined the street on both sides: mausoleums for the homeless. In contrast to Borough Park, which was predominantly residential, Williamsburg seemed to Rhoda to combine all of the despicable features of the East Side with none of its vibrant life: a fine place to die in, but one hardly propitious to begin a new life in. The ugliness of this Gravesend area was so nondescript, so passive in its function of providing quarters for people who had been pushed to the edge of Brooklyn, that Rhoda's spirit—geared to withstand most of life's adversities and come back with a smile and a quiet shrug of the shoulders—fought against it.

Somebody had been cooking fish in the building. A fortywatt bulb, flickering and amber, provided what light the entrance had. Jay went ahead of her—her suggestion lest he fall backwards—up the three flights of stairs to their apartment. She had seen it only twice and for a total of twenty minutes; she had been too excited during these furtive visits to take it in, to compose a picture of the way it would look once the right type of furnishings were brought in. Jay toyed with the key and lock for some minutes until Rhoda took the key away from him and with the help of a match opened the door. A gust of damp air escaped, as though from a cylinder, and hit her in the face. Jay stumbled in over the threshold and she behind. He switched on a light and flopped onto a sofa and she saw what the apartment was really like. It wasn't quite a flophouse, but it appeared to be worse because it pretended to be more—a home! What set her against it was the realization that additional furniture, colorful drapes, would only serve to heighten the inhuman quality of the surroundings and that the landlord who had sparsely furnished the apartment with remnants from fire sales and bankruptcies had done all that could be done with the place. There were three rooms and a bathroom, free from cockroaches—at least she did not see any; she examined the bath which was shaped like a cauldron and would only accommodate the full body of someone under three feet; the enamel had eroded and a dull metal sheen appeared from underneath; the faucets leaked and the sink had rust stains. The bedroom contained a fair-sized double bed with a sagging mattress from which feathers were escaping and a wooden headboard machine-carved in a design of some kind, intended to draw attention away from the quality of the wood which, if rubbed, would reward the rubber with splinters. She examined a series of regular marks on it; something with teeth, not necessarily biped, had used it to sharpen its fangs. She got out clean sheets and made the bed, then went into the living room, where Jay lay snoring on the sofa. She shook him gently. Stirring and blinking his eyes, he rose with her assistance and staggered the few feet into the bedroom. The bed moaned under his weight; methodically she undressed him. There were no hangers in the closet so she opened the top drawer of the dresser and forced the cuffs of his trousers in, then closed the drawer so that they would hang straight. His eyes opened and there was a flicker of recognition in them, and then they sank into oblivion. In the kitchen she boiled some water and made them cups of tea and put some saltine crackers on a cracked plate. He was already under the blankets, his head hanging off the edge of the bed as though waiting for decapitation. She had never seen him so helpless, so lacking in aggression, and she discovered, when she cradled his

head in her arms and fed him tea in a saucer, that when she
assumed a maternal role the state of war which existed between them was suspended and a truce filled with affection,
warmth, mutual appreciation, if not love, drew them closer
together than they had ever been. His gratitude was real, and
his reliance on her strength had become not the admission of
weakness, but recognition of a function he had delegated to
her which would permit them an uneasy peace. Secondhand
and vicarious, it was hardly the form of love she wanted, but
it was a state in which she could feel some security and dom-
inance. He had stopped competing and was allowing her to
love him, and indeed loving her in return. She changed in the
bathroom into a nightgown which Myrna had bought her for
the occasion and studied her reflection in the tarnished cracked
mirror attached to the back of the bathroom door. Her hair
had a faint glow and a reddish tint and fell down to her waist;
her face was fuller and she had begun to bulge all over, but
she thought that she was prettier than she had ever believed
possible. Men stared and smiled at her and she knew she was
desirable. When she and Jay made love she never held back,
giving everything that it was possible to give, doing whatever
he asked of her and making the act itself something beautiful,
transcendent, an act of homage to an ideal state of existence.
Her eyes, green and luminous even in the poor light, revealed
as nothing else did how far away she was from any ideal state
and how unhappy the last few months with Jay had really
been. Like a file he had worn away the edges of her personality
so that what lay underneath was raw and sensitive to every
emotional prick. She cried more easily, worried about what
people thought, had dirtied herself forever by abetting him in
robbing the defenseless Finkelstein who, had she wanted,
could have been her prey for the seven years she had been in
his employ. She didn't need Jay to tell her that he was a sucker
and like all suckers dependent upon human decency. At the
same time, she did not harbor any genuine grievances against
Jay for forcing her to conspire against him, to bleed him, for
it seemed the natural, the obvious, way for them to improve
their position. Her principles had not suffered as a result, but

her mind and body had, she thought, because she could not
undo the act of deceit without further dirtying herself, and
destroying any hope of happiness she and Jay just might have.

When she got into bed he moved closer to her and touched
her face.

"I'm practically dead," he said.

"It's okay, honey, I know."

"Do you want to . . . ?"

She was silent.

"You must want to, and if we don't you'll hold it against
me always."

"I won't."

"You're just saying that." He supported himself on his elbow. "The mystery's gone, isn't it?"

"I don't think it is."

"Well, it's not like the first time."

"Would you want it to be the first time?"

"I would and I wouldn't. There's a feeling of doing something dangerous when it's the first time, and here you are as
undangerous as can be."

"Well, that's the way it is when a woman's pregnant on
her honeymoon."

"It's my fault."

"It's both our faults and not our fault."

"I'm glad you didn't go through with it in Scranton."

"You wouldn't have married me, then, would you?"

"I think I had to marry you, Rhoda, no matter what."

"Not because you love me, that's for sure."

"I have a feeling for you. It's just not the same as you have
for me. You want to eat me up."

"Is that why you're fighting to get away from me?"

"Something like that. I don't like the idea of someone own-
ing me, having a claim, being responsible for them. But I don't
have much choice."

"I want to help you. You've got good things in you fighting
to get out."

"Let's wait till the morning? Okay? I'll feel better then."
He rolled over on his side.

She listened for a while to the noises coming from the river, the urgency of tug hoots, the drone of cars on the bridge. The night passage of machines and people caught in them, and the pervasive smell of the river in her nostrils, the dampness of the apartment, and the camphor of the bed ticking, and Jay's rye breath, his snoring, and the sudden inexplicable kick in her womb, irregular; she was overpowered, forced to sleep, despite the fact that she had planned to go over all the events of the most important day of her life.

In the middle of the night she felt him move out to her, and his hands, warm, crept over her body. She resisted and he increased his pressure on her thighs. Will it always be this way, she wondered, and then she gave in as she knew she would. Her reliance on him, his needs and urges, was total.

"I'm committed . . ." she said in a whisper.

"Whaaaat?"

"Nothing. Just take it easy."

The jeweler—a man in flight is concerned only with his free-dom—had left the store in chaos: a counter was turned over on its side, the showcase was smashed and huge jagged pieces of glass littered the floor; wherever the eye roamed, mounds of dirt had accumulated like small coal piles in a yard.

"Must've been a fire," a man called Shimmel said. He was the painter Fredericks had assigned the job of renovating the store. "Best idea is to make a fire and rebuild the whole place."

"I may do that next year," Jay said. "God, did you ever see such a craphouse?"

"Your funeral, my boy."

"Thanks for the encouragement. Can you do anything be-side painting, or are you just a *schmeerer*?"

"Chippendale's cabinets I'll give you if you want to pay."

"Can you wallpaper the place? It won't show the dirt so much."

"You got paper?"

"No, but I'll get some. . . . Rhoda, we'll have to go to

Macy's to get some paper and I'll stop off at Thirty-ninth Street while you're picking it out.''

"I've got to go to see Mr. F: to give notice."

"Give him nothing."

"Jay! He won't know what to do or what hit him."

"Sorry, he hasn't got my sympathy. He was born a *schmuck* and that's how he'll die. It's time, Rhoda, time that he stood on his own two feet."

"Your father-in-law?" Shimmel asked, full of sympathy.

"Ex-boss. A *putz* of the first order."

"I thought it was your father-in-law. Mine lives off me like I was grass and him a cow. Listen, it'll take a day at least to get all the *dreck* outa here before I can start *schmeering* or papering. You want I should get a *schvartzer* to gimme a hand? It'll cost maybe fifty cents."

"I'm going, Jay."

"Hire him. Rhoda, I need you."

"I'll see you in Macy's at one o'clock." She was out the door before he could stop her.

"An honest wife I've got," Jay said.

"She's a *shiksa*?"

"No, I wish she was."

"That's a woman for you, a *shiksa*. They kill for their men. Someday, you'll get lucky. We'll both get lucky."

Rhoda arrived at Modes a bit after ten. Finkelstein had by this time succeeded in jamming the register, starting a small fire in the lavatory, which Betty was attempting to put out by sprinkling sugar on it, and giving two women the wrong dresses. They were now angrily haranguing him. Another woman who claimed that Mr. F gave her a goose during a fitting, one of Jay's regulars, had brought her husband to plead for justice—a little worm of a man who was spitting tobacco juice on the floor and dancing round Finkelstein in imitation of a boxer. With all this activity surrounding him, Finkelstein, by some mystical trick of personality, had remained glacially unperturbed and was threatening to go into a trance or a swoon. He rolled his eyes maniacally when he caught sight of

Rhoda standing in the doorway. In five minutes she had cleared up the mess and Finkelstein embraced her.

"No honeymoon?" he asked.

"No, we've had to change our plans. That's why I've come to see you."

"Honeymoon?" he asked again.

"Not exactly. I'm afraid Jay and I are leaving."

He sank on to his stool, the gelatinous soft green leather had long ago hardened and cracked under his weight. He shook his head and triggered his ear as if to rid himself of a fly which had entered the orifice. He rose from his seat and went outside, rolled down the awning to shade the store from the clouds, bought himself some pistachio nuts from a nearby machine, returned to the store and took up his newspaper.

"I said we were leaving, so don't make believe you don't understand," she said, with some vexation.

"Understand, what's understand?" he groaned.

"We've decided to start our own business."

"This . . . yours."

"What do you mean?"

"Yours . . . everything, who I got?"

"You can't do a thing like that."

"Can't leave me."

"I've got to. Jay says we have to. He can't work for anyone."

"The store . . . his." Finkelstein opened his arms expansively like an eagle about to take flight. "Can't leave me."

"We've taken a store."

Finkelstein swallowed a nut whole and began to choke. Betty ran to the back of the shop and brought a glass of water most of which Rhoda poured down Finkelstein's shirtfront.

Finkelstein gave an enormous belch and the nut came out with the speed of a pellet. He searched his pockets for a handkerchief and at last brought out a dusting rag which had lived in the garment for a decade. He sniffed into the cloth, expelled some mucus from the back of his throat, jumped to his feet and commenced a rhythmical stamping exhibition which in its perfect cadences would have done a West Point cadet proud.

After some moments of this tribal gavotte, he ceased as suddenly as he had begun and stared helplessly at Rhoda.

"I've got to do what he tells me. He's my husband."

Finkelstein moaned and stretched out his arms to embrace some divine and invisible God, but Rhoda, her mouth firmly set, her eyes aimed unswervingly at the sign behind the register—NO EXCHANGES OR REFUNDS OR RETURNS—was adamant.

"Like that . . . finish?" Finkelstein declared, biting a hangnail.

"My final word."

"Partnership!" he said.

"Oh, what's the use?" she answered, losing patience with him and herself and discovering that the longer she stayed the more indefensible her position became. She rushed into the street and crossed to the other side. She could hardly believe that she had spent seven years of her life in the store and that now she had walked out and closed a chapter in her life. In a way she felt grateful to Jay, for she could not have left without him. He had made her act: he had set her free.

She got on a train and went uptown to Macy's to meet Jay. She found him in the wallpaper department making life miserable for a salesman. He showed Rhoda twenty different types of paper and she decided on one which would wear like iron and was washable. They had lunch at a Nedick's hot dog stand and walked up to Thirty-ninth Street, where Jay planned to launch himself on anyone who would give him credit.

7

It soon became apparent to everyone who knew Jay, did business with him, or was related to him, that he was destined for success. The store's new windows gave it a display area and people who passed by could see that some kind of business activity was going on inside the brightly lit cavity. The wear-like-iron wallpaper had a greasy luminous quality and was the color of rancid butter. Two false walls had been liquidated by the industrious Shimmel and according to Jay's count, forty people could be crammed into the space. Like most semiliterate people, Jay was sign crazy, and Shimmel's assistant, a young Negro art student, with a predilection for unspeakably tasteless calligraphy, had plastered the walls with such inventive admonitions as: "Buy here now. Tomorrow may be too late." "All dresses one price: cutprice." "Two Dollars Only." "Original models as worn by the French." The winter months marked the watershed for J-R Dresses and during the post-Christmas sales his business increased. On a slow week he was able to move at least a thousand dresses, and by February the number of sales shot up to fifteen hundred. He bought with the astuteness of a gypsy and he always seemed to know which jobber or manufacturer was in trouble and would therefore be vulnerable to price shaving, an art he had perfected. Everyone wanted his business because he paid promptly, often in cash, which enabled whoever got his order to cheat the internal revenue of a substantial sum. His first coup was pulled during the month of December, when with information provided by Marty Cass, who got twenty percent, he finagled his way into New York Fashions, owned by Marty's father-in-law, who desperately needed to move his winter stock and was ripe for a cash sale. With $4,000 in his pocket, Jay succeeded in buying two thousand six-dollar dresses at *his* cash price. He was making tremendous dents in the business of his competitors. Manufacturers who dealt with him were blacklisted by the big chains, the Better Business Bureau investigated him after numerous complaints that he lured women into the store by window displays which suggested that twenty-dollar dresses were being sold for two. Nothing from the window was for sale, of course. Jay never had the right size of the come-on dress, as it was called, but shrewdly switched a customer to something he had in stock.

Rhoda still took an active part in the business even though she was now in the middle of the ninth month. She had always had a tendency to put on weight easily, and a combination of indifference, frustration with Jay as a husband, and simply the peculiar urges of pregnancy, forced her weight up, so that she had become massive. She worked in the store twelve hours a day and took no lunch or dinner hour, living on enormous meatball sandwiches and black coffee. To Jay she had become an object not merely of derision, but of disgust. Her obesity revolted him, although to others she still seemed attractive in spite of being overweight. As her time drew nearer, his attitude towards her altered slightly, for he realized that she would be in the hospital for at least ten days and he would be free to conduct his little campaigns with customers, shopgirls, staff, showroom secretaries, with less than his usual discretion. He had begun to live a dual existence from the first week of his marriage, using the excuse of a visit to his mother when he met women whom he had picked up during business hours. His affairs were indiscriminate and meaningless until for the second time Eva Meyers came into his life.

They met accidentally at a party given by Marty Cass. Jay had explained hastily to Rhoda that he would have to leave the store early because he had to meet some people who wanted his business.

"Here"—he gave her a five-dollar bill—"don't take the subway, grab a cab."

"Can't you drop me first? You've got the car a week and I've been in it exactly twice. Where're you running all the time, Jay?"

"I can't stand here talking all night. As it is, I'm late already."

"What's so important?"

"The business of course! I mean look at you. Do you expect me to take you with me? Honestly, Rhoda, buy yourself a mirror—you're a sight."

Conspiratorially she whispered: "Don't make nothing out of me in front of the girls. I'm supposed to be the boss also and if you treat me like dirt, they'll take advantage."

"Then stop nagging me, will you, please? Do you do anything but piss and moan?"

"You're my husband. I know it's a fact you'd like to forget."

"What're you talking about?"

"What happens if I have pains while you're out?"

"Pick up the telephone and call the hospital. What do you think I had a phone installed for? For its own beauty?"

"Please don't be late," she said, conciliatory. "I worry . . ."

"See you."

He lit a cigarette when he got inside his car, a brand-new maroon Chevrolet which he loved possibly more than anything he had ever possessed. He breathed easily, delighted that he had gotten away so easily. *Housebroken* was the word he used to describe Rhoda to Marty. The smell of the new leather seats excited him and he rubbed his fingers lovingly on the glinting steering wheel. He pulled out from the curb, taking pleasure in simply changing gears and revving up the engine when he stopped for a red light. It was *his* car and he was moving in the right direction: up. Luxury resembled a bottomless well: the more you got, the deeper the well appeared to be. Most of the people he had grown up with were still on Relief and none of them had a hope of achieving so quickly—in the space of barely a year—all that he had. The thought comforted him.

He had passed Marty's apartment house a number of times, but this was the first time he had been invited in. A doorman who looked like General Pershing opened the door for him.

"Can I leave the car here?"

"Yes, sir, I'll look after it."

Jay handed him a dime and the man doffed his cap, revealing a pink-ridged scalp. Not Pershing after all. The lobby had an odor of floor wax and carpet shampoo and Jay was greeted by another flunky who asked if he could help him.

"Mr. Cass," Jay said. "Which apartment?"

The man picked up a phone and pressed a button on a lighted switchboard which had all the tenants' names. He waited and then said: "Your name?"

"Blackman."

"There's a Mr. Blackman in the lobby. Right, sir." He put down the phone and gave Jay a smile of approval. Jay followed him to the elevator and held the door for him, but the man said: "After you, please, sir." The elevator shot up to the eighteenth floor in a matter of seconds and Jay was led to the apartment. He hesitated about tipping the man and finally took out a dime, but the man smiled at him and said it was just service and something about being paid to do a job, which Jay didn't catch. He pressed the buzzer and a maid, dressed in a black satin uniform that must have cost at least ten dollars, opened the door for him.

"Yes?" followed by a display of teeth.

Must look like a heist guy, Jay reflected.

"I'm Mr. Blackman."

"Please come in," she said, all polite and with an ass wiggle that gave him ideas as he followed her through a long foyer with about ten wall lights on either side. The walls were painted mauve and Jay's lips puckered in an incipient whistle but he caught himself at the last moment. He adjusted his tie in the mirror and the maid asked him if he'd like to wash his hands. Jay turned them over for her inspection.

"No thanks, they're clean." She tittered and he thought of asking for her phone number.

Marty, dressed immaculately in a midnight blue suit, a white silk tie, and a white-on-white shirt with a pattern that made Jay dizzy, greeted him with an affectionate hug. He touched Jay's suit.

"Klein's had a fire sale?"

"No, handmade by Jewish peasants. You didn't tell me it was formal. I would have worn my jock strap with luminous nailheads."

"Tonight we're on good behavior. My father-in-law's here."

"Never met him, but I don't like him already."

"By the way, why didn't you bring Rhoda?"

Jay reddened slightly and lit a cigarette.

"I don't take a salami sandwich to a banquet."

Marty pulled Jay by his sleeve into the living room as though he were an entertainer. A small man with an enormous head and sparse grains of red hair sutured onto his scalp was playing "Smoke Gets in Your Eyes" at a concert Steinway and a woman was leaning on the piano gazing at him like Proserpina en route to the underworld. Her elbow slipped and Jay said:

"Who's the drunk woman? She looks unconscious."

"My wife."

"Oh?"

"She's supporting a quart of scotch."

A barman behind a small but elegant mahogany bar in the corner of the circular room was crushing ice, and two people whom Jay recognized as a manufacturer of expensive dresses and a model who worked in his showroom some of the time seemed to be plotting the death of his wife. About five people stood in the center of the room, all dressed to kill, sipping long highballs and munching cashew nuts. It was the largest room Jay had ever seen outside of a movie set. Marty's wife approached them; she was carrying two drinks, both of them hers. She had raven black hair, a nose which had formerly been a chicken wing and which now, through the miracle of modern science, had become a shiny pearl onion. She wore a red evening gown with a slit down the side, revealing eight inches of sun-tanned calf. The gown had enormous square full-back shoulders, and she reminded Jay of a courtesan he had seen in a recent French Revolution epic which he had never for a moment pretended to understand. She looked like the sort of woman who spent most of her time in league with bishops, planning to murder the king.

"You forgot to introduce us?" she said, screwing her face up into a perfect tomahawk. She peered at Jay's speckled tie as though it were a curtain fabric she wouldn't even consider for the bathroom. "And he's the best-looking guy in this whole dump."

This whole dump had an authentic Dresden chandelier lit by about two hundred candles, two elaborately fluted French settees which looked as though they were made from lobster skeletons and were covered in a kind of minstrel-playing-lute-to-milkmaid tapestry which he had once seen in a Viennese museum during his electrical days with Uncle Klotz. Three spindly tables supported Meissen lamps, and the walls were covered with a satin fabric and a number of paintings showing bearded men on horseback, which probably cost more than he would earn in five years.

"Jay Blackman, my wife Paula," Marty said through the haze of her breath.

"You look like a bookmaker, Jay. Are you a bookmaker?"

"I'm a bookmaker like you're Sylvia Sydney."

She stared at him sullenly and took a sip of her drink.

"I'll bet it's the chaser that gets you," Jay said.

"Hey, tha's good," she said downing four ounces of chaser.

"Paula, tell that guy to play 'Hatikvah' or something. He's falling asleep."

Two funeral attendants marched through the room bearing trays of drinks and bull's-eye and sandwiches.

"I'll have a scotch and water," Jay said. He swallowed some and refrained from spitting it out, because Marty was watching. His rye days, he thought, unhappily, were over. An enormous blonde and a little man who had probably been her patient attempted a foxtrot in the corner of the room. A saxophonist and a weary bass player appeared on the scene and tried "Stomping at the Waldorf" with the pianist who gulped down a drink and began bouncing on his rump. Everywhere people chattered excitedly and there was a tension and electricity in the air which Jay had never before experienced at a party; the type he was accustomed to usually started at seven o'clock with everyone fighting to get at the food, drinking suspiciously from his own bottle, and then taking a ride to Canarsie in someone's jalopy with three girls: sex and heartburn in the backseat squashed between another couple who were trying to move up and down when he was moving sideways, and the girl invariably winding up with a mild concussion because her head had been banged so regularly on the

roof of the car. He succeeded in banishing Rhoda from his
mind. She didn't fit in with people like this, and he resented
her now even more.

Paula shoved a plate of sandwiches under his nose.

"Here, have some."

"No thanks, I never eat on an empty stomach."

"Whaaaaaaa . . . gee, you're a funny man." She stretched
out an arm which looked as though it had been designed to
be a coat hanger. "Daddy, say hello to a funny man."

A pudgy balding man with concentric groups of freckles on
his scalp undid her arm from his jacket and wheeled around.
Jay wondered how he got his tan and who sculpted his mustache which was so carefully penciled that he must have kept
a make-up artist. The man adjusted his horn-rimmed glasses
and tried to pick Jay out of the line-up. Yes, officer, he's the
one who had the gun, his eyes seemed to say. He wore a black
mohair suit which matched his brooding eyes.

"You all right, Paula dear?" he said, paternally solicitous.

"Oh, marvelous. Never better," she said, collapsing on the
edge of a table.

"Don't let her have any more to drink, Marty," he said in
a commanding, low voice, which impressed Jay by the authority behind it.

"Yes, sir," Marty replied. "Better get her something to
eat."

"Good idea. She likes the white meat on the turkey."

Jay found himself standing with Paula's father and unable
to make up his mind what to say. When he had made his
buying raid Harry Lee had not condescended to come out of
his office to meet him; one of his assistants had dealt with
Jay, and when he had asked about Mr. Lee the assistant had
laughed in his face and said that the boss couldn't care less
about peanut orders. If he had been Sears Roebuck, Montgomery Ward, or Saks, Jay would have been sure to get theater
tickets, dinner at Twenty-One, and the best looking call girl
money could buy, but the boss didn't waste his time on peasants who spent a few thousand for the old stock. It was ru-
mored that Harry Lee had ten million dollars, most of it in

cash. He had got out of the stock market in time, ignoring, in 1928, the advice of his brokers, lawyers, and investment counsels. He had new brokers now and six large factories which were never idle. Every big store in America carried his dresses and indeed so great was the demand that he could not fill all of the orders.

"You a friend of Marty's?" he asked, as though it were a criminal act.

"I do a bit of business with him."

"What do you call your outfit?"

"J-R. I've got a store on Fourteenth Street, near Klein's."

"Good spot. You doing business?"

"I can't kick."

"What do you push out a week?"

"I think that's my business."

Lee gave him a surprised smile and moved his head reprovingly from side to side. His fingers had that well-cared-for look which five thousand manicures tend to give a hand. His tie had cost more than Jay's suit—wild silk or something—and Jay suspected now he had been born with that suntan. He jiggled the ice cubes in his glass, then lit a thick Havana cigar whose odor almost floored Jay.

"A small guy doesn't like to talk numbers, but a big man always."

"I'll carve that on my heart."

"Pretty cute, aren't you?"

"You wouldn't be impressed with any numbers I could mention."

"Try me."

"Fifteen hundred a week."

Lee puffed his cigar pensively and blew some smoke over Jay's shoulder.

"One store?"

"That's right."

"See, you're wrong, I am impressed. If I'd asked you how much profit you were making or what the mark-up was, that would be personal, unless you were so big that it didn't matter." He flicked some ash on the carpet. He must've bought it, Jay thought. "That's department store figures. How many girls on the floor?"

"Six. Me and my assistant make eight."

"Big store?"

"Narrow but deep."

"Where else are you opening up?"

Jay pondered the question. It hadn't occurred to him that he should be hunting for new stores. He had been so amazed at his rapid success that he thought he would consolidate for several years.

"Where do you suggest?"

"I don't know a thing about the retail trade. But if you're selling cheap, then a Sunday street wouldn't be a bad idea."

"I've moved pretty fast and I thought of taking it easy for a while."

"Bad thinking. Now's the time to open up all over the place. Cheap rents. In two or three years, the way Roosevelt's going, the rents will've tripled. There's going to be a war and people'll have money again."

"You think I ought to look out of New York?"

"Every place is good. The more stores you've got, the greater your buying power. You can dictate price to a manufacturer. That's the thing of the future—big organizations, volume sales. People aren't going to want to pay high prices when they've got money. That's a mistake a lot of people make. You've got to get the masses to buy—that's business. When you sell expensive stuff you've got to contend with fickle customers."

Jay blinked with astonishment when Lee took his empty glass out of his hand and said: "I'll get you a refill."

He surveyed the room for the first time since he had come in. People were coming and going, and the festive, abandoned quality of the evening seemed more like New Year's Eve than an ordinary Saturday night. People simply gave parties; they didn't, he realized, have to have a definite reason for them. A low anguished moan came from behind him and he moved up to see what had happened. Harry Lee's even suntan appeared to have been swabbed with calamine lotion. His hands shook and he put his drink and lit cigar down on the end of a table. He lifted Paula off the sofa where she was sprawled like a trussed chicken and began anxiously trying to undo her red evening gown. Finally with Marty's assistance they got her to her feet and marched her court-martial style down a long corridor which led to the bathroom. The band played on, and no one appeared to be unduly concerned by the collapse of the hostess.

A familiar face emerged from a group of people who were in a huddle in the corner listening to someone's jokes. The face was connected to a body he was unable to see. It was a beautiful face with red hair done in an upsweep with a crown of curls. The lips were a trifle thickish, and the nose was tilted up slightly. He couldn't tell what color her eyes were because she was too far away, but then one of them winked at him and he smiled, hoping she hadn't made a mistake. He had prickles under his skin and his temples pulsated so that the whole room became hazy and gray. He finished his drink quickly and moved towards the face, asking with his glass if she wanted a drink. The face nodded and now he saw her body. She was wearing a startlingly simple high-necked black dress and a large pearl clip just at the right point on the bodice, and her red hair acted like a shock on the black dress. She had smallish well-shaped teeth and her tongue flicked out when she spoke to him.

"You were very rude to me once."

"My mother should punish me then." He handed her a scotch highball. She had a small waist and a full bosom which was out of fashion that year and the dress was doing a poor job of concealing it.

"We met at the elevator in Marty's showroom, and you said—"

"Don't go on. It's all come back to me. Let's go to the bathroom and you can wash my mouth with soap. I deserve it. I'm sorry."

"I got the job."

"When?"

"Marty called me last week. The girl he hired originally didn't work out."

"He's kept it a secret from me."

"Well, I'm there now."

"I don't want to put my foot in it again, but please tell me why a girl who looks like you would want to get into this lousy business?"

"I went to Cooper Union."

"What's that, a railroad?"

She laughed very warmly, and her eyes caught the light from the chandelier and he could see that they were a fine shade of blue like a cornflower. He could hardly believe that anyone could have eyes that were so clear and so alive.

"It's an art school," she said. She touched him on the shoulder with her index finger. "And remember it for future reference."

"Do you accept my apology?"

"You're so serious," she teased him. "I'll bet you don't apologize very often."

"That's a fact."

"All forgiven, Jay."

"Eva . . . Eva Meyers. I won't forget it again."

"That a promise?"

"An oath. Where do you live?"

"Brooklyn."

Not again, he thought to himself. Geographically undesirable.

"On Ocean Avenue."

The gateway to Canarsie and Plum Beach.

"Why did you get a job with Marty?"

"Have you tried looking for a job lately?"

"You've looked around?"

"Everywhere. Nobody wants untried designers, so I'm starting in the showroom and Marty promised to let me do a bit of designing."

"I'll bet. On couches."

"You've got a one-track mind. And Marty's as safe as they come."

"I'd get that in writing if I were you."

"You worry too much. Let's dance."

Jay led her to where a few couples were lazily keeping up with a lisping rendition of "Blue Moon." He couldn't dance, except for a shuffling two-step picked up from Barney Green. She led him easily without his being conscious of what she was doing. He pressed close to her and she put her hand on the back of his neck. Her fingers were warm and she wore a faint scent which excited him because it continually eluded him. He wanted to press his cheek against hers, but he was frightened that she would resist and make him feel awkward. She spared him the ordeal of testing his luck by pressing her cheek against his mouth but he was uncertain whether this came under normal dancing procedure or represented interest on her part. He had a strong urge to kiss her, but feared that she would object. He wondered what it would be like to be at ease with her. She moved well and gracefully on the floor and he put both arms round her and swayed with the music.

"Your store's doing very well," she said. "Everybody talks about it."

"When I start talking about it, I'll be on my way to the bankruptcy court."

"Do you like the business?"

"I like what it can buy. For my part I could be selling nails. Same difference."

"That's honest enough. The wise guy doesn't really become you." She tightened her lips. "I'm sorry I said that. It's none of my business, is it?"

"It could be if you wanted it to."

She drew away from him and dropped her arm and her mouth half opened in surprise.

"But you're married, aren't you?"

It was not really a question and Jay's hand went limp, the lights spinning round him as fast as a mechanical top. He was overwhelmed by the sadness of the situation and almost walked off the floor leaving her there. A sense of outrage made him tremble and she watched him anxiously and with sympathy.

"You weren't trying to conceal it from me?" she asked.

"I suppose not, you would have found out. It's just that . . . dancing with you and this is going to sound stupid—I don't feel married. I don't feel anything except that I'm holding you."

She led him to the settee and he fell heavily on a smiling minstrel's forehead.

"I'll get us something to eat. Turkey okay?"

"Fine." While she was fetching it he became distracted and confused, got to his feet and decided to leave. He fished in his pocket for his car key and held it tightly in his fist. A barrage of guests had arrived, and Marty and a resuscitated but deathly pale Paula stood at the entrance way and he lost his nerve. He returned slowly to the room and Eva met him before he got inside.

"You forget something?" She was carrying two plates and he took one from her. She waved some smoke out of her face with her free hand, then intertwined her arm with his. A couple brushed by them and the man touched Eva's dress and said: "Oh, la-la, it's a living doll." The woman said: "If you make one more pass, I'll cut it off."

"Well, were you going to walk out?"

"I think I was."

"Do you want me to make believe I didn't see you?"

"I really don't know what I want."

He followed her to the window which overlooked the park. The cars looked as small as Macy's toy fair exhibition at Christmas. They picked at their food and someone handed them glasses of wine.

"There's a restaurant that I like to go to in the park," she said.

"In the park?"

"Yes, Tavern on the Green. You can dance outside in the summer and they have a long sweeping bar that makes me dizzy just to sit at."

"I'll have to"—he stopped and sipped his wine. It wasn't sweet and he thought it must be Chianti.

"This isn't meant to shock you or to console you. But I'm married also."

"Christ, that's the joke of the year." He became confident and at the same time miserable.

"I'm glad it amuses you."

"No, it's not funny. It's just that I didn't expect you to be married."

"I've got a little girl who's two. That should make you howl."

"Do you love your husband?"

"Do you love your wife?"

"No. I never did."

"Then why'd you marry her?"

He ignored her question and drank more wine.

"Sorry I asked. Looks like we're both in the same boat," she said stoically. "I love my little girl very much, and I'm afraid I'll have to leave in a few minutes. One of the neighbor's kids is baby-sitting and I can't be home too late."

"What about your husband?"

"He's in Cleveland till next week. He sells sporting equipment on the road."

"I'll take you home."

"What'll your wife say?"

"The same as your husband."

They left separately in an effort to avert suspicion, and Marty held Jay's coat for him.

"You've made a hit with my father-in-law. Like to marry his daughter? You can have her for nothing and I'll pay the freight charges."

"She better?" Jay asked out of politeness.

"Much . . . she's drinking herself sober. It always happens with the second bottle. Amazing constitution. I'm hoping she'll walk through the window one of these nights."

"See you, and thanks. I enjoyed myself."

"Come up to the showroom next week."

He got his car back from a different doorman after produc-

ing his driving license and registration. Jay held the door open
for Eva and with some embarrassment got in.

Eva lived in a small apartment house on Ocean Avenue. It
was well-kept and had a night man who watched them curiously out of the corner of his eye while rolling a cigarette. A
sixteen-year-old girl who looked about thirty-five, and had
spent most of the evening eating everything in Eva's icebox,
gazed cross-eyed up at them from a copy of *Silver Screen*. She
continued with her reading even after Eva had paid her.

"Baby quiet?"

"Dead to the world."

"You can go now."

"When I finish this," the girl said, flipping a page.

"Your mother'll worry."

"Her worry? She's playing Mah-Jongg. They never break
up before two."

Eva led Jay into the kitchen, which was small but obses-
sively tidy; it seemed more like a W. & J. Sloane ideal kitchen
than a place where people ate. Copper frypans, the type used
in all-night ham and eggeries, hung from a wooden slat on the
wall opposite him. She ground some beans in a coffee grinder
and put the water in the percolator. He watched her with avid
attention, marveling at the fact that she appeared to do everything with a style peculiarly her own. He got the impression
that she had a method for everything she did.

"Like it strong?"

"Any way it comes."

"Sandra'll go soon, I hope," she added.

"I could always push her out the window."

"Not worth it. I may need her again."

"Who looks after the baby when you're working?"

"I drop her at my mother's every morning and she brings
her home in the afternoon. Not a very satisfactory arrangement
really, but frankly we need the money. Herbie's been on the
road for five years now and things have got a lot rougher.
People don't want to buy things to play with when they
haven't got enough money for food."

"So he sends you out to work?"

"It was my idea . . ." She sat down next to him in the coffee nook and put a cigarette in her mouth. She looked tired of life but she still maintained an air of buoyancy, but without bubbles.

"What kind of guy is he?"

"Honest, hardworking . . . dull. I always wanted to be a dress designer . . . funny ambition, I suppose, but that's what I studied for. I never had it in me to be a serious painter. So here I am at twenty-two and slightly tarnished with a new career in front of me. I'll tell you something: even if Herbie was doing well, I couldn't stand staying at home full time. I'd have to do something to get out of the rut of being a house-wife."

He touched her hand tentatively and watched the blue smoke filter through her nostrils. The smoke reminded him of sky writing. The water boiled and she got up slowly, patting his hand in a comradely way, and took out cups and saucers. On the way back to the table she kicked off her high heels and he realized that she was only about five-foot-two and very compact. Her legs were long and that made her seem taller.

Sandra entered the kitchen, yawned adenoidally, scratched one of her chins, and stared blankly at Jay out of small brown bloodshot eyes decidedly oriental in shape. She looked like an Indian squaw, the fat pregnant one who's always the last one to leave the reservation when the cavalry start to attack.

"Guess I'll mosey over to Apartment 4B and see if my mother's still alive."

Jay could have kissed her if she had a place to kiss. He took out a silver-dollar piece and handed it to her.

"My treat," he said. It was worth a dollar to get rid of her.

Sandra examined the coin, stuck it in her teeth, then in her eye as a monocle. A living goon.

"T'ain't gold, pardner. But I'll take it jus' the same."

"Buy yourself a mask."

"Yeah?"

"For Hallowe'en."

"That's different."

"Good night, Sandra."

After Sandra had gone, Jay said: "That's gonna be somebody's mother, someday."

"We can't all be born as beautiful as you, can we?"

"You were," he said, edging closer to her.

"You're a nice guy, Jay. In spite of yourself. But just for the record: I'm not a fast pickup. I never was, and I never will be. I made one mistake in my life. I felt sorry for Herbie and I married him. But that doesn't alter the fact that I haven't cheated on him, and I didn't sleep around when I was single."

"Would you have felt sorry for me?"

"I doubt it. No, I couldn't have *that* kind of relationship with you."

The coffee was hot, bitter, and strong, and he sipped it slowly, anxious to prolong the night. His demands on women were usually straightforward and elementary, but he found himself enjoying her company, and his desire for her increased out of all proportion. She leaned her head back against the stretch of leather head buffer behind her, and he kissed her softly on the cheek.

"I had to do that."

"Did you?" she replied in a toneless voice. "You strike me as the sort of man that doesn't have to do anything except what he wants to."

"You're too smart for me."

"That sounds like a challenge but I'm too tired to accept it, so I'll put it down to flattery and be very feminine about the whole thing."

"Can you sleep late tomorrow?"

"What do you want to do, take me night-clubbing?"

"Another night. I just wondered . . ."

"Lorna gets me up at seven and as I don't see much of her during the week I spend the whole day with her."

"Where do you go?"

"We walk up to Prospect Park, and about two hundred men, usually with their wives and children on their arms, try to pick me up. But I manage to resist them all."

"Could I meet you one Sunday?"

"Sure and bring your wife; Herb and I'll have tea with milk

ready and we'll all talk about the weather and the view of
Ocean Avenue we have from our living room.''

"I have to see you again.''

"Why?''

He put his arm around her and kissed her roughly on the
mouth. She neither protested nor gave anything and when his
hand moved to her waist she pulled away and held his wrist
firmly against the side of the table.

"It won't work, you know.''

"How do you know?'' he said angrily, at the top of his
voice. "You don't love your husband. I think maybe you
could love me.''

"That's a charming solution to my problem. Why didn't I
think of it myself? All I have to do now is fall in love with
you and we'll live happily ever after. Oh, boy, this is a George
Raft scene if I ever played one. All that's missing is the tango
music and you haven't got a .45 in your hand.'' She shoved
a teaspoon in his fist, ruffled his hair, and threw her beautiful
red head back and laughed.

"I don't think you're very funny and if you ever get smart
with me again I'll knock your head off.''

She put up her fists and sparred against the air, and he
started for the door.

"You're really serious. Hey, Jay, aren't you?'' She got up
and chased him through the living room. He was almost out
the door. "Hey, honestly, I was only teasing you.''

"I don't like to be made a schmuck of. Better people have
tried it and wound up laughing on the other side of their face.''

"Wait a minute, I didn't mean to upset you.''

She didn't finish the sentence, but fell against him. He
raised her face and looked at it with loathing, then kissed her
with a sense of anguish which almost made him cry. He forced
her mouth open, and her breath tasted warm and sweet and he
clung to her as though to a life preserver in the open sea. He
looked at her closed eyes and she came away slowly and surprised as though she had received a shock from a live wire.

"Call me,'' she said, as he started to go. "Oh, and you
better comb your hair, or your wife won't believe that you're

telling her the truth about it being an innocent little party."

"I'll see you on Monday when I come up to the showroom. We'll have lunch," he added matter-of-factly.

It rained on Sunday and Roebling Street seemed dirtier, drearier, and even more nondescript in the pelting gray thunderstorm. A street designed to support traffic and not much else. In the bedroom Jay slept fitfully. He woke from time to time to listen to the rain, breathe in the heavy odor of sleep and unaired bedclothes, then decided it was one of those lost days in which one's personality and the elements find each other at odds and the usual activities reserved for the day, visiting relatives, an early movie, a longish drive, dinner at the local Chinese restaurant, are of such overwhelming futility that sleep becomes an end in itself.

It was about two-thirty when Jay, his beard itching, his tongue parched, his disenchantment with his surroundings at a new and dizzy height, stalked out of the bedroom to the bathroom. On the way he passed Rhoda, who was glued to the radio absorbing the weather report. If she had been standing by the window he could have pushed her out, without remorse and without thinking. Pregnant women have accidents, he reflected, so she becomes a statistic, somebody has to.

"It's gonna keep up all day, the rain," she said.

"That announcer must be a genius. Must've had a college education, like you."

"You're in a great mood."

"Put on some coffee, if you can tear yourself away."

"You might ask me how I feel?"

"Well?" He paused in mid-stride.

"Rotten. I was sick half the night."

"That's what happens when you stuff yourself like a pig."

"Oh, Jay. Cut it out, for God's sake."

"Any plans for today?"

"I thought we could drive over to see my family, then maybe go to a movie."

"Good idea." Her face brightened. "I'd get an early start

if I was you. So don't bother with coffee, I'll make it myself.''

"Sure, get me out of the way, so you can go to see one of your whores."

He slammed the door in her face and ran the bath to drown her voice. A bath and a shave, although refreshing him and reaffirming his status in the human race, did little to improve his humor. He sat down at the table and drank three cups of coffee, and ate two slices of dry toast. The butter had gone rancid. Only one thing could improve the day: Eva. An afternoon in bed with Eva, safely locked in her arms, with perhaps a bottle of rye nearby.

"So what do you say?" Rhoda asked.

"If you want to see your family, you can go. I'll release you from custody. And if you'd like to make it more than an afternoon visit, I'll help you pack a bag."

Her bottom lip trembled and she fought to maintain a show of composure. Tears got her nowhere with Jay and they gave her gas. She poured herself the dregs of the coffee and flopped down in a chair. He picked up the *Sunday Mirror* and examined the dress advertisements to see if anyone was underselling him.

"What's got into you?"

He looked over the paper.

"You."

"What's that supposed to mean?"

"I'll draw you a picture."

"All of a sudden you're picking on me whenever you get the chance."

"Not all of a sudden."

"Since we got married then."

"The day we got married."

"For months you ignore me. You don't come near me."

"You sound surprised."

"There was a time when you were nice, when you cared."

"People make mistakes. And to set the record straight: I never cared a whore's drawers for you."

"Jay, you can't talk to me like that. Not after what I've gone through."

He threw the paper savagely on the floor and she recoiled as though from a slap.

"You could've saved us both a lot of aggravation if you'd done what I wanted you to in Scranton. You could've gone back to Borough Park as good as new and married somebody more your style."

"What I've done for you! I mean what were you when I met you! A porter freeloading meals at weddings you weren't invited to. I've made something out of you, given you a trade, tried to teach you manners. Everything I've given."

"If that's supposed to bring tears to my eyes, it's failed. I'm grateful and I'll always be that, but I don't feel a thing for you. You're like a dead lump of meat to me. I've learned everything you can teach me and that wasn't as much as you think because frankly, Rhoda, I've outgrown you already. Now if you want to run home to your parents, I'll drive you."

She began to wail slowly and hopelessly. He was too strong for her.

"I'm having your child!" she shrieked. "Your child, you low-life bastard. What did I ever do to deserve someone like you? God must hate me."

"Don't blame God. Blame yourself. Your child'll have a father and a name and I'll provide for it. But if you want sympathy, get it from that old pimp Dobrinski or your father."

She slapped him with the back of her hand across his face and his nose began to bleed. He caught the dripping blood with the palm of his hand, and he was more startled than hurt. He lifted his foot and with all his strength pushed against her chair. The chair thudded to the floor and Rhoda hit her head against the leg of the stove. She lay without moving, dazed, her face frozen as though caught in that last moment between life and death. Jay picked up his overcoat and walked out of the room. He paused in the hallway, hoping she was dead. He'd say it was an accident—she must have lost her balance standing on a chair. As he descended the stairs he heard a yelp that sounded less than human. He pulled up his collar and dashed out into the street. He had the key to his car in his hand but decided first to go to the bar opposite. He had never noticed it before.

The bartender gave him a warm hello, a moan about the weather, lit his cigarette, and told him to keep the matches which had the name of the place on it. Jay stared dumbly at the matchbook: SAL'S BAR AND GRILL: SPECIALIZING IN STEAKS AND SEAFOOD. It smelled like a cat morgue and the bartender seemed the sort of man who never washed his hands after going to the toilet and who cleaned the glasses with spit. Jay had three double Harwood's in quick succession. He wondered if he ought to use the telephone, but decided against it, then rushed out into the street leaving his change on the bar and started up his car. He drove wildly, passing two lights. A patrol car at the curb with two cops made him stop for one.

Eva would be happy to see him. She had to be. The hate in him welled up and he felt a distinct glow as though the bitterness had reached its limit. He realized with an apprehension so sudden and inexplicable that he gasped: he didn't hate Rhoda, he had fallen in love with Eva.

8

Eva was wearing a gray tweed skirt and black sweater when she answered the doorbell. Her hair was loosely combed in a page boy and he thought she was the most exquisite creature he had ever seen. She had an easy swaying grace and her mouth was irresistibly sad. He swallowed the mint he had been sucking and almost choked on it. She blinked her eyes unbelievingly when she put the hall light on.

"Oh, God. I don't know whether to laugh or—"

He kissed her and she almost lost her balance.

"Are you glad I—?"

She rubbed her sleeve over his wet hair and wrinkled her nose.

"I never would've believed . . . Crazy isn't it? Only seen you a few hours ago."

He brandished a paper bag which contained a bottle of rye and one of scotch. The apartment was just as neat and clean as it had been the night before and he noticed that she was making a pair of striped kitchen curtains. The material was spread out on the settee.

"You might've called."

"I didn't have your number. No reprimands today."

She rubbed his face affectionately.

"I would've made you lunch."

"You didn't do much walking today."

"I only walk in the rain when I'm in love."

"Could you get that cigar store Indian to baby-sit?"

"I'll ask her. Gee, I am glad you came. Did you kill your wife?"

He fumbled awkwardly with his coat and avoided her question. She took his dripping coat and hung it in the bathroom on the shower curtain rail, then she went into the kitchen and brought out some glasses and a hunk of salami.

"We'll both smell of garlic," she said, "but so what?"

She had long reddish-brown eyelashes and her complexion had an ivory hue under the light. He poured them drinks and opened the large bottle of ginger ale he had bought at the last moment. She reached for his hand and toyed with his fingers, then ran them along her cheek.

"So? What's on your mind?"

"I thought we might go out and have an early dinner or something."

"Do you like seafood?"

"Love it."

"We could go to Lundy's then. It's only about a ten-minute ride."

"Where's the baby?"

"Sleeping. She always has a nap before she goes to sleep. That's all she seems to do, eat, sleep, and dirty her diapers.

You didn't come from—by the way, where do you live?"

"Williamsburg . . . by the Bridge. We get a pretty fair flow of traffic and dirty windows and the smell of fog. Otherwise it's a slum."

"Then why don't you move?"

"Maybe I will. It's only temporary, but at the time it was all I could afford."

"Well, you didn't come from Williamsburg, which sounds pretty enchanting, just to hear me tell you about Lorna's routine."

"I wanted to see you."

"Well, let's not have a rehash of last night. Friends, yes, but the other—"

Jay took a long pull from his drink and observed the room which was smallish but because it had been painted white appeared larger. The furniture, a three-piece affair covered in a heavy tweed material, was functional but without interest. A mantelpiece over a simulated fireplace supported a china cat, a pair of copper ashtrays with beveled edges, two metal soldiers with beards and red uniforms, and a weathervane clock designed not to work and which no doubt had been won in a Coney Island shooting gallery. The only item he found attractive was the figurine lamp on the walnut barrel sidetable: a Dutch peasant girl with a green jacket, which must've come from Gimbels' antique department, looking, or so he thought, for a missing wooden clog. He visualized them both living in Marty's apartment without Marty, driving a white Packard convertible.

"Do you think you'd ever divorce your husband?"

"You sound like a census taker."

"Answer me, please?"

"You're really too big for this room. Herb's a good five or six inches shorter than you. How tall are you?"

"I'm not sure."

"I'd say about six-foot-two: a perfect homewrecker. Well, Jay Blackman, what do you want me to say? That I could be mad about you if I planned to get rid of my short, slightly balding husband who travels half the year?"

"You should've been a lawyer."

"What do we do about my baby?"

"Can't you be serious for a minute?"

"I could, but I don't propose to be. What's the point"—
she swallowed her drink and tilted the bottle again—"we'll
just be making more trouble for ourselves than we could ever
get out of."

He moved closer, seized her shoulders and she fell into his
lap. Her hair trailed on the floor and much to his annoyance
she stared at the ceiling. Her ears were small and pierced. He
kissed her lightly on the lobe and when she didn't pull away
as he expected her to, he put his tongue in her ear and ran his
fingers along her neck.

"Counting my skin pores? It gets monotonous . . . there're
so many of them." She stretched out her legs and let them
dangle on the arm of the settee, and her shoes dropped off.
He kissed her on the neck and she moaned slightly; he wasn't
certain if it was excitement or boredom and his hand skimmed
along her smooth thighs. He was surprised that she had not
put on stockings. His hand seemed to be traveling light years
and at last when he touched her she jerked away. Like an
acrobat she sprang to her feet and stood in front of him, her
face red and her eyes violent. He touched her hand reflexively
and sadly.

"We're not fifteen years old and this isn't the back row of
the local movie house," she said. She rushed out of the room
and he got up to follow her. He found himself in a pink room,
dominated by an enormous dressing table running the length
of the wall, a bedspread of wild silk, embroidered with initials
that were illegible, and a white quilted housecoat hanging outside a closet which seemed to be illustrated by an oriental
herbalist. She lay on the bed with her back to the door, and
he made his entry silently. Her eyes were red, but she was not
crying. She dug her nails into the plum-colored carpet.

"I'm sorry. The last thing I want to do is—"

"Then for Christ sake stop treating me like I was a piece
of merchandise that anybody could touch. I wouldn't be human if I didn't find you attractive, but stop forcing me. It's

got to come from in here"—she pressed her hand against her heart—"and I don't know. I'm pretty confused. Yesterday you were some character who insulted me for no reason when I was feeling very sorry for myself because I knew I wasn't going to get the job, and then you walk into my life at a party and I see that you've got a nice side and that you're an unhappy man who's probably making some woman awfully miserable."

He sat down on the bed beside her and stroked her back. Suddenly she turned round, glared at him with unmistakable hatred, and reached for his head and pulled him close to her. He was too frightened to move. She lifted up her sweater, undid her brassiere, and pushed his head under her sweater so that he was in complete darkness.

His astonishment gave way to discomposure; he had never lost his balance so completely with a woman. He listened to her uneven, chortled breathing as her breasts swelled. She pushed his head away after a few minutes and he sat on the floor next to a pair of furry green slippers. He could not bear watching as she removed her clothes, carefully folding her sweater and hanging her skirt on a hanger; he was frightened of having his orgasm. She stood before him only in a pair of white panties and he was overcome by an emotion so foreign and exalted that he almost choked. He loved her, and he was appalled by the realization that he had reduced his stature and confessed to a weakness. She stood over him, swaying from side to side, her face dispassionate, yet submissive, her chalk white skin, slightly freckled, exuding a sweetness and fragrance which drew him to her. He wanted to say something, but could not.

She glared down at him angrily with tears streaming down her cheeks like little bubbles, then bit his lip. He sat there mystified, impervious to pain and thought, a victim of his own passion. He had slumped down lower and with effort lifted himself on his haunches like a jackal. He lowered her panties and there was an explosion of red hair, and his mouth went to her. She pulled his arms and he got to his feet as she moved to the bed. He couldn't remember how his clothes came off, whether she had removed them or he had torn them off and he only became conscious of them when he looked over her shoulder and noticed a pile of rumpled clothing lying by the side of the bed. His body had constricted and he was aware that she was lying on her side with her mouth on him, her head as though on a guillotine which decapitated and re-embodied in the same knifelike motion, and that he was climaxing, agonizingly, and she would not release him. He pleaded with her to stop, but she ignored him, stopping at last of her own accord when he went limp and screamed.

He grabbed her by the throat and she said: "I'm dead."

"Dead?" He couldn't believe his ears. Slowly he released his grip on her. "I love you, don't you understand?"

"It'll be like death . . . your love," she said. "You'll destroy my life."

"I won't," he protested.

"What do you think we've done already? It's less than human."

"It's *only* human."

"My little girl is in the next room and I let you come into my home and I let you destroy what I've got—in my own husband's bed."

"You didn't have anything, but now you have."

"Oh, Christ, what's the use? I'm not talking about the morality of what you've made me do—what I wanted to do," she added. "I'm talking about the wreckage that you can't see yet. But it's there, right in front of us."

"I want to marry you."

"You've said that already, but I'm not prepared to give up my life for you."

"Why?"

" 'Why?' " she shouted. "Is this the sort of thing you want to build a relation on? What do you plan for me? A little two-room apartment somewhere convenient so that you don't have to travel too far and can visit me, drop your load, then go home and have dinner with your wife? I hate you. If by some crazy mischance I should ever fall in love with you, I'll hate you for what you've done to me."

"You're crazy. I don't want a fast screw, then good luck, good-bye, I want you to be my wife and have my children."

"This is getting stupid and repetitious. We're both married and we've got ties."

He tried to think of a solution, but nothing occurred to him and he felt mentally depleted. When he turned to her, he saw her adjusting her brassiere from a squatting position on the pillow. He reached out and squeezed her arm, so that the strap slipped down. He forced her down beside him. She did her best to pull away but he would not ease his grip until he was on top of her. When he let her go, her arm was black and blue and she could hardly raise it. Her eyes remained closed and he kissed her breasts. She opened her eyes slowly.

"Do it! You're torturing me."

They spent the night together, and Jay in his agony and joy could not leave her alone for more than an hour. She fed the baby and returned to him.

An alarm clock woke them at seven in the morning and the day, February twenty-first, 1937, was the happiest of Jay's life. The wintery sun sent a spoke of light into the room which illuminated her red hair and bored into her closed eyes. When she opened them with a faint fluttering she saw him propped up on an elbow, smoking and smiling. She held up her face and he came to her and kissed her.

"God help us both," she said wearily, "I love you."

Jay drove Eva to work, then went back downtown through the stream of traffic to his store. He hoped that Rhoda would not be there, and yet when he went into the shop which was already filled with early morning customers, he became vaguely alarmed by her absence. A short fat woman with spectacles attached to a silver chain attacked him with a kiss when she saw him. She brimmed with happiness and her short body stretched to reach his cheek. He didn't much care for physical affection from his staff but Helen was his star saleslady and he couldn't pull away without offending her.

"A boy, you lucky man. Eight pounds, four ounces," she exclaimed, slobbering over him. "Your mother rang us from the hospital and said would you go straight back.''

He was overcome. A mixture of relief and shock, and his hands trembled. He felt grateful to his mother for saving him from the ignominy of arriving without knowing about the baby. His staff left their customers and gathered round, congratulating him, and he felt small and cheap.

''We've all chipped in to buy you something for the baby. A carriage, a genuine English one that they call a perambulator. It's better than a carriage,'' Helen said proudly, and was seconded by the girls:

''Yeah, what do you think?''

''It's a perambulator.''

''Such a big boy.''

''What're you gonna call him?''

''You better get back to the hospital!''

This came at him all at once and he hardly knew how to reply. He threw up his arms.

''Don't worry about the store today, Mr. Jay, we'll see that things go smoothly,'' Helen cried.

''Thanks,'' Jay said in a strained and croaking voice. ''You shouldn't have spent so much money . . . Honestly it must have cost a fortune.''

''You're a good boss,'' Helen replied. ''The best one I ever worked for, a decent man. How could any of us have done less? So we're just showing our appreciation.''

''I better get moving.''

''Give Rhoda and the baby our love,'' several voices called after him.

He got back in his car, took a pull from the bottle of rye which Eva insisted that he take with him, as her mother might wonder about it. He shoved the key in the ignition and began to blubber, uncontrollably. It seemed impossible to reconcile his new feeling for Eva with the experience of fatherhood; the two jarred each other in his mind. If only he could be on his way to the hospital to see Eva . . . if only she had had his baby.

He had regained his control when he walked down the corridor of the hospital, but inside him there was a sense of relentless anxiety. He stopped by a desk and gave his name to a tall Swedish nurse who was built like a weight lifter.

"Just a sec, Dr. Rosen wants to see you," she said glumly, and he froze.

"What about?"

"I really wouldn't know." She glared at him impatiently.

"Is the baby okay?" he asked.

"I'm not at liberty to discuss the matter with you."

She picked up a telephone, whispered something into the receiver and he heard Dr. Rosen paged over the public-address system. A thin wispy man with a mustache as long as a licorice stick, a loping gait, and bushy eyebrows which lived a life all their own, came up to the desk. He turned his stethoscope round his finger with the confident air of a snake charmer.

"Yes, nurse?"

"Mr. Blackman"—she pointed a gnarled twig of an index finger at Jay, who stood looking out of the window at the air shaft.

Dr. Rosen loped over to him.

"We met, I think, once, when you brought your wife in for an examination."

"Uh-huh. How's the baby?"

"That's what I want to talk to you about."

"Oh, no, he's all right, isn't he?"

"Satisfactory. He's a normal baby—good size—but I don't want you to be alarmed when you see him." Jay's face lost its color and he began to sweat. "He's had a bit of trouble breathing. But there's nothing to worry about."

"How long will he have this trouble?"

"It's difficult to say. The resident pediatrician examined him and diagnosed it as a pulmonary infection. Has your wife had any shocks that you recall?"

"I'm not really sure."

Dr. Rosen shifted his weight from his right foot to his left, pressed his palm against the wall, and said skeptically, "She had a fall of some kind last night, didn't she?"

Jay's attitude altered from concern to "search me." The doctor did not press the point. He realized that Jay was lying.

"My wife mention anything?" he asked innocently.

"No. But she had a laceration on her scalp. Your mother brought her in. I suppose you do a lot of traveling in your business. She said you were in Philadelphia."

"I move about," Jay agreed.

"Well, the baby was premature because of her fall."

"But he's all right?"

"He is."

"Can I see him now?"

Dr. Rosen sneered ever so slightly and led Jay to the nursery. Through the glass window, Jay saw him, flat on his back, in a translucent tent that covered most of his body but revealed the face.

"Your wife's in room two thirty-eight." The doctor turned sharply and walked away.

"Thanks a million for everything."

A nurse wearing a mask gave him a thumbs-up sign from behind the window, and tilted the small basket towards him. After a minute she lowered it and he reluctantly started in the direction indicated by an arrow on the wall. He rapped softly on the door of Rhoda's room and waited. There was no reply from inside and he pushed the door open and saw that she was sleeping. Five bouquets of flowers with cards attached were in vases around the room. He had forgotten to buy flowers and was just about to rush out to a florist to get some when Rhoda awoke. He was trapped. She had a drugged smile on her face, her eyes had deep brown rings under them, and her skin had a sallow shiny glaze.

"I forgot to bring the flowers. They're in the back of the car."

"That's okay. Did you see him?"

He wondered if he ought to say anything about the oxygen tent and she sensed his anxiety.

"He'll be okay. He just needs love."

Jay approached the bed and sat down in a straight-backed wooden chair with an uneven leg which made it wobble.

"I'm sorry about last night."

She touched his hand lightly with the tips of her fingers.

"You're a man ... you mustn't lose your self-control. I

guess I just got on your nerves. Things'll be much better now. Your mother's been wonderful to me. The superintendent called her, and she came over in a taxi. She's told me all about the trouble with your father and I think I understand you much better than I did before.''

He went over to the sink in the corner and puked. Tears came into his eyes and he washed his face with cold water.

''Have you been drinking?''

''A bit . . .''

''Have something light to eat . . . some boiled eggs. Your mother expects you for dinner tonight, so don't disappoint her, okay, darling?''

''Do you want to sleep?''

She thought for a minute, and realized that he wanted to leave.

''I guess you have to get back to the store. They'll be very busy and with both of us not there—''

He gave her a light peck on the forehead and made for the door. She waved at him, and he strode morosely into the corridor. He passed the nursery and paused to catch another look at his son, but he could not see much even on tiptoe. The child was too far away. He walked about for a few minutes in the hope of finding a nurse who could go inside and hold the child up or push it closer to the window. The nurse at the desk was not there. The long corridor was poorly lighted and stretched to infinity. A vague, nagging worry crept up on him: could the baby really breathe in there? What would happen if something went wrong with the apparatus? Why weren't there any nurses about? He trotted down the corridor, turned a corner and came up against a blank wall. Retracing his steps to the desk and still finding it unattended he ran back to the nursery. He shimmied up a small two-inch wooden platform which jutted out from the window, but he could not keep his balance. In a panic he raced around the side, opened the door and tore in. His entrance disturbed some of the infants. Several whines created a chain reaction and then all of them began an exacerbated caterwauling screech. All, except his. He bolted out of the room and shrieked for help, then went back inside. In desperation he rocked the child's crib. Through the glass he saw Dr. Rosen and a nurse. The doctor came in, his face red, and his eyeballs popping out of his head.

"You get the hell out of here," he shouted.

"What kind of hospital you running?"

"I'll have you arrested if you don't get out."

"My kid! Something's wrong with my kid."

The doctor pointed to the door and Jay walked out. The doctor examined two dials attached to oxygen tanks, peered through the plastic hood, then closed it.

"Is he okay?" Jay demanded, grabbing the doctor's sleeve.

"Yes. As if you give a damn!"

"Just who the hell do you think you're talking to? I'm not a charity case. You people are guilty of criminal negligence."

"Are we now?" Dr. Rosen measured him as though for a coffin. "Did you know we gave your wife ether?"

"So, get to the point."

"People talk under ether—when they're going under, and when they're coming out of it. Your wife had quite a bit to say." Jay's face lost its color and his mouth twitched. "In front of witnesses she talked: the anaesthetist, a nurse, and myself. She kept saying: 'Jay, don't hit me . . . I'm pregnant. Jay I can't get myself off the floor, help me. I've hit my head. Jay don't leave me. Help me.' Let me tell you something, tough guy, if anything had happened either to your wife or the baby, I would have reported the matter to the police. At the very least you're guilty of first-degree assault, but your wife has to make a complaint for the police to take action. In short, Mr. Blackman, I think you're the worst shit I've come across in my life and I've met a few unpleasant people in my day. And if I catch you around here, except during official visiting hours, I'll report you to the hospital authorities and provide them with a complete report."

Jay stumbled out of the hospital. He didn't know where he walked, but after a few hours of aimless wandering he discovered he was in a bar on Second Avenue. He sat crouched in a booth by the men's toilet. He was feeling no pain and he

stared at some money in front of him. He counted the money:
six dollars in bills and some silver. He lurched to his feet and
drifted over to the bar.

"You got the time?"

The bartender, a short beerbarrel of a man with axle grease
on his hair, held his watch to the light by the register.

"Seven o'clock."

"How long've I been here?"

"Look, buddy, I'm not the official timekeeper counting for
the knockdowns, I just sell booze."

Jay returned to the table, scooped up his money, leaned on
a small hand rail that led up two steps to the street, and came
out into a biting wind that almost blew him back downstairs.
He watched a few people chase their hats across the street and
hailed a taxi. He gave the driver his mother's address and
promptly fell asleep in the back. When he awoke, the taxi
seemed to be rolling around like a light craft in a choppy sea.
He paid off the driver on Delancey Street and then bought a
bottle of rye at the corner liquor store. His legs were rubbery.
He walked down the long crooked street and the wind coming
up from the river had a gelid deathly touch in it which cut
through him. Climbing the creaking stairs of his mother's
house, past the doors of inquisitive neighbors who when they
recognized him smiled the smile accorded one of the locals
who had made good, he thought his guts would cave in. He
rapped on his mother's door and when she answered it, he
stood for a moment peering into her doleful eyes which revealed a degree of suffering he had never before noticed. She
seemed frailer and her arms stretched out towards him like
broken twigs. He fell into her arms.

"Momma, what have I done? The baby's gonna die because
of me."

"He'll be all right." She sat him down in his father's chair.
"It's a good thing she had the phone number from the candy
store. The super called me and I went and got her."

"Does Poppa know? Did you tell him?"

"No. I just said that I had to go with you to the hospital."

She stood by the window and stared into the street. "Jakie, what's gonna be with you? She coulda died. Tell me why? You can't hate her so much."

"I can't explain. She brings out the worst in me. I behave like an animal with her. I lose all control."

"She said you had another woman and that you go out all the time with women. Is it true? Jake, Jake, answer me!" She pushed his slumping head up to the light, but he had passed out, his hand tightly clutching the bottle in the brown paper bag.

Faced with a problem too monstrous to solve, Jay abandoned any hope of a solution. He continued to cross wires in a desperate effort to hide Neal's birth from Eva. He remembered alluding to Rhoda's pregnancy when he had met her at Marty's party, but as she never asked him about it, he kept quiet. Eva, who had a fine and sensitive grasp of character, already knew more about him than she was prepared to accept, but she could not keep away from him, and whenever he came, she was there, waiting, tense and aroused, for him to do as he pleased. She believed she loved him. Three weeks of his violence, his childlike need which drained her energy, had made it clear that her destiny, for what it was worth, had Jay as its focal point. Her relations with her husband had become static before Jay had come into her life, and now if she needed any justification for being a wife in name only, she had it; but as her husband was a man incapable of any kind of defense, a branch floating in a fast-moving mountain stream, he accepted his new position without complaint or comment. Jay had met him three times, giving spurious reasons each time for being with Eva, and Herbie had merely shaken his head, rolled his eyes passively, and looked away. Complications had increased Rhoda's stay in the hospital to three weeks and Jay used his liberty like a sailor coming ashore after an eight-month stretch at sea.

At three o'clock one morning, after an evening of heavy drinking and a tour which began at the St. Moritz and ended at the Copacabana, Jay finally brought Eva home. It was a shock to find Herbie sprawled on the sofa wearing a woolly bathrobe with unnaturally large shoulders which made him look like a jellyroll, a pile of *Saturday Evening Post*s by his side.

"You still up?" Eva asked.

"Yeah, a bit late for you, isn't it?" Jay said.

"Couldn't sleep." He sat up and peered at them out of liquid brown eyes. His forehead was decorated with sweat-beads and when he lowered his head he showed a perfect isthmus of pink scalp.

"How's tricks, Herbie? Let's see, you're pushing off to-morrow to where did you say, Eva?"

"Charlotte, North Carolina. It's his southern route."

"You need your sleep, Herbie. That's a long drive."

"Where've you been?" he said, lighting a cigarette with a shaking hand.

"We had a business conference with Marty. Jay's opening two more stores next month."

Herbie nodded his head and blinked, as though the light was too strong.

"Smells like it."

"Well, we had a few drinks; anything wrong with that?" Jay said defiantly.

"Big businessman."

"I'm doing all right. Why, you want a job? Maybe I can find something for you."

Eva giggled drunkenly.

"He could get the coffee and sandwiches for the girls."

"Hey, that's a great idea. It's worth at least a sawbuck a week. What do you say, huh?"

"What's the matter with you, Eva? I think I'm entitled to an explanation."

"Here, have a drink, it'll settle your nerves." She handed him four fingers of rye.

"I don't want a drink."

"Sure, have one, your balls are in an uproar," Jay said.

"Don't use expressions like that in front of my wife."

"I don't object. It's colorful."

"I suppose the people you work with all talk dirty in front of you."

"What if they do?" Jay interjected. "If you made a living, she wouldn't have to go out to work and hear all those nasty words."

"She could manage on what I make . . . if she wanted to."

"And do what? Live on peanut-butter sandwiches all week."

"Maybe you haven't heard that we're having a depression. No one's making money."

Eva pointed her almost empty glass at Jay and said proudly: "Jay is. Nothing stops him, bad times, good times. He's got the golden touch."

"That's reassuring." He cocked a finger at Jay. "Look, Blackman, I want you to leave my wife alone. From what I hear, you're married. So if you want to cheat, find somebody else. Not my wife. Do you understand or are you too drunk?"

"That's a pretty serious accusation. I don't care what you say about me, but you should have a little respect for your wife."

"Like you do?"

"I don't think I like your tone, Herbie. Jay's a friend of mine, and he does a lot of business with us. *Business*, that's what I get a commission on."

He looked from one to the other—the Lady or the Tiger— and in a quavery voice said: "That doesn't mean you have to become a whore."

"Hey, listen, you little shitheeler, if you were a bit bigger I'd put you through that wall, but I might kill you if I hit you. Eva can pack her bags anytime she feels like it and take the kid with her. I'd set her up in an apartment tomorrow, but she's too nice to leave you, so be grateful, and don't take your complexes out on her." Jay waited for the silence to explode, but the argument seemed to drain all the color from Herbie's face, and he shook his head disconsolately.

"I'm sorry, I didn't mean anything. It's just that I never see her much and I'm going on the road for six weeks." Pathetically he held out his hand to Jay. "No hard feelings. It just looked funny seeing you and Eva together so much.''

"Okay, okay, Herbert, but don't get any ideas. It's strictly business.'' Jay shook hands with him, and couldn't quite believe that he had foxed him so easily. He wondered uneasily on his way down to the car if Herbie had allowed himself to be tricked, and then dismissed it from his mind. He drove home slowly; he had to find a way out, before Rhoda and Neal came home.

The next day when he got home from the store he thought he heard someone moving around in the apartment. He put his ear to the door, heard the bath running, and the radio blaring something heavy and classical. He opened the door silently, crept into the passage on tiptoe, both fists clenched, prepared to fight. A voice, a female voice, trilled along with the music. He loosened his tie and removed his jacket, flinging both down on a dusty chair which was a repository of a month's supply of newspapers. The voice was in the bathroom and he eased the door open.

"What . . . ?''

"Christ, you scared the life out of me.''

"Well, Myrna. Can't say I expected to find you in the toilet.''

The air was heavy with disinfectant and Jay held his nose.

"Rhoda gave me the key, so I thought I'd give it a quick clean before she came home.''

"You're too good to be true.''

She glared at him, her eyes hesitant and a bit frightened.

"A goodwill gesture?''

"Whatever you like. I could hardly expect Rhoda to start cleaning the minute she walked through the door.''

"It must be something more to make you come up here!''

"Like a jungle here. Who's been eating all the bananas?''

"Monkeys. Didn't Rhoda tell you I keep three monkeys? Gotta lock them in a closet when I leave. We play poker when I get home.''

"Same old Jay.''

"You want to be friends, don't you? You want to be forgiven,'' he added.

"Oh, boy, you've still got a God complex." She brushed her hair back with the back of her hand and sighed. "Money hasn't improved your disposition one bit."

"Hey, you're going to pick a fight. I don't want to fight with you and I only said what I did because we ought to clear the air. You dropped me in the shit with your family and anything I do, not that I intend doing much, won't make them like me any better. You stuck your nose into somebody else's life and changed that life, so I'm entitled to a beef."

"You never would've married Rhoda, if I didn't butt in," she said a bit forlornly.

"Of course I would've. I had to, didn't I?"

"It didn't look like that from where I was sitting."

He put out his hand and she looked at it for a moment, puzzled and unsure of herself.

"C'mon, shake. I'm not gonna throw you over my back."

She smiled uncertainly, and extended her hand. He could see how attractive she had been when she was younger. Her figure was still good. It had set like plaster of Paris, but the shape, the allusion to an earlier grace, still remained. Rhoda, a later model from the same mold, had a coarseness that Myrna had avoided. She had a firm nose, hooked in structure, but not exaggerated, and finely-stranded hair done in a bun which had a silky sheen in sunlight and was by turns reddish and brunet. Her face had an alertness and a fine sense of intelligence which because of bitterness and her wary attitude towards people never quite relaxed; and her laugh sounded like a jeer. When Jay held her hand for a minute, she became sullen and cautious.

"I've still got a lot to do. Kitchen floor needs scrubbing."

"Oh, yeah. Well, you don't have to bother."

"I always finish what I start."

"Hey, what're you doing for dinner? Date or something?"

"Don't be sarcastic." She flushed and flung her hands in the air.

"Wait a minute. You take everything the wrong way. I was only trying to be nice."

"It's difficult to tell with you."

"What I thought was we could have a deli dinner. There's a good one down the block. I could get some hot dogs, corned beef, anything you like and we'd eat here when you want."

She raised her eyebrows and her chary expression turned into a full smile. He patted her shoulder amicably.

"What do you say, huh?"

"That sounds swell. But honestly if you've got other plans I don't want you to change them for me. Rhoda says you're busy trying to get two new stores into shape."

"Not tonight. I'm knocked out."

She considered the proposition as though her future hung in the balance and one false move would mean irrevocable bondage.

"Be an executive, make a quick decision."

"Yes, then." A great load had been lifted.

On his way out, Jay saw a rectangular black leather case. He studied it curiously for a moment, then opened it. Inside he found a clarinet, dismantled, and like a child, unable to keep away from a strange object, he began to assemble it. He laughed guiltily to himself, then went to the mirror, stuck it in his mouth, and blew with all his strength. A strange muted duck call was emitted from the instrument, and his cheeks became inflated once more as he tried to blow it. In the mirror, he saw Myrna approach him, her face white and tense and her hands shaking while she tried to control her anger.

"Please, please stop it."

"I was only kidding around."

"You mustn't touch it." She took it from him, her eyes panicky and suddenly feverish.

"I didn't break it, or anything. Just wanted to try blowing it."

She took a red cloth out of the black case and gently, with deft, loving strokes, began to polish it.

"You shouldn't have touched it."

"Did I get germs on it?"

She seemed hypnotized.

"Germs? I'm not sure."

"I thought you gave it up?"

She came over to him and in a lost, faraway voice whispered conspiratorially: "Please don't tell anyone. I've started taking lessons again."

He was puzzled and uncomfortable and sorry for her. He touched her face with his fingers and she shrank away into a corner.

"I've found a wonderful teacher. She's at the Juilliard School of Music."

"Oh? Well, I'll forget that you told me," he said at last in some confusion.

On the way to the delicatessen he telephoned Eva and learned with some irritation that she could not see him because her mother was spending the evening with her. She sounded remote, and Jay was troubled and disgruntled and accused her of duplicity. She swore at him and he slammed the receiver down and bought a bottle of rye to assuage his virulent anger. When he returned, Myrna came to the door with an expansive smile and an air of passionate reunion. She had used the time to comb her hair and had put on fresh make-up. Jay sniffed her perfume which had a touch of jasmine in it, and was glad he had come back to someone. The prospect of a night alone terrified him. He opened the bottle of rye and poured huge drinks, mixing them with ginger ale. They clinked glasses like confidantes of long standing and Jay enjoyed the sense of intimacy and friendliness. Her mood had changed from one of saturnine resignation to one of almost insouciant gaiety, and the alteration had been smooth so that he could not even refer to it without sounding foolish.

"What a spread!" she said with delight as she put the cold meats on a platter. She opened up a cardboard container and shrieked with delight. "This is silly, but what possessed you to buy so much cole slaw? Did I ask you for it?"

He threw back his head and laughed.

"Remember that dinner at your house?"

"How could anyone forget it?"

"The only thing you ate was cole slaw. In between screams from your father I kept watching you eat it all up. I wanted to tell everybody how funny I thought that was, but I lost my temper before I got a chance."

She wrinkled up her nose and chuckled.

"God, what a case of nerves I had. And my lip hurt something awful. It was swollen for a week and Poppa insisted that it was a bee bite and made me a concoction of vinegar and witch hazel to put on it. I couldn't stand the smell."

"I'm sorry about that. I just wanted to do something to hurt you."

"You succeeded. Boy, did you . . ."

Jay filled their glasses again, and Myrna put the radio on. Mercifully, from Jay's point of view, the program was of music "enjoyed by our Latin cousins in strange lands." Myrna shuffled on the linoleum, shaking her hips from side to side in a Conga step, and Jay got up and placed his hands around her waist, and followed her lead.

"One, two, three, La Conga, one, two, three, La Conga," she sang in a husky voice, thickening from the whiskey. They danced through the passageway around the telephone table, returned to the living room when the tempo quickened, and picked their way through a coffee table and two high-backed chairs; when the record ended they fell breathlessly on the sofa, the wheels of which turned suddenly, slamming them against the wall with a dull thud.

"And now from Argentina," the announcer said with a pomaded lilt in his voice, "the music of Valentino and the romantic Tango." Like a nagging schoolgirl, she made Jay get onto the floor again and he led her into a series of furious dips, spins, and sharply cut corners.

"I don't remember the last time I danced," Myrna said enthusiastically.

"You're pretty good."

"Not bad for an old lady."

"Old lady? You look five years younger than me."

"Jay, you are sweet when you want to be. But I'm about seven years older than you."

"No one'd believe it."

"Here's to youth," she said, holding up her glass, and spinning dizzily on the floor. "Whoa, whoa, boy," she addressed the air, but could not stop herself. Jay held on to her and directed her to a chair. She flopped down, tried to catch her breath, and Jay lit cigarettes for them both. He poured what remained of the bottle into his own glass and downed it straight. She gave him an eerie, dazed look when he put the cigarette into her mouth, then closed her eyes. Her head fell on his shoulder and she puffed the cigarette furiously.

A sound. He could not identify it. It tore through his dream like a muted whine and his body tensed. The cold, the wet, the smell of rain. He climbed up a shaft on greasy metal rungs which jutted out from the rough-cast walls, scraping his shins and his chest. He shook his head furiously, trying to revive himself, then half awake, shrank back in terror. Something inside his skull kicked out at him; the throbbing nearly drove him mad. The sound again, low, plaintive, a moan in the darkness. She sat on the edge of the bed in a squatting position. The window was open and the rain pelted down on her bare shoulders and he retreated under the blanket, blinking, lost. She had the clarinet in her hands and was running through the scales. A tune emerged, something mournful and sad, a dirge to recapture something remote and dead.

"It's cold," he said. "Myrna, close the window, you're getting soaked." She stopped playing with a suddenness that alarmed him. He heard something hit the pavement outside. A metallic thud. It had smashed.

"What'd you do?" he protested.

"Threw it out," she said in a lifeless voice. "Useless to go on. I'll never play well."

9

I'm scared. Please, Rhoda, tell me what to do."

"That's it"—she moved his hand up along the baby's spinal column—"you support his head so it doesn't wobble. It suits you, being a father."

Jay looked down into the sleeping face of the child and sought to discover physical resemblances between himself and Neal.

"I can't see that he's like me."

"You can't see yourself, but feature for feature, he's the image of you. Everybody says so. Jay, he's such a beautiful baby. Are you happy . . . now?"

"I guess I am," he said thoughtfully. "Neal makes it all worthwhile."

Neal's breathing had improved, but whenever he became agitated either through hunger or irritability, he would wheeze and gasp for breath. Jay had considered hiring a nurse, but the doctor advised against it, and suggested that it would be better to get to know the child on their own and cope as best they could with the condition. Reluctantly Jay agreed, but secretly he remained terrified. He spoke softly to Rhoda and treated her with a mixture of subdued insolence and fraternal concern. He could not be a husband to her, but he made an effort to conduct his affair with Eva with a measure of discretion although the pretense irked him. He succeeded in controlling his periodic rages and he usually came home before two in the morning, but the deception and the simple animal fact of sleeping in the same bed with Rhoda brought on frequent bouts of moodiness which drained his energy.

He worked longer hours now, and had opened his two new stores, one on King's Highway—the gateway to upper-class

Brooklyn—and the other in the downtown business section in
direct competition with the big chain stores who made the
same complacent mistake as those in Manhattan and ignored
him, until it became too late to do anything about him, for he
had purloined their customers. Frantic reductions in prices
came when the battle was lost; either they had to sell cheap
dresses or expensive ones, for the popular-priced business—
the guts of the business in which sales volume and actual profit
were commensurate—belonged exclusively to Jay. His business psychology was so simple as to be obscure to the high-
powered executives who interested themselves in charts,
trends, trade cycles, and economic factors: he treated his customers as whores, a starkly primitive assessment, but in prac-
tice dynamically effective. Women wanted bright cheap
dresses that looked as though they were expensive; they liked
the idea of a one-price shop because many shops charged
whatever they could get, the prices fixed by the saleslady who
had to be one part private detective, one part talking machine.
A big operation could not depend on high-pressure sales pat-
ter, but only on merchandise which sold itself, and therefore
cut staff requirements down to the bone. There was as well
something democratic in the idea of a one-price technique, and
Jay instinctively realized this. ''Treat 'em like whores but
don't have favorites'' was the business commonplace he repeated to anyone who would listen to him, and many of the
important manufacturers did exactly that. Every retailer within
a radius of three miles of any of his stores complained to the
wholesalers and manufacturers and did what they could to stop
his supplies, but despite threats and sanctions, everyone vied
for his business.

In spite of the rapid success Jay achieved in a short time,
he was unhappier than he had ever been. His involvement with
Eva was as deep as any emotional relationship could be, and
the regular demands she made on his time had begun to create
more suspicions in Rhoda's mind. She had always known, or
at least he thought she had known, that he had affairs, but as
long as they were isolated and intermittent she had avoided
referring to them; the problem of keeping her in the dark about

Eva became more urgent daily. He had been prepared to leave her before Neal's birth, but the child now became the center of his universe and it brought out a special tenderness in him. It was the love that is more than love. He regarded the child as his responsibility to protect, and he believed it to be sickly because of his treatment of Rhoda. He managed to repress the direct guilt associated with this, but occasionally, when he least expected it, it floated to the surface of his conscious mind. In the middle of a business conference he would dash out of the room to phone Rhoda and find out how the baby was. Was he still alive? It haunted him, a gray wraith, dumb and helpless, that he had almost destroyed, the way his father had tried to destroy him. His attitude to Rhoda, when she suggested going back to business, was therefore a compound of outrage and submissiveness.

She put Neal on top of the bassinet and changed his diaper, and Jay watched the child with its head thrown back sucking at the air, trying to fill its lungs.

"Sit him up," he said sharply.

"Are you taking over?"

"No, but can't you see—?"

"He does it all the time."

With professional, unruffled deftness, she changed his diaper, massaged his back for gas, then placed him in the wicker cradle in the living room.

"That's that," she said. "I'll be glad to get back to the store."

"You'll be what?"

"Surprised? I am too. I thought I'd love staying home, but I'm not really a housewife. It bores me to death."

"Fine, Neal's a month old, he can look after himself."

"Oh, Jay, you are a fool sometimes. I've hired a girl."

He maintained a show of composure because his position was indefensible: she could demolish any argument he put up, merely by throwing in his face his earlier reaction to her pregnancy. Squirming uncomfortably and with his back against the wall, he exercised what he vaguely thought of as diplomacy.

"You never said a word to me."

"You're so busy all the time," she said without guile and looking evenly at him, "that I thought I wouldn't bother you with these little domestic arrangements."

But he's my son! was on the tip of his tongue.

"Rhoda, he's a sick baby. He needs you to be with him."

"Nothing anybody can do about his asthma. He'll outgrow it. But you need me. The way you've been working lately isn't normal. I don't want to be a rich widow; and I'm good in the store. I can take a lot of responsibility off your shoulders—you could give me the jobs you're too busy to do. It'll work, you'll see. Oh, Jay, I'm so proud of you—what you've only done. Three stores and they're ours. I never thought in my wildest dreams that I'd ever be anything but the manageress of Modes Dress Shoppe."

She approached him, placed her arms round his neck, and hugged him.

"Honest, there's nothing to worry about. Neal'll be all right. This girl has good references and she worked in a hospital for six months."

"Wait till he's a bit older . . . at least a year old."

She drew away from him and her eyes darted wildly around the room.

"I'd be in the bughouse in a year. I couldn't stand it. I've got too much energy."

"Then for Christ sake stop taking those pills."

"What are you talking about?"

"Benzedrines!"

Her eyes rolled, lifeless and enlarged. She was of two minds: to get angry or laugh. She had enormous confidence and she smiled complacently at him.

"It's just till I get my figure back. I remember you saying to me once: 'Look at yourself in a mirror.' I did just that and I didn't like what I saw. I understood how unattractive I was to you and I had to change that. I was too fat, but in another month or so I'll be back to normal. 'How could I make you happy?' That's the question I asked myself, and what have I got in life but you? I mean, God, I must love you to—" she faltered.

"But ten-grain pills, four a day. I asked a druggist about it and he said it was habit-forming."

"I take what the doctor prescribes."

"And a little booster in the evening just to pep you up."

She twirled round like a ballerina.

"Ten pounds I've lost."

"Oh, what's the use of arguing?"

"It's for you, silly. In a month I'll be finished with them."

She sat on his lap and rubbed the back of his neck and kissed him coquettishly. She opened the top of her dress and he stared sullenly at her.

"Ooooh, I want you so bad," she said. "It'll be like it used to be soon, when the doctor gives me the all clear." She rubbed her hand along his trousers. "But I could give you a little treatment in the meantime."

He pushed her up abruptly and got to his feet.

"Not now, honey. I've got to go to the store."

Marvelous to have an honest-to-God excuse: verifiable.

"I'll wait up for you."

Exactly what he was afraid of.

"I may be late. It's a ten o'clock street, or did you forget?"

He fled.

Brooklyn, cold, black like a huge spider in a web of crooked streets, spread out before him. It took him almost a half-hour to get to Eva. She waited outside a candy store, a block away from her house. He pulled in to the curb and she opened the door and got in.

"I'm frozen."

"Have you eaten?"

"I have. Herbie came home this afternoon."

"Surprises never end."

"I had to make dinner when I got in."

"When are you gonna cook for me?"

"Anytime you like."

"How'd you manage to get out?"

"Said I had to see a buyer. He believed it because I came home first. If I'd stayed in the city actually seeing a buyer he wouldn't have worn it for a minute. He's got a logical mind

and that makes him easy to fool." She lifted Jay's hand off
the steering wheel and rubbed it across her cheek. "Ooooh,
such a cold hand. We going anywhere special or just driving?"

"I want to show you the new store on King's Highway,
then we meet Fredericks for a drink at the Bedford, after ten.
I'm gonna persuade him to do business my way."

"No love tonight?"

He felt sick to his stomach at the thought of returning home
to Rhoda.

"Where? When? How?"

"You ask too many questions, Mister. Not a single idea in
that clever head?"

"Let's talk about it later," he said with exasperation.

"You bet we will."

A luminous sign ten by four, as though announcing the end
of the world, stood out starkly from the black background:
J-R DRESSES, it screamed to an indifferent world. Jay's incon-
trovertible rise to power—one of the arches of his empire.
They went into the store which was brightly lit and crowded
with women shoppers and a few bored, dazed husbands who
were surreptitiously peeping into changing rooms as fat-
thighed, becorseted matrons forced themselves into dresses
which refused to conceal their moving parts. A tired businessman's idea of a harem, and dollars and cents to Jay, who
strode in like Caesar inspecting his legions. A hundred-dollar
camel's-hair overcoat which revealed the knot of a black
speckled tie against a white-on-white background of Egyptian
cotton and a beautifully fitted black flannel suit of recent vintage reduced the sales staff to sycophancy and awed obedi-
ence. Even the customers cast delighted gazes in his direction.

Jay was aware of the effect his entrance had made on everyone in the store; it gave him a physical thrill, for the idea of
possessing a public presence, an air of importance, reinforced
his own identity. He stretched out his arms to grasp life but
what he hoped he would take hold of was himself. He made
a note of the day's receipts, smiled to himself, and showed the
figure to Eva, who patted him on the back. He did a quick
stock check, quizzed a few of the girls about what was selling,

and then threaded his way out through a crowd of women. A dark phantom in a dark night.

They arrived at the Bedford a bit after ten. It was a dimly lit little bar with green fauna on the walls, an aquarium stocked with guppies, two smiling bartenders who still spoke with a Sicilian brogue after two decades of residence, and occasionally were responsible for an unsolved murder or two, and a short thick-set manager called Topo who supervised the kitchen with the nervous fastidiousness and pomp of an honors graduate from the Lucerne Hotel School, but who administered the other side of his business—Brooklyn's call girl service— with a calm astuteness and a celerity that would have been the envy of an Old Testament prophet. The restaurant specialized in a wide variety of heartburn—even the pizza brought tears to your eyes; a month's regular consumption of the Bedford's inimitable cuisine could wreck the gall bladder of a jackal. You didn't die with a cry for justice, or come take me sweet death, on your lips, but with a request for bicarbonate of soda. The racket atmosphere of the place appealed to Jay's second-feature sense, and it was a source of some small pride to him that he was on first-name terms with a pair of acid throwers.

Douglas Fredericks sat at the bar, dangling a pair of long legs encased in knife-creased midnight blue cashmere trousers while a Milwaukee milkmaid explained with just the right note of piety and mournfulness how her stepfather had tucked her in on the night of her sweet-sixteen party. Fredericks' face had a somnolent yellow texture under the green light which shone through narrow cracks in the ceiling.

Jay tapped the milkmaid on the shoulder and she turned on a buttery smile; definitely her night.

"Hey, what are you selling, cancer?"

"What wuszat?" The smile congealed and hard-knock exasperation took its place. "You a wise guy?"

"You see that?" Jay pointed to a table near the door.

"Yeah, so?"

"Well, that's first base. Now why don't you show us how fast you can run around the bases."

The blonde got up, clenched her fist in Jay's face.

"Vince," Jay said, "throw this douchebag out."

The bartender indicated the street with a jerk of his thumb and Jay took her vacant stool.

"Thanks," Fredericks said, "I didn't want to embarrass her. Actually, I would have preferred the St. Moritz."

"Next time. I had to go to King's Highway tonight. What are you drinking?"

"Bourbon."

"Vince, two C.C.'s and ginger and bourbon and Coke."

Fredericks looked faintly surprised.

"I'm with . . ."

"Me," Eva said. "Just had to powder my nose."

"Your . . . ? No, it wouldn't be," Fredericks said, stretching his suntanned neck around and tensing it so hard that the white creases showed.

"Eva Meyers, Douglas Fredericks. We're—"

"Engaged . . . to wait," Eva replied.

"That sounds very pleasant."

"See, Eva, he's impressed. Even millionaires have pipe dreams."

"Are you in the same line of business?"

"I work for Marty Cass."

"I know his father-in-law. He thinks Jay's pretty sharp."

"I buy most of his rags and pay promptly on the tenth, so he loves me like a son. If I'm two days late, he'd send the collection agency down to see me, which only goes to prove that money's thicker than blood."

"Are we going to eat?" Eva asked.

"Only if you promise to kiss me with garlic on my breath."

"Ah, Jay, have a heart."

Jay wrapped his arm around her and pecked her on the cheek.

"I love her. What can I do?"

"You don't need my advice." Fredericks gave a deep, throaty, Hershey syrup chuckle.

"Hey, Topo," Jay called, catching sight of the manager. "Hey ladrone."

"Ey, Jaya." Topo walked across the room with his hand

extended. The creases on the back of his neck were like the inspiration of a mozzarella cheese sculptor. He removed his tinted steel-framed glasses, gave them a blow, and reached for a cocktail napkin to wipe them. "Ey, Jaya. Good to see yuh! Wha kin I do?"

Jay introduced him to Fredericks and Eva, forced a drink on him and he sat down next to Eva.

"Topo, fix us something beautiful to burn our *kischkas* out. Mr. Fredericks's got an ulcer and he wants to play Russian roulette with it."

Topo rattled off a menu of Palermese comestibles that could blow a safe.

"And two bottles of Chianti, but not the stuff you dilute with vinegar."

"Ey, Jaya. Would I do that to yuh?"

"I'm kidding. We'll have the back table."

Eva watched him move a couple of after-movie diners, spaghetti and all, and under protest, to another table.

They had three more rounds of drinks, exchanged pleasantries, accepted an invitation to go to Miami and spend a week on Fredericks' yacht. They nibbled hot breadsticks until the shrimps diavolo and clams à la casino were placed before them.

"It's marvelous," Fredericks said, "if I survive."

"I'll bet you're wondering why I wanted to see you?"

"To ask me to be the best man at your wedding?"

"Apart from that?"

"You like my company."

"I love it. With the single exception of F.D.R. there's no one I'd rather be with. I'll tell you. You're building, Doug. In Long Island and Westchester. You've got five sites altogether."

"You're pretty well informed."

"I gave Warner fifty bucks."

"I'll have to get rid of him."

"Whoever you go to, I'll get to, so he's just as useless as the rest."

"So we've ascertained that I'm building."

Jay squeezed Eva's hand under the table and rested it on her thigh.

"Anyone ask you about stores yet?"

Fredericks gulped a clam down, smacked his lips approvingly, poured some wine for Eva, and said:

"It's a great way to die."

"That's really why he brought you here," she said.

"C'mon, Doug."

"What makes a potentially nice young man such a hard nut?" he asked Eva.

"Who do you mean? You or Jay?"

"My protection," Jay said.

"I can see that I'm in for it. Walked into a trap. Old Douglas Fredericks walked into a trap. I didn't make that mistake when I was younger."

"You've made too much money, Doug."

"So here I sit in Brooklyn, getting my brains picked by a youngster. Let me tell you something, Jay. The Fourteenth Street store didn't mean a thing to me. I could have let it stay empty for ten years without its having any effect on my affairs, but I liked you so I gave you a chance. You've improved the property. That goes without saying. But what we're talking about now involves quite a substantial investment. We're not talking about five-hundred-dollar-a-year rent and split the difference. The properties you're referring to can bring in something like a quarter of a million a year in rent, and quite frankly with all due respect to your business acumen, the type of operation you run hurts the big boys. In every one of these sites, there's accommodation for a department store. They wouldn't be interested for a minute if you came in. And I don't want to break one large store into a dozen small ones. So I'm afraid you're out."

Jay grasped Eva's knee tighter. He drained his glass of wine in a single gulp and refilled their glasses while the waiter put down an enormous platter of chicken cacciatore.

"I hoped," Jay said, "that you would've had more faith in me."

"Why, I've got all the faith in the world in you, but this isn't your kind of deal."

"I'd like it to be."

"Well, possibly in the future we can do something together."

Topo strolled by with another bottle of Chianti, and Jay beckoned him to sit. Fredericks gave him a supercilious smile and told him how good the food was. Topo agreed.

"Maybe you come again?" he suggested.

"I wouldn't be at all surprised."

"Did you know that Topo's quite an expert—if you'll forgive me mentioning this at dinner—on sewerage problems?"

Topo shook his mozzarella head, speared a cold shrimp, and sipped a glass of wine with the aplomb of a Roman count. Fredericks glanced from one to the other, somewhat nonplussed, and said to Eva: "Jay's really rather extraordinary."

Somewhat in a quandary herself, she turned to Jay.

"What're you talking about, Jay?"

"Well, I'll explain. You've gone into the property business as of this afternoon, Eva."

"Is this some kind of joke?"

"No, you're going to build shopping centers in Hempstead, Larchmont, Rockaway, White Plains, and Great Neck."

Fredericks shoved his plate away angrily and rose.

"I think this has gone far enough. If you'll excuse me."

"Doug, relax. You haven't heard the whole story and as so much is at stake, you ought to want to listen. You see, I've got some bad news. Your building permission is going to be refused. Something about inadequate sewerage on those sites. The State Building Commission will have to look into the matter and official bodies can be terribly slow, but in any case they'll probably decide in your favor with the proviso that you bear some of the costs, probably the bulk, of providing new sewerage. Do you know much about sewerage contractors?"

Fredericks' face was a study in burnt ash: "Okay, get on with it."

"Well, a firm that calls itself Topo Contractors are the biggest in the business."

Topo tittered and Fredericks glared at him.

"Do we have to discuss this in front of a restaurant waiter?"

"Manager," Topo, a bit hurt, corrected him.

"Well, Topo Contractors is Mr. Topo, so I thought it might be a good idea to bring you two together to see if we could all iron out our differences."

"Mr. Fredericks, more wine?" Topo said, all affability.

Fredericks sneered at him.

"What the hell's this all about?"

"Jay, I don't get it," Eva said.

"Simple. The sites that *you've* taken an option on, or rather that I've taken in your name, have, according to Topo Contractors, adequate sewerage, which means you can build once you provide plans. Doug isn't so lucky with his sites, so he'll just have to wait. And when he finally does get the go-ahead, he'll have to use Topo Contractors because nobody else will tender for it. Most of the other firms don't feel they could compete with Topo, and he's got an awful lot of work on his hands so it might take him five or six years to do the job."

"That's ridiculous; they've got to be ready in twelve months at the latest," Fredericks said hotly. "I've committed myself."

"That's why I thought we ought to meet over a drink and dinner."

Fredericks pushed the table away from him and slid out.

"You're not going to get away with a goddamned stunt like this. I'll see you in hell first."

"If I'm not there, start without me. In the meantime, let's make it Rumpelmayer's at the St. Moritz tomorrow about one. Give you the night to think over the situation."

Fredericks tore out of the restaurant and Jay rolled his head from side to side, laughing triumphantly. Topo clasped Jay's hand as though it were a pearl and grinned through brown stained crooked teeth.

"He's such a smart boy. We gonna make money."

"I don't take any credit—your people did all the work."

"But issa your idear."

They parted without kissing, but Topo was under his spell.

They sat in the car under a lamppost opposite Eva's apartment. The light in the living room was still on, and every now and then they saw Herbie come to the window, survey the street, and finding it deserted except for the drone of a lonely car unsettling the quiet, he would shrug his shoulders and return to the *Saturday Evening Post* to pass the time. They sat for fully half an hour without talking, for Eva was both puzzled and shocked by Jay's tactics. She had no sympathy for Fredericks, but something inside her, a small voice, which her physical passion for Jay could not silence, told her that she must speak up. It wasn't so much that she was outraged, but that she had been forced to wear moral blinkers; although she could justify the deception she had perpetrated against her husband on the grounds of love—and she wondered vaguely if it was simply sex, but this was too painful to accept—there seemed something particularly odious about Jay this evening; not only a total divorce from the simple plane of human emotion, but also some uncontrollable lust that could be fed only by using other people.

"It's late," she said finally.

"Huh?"

"Busy counting your money?"

He laughed: he could afford the luxury.

"No, just trying to figure out what I'd do in Fredericks' position."

"You'll outsmart yourself."

"He'd go to see his lawyer, and his lawyer is my lawyer. He made the marriage."

"You're really having a good time tonight."

"What do you mean by that?"

"Not important."

"Sure it is. Come on."

"Would it matter?"

He put his arm around her and forced her to him. He was

a bit surprised when she resisted, and he kissed her against her will.

"Good night." She opened the door and he reached across her lap and forced her to close it. "I want to go . . ."

"That sounds awfully final."

"Okay, if you want to know: you made me sick tonight. The way you treated that man. And why did you have to involve me?"

"I had to take the options in your name."

"Why didn't you ask me about it?"

"I wasn't interested in your opinion and I thought there was enough between us for me not to have to ask. It was business in any case. Maybe not very nice, but then again Fredericks isn't a very nice man. He didn't get where he is by winning popularity contests. He's cut plenty of throats in his day. Today he doesn't have to." He loosened his tie, and had difficulty catching his breath. "Christ, look at me. A little while ago, I was a bum living on the East Side, and now I'm a somebody, or starting to be one. I come from nothing . . . no background, no letters of introduction, no special favors. All by myself. You wouldn't have talked to me, then."

"You've got a lot of excuses for yourself. I'm not God, so you don't have to defend yourself to me. What I'm worried about is the kind of effect it's going to have on us—this callousness of yours. It's as though every decent emotion you have dies inside and what comes out is hate."

"Eva . . . Eva . . . Please, please, don't say that to me."

She couldn't believe what was happening: he was shaking.

"Jay! Jay! Stop, darling, stop."

"I love you. I've never had this kind of feeling. It eats me up—"

Her momentary revulsion was displaced by a wave of sympathy, part of it exclusively for herself. She had been drawn into his life by a force greater than herself—the irresistible impulse to destruction which had been created by his cannibalistic hunger for her—and she recognized this from the first afternoon that he had taken her, against her will, but not against her inclination. In her husband's bed—a bed that had never been a theater of love or desire, but still a bed, in which two people shared a hostile intimacy; Jay's sperm had stained the sheets of an unsuspecting and defenseless creature whose only desire had been to make her happy. She had felt afterwards as though she had been eaten by worms and after that she had grown to like the feeling because the terror of it—the worms on her breasts, tearing away at her nipples—had made her feel dynamic, a well of infinite depth and darkness which *was* life. She cradled Jay's head in her arms and soothed him. Then with a clairvoyance that amazed her he said: "How do you think I feel when you go back to him? To his bed . . . ! Stealing my manhood."

"Who's stealing what?" she said softly.

"I haven't stolen you from him: he never had you."

She sighed fitfully; the discussion, like a bout of lovemaking, had drained her and her body was limp and exhausted.

"Oh, Jay, what's going to happen to us?"

"I'm going to marry you, if I have to kill your husband."

She let him kiss her on the cheek.

"Make sure I'm still alive afterwards."

Rhoda was waiting up for him. He saw her perched on three pillows with an Ellery Queen in her hand, a bowl of gnawed fruit by her side, and a chocolate stain across her lips. He went over to Neal and covered him. His breathing was raspy, but he was sleeping soundly.

Rhoda pointed guiltily to the fruit bowl when he came in.

"I got bored and well—I had a ball."

"Better than taking pills—they can kill you."

"Maybe it wouldn't be such a bad idea, huh? Make things a lot easier for you."

"The minute I walk in, you start. I'm tired—"

"She gave you a workout?"

"Aw Rhoda, cut it out. I met Fredericks tonight at the Bedford."

"Fredericks?" she said, incredulous. "The landlord? What for?"

"To talk business."

"What kinda business?"

He slipped off his jacket and threw it on a chair which was losing horsehair, and was Rhoda's idea of an antique.

"You wouldn't understand."

"That's you to a T. Why bother to explain to her—she's only some idiot I live with." She paused, her eyes darting nervously from side to side. "Tell me the truth. He's asking us to get out of the store; isn't he?"

He wished she would swallow her tongue.

"We've got a lease, remember?"

"What then?"

"I've taken five more stores."

"Whaaaaaaat? You crazy, or something? We've got three stores already, what do we need more for? Jay, I don't claim to understand you, but I think you're losing your mind. You're opening stores like cans of sardines."

"Are we making money?"

She looked at him cautiously.

"We are . . . but why spoil it?"

"Rhoda, do me a favor, read your comic book."

"It makes more sense than you, at least. All of a sudden, you're a big business expert, and I don't know a thing."

"When I fall on my ass, you can open your big mouth. But right now remember that you've never had this kind of money in your whole life. So just keep that big mouth of yours shut."

"Back where we started from, aren't we? When's it gonna end, Jay? When? When? Are you gonna treat me like a human being—your wife—?" she shouted angrily.

Neal began to hiccup loudly, then worked himself into a raging tizzy. Jay felt very tired and forced himself up from the bed and went inside to him. With trembling hands he picked Neal up and tried to soothe him.

"Wunnerful father, you are," Rhoda's voice rang out. "I must tell him someday, how lucky he is to have a father like you."

He stood with Neal by the window and the child gave him a gas smile. The street was empty and in the darkness less actively ugly than in the daylight. Jay wanted to move to another apartment, but the thought of taking Rhoda with him forced him to abandon the idea. Sooner or later, she'd get around to asking him about moving, and when she did, he'd accede, because there could be no logical case for staying on at Roebling Street. Neal calmed down after a five-minute vigil at the window and Jay kissed him tenderly on the head and placed him back in the crib.

"So you went to the Bedford?" Rhoda exclaimed, as though the fact was some sinister corroboration. "And introduced him to your gangster friends? Must of made a good impression on Mr. Fredericks."

"Can we go to sleep, or are you going to read all night?"

"The Bedford, huh? You stink from garlic. I guess it covers the smell of the woman you must of been with. That dope Rhoda couldn't figure out a thing like that, could she? Well, when I get back to the store, you won't be leaving me home, so that you can run around whenever you feel like. I'll be included wherever you go."

He turned off the light and rolled over on his side, and Eva's face flashed before his eyes: the flaming red hair, her enormous opaline eyes that lingered on his face speechlessly for minutes, the swell of her breasts when he was inside her and she could not breathe, and her anguished cry when he had satisfied her. He heard Rhoda rustle the pages of her book, then close it, groan irritably, and chomp a chocolate marshmallow. He mustn't lose Eva. God help him . . .

Douglas Fredericks had pouches under his eyes and his skin was a jade color when he entered the office of Robertson and Clay, Attorneys at Law. The receptionist was a slim, middle-aged woman who used witch hazel behind her ears and lived on cottage cheese. She got up to greet him with the kind of open-faced embarrassment women accord distinguished clients who give them pen sets every Christmas when they want those pen sets, six in her case, to turn into an engagement ring.

"Good morning, Miss Berry," Fredericks said briskly, gritting his teeth, but squeezing a smile out. Miss Berry did him a lot of favors.

Miss Berry was about to remind him that he had called her Cynthia last Christmas, but instead she extended a slightly gnarled hand, an honored veteran of twenty years of shorthand, and said:

"Oh, good morning, Mr. Fredericks. It's so good to see you. You've brightened my day. Mr. Clay will be free in about five minutes—he's tied up with someone at the moment. Can I get you a cup of coffee?"

"Yes, thanks, but—"

"—No sugar, I remember. I've never given you sugar once, now, have I?"

A pyrrhic victory, definitely, for Miss Berry.

Fredericks had to admit she was right, and now realized why enraged janitors murdered innocent spinsters with hammers.

A few fond glances later, Miss Berry received two sharp reports on her telephone and Mr. Nathan Clay emerged. He was built like a wine tun with a gold watch hanging from one of his bellies, a scalp that looked as though it had lived through a drought and could support no form of vegetation, least of all hair, and a smile which revealed two buff-colored caps which had been necessitated by a disagreement with an outraged criminal whom Clay had represented during his younger days when he had to work for a living. The experience had turned Clay to corporation law and real estate for which a talent for finding obscure loopholes, snaring parcels of land almost before they were put up for sale, and interlocking directorships so cleverly fitted him.

He shook Fredericks' hand warmly, and led him into a booklined office which he only used to entertain clients. Four young clerks, two doors away, did all of the research.

"Sit down, Doug. What're you looking so worried about?"

"You know that little sonovabitch I introduced you to some time ago, and asked you to act for: Blackman."

Clay wrote the name down on a pad, then ran the name across his lips like a hock.

"Dress business, or something?" he said through his nose.

"That's right. I rented him the store I had on Fourteenth Street."

"Of course, now I remember."

Fredericks launched into an account of the preceding evening, citing every one of Jay's nefarious tricks: the blackmail, the implicit threats, the swaggering air, which wasn't really an offense except against good taste, the hoodlum in the background. He stopped peremptorily and cast an angry glance at Clay, who had not uttered a word.

"Well, what are we going to do about it?" he demanded.

Clay did a few somersaults with his pocket watch; the chain was inordinately long and Fredericks imagined it coiled around Clay's belly like a sleeping python. He got up, walked to the window, and gazed down at minuscule New Yorkers crawling on the pavement forty stories below.

"It's a tricky situation."

"What's tricky about it?"

"Has he actually said that he would do you bodily harm?"

"Does he have to mug me first?"

"No, but someone has to witness a threat. He'd probably—if it came to it—have two witnesses backing him up."

"Can't we swear out a complaint?"

"Not so simple. The State Building Commission would deny any suggestion of collusion and you'd have to prove that. It would be very difficult—even with Dewey as the D.A. If you didn't prove your case, I think you'd be in a great deal of trouble, because in a situation like this—that is with an official body under investigation—they could well go through your affairs with a fine-toothed comb. It's not a very pleasant business. Every business deal, every tax return of yours, your whole business life would be put under a microscope. And when these people start looking, they find little discrepancies. No one's life can bear that kind of scrutiny, and yours especially."

Breathlessly Fredericks said: "Nat, I can't believe this is possible. Little shits like Blackman don't push me around."

"Doug, we're all vulnerable. It just takes the right combination of factors. The point of all this is this: is Blackman offering you any less than the big department stores for the locations?"

"No, he's prepared to negotiate the way they would."

"He's a smart young bastard, but a greenhorn about leases. What you must insist on is a percentage of his gross profit—it could be anything between five and ten percent, plus the rent. You could never get a deal like that from a big chain. I think he's going to do very well. He's got a gimmick and he always seems to have something up his sleeve. If his gross profit runs to a million between the five stores it could be that he's doing you a favor. So long as he believes you're at a disadvantage, you've got him by the balls."

Fredericks weighed up the advice and reluctantly accepted it.

"Send me a bill, will you, Nat?"

"A bill?" Clay embraced Fredericks warmly: he might have been the school's star student at a nationwide spelling bee. "We're friends . . . so I've given you a little advice."

"I've got to do something to repay—"

"You'll buy me lunch one day at Rumpelmayer's and we'll talk about old times and the future. It's important to old thieves like us to talk about the future."

The elevator shot down at a speed of fifty miles an hour and Douglas Fredericks had a small ungainly gremlin dancing around in his stomach. He blamed it on the elevator, and then when his chauffeur dropped him in front of the St. Moritz for lunch, he realized that Clay had been working for Jay as well.

10

In the summer Brooklyn was hot and sultry, a sargasso of crowded apartments, of people sleeping on fire escapes, trying to breathe, of suicidal flies dying in midair before they could reach the rotting fruit, of rancid effluvia emerging from the river, of old people dying in subways. Jay watched Neal's asthma gradually become worse, and finally, with an urgency and desperation that had escaped Rhoda's detection, he persuaded her to take the child away to the mountains for the summer. She held out till the last week in June, for the thought of leaving Jay to his own devices in the city spelled death to the crumbling tenement their marriage had become. Hurried family councils with Howard and Jan buoyed her spirit: ''He'll miss you, you'll see,'' was the reassurance Jan gave, and Howard, totally enthralled by the huge success Jay had made—''An empire out of dust'' was how he described it—advised her that Jay ''needed a bit longer than most to settle down.'' A surprising decision made by Jay at the last moment—to send his mother along with them—brought Rhoda to her knees; but she gave in only when he promised to visit them without fail every weekend and she knew that he would keep his word because the two people he loved, if he loved anyone, would be with her.

The journey to Ferndale on a humid, stifling morning, as though the city refused to wake from its coma, took nearly seven hours. Celia cradled Neal in the back seat for most of the morning, and the movement of the car lulled him to sleep. The mountain air had a crisp cool dryness which made them all feel better, and Neal's racked breathing became less labored.

The countryside spread out before them in a porraceous wild mass of furze and boscage, with forests of ash and maple stippled on the mountainside. The road twisted through the mountain like an artery trying to find its way to the heart, through valleys where alfalfa, haystacks, red stiles, and morose cattle receded from their field of vision almost before they took them in.

Jay had a dim recollection of an afternoon in Kalenberg: eating chicken in a field with a young German girl he had met outside a cinema in Vienna. The lowing cattle and the thick corn ears and the greensward by the weir were before him again, just beyond the windshield of his car, haunting him as he shot past them because they came from another life, a life that was now dead and which represented the best part of his memory of youth, also dead, never to be resuscitated except in the smell of cow dung which was unbearable and the image of chalk white naked legs on a red polka dot skirt and saffron hair, straight and braided, and the distant toll of laughter which now sounded like a jeer, and a smile which revealed a chipped tooth, an arm with a dog-bite scar: an afternoon which had ended with a despairing revelation when he had taken the girl back to Vienna; back, or so he thought, to her parents' home. He had been shaken to see half a dozen soldiers emerge, cackling and drunk, their black boots shining like seal-skin, their scabbards lewdly over their stomachs—one of the soldiers hopped on his to the amusement of the others—and a girl, red-faced and slovenly, hanging out of the window, one of her breasts outside a muslin slip, shouting to him and the girl. He froze when he realized that the girl had said: *"Heidi, wie geht es?"* for he had been with Heidi and Heidi wasn't . . . country memories, on a country drive with Neal wide-eyed, staring at an opalescent sky which had patches of sapphire in the west, and Rhoda's voice, cranky and pitched low, so that she always sounded as if she were trying to transcend some physical pain . . . he was brought back to the narrow curving road and the mud huts and faded bistre bricked farmhouses set back from the road, visible only peripherally.

Lieberman's Farm rested on an acclivity which overlooked Ferndale, a sleepy Catskill hamlet which came to life in the summer. The farm was about a mile from the town, and although its principal source of revenue was from summer guests, it still maintained a semblance of bucolic innocence. Half a dozen Jerseys munched in the small green lea in front of the main house, and about twenty lambs bleated welcomes to the new visitors. Hens squalled in a chicken run behind the house. Jay helped his mother and Rhoda out of the car, and Celia held Neal tightly in her arms, crooning with joy. She had never had a holiday in her life and she couldn't believe that she was about to have one now. The porch squeaked when anything heavier than a robin trod on it; the façade of the house was an unequal mixture of flaking brown wood and red brick, testimony of man's ability to improvise when money is

at stake. The lobby contained two second-Empire sofas—
vintage Salvation Army—a writing table precariously bal-
anced on two bricks to make up for height deficiencies, a
brown leather chair which could accommodate a gorilla, two
rugs made out of remnants, and an official-looking mahogany
counter which had once been a bar. Behind the counter, Mrs.
Lieberman sat chicken-flicking. The feathers were all stuffed
in a huge laundry sack, to be used for pillows. Mrs. Lieberman
lifted herself out of a rocker to greet them. She was a large
thick-set woman, with ruddy cheeks, a stevedore's forearms,
curly blonde hair which she had given up brushing a decade
before, and a rear end which appeared to be an extension that
was still being built. She had served her hotelier's apprentice-
ship in a Munich *wirtshaus* and she had been grabbed, or at
least her behind had been, by every workman in the city.

"I spoke to you on the phone, the other day," Jay said.
"Blackman."

She opened her arms to embrace him, and dropped the
chicken on the rocker.

Celia pointed to a sign behind the counter.

"Strictly kosher . . ." she said, reassured. She suspected that
gentiles were all trying to poison her with unkoshered food.

"Ebsolutely," replied Mrs. Lieberman, striking a sympathetic chord. "For suppa tonight we got gefilte fish, chicken
soup, and boiled or roast chicken."

"Satisfied, Momma?" Jay said.

"I've got some baby food for Neal that has to be heated
up," Rhoda said.

"Everythink we got for der chillden."

A small gray man in a pale blue smock appeared. He had
a vulpine snout, thin gray hair under a peaked cap, and small
slate-gray eyes which peeped out from cowlish eyelids.

"Mine usbin," Mrs. Lieberman said, indicating the man.
"Say allo, Mex."

Max said hello and then picked up their cases and beckoned
them to follow him down a corridor. He swung open a door
and said:

"Your rhum. Plenty yair." He pointed to the double exposure with a flourish.

"Nice and big," Rhoda said.

"And clean," Celia added.

Max smiled gratefully.

The room was better than Jay had hoped for. It had two largish double beds, and a small crib for Neal tucked away in the corner behind a huge wardrobe which acted as a room divider and would give them a bit of privacy.

"I think this is a better setup than a hotel. Plenty of fresh air and good food," Jay said apologetically. Rhoda had wanted to stay at a hotel, and had accused him of cutting corners on his family, but a doctor had recommended the farm and he had insisted that Neal's health was the most important factor.

"I guess maybe when you come up weekends, we can get out a bit to some of the hotels," Rhoda said.

"Yeah, sure."

"Beautiful . . . like the old country," Celia said, peering out of the window at the green field behind the house. "You can see in front and behind. Oh, Jakie, you're such a good boy. Isn't he, Rhoda? So thoughtful."

Rhoda stared at him and reluctantly nodded. Her attention was drawn to Neal, who awoke abruptly in Celia's arms and commenced squalling for food. Rhoda took him from her and started out the door.

"You unpack, Momma, and I'll feed the baby."

"Oh, Jakie, see I told you it would be better when the baby came. You and Rhoda are gonna be happy . . . I know it in my bones. I'm sucha proud momma because of you, the way you make a success of everything." She put her arms around him and hugged him with all her strength and for the first time in months he felt safe and at peace.

Blobs of hot, dirty air hit Jay in the face when he got back to the city that night. The traffic pile-up choked the bridge. It was about ten o'clock when he reached his apartment. It was silent and empty and there was the lingering odor of fried egg.

He opened all of the windows and ran a bath. A pair of the maid's stockings were hanging over the faucet, and he rolled them up in some old newspaper and stuffed them in the small garbage can under the sink. The bath cooled him off and brought him back to life. Eva had been unable to get out of a family dinner and he had not tried to pressure her, for he realized that it would only make her position more untenable. By the time he was dressed it was eleven o'clock and like a wild animal on the hunt he decided to go out. Just as he was about to slam the door behind him, the phone rang and he retreated back into the apartment; the open windows had done nothing to counteract the stale egg smell.

"Hello?" he said.

"Gotcha at last . . . where the hell you been?" Marty's voice had a querulous tone.

"Took Rhoda and Neal up to the country."

"You free then?"

"Yeah. Why, something exciting happening?"

"It could. Listen, drag your ass out of that *schwitz* bath you call home and come up to my place."

"Where's your wife?"

"Atlantic City for the weekend to visit her sister."

"See you in twenty minutes."

He went back to the bedroom and put on a lightweight gray gabardine suit, and a dark blue tie, fastened his pearl stickpin, a recent acquisition which like a beacon announced his entry into moneyed society. When he got behind the wheel, it occurred to him that he had driven for nearly fourteen hours during the day; his legs were stiff and he took a cab uptown.

Marty was behind the bar, minus the barman, mixing himself a drink. He poured about four fingers of scotch in a tall glass, tried to get the ice tongs to close, but they resisted, so he used his fingers and carried it to the door with him. He handed the drink to Jay.

"You've got a future in room service," Jay said, sipping the drink, "so if you have a bad season I'll give you a reference for the Statler."

"What're you doin' tonight?"

"I'm going to a military ball, if it's all the same to you."

"*Putz* . . . I mean do you have to get home at a certain hour?"

"No, my mommy gave me a letter saying I could be out till midnight. What's all the Hollywood production for?"

Jay sat down on the lobster-shaped settee and stretched his legs out. The room didn't seem quite as large now as it had the first time. He could afford to put his feet on the furniture, and he wasn't worried about being told that he had no manners. In a sense he regretted his quick success; if it had taken longer he might have learned how civilized people comported themselves and he was full of admiration for men who made amusing small talk, used the right knife, and wore women down by a process of silk-tongued attrition. He was still a bandit. Marty traversed both worlds with skill and finesse, and Jay liked him for that and his freedom from hypocrisy. He gave Jay another drink and Jay felt a sudden burst of energy.

Marty paced the apartment edgily and Jay wondered what he had on his mind.

"So, what's happening."

"Am I a friend?" Marty demanded.

"Sure." Jay was taken aback. "Why the question?"

"If you'd heard something that might hurt me, would you let me know about it?"

Jay reflected for a moment, and loosened his tie.

"I think I would."

"Eva knows you've got a kid."

Jay sighed despondently. He hated to have anyone catching him out in a lie and he realized that he should have told Eva the truth, but he was afraid that it might damage their relationship, which drew its energy from the fact that he was an unhappily married man who had been deceived by a girl who wanted him at any cost. He had dodged around the issue when Eva had asked him about Rhoda and assured her that Rhoda had a false alarm, but he had learned about it too late. She regarded the story with some skepticism, for it was difficult to believe that Jay could be duped by anyone. She had not, however, pressed him further and he had let it die.

"You got any brothers or cousins?" Marty asked.

"Who told her?" Jay said in a resigned voice.

"I asked you if you have any brothers?"

"One. A half-assed bookkeeper. But he doesn't travel in my league."

"Well, someone who says he's your brother got a job with Harry Lee last week."

"Impossible."

"Stoops. Parts his hair on the wrong side. Steel-rimmed glasses, carries fruit in his pocket and thinks he's the hottest accountant in the world. Says his name is Al Blackman."

Jay jumped up unsteadily. He walked over to the bar and poured himself another drink. He hadn't eaten for ten hours and the whiskey hit him harder than he thought it would.

"It's Al. But how the hell could he get a job working for Harry?"

"I asked Harry the same question, and he said that last Monday this guy turns up in his showroom, asks to see him, and goes through a whole spiel about you and him and how much alike the two of you are and how he taught you a lot of tricks. Harry didn't like him much, but he figured that he might be a smart boy and he needed a good bookkeeper, so he hired him. He figured that if he was your brother, and had one tenth of your ability, he'd be getting his money's worth. Can't really blame him."

"Why didn't he call me about it?" Jay said bitterly.

"Seems your brother told him that he'd rather you didn't use your influence, that's why he was doing it on his own. We don't usually work on Saturdays, but this morning I asked Eva to come in because I had to see a few buyers from Atlanta and she's sudden death with Southern idiots. So we grabbed them for a few thousand p.m.'s. They'd buy pinafores for velvets. When they left, Eva and I had a little talk and she showed me some sketches she'd done. Better-priced stuff, really sensational, but Harry's kind of stuff, not mine. That girl's really got a talent, very shy though about her work and unsure of herself. The fact is, I was very grateful for what she did . . . I mean moving dead stock without a fire's a miracle, and I was

in about two thousand on that little sale. Naturally I gave her
fifty, but I could see that she was more interested in what I
thought of the sketches than the money she was going to make.
So I picked up the phone and gave Harry a tinkle and he told
me to come up with Eva and to bring the sketches. He's got
a soft spot for Eva. We went up to the showroom and Harry
gave us a few drinks and insisted we stay for lunch. He was
pretty busy too with his export stuff—whole load of European
buyers in the place. He looked at Eva's sketches and he loved
them—bought them right then and there—and told her that
she could work for him any time. The thing is, he wouldn't
steal her, because he knows she's my right hand and he's got
his dough invested in my place, so it's like stealing from one
pocket to put in the other. But he said he'd give her fifty a
week for any sketches she did on her own time and she was
singing. As we're about to leave—twoish—this wormy-
looking character comes over. I'm sorry, Jay, even if he is
your brother, there's something about this guy . . . He tells
Harry that a few people are waiting to see him, and Harry
realizes that he forgot to tell me about how he hired your
brother. I almost fell over. It's peculiar . . . you do business
with people for years and except maybe for a wife, you never
think of them having families. Silly, isn't it? Well, this brother
of yours starts drooling all over Eva, not suspecting a thing
about you and her, but he wants to impress her about how
close the two of you are. I shove off with Harry for a minute,
and when I come back I see her standing there like a display
dummy, white-faced and ready to faint. So I tell Al that we've
got to go and in the elevator she doesn't say a word, but as
soon as we hit the street she starts to cry, bitterly. Everyone
in the street begins to stare at me like I'm the heavy, and I
plead with her to tell me what's wrong.

   " 'It's hopeless,' she says. 'I knew he was married, but he
never mentioned that he had a child.' I give her a handkerchief
and she just holds it in her hand so I take it out and wipe her
face and I was sick, because she seemed so helpless and I
don't have to tell you how self-possessed she is. So to see her

standing there as though the end of the world's come, upset me.

" 'His name's Neal,' Eva says. 'Marty, why didn't you tell me?' I couldn't answer her and I couldn't lie about not knowing.

" 'What am I going to do?'

" 'Jay probably had his reasons. He loves you. He'll explain . . .'

"Then she turns to me with her hands stretched out and says: 'But Marty, I'm pregnant . . . with Jay's child.'

"She ran away from me and I watched her duck into the subway. I tried to call her all afternoon, but her mother says she hasn't heard or seen her all day."

Jay wobbled on his feet and fell into a bar stool. His hands were limp and his legs ached. The room began to spin and he realized that he had had too much to drink in too short a time. He wanted the room to stop moving and he held out his hand ineffectually.

Marty lifted Jay up under his arms and helped him to the settee.

"I'm sorry, Jay. I hated to be the one. But I'm your friend . . . I care." He shook Jay anxiously. "Say something. You're not sore, are you?" Marty waited for a response, but Jay stared at the ceiling. He helped him to his feet. "You need some fresh air and something to eat."

The humidity still hung over New York and the air in the street tasted stagnant and dirty even on Central Park West. A major-general got them a taxi, and Marty told him to take them to Lindy's. The taxi swung around the park at Columbus Circle and the numbness in Jay's brain wore off.

"I think I better drive into Brooklyn to see her," Jay said. "Will you come with me?"

"Of course I will." Marty patted him on the shoulder affectionately.

"Nothing ever seems to work out. Nothing ever means anything. It's all a big joke because you're always trying to fight something that gets bigger all the time. What the hell am I struggling for?"

"I don't get you. Sure, you've got yourself into an unpleasant situation, but what do you want out of life?"

"I want not to want . . ."

Jay gave the driver his own address and the taxi shot down Fifth Avenue in order to avoid the Broadway traffic. Jay felt a bit more secure in his own car, but his hands were shaking and he gripped the wheel tightly. He drove carefully and slowly under the Broadway Brooklyn El and turned off at Reid Avenue, then cut into Utica and finally headed down Remsen Avenue. He had never driven to Eva's place using this long, circuitous route and he dimly wondered why he had chosen it, but when he passed his King's Highway store it became apparent to him that he needed some physical reminder of his existence, and the largish lateral sign, striking out luminously in the dark street, assured him that he existed—perhaps not as a living, breathing man, but as a name, an identity.

They were both surprised to find that most of the lights in Eva's apartment house were on, and the road was alive with activity. Three police cars were parked at the curb, and an ambulance drove off past them. The whine of the siren faded as it passed a red light. They got out of the car and walked over to a candy store which was open late. A man in a filthy white apron was sorting out the Sunday papers. Jay asked him for some change and then handed it to Marty.

"Just in case her . . . you better call and tell her that she's got to come in tomorrow. An emergency . . ."

Marty took the coin reluctantly and dialed her number. He emerged a minute later.

"Busy."

"This time of night?"

They sat down on the two rickety counter stools and waited. Flies had established a colony on a box of sweating chocolate jellies, and the counter was wet with the white foam of an ice cream soda which had spilled over. The man in the dirty apron drifted behind the counter. He ran some water and washed the black newsprint stains off his hands; they were still dirty when he dried them on the apron.

"You gentlemen thinking of buying the store or are you reporters?"

"Gimme a two-cents plain," Jay said.

"And your friend?"

"The same."

"I won't become a millionaire at this rate."

"What's all the excitement across the street?" Jay asked.

"Do I look like the news bureau? You want news, then you buy a paper."

"Okay, let's have a *News* and *Mirror*."

The man handed them the newspapers and he became more expansive.

"Shamed you into it? Well, it don't matter. Won't be in this paper what happened."

"So, get to the point," Marty said, irritably.

"Somebody got murdered or something. Somebody's always getting murdered."

Marty tried the number again, but it was still busy, and Jay suggested that they go across and see if they could get the janitor to give her a message.

The lobby was ablaze with lights and two cameramen were popping off flashbulbs and looking extremely bored. A police sergeant stood scratching his nose. Jay recognized the janitor with him. He was a man with a craggy face, a sharp pointed nose, freckled arms, and an air of seedy dissipation. He wore a blue striped pajama top over a pair of green corduroy trousers and he appeared to be in a highly agitated state. Jay approached him and the man forced a smile to his face.

"'Lo, Mr. Blackman."

"Hello, George . . . What's happened?"

"It's terrible . . . and in my building."

The sergeant stopped scratching his nose and clumped over to them.

"You live here?" he said sharply.

"No, I want to see a friend."

"Well, you better make it another night, buddy."

"I've worked in six buildings in twenty years and this is

the first time anything like this ever happened,'' George said
sorrowfully as though it reflected on his character and would
damage his prospects.

"Who'd you want to see?" the cop asked.

"Mrs. Eva Meyers."

The cop stared at him and his face lit up as though Jay had
set off a whole network of ideas in his thick skull.

"Inter-resting . . ."

"Mr. Meyers in 6A—" George started to say.

"I'm a friend of hers"—he pointed to Marty—"and this
man is her employer."

"Nice, quiet man," George said. "Didn't see much of him
. . . he used to do a lot of traveling. Gave me a baseball glove
for my kid last Christmas."

"Christ, what's happened?" Jay said, stunned. He tried to
get past the fat cop, but he had his sleeve grabbed.

"Just a minute. If you're a friend of the family, you'll have
to give me your name and then I'll see if they want you to
come up."

Marty and Jay gave their names and the cop squiggled them
in a little notebook.

"Stay right here till I get back," the cop said.

"I didn't hear a thing. What with the traffic all night and I
had a few drinks at my sister's, so I was sleeping." He rubbed
his eyes sleepily and looked from Jay to Marty in puzzlement.

"George, for God's sake, tell me what happened?"

"I thought you knew and that's why you come over." He
waited for a reaction, and received none, save incredulity.
"Oh, me oh my, you haven't heard . . . Mr. Meyers shot his-
self with a forty gauge. He used to sell sporting goods on the
road . . . and rifles was one of the things—"

Jay and Marty tore through the lobby and rushed up the six
flights of stairs. The door of Eva's apartment was open and
they entered past a throng of neighbors who were in bathrobes
and "tch-tching" through their teeth. A tall studious man was
writing something down. He picked at his mustache as though
it were a sore. Two other men were roaming around the apartment like exterminators.

"Who the hell are you?" the man with the mustache asked.

"I'm a friend of Mrs. Meyers," Jay said; his words hung on the air like frost and he couldn't believe he had spoken them.

"I don't think she wants any visitors at the moment. You should've called up first—saved yourself a trip."

"Where is she?"

"In the bedroom. The doctor's giving her something."

A thin red-eyed woman of about fifty came out of the room. Her hands shook uncontrollably. She puffed at a cigarette with an inch-long ash which finally fell on her black dress. She wandered around the room for a full minute before anyone said anything, then she sat on the edge of the sofa, and started to cry, noiselessly. The cigarette burned her fingers and she let it fall on the carpet. Jay stooped to pick it up, and there was a flicker of recognition in the woman's eyes.

"You're Jay, aren't you?" she said.

He nodded and held out another cigarette. She slapped hard at the pack and knocked it out of his hand.

"It's your fault. This wouldn't have happened if—"

There was a loud wailing call from the bedroom and a voice, ghost-like and cracking, cut her off.

"Jaaaay . . ."

He went into the bedroom, past the mustached cop who did not try to restrain him. Eva was lying fully dressed on top of the bed, and a man with a hypodermic needle was squirting it into the air. She rolled her eyes up to the ceiling when she saw him and he moved to the edge of the bed so that she would not have to strain herself to look at him.

"She's lost a lot of blood," the man said, matter-of-factly.

"Did he shoot her?" Jay asked, panic-stricken.

"No, but she's pregnant and we're going to have to get her to the hospital. Would you please wait outside!"

Jay started for the door and her eyes followed him out of a white, bloodless face. Her hair lay like blood-red swabs on the pillow and her eyes turned back to the ceiling.

"Oh, would you ask Lieutenant Collaro to get King's

County to send an ambulance over. I'll stay with her till the ambulance comes.''

The next two weeks were among the most agonizing of Jay's life. He walked around, and went through his daily routine of checking the stores, buying, in a daze, like a somnambulist. No one remarked about the sudden change in his manner. The harshness, the vitriolic gibe, were absent and a new, softer man emerged. The fire in him had died, and when he went up to Lieberman's farm for the weekend Rhoda was filled with new hope for their future. Something freakish had happened to change Jay—he had received a severe buffeting, of that she was certain, but she did not want to verify her surmise. It wasn't that the balance of power had shifted and she had gained a new and meteoric ascendancy, for she knew him too well to deceive herself. His attitude towards her had become more passive. The old arrogant manner had disappeared, the megalomania was not quite so pronounced. She wondered what had happened to alter the center of his universe, and she tried to confirm this impression by questioning Celia, after he had returned to the city.

They were walking along the road to Ferndale. It was still light, and the air was heavy with the fragrance of roses. The diffuse light lit a small section of firs on top of the mountain as though with a halo, and Rhoda had a sense of contentment that seemed to wipe away all the bitterness and agony of her life with Jay.

"He looks very tired," Celia said. "I esk him to stay over, but he won't. He works too hard."

"I tell him the same thing, Momma. But he doesn't listen to anything I say."

"Rhoda, you think Neal'll be all right?"

"Mrs. Lieberman's sitting right outside the room on the porch."

"I shouldn't worry, but I do. I worry all the time about Jakie. He looks so old all of a sudden . . . so much responsibility on a young man's shoulders. I told him to take some time off, but he said he couldn't." She stopped in her tracks and looked out over a field of daisies and breathed deeply. "You know what he esked me the other night?"

Rhoda shrugged her shoulders.

"He wanted to know what would make me happy, and I said to have his father here with me. He hasn't had a vacation in thirty years and he's sitting in that hot apartment all by himself even though he wouldn't be mad on me or Jakie for not coming. I know a few days here would mean a lot to him. Jake said he would send him up on Monday if that's what I wanted. It's time we was a family and . . ." she faltered and resumed walking.

"Momma, tell me the truth. What happened to Jay to make him the way he is?"

The question surprised Celia, but she managed to conceal it.

"What should hev heppened? He had a hard time when he was young. Never any money, never enough to eat."

The answer did not satisfy Rhoda.

"Is that all?"

"What else?" She had avoided Rhoda's question, and none too skillfully.

Rhoda did not press her, for she knew that Celia, who did have the answer, would never reveal it, and she was aware of Celia's desire to help secure her marriage.

"Then what's bothering him? Did he tell you?"

Celia's steel-blue eyes flickered as she cupped her hand to ward off a shaft of light which cut into her line of vision just after a clump of serried maples. She also had witnessed the abrupt and inexplicable metamorphosis Jay had undergone, and with sphinxlike wisdom, or at least the semblance of omniscience, she had turned her back on him, refusing to be drawn into a crosscurrent of conflict which she sensed was at the bottom of his change of heart. She had localized his affliction almost at once—something had stretched out to hurt him, but not in any normal, manageable way, the type of experience which assails all men every day of their lives. This was an event so devastating, so unnameable and terrifying in its impact that she dared not even allude to the possibility of its existence, for she had seen it once before on his face, a variation admittedly, but the essence, the quiddity, of the experience was substantially the same, and she had turned her back on it then—to survive.

"It's overwork, thet's all," Celia said, forcing herself to accept her own account at face value. The walk was tiring her now, and she felt the first chill of evening break through the buzzing air and she placed a black shawl on her shoulders, a present Jay had given her that weekend. He had said: "Momma, pray for me." His face had been tense and strained, an ivory mask of lined skin, and pale blue protuberant veins, stretching the skin of his forehead, but he had forced himself to smile, as though aware of some subtle paradox in the request, and the effort had almost broken him into small bits. There was always Jay, Celia reflected, at the back of every meaningful event of her life—the *angst* and the awful febrile joy which he brought with him like a mule in a desert, riderless, with its panniers of pure gold . . . She remembered how he had come home that day, on that long-forgotten day in Lvov, drunk, and his clothes reeking of the sweat which accompanies the sick vomit of drunkenness, all control lost, with frantic gorgon eyes, his trousers sopping with his own urine, and how she had washed him, changed his clothes and eased him into a pair of his father's long winter underwear which were gray from washing. It had snowed for a week, a deathly blizzard with a Siberian impetus that froze the marrow, and when he walked away from the pot-bellied stove's direct heat, he was overcome by chills. The gelid cheeselike mass of ice on the windowpanes. The cold that tore him apart so that he cried out in pain . . .

"Maybe he does need a vacation," Rhoda said.

Celia leaned against the stump of a poplar, an old one by the look and smell of it, which was decaying. She saw something move in the cracks and she wanted to throw up: a host of moving white maggots, squirming and undulating, while a phalanx of red ants moved inexorably forward for the kill. Rhoda saw them also.

"Uch. Let's move, Momma."

They walked downhill through the dales and flickering streams which caught the last aureole gold of sunlight before night came.

The hospital, King's County, was a complex of gray interweaving buildings which twisted like a snake through the King's Highway section of Brooklyn. It shared with Rockland State the questionable distinction of synonymity with madness. Jay nervously sat on a bench in front of the hospital's emergency wing; a hot, sultry morning, typical of Brooklyn's summer. He had in his hand a small bunch of violets. He could have purchased a gross of roses, but had thought them inappropriate. Eva came down the steps, carrying a small plaid suitcase. Her lips were a startling cherry red in contrast to the pallor of her skin; her cheeks had lost their healthy appearance. The bones had moved up and the face had shrunk somewhat, and she moved shakily with uncertain jerks in her walk, which had become the exaggerated gait peculiar to the old and infirm. He had been unable to see or speak to her for two weeks, and Herbie had been buried at Beth David Cemetery while she was still in the hospital. She walked past him without turning her head; he jumped to his feet and caught her by the arm.

"I tried to see you, but your mother . . ."

"She meant well, I guess."

He took the suitcase from her and put his arm around her shoulder.

"Well, I survived. Why, I'll never know."

He kissed her on the cheek and his mouth sank into her flesh and he hated to move away.

"Baby, I love you. Baby, baby, baby."

"Funny word to use," she said.

"You want to go home?"

"I don't live there any more. My mother's got Lorna."

"I took a suite at the Peter Hamilton . . . for you," he added.

She sighed and looked into the glare of the sun.

"Well, if I'm going to be somebody's kept whore, it may as well be there."

She allowed him to lead her to the car and got in without

speaking. He drove to the downtown section of Brooklyn through a stream of marauding traffic, keeping his eyes firmly fixed on the road. A number of times he wanted to speak but when he caught her out of the corner of his eye she was staring out of the window.

The Peter Hamilton was an ochre monolith which sprawled over most of a city block; it was off to the side of the Manhattan Bridge and had a well-earned reputation for specializing in matinees and one-night stands. Twelve resident call girls did shift duty; and the bar, a noisy, dim, green room, known as the Aquamarine Room, with French Provincial frames on the backs of the booths, was the invention of some goggle-eyed subaqueous creature who was obsessed with goldfish, guppies, and myriad varieties of seamoss and rock all brought at great expense from Sheepshead Bay. The oceanographical motif extended to dressing the waitresses as mermaids and the barmen as deep-sea divers. The centerpiece of the bar was a plaster of paris bathysphere designed after Jules Verne. Jay and Eva went in for a noonday cocktail. A neanderthal in a diving outfit, with a face like a crushed flounder, sidled over to them. Jay ordered a couple of whiskey highballs and lit a cigarette. Toying with a dessicated olive, he waited for her to say something. Nervousness and anxiety made him reach out for her hand, and she let him hold it. Her face under the green light was drawn and tired, with small pouches of shadow under her eyes which were strangely lifeless and drifted from one mounted swordfish to another and finally rested on a shark.

"What have you been doing?" Eva asked, without curiosity. It sounded to Jay like the end of something; two people, who had shared something that had become unmentionable, meeting awkwardly after a time gap in their lives.

"Worrying about you, and wondering . . . and dying."

She gave him a sharp look.

"How's Neal?" She sipped her drink hungrily and he called for another.

"The mountain air agrees with him and my mother's there too . . . out of the hot city."

"You're a good son, and a good father, aren't you?"

"Not good, but I care."

She swallowed her highball almost as soon as the barman had put it down.

"You want to get drunk, don't you?"

"You're paying, aren't you, Jay?"

"It isn't a question of money. But you've only come out of the hospital . . . what did the doctor say?"

"That I'll live." She took a cigarette out of his pack and tamped it on the bar until it broke. She threw it away and took another and he lit it. "Well, have you got any master plan for me today? Fredericks or somebody like him whose throat we can cut?"

"That isn't fair."

"Sorry, I didn't mean to hurt your feelings."

"I may have got Fredericks in an unethical way, but the simple fact of the matter is that he's going to make about fifty thousand a year more out of me than he would have from a prestige outfit. He didn't cry his. eyes out when he signed the contracts."

"I guess you're just a misunderstood good Samaritan."

"Eva, please let up. The last thing I want us to do is argue."

She took another pull from her highball and then laid her head on his shoulder, and started to cry silently with a kind of forlorn resignation which enveloped him in a web of despair.

"The terrible part of it," she said, "is that I'm to blame. I tried to reason with him, to be logical. We went to dinner at his brother's house and it was all very pleasant and harmless and we all had a few drinks after dinner and then we went home. Herb wasn't much of a drinker. You'd never believe to look at him that he was an athlete when he was younger—the fastest sprinter on his high school track team. Oh, Christ . . . So, when we got home, he got a little romantic and I told him I couldn't—he hasn't been near me since the day . . . He started to plead with me, and then he said: 'If I was that nigger-rich, East Side gangster, you wouldn't hesitate.' There it was, out in the open. We sat down in the living room, and I said: 'Let's see if we can straighten ourselves out . . . We're

both young enough to make new lives.' I asked him for a
divorce and he shook his head stubbornly. Said something
about Jewish people never divorcing, oh, I don't know. I was
very calm and I told him that I had to have one—that I was
having your baby and we couldn't live together—it wasn't fair
to him or you. He smiled at me, as though the whole thing
was a joke that I had made up . . . he smoked a cigarette, then
did a crazy thing for him, because he was so fussy and house
proud in a childish sort of way. He took his cigarette and
stubbed it out on a silk cushion. I just couldn't believe my
eyes. When I pulled the cushion away from him it had a hole
in it and the feathers were smoking inside. He got to his feet
and started to walk past me. Then he stopped and said: 'Eva,
you decide who loves you more: me or Blackman. Just you
decide, and if it's Blackman then put a sign on the door in
big black letters so that everybody who walks in can see it.
God is my enemy, that's what you put on the sign.' He pushed
me out of his way and went into the bathroom and got into
the bathtub. I didn't know what to do. I heard him stomping
in the bathtub and then there was a shot . . . and oh . . .''

Jay's mind drifted away from the scene. He had a vision of
Neal at thirteen on his bar mitzvah day wearing a blue serge
suit about four sizes too large for him, and a rabbi with a long
gray beard of gnarled and twisted hair, touching both his
shoulders. But he couldn't see Neal's face. In the synagogue
was a gaping hole in the side window which allowed a current
of wind to blow the silken curtains that covered the Torah. It
irritated him and he could not lift his eyes from the curtain.
Then someone said in Polish: "Today you are a man." He
knew why he couldn't see Neal's face, nor imagine what it
would be like thirteen years hence, for it was his own face
that he was trying to piece together in the tangled strains of
his memory. His own face . . . and he could not see it. He felt
an awful chill cut through his bones.

"I . . ." He started to say something, but his tongue was
thick and felt like a piece of cracked leather.

"We're in it together," Eva said, after a long silence. Her
eyes darted nervously around the room. "Nobody's said 'to

have and to hold . . .' but it doesn't much matter.''

He took hold of her hand and ran it along the side of his face as though it were the beginning of an enticement, cold and bloodless and without joy.

"Eva . . . Eva . . . you should have told me you were pregnant.'' She pulled her hand away and picked up her drink.

"I had some crazy idea about telling Herb that it was *his*. But that would have meant, well . . . and I was in the third month so it was too late. But you see, when he came close to me and touched me, like I was an old possession that he'd suddenly found again, I couldn't . . . It was a case of you or him and maybe a question of character, of trying to do the decent thing. Of thinking to myself: 'I'm cheating on both of them if I do it. And me, I'm lost somewhere in between in a kind of spittoon.' I kept thinking of a spittoon I'd seen in a western where dirty old cowhands used to stand with a foot on the brass bar rail and aim at the spittoon. And God, it made me sick. Maybe I wanted to make up to him for all the times I've lied about where and who I was with and telling the truth to make up for lies is like forcing poison down someone's throat. He only wanted to touch me and I suppose I should have let him, but the thought nauseated me.'' She pointed an accusing finger at Jay: "It's what you've done to me''—he turned his face as though to avoid a slap—''the way you've made me feel. With Herb when we first got married I had to be the boss, do the leading, and I never much liked it and after I met you, well it was different, fantastic . . . I didn't have to be the man. At first I hated the idea of letting you take over because there was something humiliating about being told to sit at the foot of the table and then I realized that I liked the idea—talk about knowing yourself, I didn't know or understand the first thing about myself—that it had to be *your* way.''

She stood up, her eyes glassy and her face twitching, and he got up after a minute and dropped some money on the bar and followed her out.

The hotel apartment he had rented for her was expensive and well-furnished. There were two rooms, and a small kitchen in an alcove off the sitting room which was a low-toned dove gray with a white ceiling and fussy wainscoting of embryonic swans and ducks. Three armchairs, a settee in gray velvet, and two end tables with lamps completed the room. A reproduction of an eighteenth-century pastoral scene somewhere in rural England hung over a defunct tiled fireplace; on the wall opposite there was a faded picture of the ruined façade of a classical building. What the room lacked was even the suggestion of character; in fact, it was this total lack of any distracting feature which in the end distracted the eye and forced it to search feverishly for a place to rest. Jay opened a closet and showed her about twenty expensive dresses he had bought her. Her eyes rested on a gray Persian lamb coat, also new. She put it on and looked at herself in the full-length mirror behind the bedroom door.

"My trophies. You get away with murder and you get presents. Who says that crime doesn't pay?"

"What's the point of holding it against yourself? You wouldn't have told him if you'd known . . ."

She threw her head back and laughed.

"But that's exactly what I would have done. I couldn't save the man's life even if I wanted to."

She brushed past him and walked into the sitting room. Two bottles of whiskey, like sentinels, stood on the mantelpiece and there was a bucket of ice on a table and a bottle of soda. She poured them drinks and swallowed hers before he took his from her.

"Well, what's it to be?"

"What? I don't understand."

"Do you want to make love or don't you? It's your money, honey."

"Just what the hell are you talking about?"

He started for the door angrily and had his foot in the corridor before she rushed to stop him.

"Jay, please don't walk out on me. Please don't . . . I can't help myself."

His face was ashen and his eyes cloudy and he bit his lip to control himself.

"Honestly, Eva, I can't bear to listen to you. Do you think I don't know it's my fault . . . It's on my conscience. I love you."

She pushed the door closed and led him to the settee.

"I've got you in my bones and when you say . . . I feel like my stomach's been cut open and my guts are hanging out." He sighed fitfully. "I've made a wreck of everything. What I'm trying to say is that I'm not sorry for myself or for you . . . It's just that you're my life and . . ."

She kissed him lightly on the mouth and then there was the sound of a rattle deep in his throat as though a machine had broken and he began to moan with a destructive force which nearly crippled him.

"Sorry," he said. "Only once before . . . and that was a long time ago and for a different reason. Or maybe it was the same reason. When somebody else's life was ruined."

"It's okay." She rubbed his back affectionately. "You do have some guts and character. People live through tragedies, I guess. It changes them, but they go on when they've got a reason to go on . . ."

"It's summer and we should be happy, having some fun. Crazy the way things work out. When you haven't got a penny, money is the big problem, and the obstacle to get over—and, when you do make some, all sorts of other things take its place."

"Couldn't we go away for a while?"

"I only wish I could, but I've got to keep on top of the business and to see how the new sites are taking shape. It's full time."

"A few days?"

"I'll try."

She hugged him and his body relaxed. They were together and she knew that whatever he was, whatever he stood for, if he was anyone, if he had any scruples, that she would be pulled along by him and that there was no way one could swim out of a maelstrom, one simply had to accept the fact that one would be drawn into the eye, and the hideous acceptance of this fact, whether one protested or submitted, had no bearing on the final and inevitable outcome. For good or ill, Jay had become her family, the center of her universe. Without him her life would be unendurable, a misshapen and warped controversy with time, a divorce from reality so deadly in its consequences that she might as well never have been born.

11

When Jay had had a few days to consider the situation he came to the conclusion that his brother's betrayal—and he was convinced that it was a betrayal—of his secret had somehow arranged destiny, or rearranged it, and had been the direct cause of Eva's confrontation with her husband. His first impulse was to beat Al's head in, but by the time he saw Harry Lee, he managed to simulate a degree of calm.

Harry's office was a study in muted stripped pine—a small desk overlooked the frantic commerce of Thirty-ninth Street, and if you stretched your head you could see the wide junction it made with Seventh Avenue.

Harry poured him a drink and put his feet on the desk.

"Frankly, I'm puzzled," he said. "Haven't you got enough on your plate, without looking for trouble?"

"I want to be my own supplier. I've got my own retail outlets . . . what do I need a middleman to get twenty percent?"

"It's an entirely different kind of operation . . . manufacturing. You don't know a thing about it. And I don't like partners."

"You've got a factory in Syracuse that isn't paying."

Harry sucked an ice cube until it melted in his mouth.

"How do you know it's not paying? Everything I do pays."

"This one don't. You've got two hundred people sitting on

their behinds because they haven't got enough work. They make for Marty . . .''

"Did he say . . . ?"

"Not a word . . ."

"I'll cut his balls off if he's opened his mouth."

"You've got a lot of faith in him."

"He's my son-in-law, isn't he?"

"But the fact is he's a great salesman. He could sell glasses to a blind man. The trouble is, he makes a shitty dress and he doesn't know how to run a business, but that doesn't mean he isn't valuable."

"So what happens? He makes for you exclusively . . . is that what you're suggesting?"

"No, he makes for me and the trade as well, but the stuff he makes for me is exclusive . . . originals, no knock-offs."

"You ought to write for the Marx Brothers, Jay. Who ever heard of a five-dollar exclusive?"

"Eva'll design them. But what she designs for me she doesn't sell to the chains. They'll have to buy the knock-offs and you can make them in a better-priced dress."

"But that's turning everything upside down."

"That's the gimmick. If you get a runner in a cheap dress you can do it for the higher-priced stores. The whole point is that you've got to give the public what it wants—cheap or expensive, so long as it's what they want."

"Don't quote my own words at me. I'll say one thing for you, Jay: you may be a nut case, but you've got some good ideas." He picked up the telephone and said: "Lemme have the Syracuse factory records."

A few moments later there was a soft tapping on the door and Al walked in carrying two ledgers and a sheaf of production schedules in a manila envelope. Jay had his back to him.

"You wanted these, Mr. Lee?" Al said, holding up the books.

"Yeah, that's right."

Al walked over to the desk and his eyes bulged when he saw Jay. He stood riveted by the side of the desk, his mouth slightly open.

"Why, if it isn't . . ."

"You can go now," Jay said without looking up.

Al picked up the books and started to take them away when Harry grabbed his arm.

"You're supposed to leave them, not take them away," he said.

"Don't confuse him, Harry. He confuses easy."

"Yes, Mr. Lee," Al said with a quiver in his voice, and closed the door softly behind him.

"So that's the way it is," Harry said. "Funny, I didn't get that impression when he asked for a job."

"We're not the best of friends . . . never have been. It's like that with brothers—sometimes."

Harry's face screwed itself into something that might be called a smile; it was more a rearrangement of the deep sun-encrusted lines.

"I could give him the push, if you like."

For a violent man, Jay exercised some restraint in the face of this open invitation. Revenge is mine, he thought. He'd build up Al before he cut him down. A strange expression of puzzlement crossed Jay's lips for a fleeting moment. Perhaps Al hadn't known about him and Eva—perhaps he had told her about Neal innocently? The possibility existed. He and Al were brothers, after all, flesh and blood of the same union. Why should he be the one to stick his knife in when he could not be quite sure? Hadn't Al abandoned his pride and self-esteem by using him to get a job, by riding along on his coat-tails? Wouldn't he have done the same thing, if their positions had been reversed? There was also his mother to consider. She would be sure to ask him to help Al, and if Al lost his job suddenly she would know that Jay had interfered.

"He's all right," Jay said. "I don't love him, that's all."

"You've got my sympathy . . ."

"Why? I don't get it. Isn't he doing his job?"

"Yeah, he's fine. Pretty good bookkeeper in fact. Conscientious. It's only that I had a brother, dead now, and I can appreciate your position. We started out together in business. He was older, by four years, and the only reason we joined forces was because neither of us had enough money to start on his own. It lasted two years.''

''What happened?'' Jay asked. He had never suspected that Harry had ever had a problem in his life.

''I drove him out of the business. I got what I wanted and I got rid of him. He ran the production side, and very well at that, but he didn't know the first thing about selling or design, and he was color-blind. So for this he got fifty percent. Who needs a partner to run a factory? You get yourself a manager, pay him a salary and *fartig*. He started telling me what to do, what to buy. An absolute idiot in business . . . he kept trying to pull his money out after the first six months.

''All he could think about was that his thousand dollars was outside a bank. It cost me money to get rid of him, much too much. I raised five thousand dollars from the bank and gave him twenty-five percent of the net profits for five years.'' He shrugged his shoulders. ''Who knew I was gonna make a quarter of a million in my first five years? Almost seventy grand, the sonovabitch cost me. He never worked a day in his life after he left. Put it in the stock market and got out with half a million in 1928 on my advice. I told him to put it in government bonds or else he'd lose it in 1929. He thought it was God talking so he did it. The crazy thing was that when the crash came he was sitting on the sidelines with all his *gelt* while brokers were jumping out of windows. But the market was in his blood, and he used to go down there every day to watch the tape, and keep on top of the prices. You'd think he'd be laughing, but it aggravated him to death. He'd hustle into the Corn Savings Bank every day to find out if they were going broke—he had a small savings account there, and the manager would reassure him, even offer to give him his money back to put in a safety deposit box, but my brother wouldn't have the nerve to ask him, especially when the manager knew he had half a million. Finally he went down, the Monday after Black Friday, and found out that the bank had folded up.

''That night he went home and told his wife about it and she said: 'So you lost five thousand dollars, does it matter? Harry gave you good advice. We're still rich. We'll never want for anything.' He flopped down in a chair, white as a ghost, and said: 'It don't matter that I've got a half million, my luck's changed, I'm jinxed. You see it's Harry's five thousand that I lost, the money he gave me when we broke up. I never even touched the money, and everything I made was because of that money. It don't mean a thing that I'm rich . . . the five thousand was everything.' The same night he had a stroke and died in bed.

"My sister-in-law and I became friendly again and I put her into a few special situations in 1932. I hate to tell you what she's worth today. The brokers wait for her to buy before telling their other customers. When she goes short, Dow Jones is down a point on the day. She's got a seat on the exchange, and she's a silent specialist in steel. Brothers . . . partners, they're a joke." He sighed philosophically. "What do I need a partner for, tell me, Jay?"

"Because you like to make money and I can make it for you. When I get through, I'm gonna have the biggest retail combine in the country and I have to get into your end of it now. It's a pattern I'm building: stores, factories, property, and then when we're nice and big, we go public and open at fifty on the market."

"It sounds very nice . . . it sounds possible too. But I'm sixty-two. I'm tired of knocking my brains out. I don't have to, but this showroom is me. If I can't have a place to hang my hat, I'd wind up in the bughouse. So I come in every day and work . . . not as hard as I used to, but a decent few hours. I can't stay in Miami all winter, cause the sun fries my brains. California bores me. Europe I been to three times. So I may as well spend the time here."

"Six factories you've got that are busy all the time. The one in Syracuse's a dog. You let me do what I want to with it, and you'll see a dream come true. Right before your eyes."

"You want to buy it?"

"You know goddamn well that I haven't got the capital."

"I get fifty-one percent of everything from the factory."

"You get forty, and you can't make an executive decision without my say-so."

"I'll say one thing for you, Jay. What you don't have in brains, you make up in nerve."

"Forty percent . . ."

"For a year."

"Two. I've got to have two years."

"Eighteen months."

Jay extended his hand and shook Harry's.

"Two years, it's a deal."

"Okay. I must be getting old. I give you my factory on your terms and all I get is a handshake."

"And youth."

"I'm a gambler."

"An investor."

"Can't even win an argument with you."

He and Jay chinked glasses. The scotch warmed Jay and made him slightly dizzy. He had been in over his depth and he had not merely survived, but won. The elation he felt turned a bit bitter in his mouth when he thought about Eva.

"One other thing. Eva's on five thousand a year, as of now."

"Are you paying, or am I?"

"We both are, partner."

"Oooh, I hate the sound of the word," Harry said, as though he had been burned with a match.

"You'll get used to it."

"You want me to do anything about that little family matter?"

"No, leave it to me."

Jay spent the rest of the morning visiting the far-flung outposts of his embryonic empire. He noted with satisfaction the progress made on each site. What had formerly been wild tracts of uncultivated land, and in the case of Hempstead a swamp which had to be filled in, now loomed in the distance, in the guise of concrete façades, new pillars of civilization. Prophets brought the Word, Jay the Dress . . . thou shalt not live by silk alone was his message to the underpaid and drably accoutred women, victims of America's black decade of depression. Like a beaten giant given a magical balm, the country slowly shook off its economic wounds and throbbed with new life. Jay, the heir to the Phoenician traders, brought the possibility of glamour to America's glamour-starved women.

When he reached the site in Great Neck, a complex of shops and office buildings, he observed a large truck with dredging equipment near the outer perimeter of the center. A man wearing a wide-striped gray suit turned when he blew the horn to get past. When the man saw it was Jay, he opened his arms expansively. Jay pulled over, then got out.

"Hiya, Jaya," Topo shouted, as though greeting the prodigal. "I ain't seen yuh for a munt."

"Been pretty busy, trying to lick everything into shape . . . I expect to be open in six weeks."

"You a magician." He put his arm affectionately round Jay's shoulder. "C'mon let's have a coffee."

They walked across the main highway to a shiny steel-shelled diner, and sat down in a booth. Topo ordered iced coffees for them and offered Jay a stogie. The diner was empty and the air was heavy with cooking oil.

"How the hell you smoke that cheap rope is a mystery to me."

"It's what yuh get used to. Like at home. I ohways drink coffee with chicory. Not trying to save money. It's the way I been brought up." He sipped the coffee noisily through a straw. "We're all pretty grateful to yuh for what yuh done."

"I don't think I've done very much. Getting you the contract was just good business. Your boys are better than the other thieves. They would've held us up for at least six months."

Topo appeared puzzled, he removed his glasses and peered at Jay through icy gray fish slits. His straw squelched at the ice cubes in his glass, and he flicked his wrist to the waitress for another one.

"That's not the whole story," he said finally. "The work's bein' done strictly legit and very fast for a different reason. What we make here is peanuts. It's the new locations that's so important to *people*."

Jay had a sudden feeling of fear and revulsion.

"I don't get it. I'm not giving pieces of my business away."

Topo blinked disbelievingly.

"Hey, you got the wrong enda the stick. We don't want no dress stores. We got our own stores on the locations. Electrical, huh."

"You mean, Fredericks rented you stores?"

"Sure he did. It's a shopping center, ain't it? People gotta buy plugs, and radios and things, don't they? We open up smart stores with all the latest things on the market. Strictly legit. Our joints are gonna give the public a service. We don't want nothing from you . . . we just want you to know you got favors coming to yuh. Whenever you want to collect 'em."

"I'm still in the dark." Jay breathed a sigh of relief.

"Hey, Jaya baby. You're a big boy now. We don't care about no radios or batteries or crap like that. You got an electrical store, you got lots of aerials and mains and hookups, right? It's for the wire service. This means we got places right near Jamaica, Aqueduct, and Belmont. And in Jersey we can cover Philly, from Passaic, which means Garden City, and Monmouth direct. In White Plains we get Terry Haute, Detroit and Chicago's on a direct line. I got the clear from the *people* to tell yuh, because they got a very high opinion a yuh."

"The wire service?" Jay rolled the phrase on his tongue. Everyone had heard of obscure big business gambling which was illegal in America. But no one knew who ran it, or what the profits were. Occasionally one read about a crusading district attorney who had a line on a gambling setup, but the story always drifted out of the papers in a day or two. Topo slid a long brown envelope across the table. His sweating hand had imprinted three fingers across its belly. He stared at it with rapt fascination, and smiled.

"That's the first time my prints've been on anything. Collector's item. To show our appreciation, but has nothin' to do with favors that we still owe. You're a lucky guy to have *people* in your debt."

The short-order cook emerged from the kitchen and sat at the counter, and the waitress served him an iced drink. They looked aimlessly at Topo and Jay sitting in the booth. It was hot and they were bored, and they weren't particularly curious about the young dark-haired man who opened the envelope.

Jay put the envelope on his lap out of sight when he noticed two people at the counter looking at him. He opened the flap, and gasped when he saw a thousand-dollar bill sticking out of the corner. His head suddenly began to ache, and there were spots before his eyes. He saw Topo sitting in a cloud of gray smoke, the corners of his mouth spread out in a smile.

"There's ten of those in the envelope."

"You must be crazy."

"It's a shock, huh? You deserve it, Jay. The setup's worth millions. *People* have long memories, and if you ever get in a jam, you know where you got friends." He got up abruptly and called to the waitress: "My friend's paying for the coffees. It's his treat. See yuh, Jay, and don't forget."

Eva had a particular dread of Thursday, for it had become the last night she and Jay could spend together. With religious promptness he would leave at eight every Friday morning for Lieberman's farm to see his mother and Neal, and of course, Rhoda. Her week ended therefore every Thursday night, and she was left in a void, a universe with no center. When Jay came in later that evening, she barely turned her head. She could see that he was excited, but she could not shake off the depression that had set in early that morning. He kissed her with exuberance and clutched her in his arms.

"What makes you so happy? Glad to get rid of me? I'll bet you're getting sick to death of me."

"Eva, what's wrong with you? What have I got but you?"

She gave him an abashed smile which conceded the point, but his mood, like the flick of a dial on the radio, had altered. When he was with her, he always had the sensation of walking on eggs. It exhausted him, but he was drawn to her, and he reflected with some detachment that the link between people who share joy is weaker and more transitory than between those who have lived through a tragedy. Herbie's death had established a treacherous concatenation of emotional ties which imposed itself completely on their relationship. It had become for them both a form of bondage so that what they were, who they were, to each other was reduced to a variation of a single charade, its subject their roles in the death of a man who was unloved and now almost forgotten, save for the silent grief of a few thin-lipped relatives who had never been very close to him in life and who had only a nodding acquaintance with Eva. Responsibility is as much a quirk of memory as of action; to be responsible one has first to remember, and Jay and Eva remembered with clarity. They could no longer live with the quiet, the unspoken—now nothing could be left unsaid, for imagination might take over; human inventories were continually being made and adjusted so that nothing between them could reside in obscurity.

"I'm gonna make you happy," Jay said.

"That's nice."

"Everything'll be changed—"

"Isn't it already?"

He paused in mid-sentence—

"Don't get me sidetracked,'cause that means one thing: too much to drink, going to bed, and waking up with nightmares."

"You've got something to show for the nightmares."

"Aw, Eva, give me a chance to tell you. I've made a deal with Harry." In a breathless voice he outlined his plans to her, explained her role in the new hierarchy, and spent a few minutes eulogizing his one-man army. She was not quite overcome with delight at the suggestion, so he was forced to reveal what he had intended to conceal.

"Here," he said, handing her a bill. "I want you to buy something for yourself and Lorna . . . something that you don't really need."

She looked at the bill with surprise and gasped when he showed her the rest of his bankroll.

"Christ."

"I did somebody a favor. The crazy thing was that I thought I was doing it for myself."

"There's a fortune there . . . You shouldn't be carrying it around in cash."

"I can't put it in the bank either. Safety deposit, first thing tomorrow."

"Should I ask: how?"

"Better if you didn't."

They had dinner at the Monte Carlo and Jay felt deflated and drank too much. He had expected her to react differently to the news he brought her, the new opportunity, but she just sat sulkily picking at her steak as though it was unpalatable. The floor show was about to begin and the waiter asked them if they wanted to order anything. Jay insisted on a bottle of scotch even though he knew he should not have any more. A group of men on a night out without their wives cackled when a dozen showgirls kicked up their heels to the can-can. They walked provocatively through the gauntlet of men and threw roses at them. One of the men got up and followed the girls. The bandleader escorted him off with a smile and a cry for audience applause for this "good sport." Jay studied the man through a haze of smoke and bleary eyes. Eva looked at Jay critically and he felt his irritation rise uncontrollably to the surface.

"Well, what *do* you want? Everything I give you ... tell me what more?"

"Divorce Rhoda!"

"I've thought about it," he lied, "but I can't do it just like that."

"Let her divorce you. She's got grounds."

"Grounds?" he said drunkenly. "What kinda grounds?"

"Adultery ... the only kind they recognize in New York State."

"What about the kid? Neal?" he said with a kind of desperation.

"They give visiting privileges."

"Visiting privileges? He's my kid ... I love him. He's a baby. It would be deserting him."

Her face colored angrily and she slammed the table with her fist, but no one in the club heard because the band was exploding through something loud and martial and the girls were dressed in drum majorette costumes.

"What about my little girl? Jay, it can't work this way—"

"Listen, I don't want to argue. We're supposed to be having a good time."

"Jay, don't you understand? I've given up everything for you . . . I can't go on living in a hotel," she said with tears streaming down her face. "I don't want to spend my life as your personal piece of ass. Monday to Thursday."

"I don't like that kinda talk," he said, pouring himself a huge drink.

"I've got to have something to hope for . . . a future." She took out the thousand-dollar bill and crumpled it on the table. "Would you give me this if I was your wife? It's conscience money. I'm grateful to you for the business chance . . . it's what I always wanted. But there's got to be more."

"Can't Lorna live with you?"

"That means my mother as well. No, it wouldn't work."

He stretched out to touch her, and she let him.

"Be honest with me. Have we got any future? Because if we haven't, you've got to tell me now."

"Sure we do. But I can't get rid of Rhoda right now."

"But will you? Ever?" she insisted.

"Yes, I will, but not now."

A man came up behind them and slapped Jay on the back, right between the shoulder blades. He lurched forward, and Eva stared blankly. Her face was seamed with running make-up, and the man opened his mouth in astonishment when he caught sight of her.

"Oh, gee, sorry."

Jay turned around angrily.

"Hey, I was right," the man said. "It is Jay, or do my eyes deceive me?"

Jay glared at Howard, then gave Eva a furtive glance.

"I'm with that party of guys, and I thought I caught sight of you."

Howard pulled up an empty chair and sat down heavily.

"My brother-in-law, Howard Gold," Jay said in a reedy voice. "This is Eva Meyers."

Howard looked from one to the other uneasily.

"Eva's my designer," Jay said.

"Oh, well. Glad to meet you." He addressed Eva, as though Jay was in need of an interpreter. "Hard man to get in touch with . . . That's what happens when you're successful." His eyes turned starry, and his manner was reverential towards Jay. "I've been trying to speak to you all week, but I guess you're never in any one place long enough to get messages."

Jay poured Howard a long shot, and Howard's gaze fixed itself on the bottle of scotch which he reckoned must have cost by his standards at least a week's salary. He had never had anything stronger than beer in a nightclub: who could afford to? Howard held the glass with an emotion bordering on awe.

"That's the thing we all admire about you, Jay. You know how to live. Everything first class . . . you want something, you go out and get it. Not many people can do what you've done."

"Did you want something special?" Jay asked. Howard's adulation bored him.

"Well, strictly speaking I hoped to speak to Rhoda,'cause it's not your problem."

"What's it about?"

"Oh, I don't want to break up your evening."

"No, tell me."

"It's Myrna, see?"

"What about her?"

Howard paused and smiled meekly at Eva who said she had to go to the ladies' room to repair her make-up. When she had gone, Jay explained that Eva had been overwhelmed by the new job he had offered her and had cried.

"I really don't know how to begin . . . it's such a strange situation. Myrna's always been a little peculiar. She was the artist of the family. Oh gee, Jay, I wish we saw you more often than we do. A while ago, around the time Neal was born—that was the last time we saw you—she came home one night and hasn't left the house since. What with all the trouble you and Rhoda've had with Neal, no one wanted to tell you. Myrna just stays in her room and mopes around the house. Finally last week, she put all the gas jets on and when Poppa came in, he found her unconscious. They came for her in an ambulance and she's been under observation ever since. The doctor had Poppa and me in the other day and said she ought to be put in an institution. She's only high-strung.

"He says—oh, I don't know what they call it—that she's a danger to herself and that maybe if she's given proper treatment she'll recover and maybe not. We didn't know what to do, so Poppa said I had to ask Rhoda what she thought we should do, and I said, if anyone could solve the problem it would be you, so he asked me to call you, because he was too embarrassed."

Slowly Jay came out of the haze of alcohol. He wondered if Myrna had told them anything, and if this was some kind of trick to implicate him. The old man hated him, and would probably like to discredit him.

"I'm not sure what I can do. One thing though: she ought to get the best medical attention possible. Institutions are probably like jails."

"The private sanatoriums cost a fortune. None of us have that kind of money."

Jay extended his hand across the table and felt for the crumpled bill; he gathered it into the palm of his hand without Howard noticing.

"Howard, if I do something, will you promise me one thing?"

"I don't want you to do anything. I need your advice, that's all."

"My advice isn't worth a damn. I'm no doctor." He handed the bill to Howard who accepted it reluctantly and held it up to the candlelight.

"Look, nobody asked for charity, and ten dollars isn't going to be much use."

"It's not ten dollars," Jay said quietly. "Here, have another drink."

"Oh, my God," Howard exclaimed. "Christ, it's not possible! Is it real?"

"Why don't you take it to a bank in the morning? They'll tell you if it's real or if I made it myself."

"How can I say I got it?"

"You don't have to say a thing. In a way it's Rhoda's money as well—if she knew, she'd probably do the same thing."

Eva twisted through the tight web of tables. She was surprised to find Howard still there, but she forced a smile to her lips.

"Not a word to anybody." Jay helped Eva to her chair. "Howard's just finishing his drink." Jay had not counted on the degree of shock his gesture would create, and Howard began talking in a loud excited voice, waving his arms wildly. A waiter came over and asked him to quiet down or leave.

"He isn't used to drinking," Jay explained benevolently.

The dance band came on, and Howard's friends waved at him from the distance, but Howard ignored them. The force of Jay's personality cast a spell over him and he sat with his chin on his elbow, mesmerized by Jay's most casual action.

"Your friends are leaving," Eva said.

"It's okay, we don't know each other really. Only met tonight . . . the ten of us won a charity raffle and first prize was a night out at the Monte Carlo. I've spoiled your evening though."

"No, don't be silly," Eva said. His awkwardness and stark innocence reminded her vaguely of Herbie. Helpless and vulnerable they come into the world, she reflected, and they leave untouched. Harried little men, who worry about paying the laundry bill, eat Chinese food after a big evening out at the movies. Sad little men: the minnows of the world. Invariably stoop-shouldered, with sallow complexions, ten-year-old suits, ink stains on their cuffs, who shine their shoes diligently, wear darned socks, and have a holiday every thirty years. They make up ninety-nine percent of the world's male population, and Eva knew them well; she had married one, borne his child, and apart from his legal identity, he was without identity, faceless, a gray body of tired, defenseless flesh. For a moment she

hated Jay, for it was Jay—the one percent—who stormed the
fortress of life, and reduced everything in his path to dust. It
wasn't Herbie who had been born faceless, it was Jay who
had stolen his identity.

"It's like magic," Howard droned, thick-tongued, his eyes
alight with a flame that belonged to Jay and was brought out
by Jay. "How a man makes out of nothing a fortune! It's a
mystery, isn't it?" He whispered conspiratorially to Jay: "Tell
me, please, tell me, what the secret is?" He didn't wait for an
answer but sought verification from Eva: "He's a magician,
isn't he? That's how he does it. Magic." Sweat beads stood
out on his forehead like bubbles on a stippled wall. "How?
How?" he asked in an imploring voice.

"I can't tell you," Jay said, after a moment's silence. "No
one's ever told me. It just happens."

"Happens?" Howard was incredulous. "You make it happen, but how do you do it?"

Jay took out a handkerchief and handed it to Howard.

"Here, wipe your face."

It made Eva uncomfortable to watch him, and she said: "It's
getting late, and I'm a working girl."

Jay paid the bill, and they started to get up, but Howard
remained in his seat, transfixed. In the glimmering candlelight
his face appeared chalk white, bloodless and defeated. He
arose with difficulty and veered against his chair, knocking it
down.

"Oh, I'm a little dizzy." He closed his eyes and held the
table for support. "I'm feeling . . ."

Jay held his arm to prevent him from falling in the aisle.

"I think I'm gonna—" He didn't finish the sentence, and
his knees sagged. Jay caught him before he fell.

"Okay, let's go to the toilet. Lean on me."

"You hear that?" Howard shouted to Eva. "Prophetic
words: 'Lean on me.' "

"Maybe you better hop a cab," Jay said. "I'll see you."

She shook her head obediently, her long red hair swinging
from side to side as though she were trying to remember some-

thing. She leaned across Jay and kissed Howard on the cheek.

"Good night, Herbie," she said, and there was a moment of recognition between Jay and her.

"I'll drive him home . . ."

She walked away quickly.

"She's the most beautiful girl I've ever laid eyes on, and she kissed me. Me! But she thought my name was Herbie. Isn't that a joke, Jay?"

The day broke bright and hot. A telephone by the bedside rang, and Jay stretched out an arm and lifted it off the cradle.

"Six o'clock," an all-night voice said. "You asked to be called."

He hung up the phone and rolled over on his side. Eva lay propped up on two pillows, like a kewpie doll. Her eyes were riveted to the gossamer lace curtains which caught the early morning breeze. Jay's face was hot and his eyes small and red with deep graven half-moon circles under them.

"You look like a bull," Eva said.

He had never been able to make the adjustment to sleeping with a naked woman, and although he thought he had learned everything there was to learn about every angle and curve of Eva's body, it still never ceased to amaze him. She had the kind of finely textured skin like parchment which he could stroke for hours, finding satisfaction in a purely obsessive, tactile way, so that when he came to make love to her it seemed to him that he was destroying, or perhaps abusing, the perfect image that existed for him.

"You're staring," she said, as he sat on the side of the bed. "You can touch them. They're yours to touch."

He leaned across the bed, bisecting it, his chest on her lap, and he kissed her breasts, ran his fingers along the soft underbelly, and kissed them again.

"Your face is all prickly."

"I'll never leave at this rate."

"That's the general idea."

"I've got such a rotten taste in my mouth." He went to the

bathroom and brushed his teeth with energy, then returned to
the bedroom.

"Why don't you have a shave, then come back to bed?"

"Best offer I've had all morning."

"The best one you'll get."

He shook his head morosely . . . the denial of pleasure always made him act like a man on the verge of disaster. He
wanted to have a bath, but decided against it because he would
then catch the morning traffic.

"Want me to come down and have breakfast with you?"

"No, I'll grab a cup of coffee at the drugstore. What are
you gonna do all dressed at seven in the morning? You can
sleep a few more hours, can't you?"

"Not really. Trouble is, you get used to sleeping with someone and if they're not there, either the bed's too hot, too cold,
the sheet's sticky, the street noise bothers you. A million and
one stupid things."

He slipped on a pair of tan lightweight slacks and went back
to the bathroom. The shave refreshed him, but he couldn't
shake his depression. It was 6:40 and he packed hurriedly. He
couldn't find his socks, so she got out of bed and located them
in the back of a bureau drawer. She put in three pairs and
stood in the center of the room by the luggage rack, with that
curious disorientated expression people get when they're faced
with alternatives at railroad stations. He took her arm and
turned her to him and hugged her.

"Gets crazier by the day, the way I knock myself out. Like
a man trying to balance both ends of a seesaw. What's the
point of it?"

"Well, you've always got an out. You can drop me, and
your life won't be so complicated."

"Christ, you talk the most godawful shit at times."

"I've forced you into this situation."

"Listen, Eva, nobody forces me to do anything that I don't
want to do. Try to think of what's ahead of you. You'll be
working with me . . . We'll get straightened out, I promise."

She walked with him to the door and stood there for a moment after he had gone. Friday to Sunday was a long wait. Years! She closed the door when she heard a maid humming to herself. She felt suspended between two equidistant walls, and running from one to the other never had any effect on her proximity to the walls because she was running in concentric circles. She pulled up the window and watched him get into the car and drive away.

"Seesaw/Marjorie Daw/Seesaw/Marjorie Daw," she sang in a lifeless voice.

III

Autumn
Black Bile
Earth

12

"Haaa—peee Burrrth—daaay to you, Haaa—peee Burrth—daaay, Dear Nee—yell," the cheeping children's voices trilled, squeakily discordant, as Neal stood dizzily surveying the sapphire blue ocean liner on the table, its five candles flickering in the gust-filled room. He took a deep breath and the air crackled in his lungs as he expelled it. The candle smoke, like discharged guns on the top of an escarpment, filled the air with the reek of melted tallow. Faces, some familiar, some strange, flicked across his view with alarming suddenness—open faces with wagging tongues, fey smiles, and a monstrous number of teeth. Why did they have so many more teeth than he had? Why were some of them lined with gold and silver bands? The teeth came towards him, the face kissed him and held him so tightly that he couldn't breathe, and the face had a funny smell, like the kind that cats have when they're wet. He reached out and tried to capture his grandmother's tooth, but it was cemented against her incisor and would not budge.

"I want teeth," he whined, and Celia threw back her head and laughed. "Dad-dee buy me some," he said in a cajoling voice that held the threat of tears.

"You wouldn't like it," Jay said, helping him to his seat. Neal gave a yawn, but before he could get comfortable Rhoda seized his hand, inserted a knife in it, and guided it over the cake, where much against his will an incision was made across the afterdeck. He tried in vain to pull his hand away, but she pressed it down again into the soft bed of sponge and cream; the jam in the middle looked like blood and he drew back nervously.

"You're the host," Rhoda said.

A small dark-haired boy called Zimmerman, with a fero-
cious mouth and the manner of a cutpurse, laid siege to the
cerise-colored smokestacks which tilted waywardly towards
the passenger cabins, and Neal swiped him viciously across
the knuckles with the handle of the knife. Zimmerman yelped
and turned to a fat disgruntled woman, who wore a capacious
black tentlike dress which, with her sallow complexion, gave
her the appearance of a hippo suffering from jaundice. She
removed a fat hand from her mouth and waved her splintery-
skinned fingers and gnawed nails in Neal's direction. She
tugged her lips and there was a hint of retaliation on some
dark stairwell on some rainy afternoon in her dark eyes.

"Well, honestly—" she began, then trailed off abruptly as
though the cerebral activity needed to lodge a more intimi-
dating protest was too much for her. Swallowing the saliva
required for her labials, she slumped back in her seat and
glared murderously at Neal.

"Gee, ahm sorry," Rhoda said, rescuing a smokestack for
Zimmerman and placing it in his sweaty palm. He sniggered
triumphantly at Neal, who in a rage, picked up a fork to attack
again, but Jay diverted him at the last moment.

"Watta stingy kid!" Mrs. Zimmerman moaned.

"He's excited!" Jay replied. "This birthday business . . .
well . . ."

"Say you're sorry, to Bea," Rhoda insisted.

"Sare-ree," Neal droned.

Jay petted Neal's head and the child rewarded him with a
captious smile. He had coal-black hair, colloid, green eyes, a
small but flared nose, and the ivory-tinted skin common to
children who are confined to their homes as soon as the
weather becomes mildly threatening. He fought tenaciously
against the semi-invalid treatment he received from both his
mother and Celia, but because Jay insisted on it neither of
them dared disobey. Jay's feeling for Neal bordered on idol-
atry and he could not keep his hands off him; the physical
presence of his own flesh and blood inspired a sensation of
religious ecstasy. His identification with Neal was so complete
and overwhelming that Eva complained regularly of it, re-

garding Neal as an adversary in the ubiquitous battle she fought for Jay's affections; but she recognized, over the years, that Jay's paternal solicitude was genuine, and that she had no alternative but to let herself be regulated and indeed manipulated by yet another human factor in the life of a man who desecrated the human factor in everyone else's life. The promise of a divorce loomed on the horizon, but repeated postponements, because of his mother's failing health, Rhoda's loyalty, and the fact of his love for Neal, had reduced it to a collation of broken hopes. She lived on nerve, even though she lived in sumptuous comfort, and was able to control her disappointment skillfully, turning it, perhaps subconsciously, into a mask of stoicism, inactive but alive.

She and Jay divided their time between New York and Syracuse, where the factory which had begun life as a failure now mushroomed out into an amorphous complex of buildings employing two thousand people, the largest mass-production dress factory in the East. Jay had even begun to use synthetic fibers to cope with the demand, and he had sixty retail outlets which swallowed with a voracious lack of discrimination whatever he produced.

Jay slipped away from the children and went into his dressing room to make a call on his private line. On the fifth buzz he was about to slam down the phone, but Eva's voice came through.

"Where the hell've you been?" he said angrily. "I've been calling all afternoon. I asked you to wait for my call."

There was silence at the other end.

"Sorry, Boss. I don't work on Sundays. It's in my contract."

"Aw cut the crap, Eva."

"I waited till two. I got thirsty and lonely."

"I couldn't ring at two, because the kids started coming."

"We could've stayed in Syracuse for the weekend, and you wouldn't have had this problem."

"Don't be funny. You know it was Neal's birthday."

"Look, if you called up to have an argument, then I can do without it."

"Just a minute . . . I'll see you at six at the apartment."

"Well . . . if you must . . ." She hung up, and he stood in the middle of the room, the phone wire coiled round him like a cobra, with a puzzled and distressed look on his face. Things had begun to get out of hand with Eva. He still occupied the central position in their relationship but she had recently started to assert herself. The door opened abruptly.

"I wondered where you disappeared to," Rhoda said.

"Had to make a call."

"She give you a stand-up?"

"It was business."

"The kind of business that gets lipstick on your drawers . . ."

"Oh, shut up. It's the kid's party, so try to behave yourself."

"From you, a remark like that sounds so ridiculous that it's funny."

He brushed past her and her head banged against the pine door without hurting her, but she became angry, and stormed after him, her eyes darkening. The children were playing "London Bridge," and she stopped, rooted in her tracks, when she spied Jay arm in arm with Neal, as though the touch of innocence would somehow redeem him and she would have him again newly born, pristine, her love enhanced by his lack of experience. It was an idle thought, and she let it slip out of her mind. They had been through too much together for her ever to recapture the quality of emotion that he had created and then discarded like a rag. She had no illusions of a renaissance of feeling on his side; she only hoped that he would tire himself out, and then come to her exhausted and bleeding, devoid of pride, and pleading for acceptance. The only avenue of attack, she realized sadly, was through Neal, for the child represented what he had never in his life found time to develop: an inviolable principle that transcended his own megalomania.

The children, bored with "London Bridge," started up "Farmer in the Dell," and Jay did a little square dance with Neal, who reluctantly allowed himself to be spun round.

Rhoda wondered whether she ought to ask Al's advice: of Jay's family he was the only one she found remotely sympathetic, perhaps because she knew that he had suffered as much as she had. Her sisters-in-law she avoided, except when a family function brought them together, and now that she could not go to Myrna, the void in her life had grown progressively larger with every passing year. Neal might have filled the hole, but he was completely under Jay's domination—Jay's personal possession, not a child to be shared and loved by both, but the object of one, the stronger one. She had a curious sensation of estrangement which occasionally became hostility when confronted with those large inquisitorial eyes, that innate *droit de seigneur* which the child alarmingly revealed in her presence. Even though he was only five, he was hard to manage, and there was a certain unconscious superciliousness about him which she traced directly to Jay's influence. Jay had won on all fronts, and she was tired of fighting. The only hope she retained, curiously enough, was for Neal; perhaps one day he would see Jay with her eyes, not with antipathy but clearly enough to make his own judgments.

Al sat in the corner on the sofa, sipping coffee, and Rhoda caught his eye.

"What can I do for you?" he said, moving over to make room.

She opened her eyes wide and sat down heavily, next to him.

"Tell me how to lose twenty pounds!"

He laughed kindly and put his arm around her.

"Your weight's okay by me. I always like a woman to be *zoftig*."

"You're a sweetie, Al."

"What're you looking so worried about? A new home ... everything the best that money can buy ... a successful husband who's on the way to more millions."

"I haven't got a goddamn thing," she said with truculence, "and you know it. I haven't got a marriage and I hate my life."

"Success does that to some people," he mused.

"Success hasn't got anything to do with it . . . he was a bastard when he didn't have what to eat."

"You don't have to tell me what I already know," he said in a hushed voice.

"It isn't that he's all rotten—"

"—Just most of him. But he's a good father, so there's that in his favor, isn't there?" Al was groping and he didn't like himself for it, but nevertheless he wanted to learn more about Jay. Hatred had had a singular effect on him: it had made him curious, and he treasured every detail of dirt he could pick up that confirmed his own opinion of Jay. At times he would lie awake at night, going over all the little slights and infamies he had been subjected to by his brother, and he had the recurring dream of confronting Jay in court with a bulging dossier in his hand, listing every act of deceit Jay had ever committed. Like all obsessions this had the effect of draining his energy and producing precisely the opposite effect on his relations with Jay; he performed the exceedingly difficult operation of removing any suspicion of personal jealousy from his remarks on Jay's character, and his public performance was so deferential, so shamelessly sycophantic, that he came to believe that the performance was a part of a master plan he had evolved with which to bring Jay to his knees.

"A good father?" Rhoda's tone was incredulous. "Shall I tell you what he's doing?"

Al's palms sweated and he waited apprehensively for Rhoda's testimony.

"He's being good to himself."

Al put his coffee cup down on the side table and peered around suspiciously to see that no one could overhear them.

"I don't follow . . ."

"He doesn't think of himself as Neal's father . . . he sees Neal as himself in miniature and as he loves himself more than anything in the world, it's easy to understand why he's so good to Neal. And he can leave me out in the cold."

Al considered the evidence and nodded his head thoughtfully. Another link in the chain of circumstances he would use

to entrap his brother. For the moment he couldn't think how
it related to his case, so he filed it.

"Typical of him. I hate to say I told you so, but I did, if
you remember."

"Hah," she made a sharp ironic sound, but it wasn't a
laugh.

"Someday . . . someday, you'll see," he said obscurely.

"I need your help."

"Anything," he said.

"I caught him on the phone just before. I'm pretty sure it
was a woman."

Al lifted his hairbrush brows in surprise.

"With who?"

"I'd like you to find out."

"That's harder than it sounds."

"You work with him."

"*For* him!"

"I know that he fools around, but I've got an idea that this
is somebody he's had for a while. He must've been pretty
desperate to take a chance on me catching him on the phone,
and right in the middle of the party."

"I've had my suspicions, but I couldn't prove a thing," he
said judicially.

The children in the background were roaring with delight
as Neal spun Jay round for "blindman's bluff." They had
joined hands in a circle and were now spreading out. Neal
dove between Rhoda's ankles and tittered, while Jay with
hands outstretched ambled to the opposite end of the room
where the record player was squalling—"Clap your hands till
Daddy comes home/For Daddy will bring you a cakie home/
One for you and one for me/And one for all of the family . . ."

"It's that Eva, isn't it?"

"Eva? You must be kidding. She's Marty's piece, always
has been."

"Maybe they take turns."

"Jay? Not in a million years. He doesn't believe in sharing.
As if I have to tell you . . . He'd never."

"They whore around together."

"Not in the office. Maybe he has someone, but I've never seen her. For a crude, obvious man, he's pretty cagy. Keeps secrets well. Half the time I don't even know what goes on in the business and I keep the books. Everything he does is legitimate. Doesn't even try to cheat the government and believe me he could with no trouble."

"What makes you so sure Eva isn't the one?"

"For one thing Marty signs a check every month for her rent; and he pays every account she's got at the department stores. They always leave together."

"What does that prove?"

"Nothing, I guess. But when you add all the little bits together, the picture you get is Marty and Eva. When a man's having an affair with a woman, he treats her in a special way. Jay looks at Eva as one thing only: a business asset. If they have one bad season, she'll be out."

Rhoda persisted although she sensed that her surmise was weightless.

"Don't they go to the factory together?"

"Don't be stubborn. He might have somebody up in Syracuse but it ain't Eva." He held her hand affectionately. "Rhoda, would it do any good if you found out that he had somebody? Would you divorce him?"

She bit her nails anxiously and sighed.

"I might if I met the right man, but I don't think he wants a divorce. It would mean breaking up the home and he couldn't see Neal all the time. He wouldn't do it, although Christ I've thought enough about it."

She pursed her lips tightly and wondered if Al realized that she had lied; she had only thought of a divorce at that moment. She had been eased over the precipice of good sense by Al's need to confirm her suspicions. She had difficulty acquiring confidantes of either sex—the function had been part of Myrna's attraction—and she was caught in a crosscurrent. Al fed her hunger for details of Jay's activities, and she was also conscious of the subtle disguises and rationalizations that betrayal assumed. But hadn't Jay betrayed her any number of times? Were there any rules in this kind of game? What happened if her suspicion turned out to be true? Would she divorce him? The word had such an ugly, debased ring to it that she banished both it and the action it prescribed from her mind.

The children were tired and rolled on the floor away from pursuing parents. Tears and a fight commenced in the foyer, and Rhoda lifted herself out of the deep sofa. An odd wave of depression, not unlike nausea, came over her and she knew she had forgotten to take her afternoon pill, without which she sank into a morass of lethargy and indifference. She slipped into the bathroom, found the pills in a bottle labelled "saccharine," and swallowed a whole one without water. She broke another one into quarters and chewed a bit. When she got back to her guests she had the slight dizzy sensation that always preceded the elation Benzedrine brought with it. The lights twinkled mysteriously at her and as she looked at the tired, dirty faces of the children a great warmth came over her and she loved them all. She saw Jay picking up the railway tracks and cars assembled in the living room which he had demonstrated to the children earlier in the afternoon. It was still light outside and she had a strong desire to go for a long walk in the park with Jay, and hear the rustle of dried leaves caught in the early evening wind. The impossibility of this hope became apparent to her when she saw Jay put on his coat, help his mother with hers, and go towards the door. Her sister-in-law Sylvia led the way.

"Momma's staying over with Sylvia," Jay said as he cautiously moved past her, a brace of children pushing behind him.

"So why're you going?"

He glared at her.

"I have to drive her, that's why."

"I thought Harry was coming for them."

"Harry hasn't got a car, remember?"

"What time'll you be back?"

"I'll write you a letter." His mouth twisted in a snarl, and she became conscious of Sylvia's sickeningly sweet voice.

"... It was such fun, Rhoda. I can't get over the apartment ... the most beautiful one I ever saw in my whole life. Lucky girl." Sylvia gave her a sister-in-lawly embrace, a compound of commiseration and envy: nobody had it easy, she wanted to say. Rosalee followed her, paid her obeisance, and trotted out after Jay.

He's got two sisters, Rhoda reflected sadly, whom he never bothers with except when it suits him ... two sisters who resent me because he's successful; and the only friend I have, the only one who could help me, is where I can't reach her, locked in a nightmare world. She made a solemn pledge to herself to visit Myrna the following week. If Jay could chauffeur his mother around there was no reason why he couldn't drive her up to Peekskill to see Myrna. She couldn't, however, in her heart, find fault with Jay's treatment of her sister, for it was he who paid for the treatment, ungrudgingly, and with absolute magnificence. The bill ran to something over three thousand a year, and the whole Gold family knew that if not for Jay, Myrna would be doomed to a state institution. What made his position virtually unassailable was that he never mentioned the cost, nor asked for thanks. As a consequence, Rhoda could never complain to her family about him, for in the ever-changing hierarchy of familial affection Jay had now become a savior to both her parents, and to Howard he was God incarnate. His manner, long held to be insolent and unpleasant, had become "his way, and you can't hate him for it," in her mother's reassessment. Everyone's life was more secure and happier because of Jay, and Rhoda's attempts to belittle him boomeranged. It seemed to her an extraordinary fact of life that money bought not only respectability and loyalty but also love. Jay had given both her father and Howard what amounted to sinecures; the old man earned twice as much money doing half as much work, as an invoice checker in one of J-R's depots, and Howard, after a six-month stint as a clerk, was put in charge of an inventory-control system that Jay had devised to prevent staff pilfering ... nice, pleasant work at twice what he was worth. The only ally she could count on was Al, and she sensed that despite his unscrupulousness, and his intent to damage Jay, Jay was several steps ahead of him. Still, when one is friendless in a hostile world, one can't be too fussy about the credentials of an ally, and one can't insist that he be motivated by altruism.

Maggie, the maid who lived with them, was busy sweeping in the kitchen. Jay had given her a dress for her birthday and two salary raises, and she would not hear a bad word about him. Rhoda, completely stymied, stared at her.

"I'll put Neal to bed," Rhoda said. "You want to go to the movies, don't you?"

"Thanks, Mrs. B. I'll vacuum first."

"Don't bother, Maggie. You can do it in the morning. It was very nice of you to give up your day off."

Maggie smiled and waved her hand graciously.

"Mr. B asted me to, and I can't say no to anything he wants. I think if he asted me to walk off a cliff I'd do it."

Rhoda gave her a wan smile. She would have liked to cut her own throat. Maybe Howard had been right when he intimated that she had a persecution complex. She went into Neal's room and saw him grinding the wheels of a locomotive against the wall. She pulled the train away from him, and he snarled at her.

"Where's Daddy?" he demanded.

"With his whore somewhere," she snapped.

The child smirked at her. There was something evil and knowledgeable in the smile, and she lashed out, striking him across the face. He rubbed his face with the back of his hand and she saw her fingermarks, like a tattoo on his cheek. Then he began to cry, not out of fear or pain, but in outrage, she thought. She undressed him and soothed him, asking for forgiveness, and chiding herself for wanting his approval. Neal averted his eyes, and when she pulled his face roughly around, instead of the expected tears he was sneering at her brazenly.

"I don't know what you expect from me," Jay said. "I should be with my mother."

Eva threw back her head and laughed.

"If you could only see yourself . . . I have to be with my mommy." She mimicked him unmercifully whenever she had been drinking, and he had begun to resent it.

"I can't stand you when you drink. Lushes make me sick to my stomach."

"You don't do so bad yourself."

He slammed his drink down guiltily on a mosaic-topped table and stormed across the room. He always had difficulty working himself up into a rage when he was in *their* apartment because the moment he entered it he dropped his usually formidable defenses. He loved the room, everything about it. Eva had selected every piece with loving care, from the white Adam fireplace to the lilac drapes. The room virtually forced him to be a gentleman and even though he moved about with a proprietary air, there was in his attitude and indeed in his mien a curiously naïve sense of awe and respect for something beautiful. His whole past and the net of deceits he had woven were swept away by the room. Although Eva was its principal constituent, she was not necessary for him to enjoy the room, and occasionally he would slip away from the office during the day, when he knew she wouldn't be there, just to go back to the apartment, have a quiet drink, and enjoy the view of Fifth Avenue and Washington Square Park. They had been happy for more than four years in the apartment, and the whole place not only exuded a quality of warmth, love, and comfort, but also of pure living joy. It had cost him a fortune, and was still not completed, because Eva took her time picking out every object in it. He had waited a year for her to find the right shaped ottoman, six months for the hairy Scandinavian rug. He disliked having to think when he was there, and Eva was making him think.

"Aren't you happy, honey?" he said, turning her around on the red velvet barstool.

"I guess not."

"But we're happy here, on our own."

"Frankly, I'm not very happy with myself, Jay," she said, waving her hand dramatically and eventually pointing to herself. "Look what I've become. A nag . . . a moaner. Someone permanently with a gripe. Christ, it's hard to believe. I used to be the most uncomplaining person in the world. And now, whenever I see you, there's only one question in my mind: when? When's he going to leave his wife? When? It colors my whole life. The other day I went shopping in Saks and I stopped at the lingerie counter and stared for about ten minutes at this poster they had up of a mannequin. She was wearing one of those negligees that don't even seem sexy in the movies and in real life are an eyesore, but women keep buying them, and the poster said: 'You want him eternally.' Terrible corn, and I stood there like some bumpkin from Wichita Falls, saying, 'Yes, I do.' For better or worse I've become a woman with a mission in life . . . a destructive one and I hate the idea of it.'' She shook her head unbelievingly. ''Crazy . . . that the only thing I want to do is break up your marriage, but that's what it comes down to.''

He rubbed her face affectionately and smiled wryly.

''You can't break up what never existed.''

In a scolding voice she said:

''It had to exist, something had to exist, for it to last this long!''

''Neal,'' Jay said softly.

''Neal? What's a kid got to do with it? Don't tell me you can't leave because of him.''

''That's exactly what I am saying. For the thousandth time.''

She reached for the bottle of scotch and poured what was left into her glass.

''It's not fair to make me suffer for your conscience.''

He turned chalk white and knocked the glass out of her hand. The drink splattered the wallpaper behind the bar.

''Now look what you've done,'' she said in a tired voice.

''It's my fucking money, isn't it? I can do as I goddamn please.''

''You think you can, but it's not true. And just remember *who* you're talking to. I'm not Rhoda!''

''Anything I want I do.''

''Above everything, aren't you?''

"I run out on Neal's party, lie to my mother, just to come here and fight with you! I must be nuts . . . not to see—"

"What? Finish what you were going to say. Let's be honest with each other just for a change. You like fucking me and that's about the size of it."

"You're just a piece of ass, like I said the first day I laid eyes on you."

"If I am it's because you made me one."

"Now listen, sweetie, you were dying to jump into bed with anybody and because I was a yokel it was all glamorous to me."

She shook her head furiously and her hair fell over her face.

"Oh, God, tell me it isn't true. Is this all there was? And I've given up my life for a man like this. You're not a man . . . you're a filthy animal. All the soft talk, the *schmooz*, what was it for?"

"Take care of yourself, Eva. It was fun."

"Fun?" She threw herself at his feet and grasped his ankles. He lifted her up.

"I can't stand begging. Come on and have some dignity."

She writhed on the floor like a wounded animal, and he felt faintly disgusted.

"You couldn't leave it alone, could you? Everything going fine, a nice life together. Friends into the bargain. But you? Were you ever satisfied?"

Her face was smudged but she had gained control of herself.

"I only wanted you."

"Only? That was the trouble. I've given you everything I'm capable of giving. More I can't do. Why does everyone want to tear my guts out? I can't please anybody. Why? Why? I've dragged myself up from nothing . . . I make my whole family's life easier, Rhoda's family as well, and you'd all like to see me fall on my face. What do I have to do to make people happy?"

"I wish I could tell you," she said.

He put on his hat and coat, and to her surprise sat down on the sofa, then stood up and paced for a minute. He picked up

his drink and swallowed it in a single gulp, then started for
the door.

"You've still got two years to go on your contract," he
said as an afterthought. "If you want out, I'll fix it. Think
about it. Entirely your decision. If you can stay, so much the
better, otherwise I'll send you your things."

"Send them . . ."

"You're the boss." She accompanied him to the door, and
with an embarrassed awkward move he clutched her in his
arms and kissed her. "If ever you need—" She slammed the
door in his face before he could finish. She could hear him
breathing on the other side of the door and she sat down on
the floor in the anteway. Her body ached, and she had a painful
constriction in her throat that almost made her choke. She
swallowed hard and stared at the iris-printed wallpaper. When
she got to her feet, she felt shaky and almost lost her balance.
She had pulled herself up by the doorknob and her hands still
firmly grasped it. She heard his footfalls in the hallway, and
the sound of the elevator door opening and closing, and she
stole into the living room, like a party guest who has passed
out the night before and awakes to find himself amid strange
and hostile surroundings, and who painfully tries to reconstruct
the minutiae which preceded his loss of consciousness. She
hummed tunelessly to herself, then began to chant:

"I'm dead . . ."

The experience left its mark on Jay, but when he arrived at
the office his business persona managed to conceal his pain,
and towards the end of the morning he began to feel jubilant,
released from a prison whose confines he had never dared to
acknowledge. The taste of freedom brought with it a curious
and inexplicable tenderness towards Rhoda, and before lunch
he bought her a mink coat. He knew that he would have some
difficulty persuading Marty that he had made the right move,
but the problem, after all, was strictly personal. In the early
afternoon he peered cautiously into Eva's office, next to his,
half hoping that the janitor had ignored his instructions to re-

move her belongings. The room was bare, except for her drawing board, a metal filing cabinet, and a small wooden desk
which she had never used, preferring even to talk on the telephone standing. He wondered now if he had ever loved her,
and concluded that he had, but the tie had been strengthened,
indeed forged, by a dead man. His volte-face was completed
when he accepted an invitation to visit Douglas Fredericks in
Miami that weekend.

When Marty bounced into his office, Jay was not only for-
tified by the promise of some fun waiting for him in Miami,
but by the fact that he had triumphed over himself, discarding
the woman he thought to be the most important person in his
life, but who, in the fresh light of the sunny afternoon, now
appeared to be a paralyzing indulgence, a form of subtle be-
witchment which had drained his energy for four years.

"You know where I've just come from?" Marty said in an
aggrieved voice.

"I can guess."

"Well, of all the idiotic, insensitive things to do. You can't
drop people just like that."

Jay snapped his fingers. "Just like that."

"With no feelings?"

"Marty, my dear friend, I'm built for endurance. When they
made me, they put iron in my blood."

"It's senseless. Personal feelings aside, she's the best designer in New York."

"I made her, and I can make someone else, but this time I
won't get involved."

Marty scratched his balding head, rubbed an imaginary
crease out of his two-hundred-dollar suit.

"Jay, be truthful with me: did you ever love her?"

Jay's face darkened, and the blood pulsated in his temples.
Marty's gray eyes stared at him expectantly, hopefully.

"I did . . . once upon a time."

"Oh, no! Don't say any more. I should've guessed when
you asked me to sign all the checks for her rent and expenses
that you'd never leave Rhoda for her. So you slept with her
because she was a good designer."

"You're putting words into my mouth."

"How'd you keep up the pretense . . . to yourself?"

"It wasn't hard, because I did care about her."

"But more for the designs."

"We've got six *pishers* in the designing room who can run rings around her. Eva was complicating my life."

"Stop, I've heard enough," Marty protested. He sat down and cast a suspicious glance at Jay who was beginning to be irked by his attitude.

"I loved her very much, but she expected too much from me. I wouldn't bother explaining to anyone but you,'cause it's nobody's goddamned business. Better this way, than a slow agonizing death when the hate sets in . . ."

"It's so hard to believe," Marty said, after a moment's silence. "Eva suddenly gone. After all, she was a part of us."

It occurred to Jay then that Marty might also have been in love with her, and he felt oddly sympathetic towards him—a smallish balding man with an accipitral head, sharp eyes, who had made the mistake of marrying for money and then discovering that he had no need to do so because he possessed ability. In a sense they had made each other and Jay, despite his occasional impatience with Marty's conscience and his endless banter, had a genuine affection for him.

"Want to come to Miami with me?" Jay asked.

"Who'll mind the store?"

"It'll mind itself for a week."

"I can't really—I've got a crowd from California coming to see me next week. But you can get away provided Harry doesn't want you for anything special."

"I'll check first," he said, obliging Marty who still took orders from his father-in-law who in turn took his from Jay. What made the situation even more absurd was that everyone knew who pulled the strings, but everybody had delicate feelings, and Jay played according to these rules. They had never, from the inception of the triumvirate, had cause to snap at each other's heels, for the power rested with Jay and he had no brief with politics. He accepted their ideas about the running of the business, so long as they didn't conflict with his

own. Both Marty and Harry had come to an understanding
early on: if Jay's approach paid dividends, there was no need
to interfere, and the retail-manufacturing setup had proved im-
mensely successful.

When he arrived home that evening he was surprised to find
Rhoda out, and he was overcome by a curious listlessness he
could not shake off. He played with Neal for an hour and then
tucked him into bed and sat in the living room sipping a drink
he did not particularly want. Like a child who had strayed
from its parents, he had the sensation of danger, and he was
anxious to see Rhoda. It was almost seven o'clock when he
heard her key in the door and he mixed her a drink.

"When did you come home?" she asked, arching an eye-
brow.

"About five." He handed her a drink and she kicked her
shoes off and squatted on the floor.

"I had lunch with Howie today . . . I figure if I don't see
my family, then they won't bother seeing me." Her hand
shook and she spilled the drink on her dress.

"Whatsa matter? You nervous or something?"

"A little surprised to find you home. I suppose you have to
go out right after dinner."

"As a matter of fact, no."

"You're going to stay in with *me*?" she said incredulously.

"I can't ever do the right thing, can I?"

"Please don't feel sorry for yourself on my account."

Rhoda's eyes bulged and she walked around the room clumsily, as though drunk.

"You haven't been drinking?"

"No, just new diet pills and they make me a little dizzy."
She sat down on top of the radiator and glumly stared out of
the window. Then she wrote her name on the misted pane,
and his irritation mounted because he disliked being ignored.
He left the room and came back a minute later with a box that
said Russek's on it and put it by her feet. Her face brightened
and she reached out and touched his face.

"You've got to lay off those pills, Rhoda; they'll kill you."

"Honestly, would it matter?" Her manner was so resigned that he became alarmed and he lifted up the box and set it on her lap. She opened it without curiosity, peeped inside the corner and then began to cry. Her body shook as though jerked by electric impulses and her dark brown hair flopped over the side of her face.

"That's no way—"

"You shouldn't have bothered."

"Why not?"

"Because I don't want presents for somebody else's unhappiness." She took a pillbox out of her purse, as though defying him, and swallowed one quickly. "Jay, I lied . . . I don't know what to do."

"What're you talking about?"

"I didn't have lunch with Howie."

He refilled his glass and heard a dim buzz of absonant words which bounced off his brain senselessly; he sipped his drink in a daze and poured another. His stomach was aflame and he moved closer to the window so that he could make out what she was saying. She had her back to him and her lips moved like those of a mute's, soundlessly. She had stopped crying but her neck muscles tensed convulsively, as though she was trying to wrest her head from her body. The room appeared to change before him: an abattoir of disembodied voices, filled with swirling gray evanescent shapes, twisting into the air like a wreath of cigarette smoke. He turned her face roughly around, and he stood transfixed, mesmerized by the shape of a word she was mouthing.

"*Eva*," she said, and repeated the word endlessly until it lost its meaning and he had to restrain himself from laughing because the syllables became nonsensical. She regained her voice.

"Not Howard . . . I saw Eva." She stared at him, and he sensed that his face had lost its color. "It's so sad."

"I had to fire her, and she's getting even with me," he said desperately.

"Please, for God's sake, don't make it worse by lying. I know everything and I believe her and I feel sorry for her, so don't deny it."

His body trembled and he loosened his tie. He could not suppress a yawn, and his hands shook uncontrollably.

"Tell me," she pleaded, "what makes you so unhappy? Is there any answer? Can anybody do anything at all for you? Do you want me to give you a divorce?"

"No, I don't think I do."

"For years, you've been meeting her, living with her. Haven't you got any guts at all, any human decency? Why didn't you ask for a divorce. I'm not an unreasonable woman." She seized his arm and shook him. "I'm flesh and blood, and you're killing me by inches. I don't pretend to be a clever woman . . . All I know is what I feel . . . in my blood. What is it you want from me? What have I done to deserve this kind of treatment? I keep going over my life, examining it bit by bit to see what I've done wrong . . . who's paying me back. I gave you a child you didn't want. I made a businessman out of a pushcart peddler. I brought you into a family that loved each other. What in hell's name have I done? I can't go out in public because I'm ashamed of the way you carry on. The last time I went to your office was over a year ago, but now I keep away because I know you've slept with every one of those showroom girls. They don't laugh behind my back but in my face! When's it all going to end?" She flung the box contemptuously on the floor and began to stamp on it as though it were an insect. "The terrible agony is that I still love you. Why I should is a mystery. When I think of the way you've humiliated me, treated me like I was a piece of dirt that got under your fingernail and could be picked out, I ask myself why, why, why?"

He had got through nearly half a bottle of whiskey by the time she paused and the room seemed to be getting smaller, moving in concentric circles around him. He had the sudden, but imperious delusion of being swallowed up, sucked into the eye of a cataract.

"Jay, listen to me. I'll do anything you want me to do: give you a divorce, get a separation, leave you, but I've got to be able to hold my head up.''

For the first time in years, since their early courtship, he felt a tremendous pull towards her, a burgeoning forth of affection and respect which made him dizzy with hope. He went over to her and kissed her with a sense of frenzy as though he was on the verge of death and his only chance of survival was in the kiss of life she could give him.

"Rhoda, please, let's try again."

She held him at arm's length and looked into his white face. His hands gripped her shoulders and pressed into her flesh. She had a vision of two heads shaking and turning around her and she realized that the pills had given her double vision.

Is it worth it, were the words that buzzed in her ears as she lay across the bed, exhausted and numb—her senses outraged. She scarcely believed that Jay was holding her, touching her, making love to her, not out of any need to placate her, but instinctively, and with a tenderness which she had been certain he was incapable of, with a depth of emotion which could not be simulated. What was the point of all her suffering, she wondered as he held her? Did this justify it? This guilt-ridden act of love? Or did it lead to more suffering? She was caught in the vise of her own weakness and indecision, and she knew with a certainty borne of grief and desperation that the situation was irreparable and that they must eventually break up. It was only a question of time.

13

Palm trees flicked in the light breeze from Biscayne Bay. The car, a pale yellow Cadillac convertible driven by Douglas Fredericks, crossed the Venetian Causeway from Miami proper to the beach. The bay, on the beach side, had a jade crystalline color which cut the glare of the sun. The red leather seat felt like a broiled lobster and Jay opened his collar, slipped his jacket off, and slumped back. Fredericks pointed to an electronic device fitted into the dashboard.

"Ship-to-shore telephone. I haven't missed a trick."

"Very impressive," Jay said listlessly. "What's it cost?"

"About five hundred . . . you ought to get yourself one."

"Yeah, it's just what I'm missing."

Douglas laughed amicably and offered Jay a cigarette.

"You've got to loosen up, Jay. You're not an old man, so don't act like one. I've got twenty-five years on you and I don't feel a day over thirty-five."

"What keeps you young?"

"Money and women. I made my first million when I was a couple of years older than you, and I've been sitting on top of the mountain ever since." He pulled the car into Ocean Drive and shot up along the front at First Street. "When you've got a million, you've got to behave like a millionaire. Imagine, you haven't been to Miami before."

"I've been too busy paying for my money."

"I'll tell you something . . . the day I met you in that real estate office, I knew you were meant for big things, but when you put the squeeze on me, I wasn't so sure."

"It's worked out, hasn't it?" Jay replied, querulously.

"Who's complaining? I thought you were going to bring your little redhead along."

"It's finished."

"I don't see any tears."

"I wear them inside."

"What's your wife have to say?"

"We're thinking of splitting up," Jay said wearily.

"Mistake . . . big mistake. Wear out a thousand women first, but don't get divorced. Once you start, you never stop. The first one's the hardest. I've had a few rough patches with my wife, but we'd never break up. The trouble is you're bound to remarry, and you never know for sure if a woman wants you for your money . . . the one you start out with is for love."

Jay looked at the tanned bodies lying on the beach; a gay

medley of swimsuit colors that reminded him of confetti, and he gradually awoke from his emotional stupor. They all appeared to be enjoying themselves, and he realized that he hadn't ever had a holiday in his life, apart from an occasional weekend in the mountains. His chin sagged and the sweat poured off his forehead, clouding his eyes.

"What's the deal, Doug?"

"How do you mean?"

"You must've had something in mind when you invited me down."

"How long are you going to stay?"

"A week maybe."

"Well, relax first . . . and have a look around Miami to see if you like it. Then we can talk. Business'll wait."

"I've got a lot to think about at the moment."

"Your wife . . . ?"

"Uh-huh. She thought it would be best for me to get away, so here I am."

They turned off Ocean Drive at The President and cut into Collins Avenue where a loud-mouthed cop was holding up traffic as he gave a ticket to a driver. Douglas pulled out of line, into the lane which had oncoming traffic. The policeman turned his leathery bull neck and was about to scream, but when he observed the license plate, and the driver, he merely smiled and saluted. The seigneurial manner which Douglas assumed made an impression on Jay, because it was a compound of nonchalance and unselfconsciousness. Perched on a raffia seat, his flowing blue scarf caught in the wind and flapping against his neck, Fredericks looked like a kindly but still dangerous form of vulture: secretive, cunning and with the patience of an idol. The elegance of the hotels they passed, white façades with dolphin, Atlantis, and Sun-King motifs, suggested a lost city risen from the sea—impermanent, pagan, a monument to man's ineluctable courtship of the elements, which he could not disavow.

"It's paradise," Jay said.

"One day it will be. When it's exploited."

They turned into Indian River Creek, and Douglas parked

the car at the edge of the pier. A tall, uniformed man in a starched collar, with skin the color of blanched almonds, lifted Jay's suitcase out of the backseat. Fredericks mumbled something under his breath that Jay couldn't quite hear, and they descended a flight of sandy stone steps to a small motor launch called TERRY II.

"The house is across the bay . . . on the island. Next to Firestone's place," Fredericks explained.

The water was a bit choppy and clapped against the side of the launch. Jay stepped in, and the chauffeur, his face a necklace of sweat beads, cast off. The water had a sapphire tint, and the air smelled of salt and lemons and mimosa, as the boat cut a steady knife-line through the water. The distance between the shore and the island appeared to be less than it actually was, and Jay, with the spray jumping into his face, was both puzzled and amused by his error of judgment. They approached the island from the west; a strip of pearl-white beach twisted around its circumference like a line establishing a tangential relationship. He could not yet see the house which lay behind an armada of trees. A large boat was moored to a silver speckled pier; when he got close, he could see that it was enormous—a fifty-six-footer, with a Chris-Craft pedigree blazoned on its arched prow. The launch angled around the boat and Jay noticed it was TERRY I. He wondered who Terry was, but his total ignorance of boats and the way they were named prevented him from asking. For all he knew, the boatwright, or the government, assigned names to them. He followed Douglas across the pier and down a shaded path which was lined with brilliant purple bougainvillea, orange trees, lemon trees, which he mistook for grapefruits, and there was a heavy fragrance of jasmine which tickled his throat. Like a perfume factory, he thought.

"We have to walk," Fredericks said.

"Don't apologize," Jay said with a laugh.

"It's good exercise, mind you."

Jay peered up at a row of enormous palm trees with swaying coconuts and walked closer to the edge of the path.

"Fifty bucks if one of them hits you on the head."

"I'll take a merchandise credit."

"It's a local tradition. The city of Miami pays it."

"I'm glad you told me . . . it makes all the difference." His feet sank into the soft black gravel which had a fresh wet odor distinct from the flowers which surrounded him. "If I didn't see this place with my own eyes, I wouldn't have believed anyone could live this way."

"Stay married, and you'll be able to buy your own island. I'm not kidding . . . divorces cost a fortune and you'll get the kind of publicity that you'll never live down."

"Thanks for the advice." Jay's mouth opened into a wide yawn of astonishment when they came towards the house. It sprawled over a wide garden; a curving green shingled roof sloped down the front of the house and there was a small rounded arch, like that of a Spanish mission's, leading to the entranceway which had a cluster of climbing roses over a wooden trellis. A twisting circular verandah ran around the house and a woman wearing gardening gloves, light gray gabardine slacks, and a white straw hat tilted rakishly over one eye sat on a chaise longue sipping a drink from a frosted glass. She got up, with military precision, when she spotted them. Her face was the color of faded saddle leather, and the skin, as though stretched beyond human endurance, was drawn tightly round her watery blue eyes. One more sagging bag, or old-age crease, might blow a hole in her face, Jay thought. She forced a smile to her lips and then dropped it, as though frightened it would cause too much skin tension.

"My wife, Denise," Fredericks said, and Denise extended her hand. Jay didn't know whether he was expected to kiss it. He shook it after a moment's hesitation.

"We've waited lunch for you," she said in a Back Bay Boston accent which sounded to Jay like someone playing a violin with a comb for a bow.

"That's very nice of you."

"Hope you're hungry," she said with some warmth, and Jay could tell that she wasn't head over heels in love with him.

"He likes the place," Douglas interposed.

"That is kind of him," Denise replied.

She rang a little bell on the table and a butler appeared, dressed like an intern, carrying two ten-inch-high glasses and a plate of olives stuffed with anchovies. Jay sipped his drink gratefully and realized that he was drinking a Tom Collins with about a quarter of a bottle of gin in it. The drink had a soothing effect on his abraded nerves, but Denise's supercilious stare, and the glum, inebriated lip purses she rewarded him with whenever he glanced in her direction or made a harmless, irrelevant remark, contributed to the alarming sense of disorientation which like a fever overpowered him. He wondered if he ought to make some excuse and check into a hotel on the beach, where he could relax and think. He was, however, reluctant to tamper with destiny; although he did not believe in a predetermined universe, he had a strong apprehension of some elaborately subtle web of plans that Fredericks had set in motion; and he did not want to upset them. Why had he been invited in the first place, and why had he accepted, unless he was prepared to listen to a business proposition which might have a profound influence on his future? Fredericks had the same significance in his life as an amulet does for a savage.

Cold lobster was set out on the table, and Denise, with a perfunctory flick of her spindly fingers, invited him to the table. The sound of wet bare feet padding on stone came from behind him and he turned reflexively. A tall, suntanned girl, with the blackest hair he had ever seen, and eyes the color of jade, was drying herself as she walked. She had a small, puckish nose and a mischievous smile danced across her mouth; she walked with a wonderful swaying rhythm which announced like a hautboy at a coronation that grace was not merely a state of mind but a physical attribute. She was quite the happiest person he had been close to, and he stretched out his hand like a beggar eager for alms and the magical touch of beauty.

"Hiya, Jay," she said. "I'm Terry."

"I thought you were a boat."

"I'm two boats." She had a soft amused lilt in her voice,

and she motioned him to sit. "You here to ski or mountain-climb"—she pointed at his wool shirt and he felt himself flush—"or swim?"

"Don't be rude," Denise said.

"I'm never rude, Mother, just aggressive." She turned back to Jay, who was fiddling with a thin, miniature fork, and trying to imagine what if any use it had. He decided it was for decoration. "You'll have to get rid of those ski togs. I'll run you down to Lincoln Road after lunch and you can get some beach stuff."

"Thanks," Jay said, munching a piece of toast that crumbled in his hand.

"See, Mother, he's not as awful as you supposed."

"Oh, sorry, are you disappointed?" Jay said to Denise.

"My daughter has a peculiar sense of humor," Douglas said, "and she's a very skillful liar."

Terry opened her eyes wide and began to laugh with child-like amusement.

"I'm a very dangerous woman, Jay, so be careful . . ."

"I came on the spur of the moment," he explained.

"Don't apologize . . ."

"When did you say you have to go back to college?" Denise asked.

"On Monday I return to the city of our pilgrim fathers."

Jay watched her spar with her mother, and he had a deep uncomfortable awareness of his own ignorance. He attempted to mask his confusion by keeping his face expressionless. He toyed with the small fork and watched her probe the lobster claws with hers. She had white regular teeth which gleamed like small beacons in her suntanned face. Douglas pinched her cheek with paternal affection, and Jay could see that although she was whimsical, irritating, and forthright, she possessed a staggering charm and originality. He wondered if money had created the aura or if the aura was innate and money merely enhanced it, like the setting of a diamond. He ate his lunch quickly and he caught her looking at him out of the corner of her eye and then winking provocatively. They moved out of the shaded dining area to the center of the verandah for coffee,

and Jay had to move his chair out of the sun. Denise seemed
to defrost slightly and she said sympathetically:

"Why don't the two of you get going? Poor Jay looks like
he's frying."

"I'll show you your room first. It faces the bay, so you'll
get a nice breeze," Terry said.

He followed her inside and crossed the living room which
was furnished in the style of a farmhouse; unvarnished wooden
chairs and a scrub table stood off to the side in a dining alcove.
A portable cane bar was set up against the wall and there were
half a dozen cane easy chairs with colorful printed cushions.
He liked the easy informality and comfort of the room, and
the gossamer curtains which floated lazily in the breeze as
though attuned to a melody he could not hear. She waved her
arm airily and took him upstairs. The servants' quarters were
on the top floor, she explained. His room was painted eggshell
and was larger than the living room at home. The bed had a
canopy and he laughed when he noticed it.

"Very sexy," Terry said. "I've always wanted to be se-
duced in an eighteenth-century bed."

"Is that an invitation or are you just passing the time of
day?"

"God, you mustn't take anything I say seriously. I'm completely nuts."

"Glad you warned me."

"I'm spoken for, or at least I think I am, if I decide to be,"
she said, giggling.

"Aren't you sure?"

She pressed her hand against her breast and in a melodramatic voice said:

"Ah, how can one be sure of anything at twenty . . . tadum.
Let me guess your age. Forty-one?"

"I've dropped people in their tracks for less than that," Jay
replied.

She stuck out her jaw, and he feinted with his left and threw
his right in the air, pulling it up short before it could make
contact, but she jumped back nervously to avoid the blow.

"Hey! Were you really going to sock me?"

"I might have."

Her green eyes were confused and she moved closer to him and flicked some sweat off his forehead. He held her arm firmly and forced her closer to him and she began to tremble; her mouth opened slightly in alarm and she was relieved to see him laugh.

"Don't tease me," he said. "I'm too tired to be teased."

She did not answer and walked out onto the circular balcony which had a table and beach chair on it and which overlooked the front of the house. The view was very fine, and he could see the irregular shape of the coastline of the bay, and beyond the bay there was the warm Atlantic, limpid and flat, and people the size of ants zig-zagging on the salt-white beach.

"It's a good view," he said, and then quickly: "Why'd your father ask me here? We don't exactly speak the same language, and I can see that your mother doesn't much like me."

"I'm sure you're wrong. Mother's a little formal with people she doesn't know, that's all. And my father didn't tell me why he invited you. He thinks you're a brilliant businessman and I guess he considers you a friend."

"Do many people stay with you?"

"Not as a rule. Mitch came for a week in September . . . God, it rained every day."

"Who's he?"

"The one I'm supposed to marry when I graduate in June. I think I'd rather go to Europe for a year though, than get married right away. I'd like to be able to breathe. I mean, what kind of life is it really? School from five to twenty, then married for ever and ever." She threw her head back as though gasping for air. "I want to fly a little or try at any rate."

"What's he do?"

"Mitch?"

"Uh-huh."

"Doctor. He's been practicing for a year or so."

"Loads of money?"

"Enough."

"Sounds like a good match."

She gripped the wrought-iron rail and began to squeeze it, and Jay saw her fingers turn white and the muscles of her arms strain to maintain the pressure. When she released the rail, she examined her fingers.

"Christ, they're numb. I must be mixed up . . . that's why I act like an idiot."

"C'mon, let's go," Jay said, taking her hands in his and pulling her into the room.

They decided to go for a swim before returning to the island. Terry had an old woolen blanket in the trunk of the car and they lay on the blanket to dry. Jay stared up at the pale blue sky and the glare hurt his eyes. The water had exhausted him. He made an effort to think about Rhoda and the new life they would have together when he returned, but he knew that the problem defeated reason, for reason is governed by instinct, and his instinct told him that the marriage had died, been still-born. All that held them together was the tenuous string of a child, a child he loved with a passion that was almost mani-acal, and whose life he had almost destroyed. Rhoda's insta-bility was a prime source of concern to him and he sensed that Neal would suffer if he left her. She loved Neal, but she could not cope with him, just as she could not cope with Jay. Bile welled up in the back of his throat; the sun had made him nauseous. Rhoda's life revolved around her pills: she couldn't get out of bed in the morning until she had taken a Benzedrine tablet, and although in his own mind he did not disclaim re-sponsibility for having created her condition, he did disavow the weakness which made her rely on them. Whether Rhoda wanted to face it or not, she had become addicted to drugs.

A hand pressed against Jay's shoulder, and he opened his eyes in a daze.

"You've been asleep for an hour. Is that how my company affects you?" Terry said.

"You're joking. Asleep?" He looked at his watch.

"You've got a burn too."

The skin on his back was hot and drawn tightly on his shoulders.

"I can take a lot of sun," he said.

"They all say that, but try sleeping tonight."

"You going to show me around this evening?"

"Would you like me to?"

His manner became brusque and impatient.

"Listen, kid. I don't ask people to do things if I'm not interested in them. I'm a big boy now. I've been through a sausage grinder, so don't put on the coquette act. Either yes or no."

"All right, take it easy."

They drove back and crossed to the island in silence. Jay wondered if he had frightened her off. She made him feel awkward and he could only conceal this by aggression. What he could not understand he tended to dominate, as though ignorance was a weapon rather than a weakness. The cool blue sky and the yawls tipping sideways, the islands with their concealed homes, were part of a design as fabled as anything he had seen in the movies when he was a boy. He wanted to belong to it all, but he didn't see how he could fit in. Money had done little to alter the cringing insecurity at the back of his mind; before, he had been nothing, his existence a gray, legal fact, but he had had a set of roots, he belonged to an environment, a tradition. Now he was like a table without legs, an object that was functionless. He did not know how he could communicate his emotional barrenness to the girl, nor was he sure he should. As with all true sufferers, the pure malaise, the actual suffering, was something that defied classification or description. In its virulent, unisolated, unidentifiable state, it haunted Jay; although introspection terrified him, he realized that one day he must examine and face his nightmare.

"You look saturnine."

Jay shrugged his shoulders.

"What do you mean?"

"Sort of sad and morose. You've got everything."

"That's the joke. I don't know what I've got. Just a bunch of mistakes weighing me down. And I'm afraid to add one more to the load."

She walked with him into his room and sat down on the terrace.

"Oh, it can't be that bad."

"Frankly, I'm dirt, and I don't belong with decent people."

"What brought that on?"

"Maybe we'd better forget about tonight. I don't think your mother or for that matter your father would be crazy about us going out . . . Especially as I'm married, and you've got the doctor on ice."

"That sounds very prudish," she said with a hint of irony in her voice.

"No, just realistic."

"Well, it's up to you."

"I wish it were, honey. I guess I'm tired as well, so put it down to that."

He had insisted on having dinner alone in his room. He skimmed through a few magazines, and then slipped into bed. His back felt raw and he struggled to sleep on his side. The ringing telephone bell jarred him as he dozed fitfully.

"Sorry to disturb you, sir. But there's a call from New York for you . . . your wife." He recognized the butler's voice.

"Put it through."

"Whoa, very impressive, like you were king or something," Rhoda said.

"Is that what you called to tell me?"

There was a silence, then he heard a rasping cry.

"Jay, we need you . . . Neal and me."

The appeal sickened him because it was untrue.

"I thought you asked me to think about it."

"Come home, please."

"At the end of the week."

"Tomorrow."

"I just can't walk out, Rhoda. I'm beat. I need a rest."

"Neal's impossible without you. I can't control him. Jay, what's gonna be with us? I'm here all by myself and I'm cracking up."

"Look, get a good night's sleep and I'll call you tomorrow and talk to Neal." He didn't wait for her to answer but abruptly said: "Good night," and replaced the receiver. He climbed out of bed and strolled around the room, then flopped down in a chair on the terrace. The air was heavy and oppressive. He switched on an overhead light and flicked through a magazine, but he was unable to read; the page of print stared back at him, meaningless. He would have liked a drink; he remembered that he had bought a bottle of scotch at the airport before leaving and he fished through his bag for it. He found a glass in the bathroom, let the cold water run a full five minutes, until an icy sweat formed on the faucet, and mixed himself a highball. He filled a second glass with iced water and carried it and the bottle of scotch out to the terrace. The drink made him even hotter, and his back throbbed violently; a million stinging nettles had entered his skin. The third drink made his head spin, and reduced the pain. Behind him he heard breathing, and he jumped out of his chair. Terry stood at the entrance of the terrace with a questioning, slightly puzzled expression on her face.

"You frightened the life out of me."

"Sorry, I didn't mean to. I heard you talking on the phone, and then you turned the light on, so I thought you were having trouble sleeping." She held out a bottle of colorless liquid. "Vinegar . . . it's the best soother for a burn. It'll take the sting out." She opened the bottle. "Ugh. It smells, but believe me . . ." She lifted up his pajama top. "Looks painful. Best if you lie on your stomach so I can put some on."

He went inside and stretched out on the bed. The harsh, acerbic smell reminded him of when his mother used to prepare pickling juice, and he had a vision of her stuffing nobbly cucumbers into a bottle and then pouring the vinegar and herbs in. Her lined face caught the light that came through the single window, a collage of filthy oilskin, rotting boards, and rusted nails. He could see the room with its chipped wooden table which teetered and had worn a lateral gash into the wall which supported it, the hissing potbellied stove never hot enough because there was never enough coal. He could smell the lime smell of the sweating walls, where a portrait of his paternal grandfather hung crookedly—the man black-bearded and glowering at a vernal scene in some nameless, forgotten Russian garden. His memory for smell was supernatural, and it was the wine-like smell of sweat commingled with atrophying slabs of salted *Kubchunka* which hung from a trestle in the larder that he remembered from that wet afternoon, and not the wood smoke or the trilling birds in the high grass as he had lain in the field. It had not been the Slivovitz he had drunk at the mill with Pyotr Markevitch which had made him vomit, but the odor of his room . . . and his mother's hands soothing him, washing him down with the faint scent of bay leaf and tarragon clinging to her stained apron where she hurriedly dried her hands.

"Does it hurt?" Terry asked.

"Nothing hurts any more."

She had dampened a large piece of cotton which was still fluffy and she skated gently over his blood-red back. He lifted his head and twisted it over his shoulder so that he could see her.

"Lie still, I haven't finished."

"It's starting to cool off."

The light from the terrace illuminated half her face and she seemed to resemble some half-mysterious goddess whose photograph he had once stumbled across in a magazine. Her tar-black hair was long and fine and straight and made a swishing sound as she moved her hand over his back. She patted him on the behind and he rolled over on his side and supported his head in the hollow of his arm.

"I'm going to wash my hands."

He lay on the bed and although his back felt as though it had been systematically lacerated, the sting of the burn had subsided. She came back, walking softly, and he did not realize she was there until the corner of the bed sagged under her weight.

"You're a nice sweet kid," Jay said.

"Praise from Jay is praise from Caesar. Are you going back to your wife?"

Her question startled him and he became evasive, but she pursued him, until he was forced to answer.

"I'm not sure."

"I don't think I want to be a doctor's wife . . . or to go to Europe. I want to live!"

"Isn't that good enough, exciting?"

"A deadly bore. It'll be skipping through life singing '*Alouette.*' People ought to trip over, get mud in their face." She touched his hand.

"Is that what I can do for you? Terry, don't act like a whore. It doesn't suit you."

"For years I've been hearing about you from my father and all sorts of people. No one has a kind remark to make about you, except my father."

"We've made each other money . . . so we've got something in common."

"You're not as tough as you'd like people to believe."

"Tougher. Years ago I used to go to the movies a lot—to learn how to behave in public, to educate myself. George Raft was my hero, and I thought I *was* him in real life, but I've learned different. I'm cast as the heavy . . . I'm not Raft, but the guy he socks."

"You're really a nice guy."

"How would you know?"

"I do . . ."

"That's the virgin talking. You want to stop wondering and you think I'm the guy. Everyone who ever gets involved with me loses. Don't throw yourself away."

She eased herself onto the bed and lay opposite him, her arms parallel to his, her long brown legs slightly arched at the knees as though she were about to thrust herself forward. Under her dressing gown she wore nothing, and the dressing gown fell open as she moved closer to him. Her skin was a copper brown, with the slippery smooth texture of satin. The soft bellies of her breasts were the flat milky color of Chinese white and they seemed to be framed. He turned away and she grasped his wrist, breaking the skin with her nails.

"Don't turn me down."

"I'm not turning you down. I'm trying to be decent for

once. You're a kid and you're about to waste yourself. For kicks," he added.

"Not for kicks. It's just that you're the first man I've ever wanted to come near me."

A small curtain hanging over the canopy drifted in the breeze that came from the bay, and there was the whirring noise of a speedboat in the distance which faded after a moment. Her hands were cold and she gave short nervous little gasps when he touched her shoulder. Her eyes opened wide, and there was a look of such pure and innocent affection and trust in them that he shrank back, as though the act itself signified a betrayal, an element of deception, which would scar him. What he feared most was the aftermath, and the responsibility of yet another woman who had woven herself into the fabric of his life, because he realized that he was a man capable only of enthusiasms. He could not sustain the sinewy quality of love.

The mouth and lips of her body were moist and he slid into her gently and without force like a man floating onto a wave. He rested inside her, on top of the small thin-skinned ball, and she wrapped her legs around him increasing the pressure herself, until the ball inside broke and she gave a little groan of pain, and then he went into her harder, unyielding. She wrapped her arms tightly around his neck and he withdrew just as he was about to come. It spurted on her stomach and dripped onto her navel, white and pellucid on her copper-brown skin. She held it against her stomach until he subsided and then still holding him she kissed him for the first time.

"I must be crazy," he whispered. "What the hell have I done?"

"I thought recriminations were the virgin's prerogative. This is a switch. Are you afraid we might fall in love? Is that what you're worried about?" she asked in a youthfully earnest way, which touched him.

"You remind me of a rainy afternoon . . . a long time ago. It was like a dream. I was in love then."

"For a full afternoon?" she said incredulously.

"You can carry one afternoon around with you all your life without even knowing that you are."

"You're going to leave your wife."

"Sounds simple, like tying my shoelaces."

"I was lying about never having seen you. Once when I was home from school—everything seems to happen to me when I'm home from school. My life at school is a long pause, like a sentence made up of a two-letter word and a hundred periods, stop, stop, stop." She paused abruptly, and her hair rested on the pillow, the black thin strands spread out like a duenna's fan, long, black, perpendicular to the cross-running brass bedstead which reflected them, and which Jay like a mesmerized cyclops fixed his eye on. Her body was so wonderfully formed that it caused him physical pain to look at it. "The mud was thick and gummy with lumps of dirty gray clay sticking to my shoes—I had to throw them away because I broke a heel and I limped around like a horse that's thrown a shoe. My father was very aggravated because of some—I don't know what—sewer or something. I kept on imagining a long gray rat with white pointed teeth running around in a mad dance underneath us. It was drizzling and you stood by a maroon-colored Chevrolet, and your trousers were mud-spattered. I asked my father who you were, and he said: 'The criminal who's responsible for all this—a sewer rat who I made the mistake of helping once before I knew he carried the plague.' I couldn't equate my father's opinion of you with your face because I thought you were the most gorgeous man I'd ever seen. And then a red-headed woman came up, quite pretty in a loud sort of way, and she took your arm. You didn't look at her and you automatically unhooked yourself. Then she sat down on the running board of your car and stared at you as though you'd just stabbed her, literally . . . I watched her face change from that terrified hurt expression children get when they're not wanted, to one of pure love. It was the most amazing transformation I'd ever witnessed . . . like you were Christ and she was a nun. I was absolutely electrified—my father kept going on and on about sewers with a little man whose face and name I can't remember. After a while she said something to you that I couldn't hear and you fobbed her off by waving your hand in her face without even turning to her, and then you did turn your face and you smiled and she walked through the gates of heaven. For weeks, months, after I got back to school I kept dreaming of the two of you in bed . . . the expression on her face changing from pain to pleasure and back to pain. For some crazy reason I imagined you had a hammer in your hand and you always bashed her head in with it after you made love and then she'd become a spirit and after a while—when you commanded her—she'd assume human form. I had a fixation or something like that on you and I hoped that one day I'd feel about a man the way she did about you . . . that I'd be crushed, destroyed, and put together again and I wanted you to be the man, but I realized that that would be impossible.

"The whole thing with Mitch was a joke from beginning to end and I never took him seriously . . . I waited and hoped, and when my father casually mentioned that he was going to ask you down here for a week to discuss business, I decided to cut school. Isn't it all a little crazy? For four years, from the age of sixteen, I've been running after you, and finally last week I flew two thousand miles because I knew that no matter what happened to me in the future I had to have a chance now to get what I'd dreamed about." She gave a short husky laugh. "So at last, here we are, you with your bloody hammer. Jay, do you understand what I've been saying?"

"You've made it all up."

She started to giggle, and he recognized the nervous schoolgirl underneath.

"Would it matter?" she said, extending a hand and rubbing his face. "Smile at me, please."

He did as she asked and she said:

"Of course it's true . . . Somehow a meeting was arranged for us on that horrible wet afternoon, and we've been unable to avoid it. Did you love the redhead?"

"It really isn't any of your business. You got what you wanted."

"You're afraid . . . that's why you won't answer."

"Afraid? Of what?" he demanded.

"Of what's happening to you. Of me being stronger."

"God, what a lot of crap you talk. Is that what they teach you in college? All this . . . You've got a line in bullshit that can't be beat."

"I don't even mind your filthy mouth. Did you love her?" she insisted.

Jay pressed his hand to his forehead; he was sweating despite the fact that the night air was cool.

"I suppose it doesn't matter now. For years I was chained hand and foot without knowing it. I thought I loved Eva, and I did for a while, before her husband died. Then it dawned on me that I was being strangled by a dead man and we were both sorry, *and* because he was dead I had a stronger feeling for him than I did for her. He committed suicide because of us and I didn't have the guts to drop her. He had to die for *something*. And just as he held us together, that's how he kept us apart, I couldn't even marry her." He turned to Terry and saw that she was asleep, and he shrugged his shoulders which sent a searing pain down his back.

He woke her at five in the morning and insisted that she return to her own room. With that exquisitely channeled balance of naïveté and belligerence and nascent power young women possess after their first turn in bed, she said: ":But my father'll have to find out." She threw back her head triumphantly and a little too magnificently for five in the morning.

"Scram," Jay said. "He'll find out when I think he ought to, and not before."

"Jay, you're a bastard."

"I could've told you that for nothing."

"No, I don't mean that. I want my parents to be as happy as I am . . . it isn't defiance."

"Well, for a little while longer let them be miserable."

Not until he sat across from her at breakfast, which was served on a curved wrought-iron table facing the bay, did it occur to him that there could be any more between them than a fugitive one-night stand. The glimmer of her brown skin, and her black hair, which seemed like coal burning in the chalk-white stream of sunlight descending on them, held out a promise of grace and hope that had not been possible two days earlier. She had a freshness and sense of joy completely new to him, and even though only a few short hours before he had initiated her, establishing a certain intimacy in the darkness, he was now ill at ease and strangely embarrassed by her. She did nothing to suggest suspicious behavior, but underneath the courtesy smile she gave her mother and the innocuous small talk she engaged in with her father, there was an underlying knowledge of something secret and personal between them. He watched with amazement his own reactions to the mask of surface indifference she assumed for his benefit, and he had a deep nagging desire to touch her, to kiss her, to tell her that she was magnificent. Later when they were alone for a minute at the edge of the pier before going on the boat she whispered matter-of-factly: "It'll be okay . . . you'll see . . ." He put his hand on her breast and she let it remain there until her mother appeared and he lost his nerve and withdrew his hand. He resented having to share her all morning with her parents who had decided to give him a tour of the islands surrounding the beach in TERRY I. He sat in a cane chaise longue inattentively listening to the endless drone of facts about alligators, Seminoles, swamps, hotels, fishing, international millionaires, all at Denise's fingertips. She continued in a monotone well on into the afternoon and he could no longer fight against the sleepiness which had crept over him. Through his doze he heard Terry say: "Mother, can't you see that you've bored the poor man to sleep." Abashed, Denise swallowed her seventh martini, and disappeared below. Terry touched his arm and he propped himself up on an elbow.

"I know why Arabs cut people's tongues out."

"She makes up for Daddy."

"Has he caught anything?"

"Only the sun. He never catches fish, but he makes believe he does. The blue marlin in the living room cost him two hundred dollars."

"When are we going to be alone?"

"Gee, I don't know," she said nonchalantly, as though the idea had never occurred to her.

"What's that supposed to mean?"

"Take it easy. You're going to be here a week, aren't you?"

"Hey, what's your story? I haven't thought of anything else since this joyride started."

She averted her eyes and leaned against the rail of the boat. Jay studied the contours of her face, slightly oval, the shimmering jade, aquamarine alchemy of her eyes, and the long curling lashes which fluttered like a geisha's fan when he attempted to turn her chin to him. The undulating littoral of the island they passed seemed carved by a shaking hand and she gazed at it as though a mystery was about to be unraveled.

"Tell me what I've done?" he asked on the edge of panic, and surprised at the crumbling weakness in the pit of his stomach. "See"—he wagged his finger—"I knew you'd be sorry. Why couldn't you've been sorry before?"

"I'm not sorry about last night. You are an ass."

"Then what?"

"I expected too much, that's all. But you've been perfect," she added sarcastically.

"What did you expect?" his voice cracked and there was a terrible rumbling in his ears as though his brain would explode.

"I want you to love me."

"Love you!" he repeated.

"Incredible to be as silly as I am."

He forced her round to him and slid into the hollow between her legs.

"But I do . . ."

"I can't stand liars," she said, "or living on illusions any longer. You gave me what I asked for, so there's no need for hypocrisy."

"I don't know what's happening to me. I come away to make up my mind about my wife and here I am involved in something I never dreamed of. I do love you, at least I think I do. No, it's the real thing," he contradicted himself. "I can reach out and touch it."

She kissed him on the cheek and he wrapped his arms around her.

"I want everything," she said with a decisiveness which surprised him. "When you're back in New York, get rid of your wife. Quickly."

He nodded and his knees sagged as he kissed her.

"What a color you are. Terry shouldn't've let you sleep in the sun on your first day. Now where would you like to go for dinner?" Fredericks asked him as they marched up the lawn. There was a fine smell of suntan oil on his wet face and his back felt less tender. "We can go to Boca Raton or Hollywood Beach and then on to the Colonial to try our luck."

"Whatever you say, Doug."

"Well, you need a tux for Boca and I guess you didn't bring one."

"No, I forgot. You mentioned it, but I was so anxious to get away . . ."

"Then Hollywood. We'll have a drink downstairs at seven and then go on."

Just as Fredericks turned to go, Jay reached out and touched him affectionately on the shoulder.

"Doug, I can't ever repay you for what you're doing."

"Don't be silly. I've got big plans for the two of us."

"You're my good-luck piece."

"You've done it yourself. You're the sharpest young man I've met in a lifetime of sharp young men."

"I just want you to know that I don't take things for granted and I'm grateful."

"Don't worry about it. Just you straighten yourself out with Rhoda and you'll fly."

Jay shook his head reflectively and went to his room where a bath and a bottle of Chivas Regal with ice cubes awaited him. He had a sudden sense of disaster and he shivered uncontrollably. "Too much sun," he said to himself.

Miami moons have a color that varies between apricot and ochre, and Jay, dressed in a navy blue mohair suit, his skin a composite of heat flushes and suntan, stood on the balcony with an iced highball in his hand, surveying one of them and considered himself to be the luckiest man on God's earth. Terry crept up on him and tapped him on the shoulder. She wore a white lace dress with a lowcut bodice.

"Caught you, didn't I? Thinking about another woman."

"About you."

"I haven't put any lipstick on, so you can kiss me."

He felt a girding in his loins and his body became as hard as a rock. He kissed her neck and then her mouth.

"Like my dress?"

"Gorgeous."

"I wore it for the junior prom at Harvard last spring. This year, you're going to be my escort at our senior dance."

Jay could not imagine himself at a college prom. It was not simply a world apart, a world he had heard whispered about but never been a part of—it was a world he was totally ignorant of. Harvard, Yale, Radcliffe were names that suggested nothing to him. He had not even seen them on a road map.

"Have you been to Boston?"

"No, never had any reason to."

"You've got one now. God, I can't wait to have you meet my friends."

Jay gave an embarrassed cough.

"You're scared."

"It's twenty years too late for me. I'm what people call a *mocky*."

"What's that?"

"A Jewish refugee and not a nice one."

"You don't talk or act like one. You haven't got an accent."

"The inner man has an accent. The outside one might pass for native born."

"You act like you've got a repressed inferiority complex."

"If I knew what you meant . . ."

"Other people aren't better than you."

"I have no education."

"That's not important."

"To some people—"

"Who?" she protested. "I'll knock their heads off."

"You sound like me. I'm me because I don't know any better . . . that's why I behave like a roughneck. The first few years I was here I thought my name was Jew Bastard or *Kike*, or *Yid*. I know different now and I don't mind if people talk behind my back because I can buy and sell most of them a hundred times over. I always wanted to tell the world to drop dead. Now that I can, I don't bother. You're not Jewish, so you wouldn't understand."

"Is your wife a Jewess?"

"Yeah. Is that what educated people call Jewish women?"

"It's like poet . . . poetess. What do you call us?"

" 'Shiksa.' There's a saying about *shiksas*: use 'em, abuse 'em, and lose 'em."

"I'll remember that when you try to get rid of me. Will you divorce your wife?"

"I'll divorce her, she'll divorce me. What's the difference, so long as I can get the kid?" He studied her reaction, but she concealed her surprise under a smile. "He's my life. I love that kid . . . and now you."

"Let's have about six children of our own."

"He's my own."

"Of course he is. And I know I'll love him."

"You better." He made a fist and tapped her on the nose then kissed the tip of it. "I wonder what your father'll say."

"He's fond of you."

"Not as a son-in-law."

"Are you going to say anything?"

"Let's play it by ear for a while."

"A schoolgirl's dream." She stood on her toes and kissed him on the mouth.

Hollywood Beach was a half-hour drive from Indian Creek, and on the drive Jay got an idea of the enormous potential latent in Miami. It was already a large holiday resort with luxury hotels, the usual paraphernalia of all-night drugstores, gambling, a string of nightclubs that permeated the downtown proper and the beach itself. The proper contained the guts of the city's businesses, the sleazy hotels and motels and the Negro section. Jay set his heart on the beach and he hoped Douglas would let him in on his plans soon. As they drove, he had an image of Rhoda sitting on the maroon davenport, her stockinged feet extended on the ottoman, smoking endless cigarettes and staring bleary-eyed at the ceiling: trapped in a haze of lost, purposeless existence. He saw the melancholy droop of her mouth, and the rolls of fat around her stomach and neck, and he wondered if she took the pills to lose weight, or put on weight in order to take the pills. Their life together was an endless cycle of boredom and petty quarrels conducted in a vacuum: a world without a common denominator, a deadening, empty world, which had never been alive. His hand brushed lightly against Terry's leg when they got out of the car and his body throbbed with excitement.

He had waited a long time, a lifetime, for the sensation.

14

Jay had never worried about separating from people. With the exception of Neal and a wistfully tangential emotion he harbored for his mother the idea of *missing* a human being had about as much meaning and relevance in his life as the fact that planets moved in elliptical paths around the earth: an abstraction. But during the taxi ride from La Guardia Airport to Brooklyn on a leaden sunless afternoon he began to miss Terry and he felt about the separation the way he would about a glandular malfunction or the loss of an extremity. In the space of a week, the concentric movement of his emotional existence had altered its course and now it revolved around her. She had given herself to him as no one else had, with a generosity of spirit and a consuming passion which reawoke the dormant fires in his heart. He couldn't believe that he deserved her, or deserved to be happy. He had caused too much

strife, torn apart too many lives, almost destroyed his child,
and now the possibility of his own happiness would wreck
two more lives. He remembered his mother once telling him
when he was very young that his father got pleasure only from
other people's misery. Had he *become* his father?

Only Maggie and Neal were at home when he arrived late
in the dying, gray afternoon. He learned that Rhoda had gone
up to Peekskill to see Myrna, and would be returning the next
day. He had a sudden flash of a rainy evening years ago, and
of the sound of clarinet music interweaving itself in a nightmare. Myrna had been out of her mind, teetering on a dangerous ledge long before then. He hadn't pushed her: she had
fallen by herself. The prospect of Rhoda hearing Myrna's account of that evening frightened him.

"She's gone to Peekskill you say?"

"Yeah. She left day before yesterday. They called her from
the hospital,'cause her sister's gittin' worst." Maggie, neat in
her white apron, stood before Jay, her face a mandolin of
creases. "You like somethin'?"

"Just a drink." He removed his shoes and stretched out on
the sofa. The doorbell rang for what seemed to be hours, then
abruptly stopped, and Neal rushed like a whirlwind into the
apartment.

"Ray, hooray." He threw himself on top of Jay. "You're
home. Oh, Daddy, I missed you so much. A million times,"
Neal shouted. He dropped his briefcase and his coat on the
floor.

"You know Mommy doesn't like you to make a mess in
the living room. Now put your things away."

Neal took his father's hand and said:

"Come with me to my room, Daddy."

Jay passed the kitchen where Maggie was emptying the ice-
tray and asked her to bring his drink to Neal's room.

"You be home for dinner?"

"Please stay with me, Daddy."

"Okay, you made a sale."

"Southern fried chicken, please, please, please."

"You're not s'posed to eat fried things, Neal."

"Just tonight."

"Broiled," Jay said. "You don't want to be up with another attack, do you?"

Jay picked up his suitcase in the hallway and carried it into Neal's room. Neal excitedly opened it and fished around under the shirts and suits.

"You bought me something!"

There was a box of candied oranges, packed in a miniature crate, a polo shirt which said "Miami Beach," a penknife which he had bought in the Seminole Indian village after he and Terry had seen alligator-wrestling, and a baby coconut. Neal examined his possessions carefully and kissed Jay.

"You're the best Daddy in the world. Oh, I love you so much."

"Would you like to live with me, Neal?" Jay asked, putting out a feeler.

Neal's brow ruckled in some perplexity.

"But I do. I always want to live with you, because you're wonderful."

"What I have to tell you is very hard to tell." He took a long pull from his drink to bolster his courage.

"I'm not afraid."

"You're a little man, aren't you? Very brave, and you know that Daddy loves you more than anything else in the world."

"Sure." Neal looked worried suddenly, his eyes brooding over the suggestion of bravery. He could not imagine what would be expected of him to prove this and he shrank back and sat on his window box. In the last light he resembled a little angel, a doomed, dark angel.

"You're Daddy's best boy, and we're really pals. The best pals."

"Yes," Neal said tentatively.

"Always will be, no matter what happens."

"Happens? Daddy, you're not going to die?"

"No, don't be silly."

"Is somebody going to die?"

"No, what made you think of that?"

Neal dropped the coconut carelessly and his eyes shifted uneasily on the floor.

"I'm afraid, Daddy. Honest, it won't hurt?"

Jay drained his glass and shouted for Maggie to bring him another drink.

"It might, just a little."

Neal put his hands on his ears, and Jay pulled his arms down.

"You're a man, aren't you?" he asked with severity.

"No, I'm not. I'm only a little boy. Please don't let it hurt, please Daddy. I'll be very good, I promise. I didn't mean to break the trains. They fell out of the closet. Maggie said it wasn't my fault."

"Why didn't you ask Maggie to get them for you?"

Neal smirked with relief; it wasn't as serious as he had feared.

"I will next time."

He jumped off his window box and flew around the room like an airplane out of control and landed in Jay's arms.

"I want to be a flyer when I grow up."

"Wouldn't you like to go into Daddy's business?"

"Ummmm, no. I can't make dresses for ladies."

"But Daddy has other businesses too. He's going to start a new one in Florida."

"You are? What kind?"

"Property."

"What's property?"

"Well, it's almost like when we play monopoly. I try to buy a street to build hotels on and if you land on me you have to pay."

"That's fun."

Maggie brought in a tray with a whiskey decanter, ice, and a glass of milk for Neal, sweetened with honey. He and Jay chinked glasses and Jay said: "Here's looking at you." Neal stripped off his sweater and put on the new polo shirt. He strutted around the room proudly, throwing his chest out.

"Will you take me to Florida next time? So I can get brown and go swimming?"

"Sure I will. I'm thinking of living in Florida . . . part of the year, anyhow."

Neal stopped in midsentence and pondered, attempting to fit this new fact into the present scheme of their lives. His sense of uneasiness returned. He had worried about his father's absence during the past week, and had had an awful dream in which his father had died. The prospect of life without Jay was too terrible for him to contemplate. His mother had mooned about for several days, then gone to the aunt he had never met who was in the hospital. He smelled something peculiar in the air: unrest. From the time that he could first remember, his parents had argued viciously; it seemed to him that his mother spent all of her time crying. He wasn't certain whether she loved Jay, for she always said terrible things about him, things he was afraid to repeat, fearing confirmation or a denial which would result in yet another quarrel. He hated the quarrels, the angry voices, the tears. His asthma always got worse after they had an argument. Occasionally the attacks became so severe that he thought he would choke to death and Dr. Rosen would be called in the middle of the night to give him an injection. None of his friends' parents shouted the way his did, and he preferred to spend whatever free time he had in their homes, even though his was nicer and had more things. Bea Zimmerman and her husband didn't argue. Why did his parents?

"Neal, you're dreaming. I'm trying to explain something to you."

"Why did Mommy go to Aunt Myrna if she knew you were coming home?"

"A good question. Maybe it was because she knew I'd be home."

"Daddy, don't you like Mommy?"

"I like her but I don't love her."

"Daddies only love children?" he asked in puzzlement. There was something enigmatic about all this, and he had to find out how these things worked.

"They love mommies too. It's just that I don't love yours."

Neal suddenly felt very sorry for Rhoda because his father's love was the most powerful security anyone could have. He wondered what his mother had done to lose his love and concluded it must have been something uniquely evil.

"Won't you forgive her, the way you do me?"

"There's nothing to forgive, Neal."

"You love me?"

"More than anything!"

"Then give Mommy a little bit of the love you have for me. I won't mind, honest I won't, if you take some of mine away."

"It doesn't work that way. You only love people because you want to, not because they ask you for it."

"I don't understand."

"When you're older . . . What I'm trying to say, Neal," he said in a voice that was uncontrollably exasperated, "is that I may have to go away."

"To Florida?"

"No, here in New York. Find another apartment to live in."

Neal threw his arms out desperately.

"Why? We all have a lot of room here. Maggie could get out."

"Oh, God." Jay sighed and poured himself another drink. "No, it's not a question of needing more room. I'm going to live with somebody else."

Neal began to cry. He stretched his mind to receive all that Jay had told him, but he could not grasp the meaning—only the significance of life without his father, and he was paralyzed with fear and an incandescent grief which lit his face like a candle. He grabbed Jay's sleeve and pulled him.

"I won't let you go. You can't leave me."

Jay made the child release his sleeve and sat down at the edge of his bed. A cowboy with a lasso in his hand was painted on the wooden headboard.

"When you're older—"

"I'll die before I get older if you go."

"You'll thank me for telling you—man-to-man—when you're a big boy."

"Daddy, please tell me why you're going?"

"Because I love somebody else. Another woman."

The room started to revolve, Neal sank to his knees and squatted in the middle of the carpet. He had never seen his dresser move so rapidly and he watched it spin. His father's head seemed to recede into the background and his body drifted up in smoke into the ceiling.

"It's spinning," he shrieked, "stop it, stop it. Help! I'm falling." He rolled over and over on the floor and Jay got up quickly to prevent him from banging into the bed. Jay held him by the shoulders and shook him. "The curtains, aach, they're going to eat me."

Jay looked at the lions and tigers colorfully printed on the light yellow curtains and propped Neal on his lap.

"No, they're not real. You were never afraid of them."

"Oooh, Daddy, I'm afraid, I'm cold . . . My head hurts, I have to go to the toilet, please." He began to gasp for breath, and Jay held him tighter.

"It's all right, don't be afraid. You're all right."

"You don't love me. You told lies. You lied to me. You don't."

"No, I haven't. I've told you the truth. I'll always love you more than anything."

"Then don't go, please, please, please. Daddy, don't leave me alone."

"Neal, you don't understand. I'll see you all the time. It's just that it's time for me to leave Mommy."

"But none of the other Daddies are going, are they?"

"Some do, some don't. You'll come and stay with me, and we'll go out as much as you like. Baseball games, Coney Island, Florida."

Neal stopped crying, but his face was streaked with tears, and the promises that Jay had made did not have the desired effect on him. Jay leaned over to kiss him, and he pulled away, knocking the drink tray over.

"You don't love me," Neal said. "You love the other lady. I hate her and I hate you."

"Oh, Neal, you've got it the wrong way around. If I love her that doesn't mean I don't love you. It only means that instead of Mommy I love her. But whatever I feel for you stays the same. It never changes, I swear."

"What'll I tell the other kids when you go and they ask me where you are?"

"We'll think of something."

"Tell them a lie?"

"Not exactly."

"Daddy, why do you have to go?"

"I just explained why."

"Does the lady have little children that you'll love more than me?"

"No, she has no children."

"Why do you have to go?"

"Stop asking me the same question over, will you!"

"I don't understand."

"You do. You don't want to accept it."

"Are you going now?" Neal spread-eagled his body across the door. "I won't let you get past me. You'll have to beat me up."

"I'm not going now."

"When I'm asleep?"

"No, of course not." Jay felt very tired, and very old. Neal looked absurdly small standing against the door, barring his way.

"I'll tell God on you," he threatened. "He'll punish you for leaving. Daddy, you can't, you can't."

"Come on, let's eat dinner. You'll feel better after you've eaten."

Maggie had made a special effort with dinner; she had charcoal-broiled the chicken and prepared a barbecue sauce that she knew Jay liked; there were candied yams in brown sugar and marshmallow for Neal, and small sweet peas and kidney beans. For dessert they had blueberry pie with ice cream. The tension was relieved by the sweet-natured woman to whom Jay was devoted, partly because he sensed that her love for Neal was as genuine as his. You couldn't buy that kind of emotion and when you found it you cherished it. He would be sorrier to leave her than Rhoda. Neal, white-faced and exhausted, almost fell asleep at the table. The ordeal had seemed like a peculiarly outrageous and intransigent nightmare which he tried to oust from his mind. He remained quite silent after dinner and did not complain when Maggie put him to bed, although he called for Jay, and Jay went in to him. He held Neal's hand until he was asleep, then returned to the living room, filled a brandy snifter half full and sat back in the large red club chair which Rhoda had bought especially for him. Terry was very far away, and their week together became part of the dream of his youth: the provincial vaga-bond and the wealthy landowner's beautiful daughter.

"Coffee?" Maggie asked.

"Maggie, would you do something for me?"

"Sure, if I can."

"Stay with Neal."

"You mean you want me to sit in his room?"

"No, I'd like you to stay on when I go ..."

"You going?"

"I've done a terrible thing, but I had to do it. I'm going to divorce Mrs. Blackman, or rather I hope she'll divorce me."

The news surprised Maggie and she wondered why she had been chosen to receive this confidence.

"I'm sorry to hear ..."

"I think I'm a little crazy. You see I didn't expect my wife to be away, and yet I'm glad she is because that gives me more time. I don't want to tell her. It's easier for me to tell you than her. And there's Neal. The last thing I wanted was for him to get it secondhand."

"You tole Neal?" she said, incredulous. "Oh my, oh my God."

"How would it have been if his mother poisoned his mind against me and said that I just upped and left and that I didn't give a good goddamn about him? He knows that I love him and it'll be easier for him to make an adjustment when I go.

It's never been any good between my wife and me—you saw that. And in the long run—if I go now, while she's still young enough—she'll be able to start a new life. I'll see Neal as much as I do now.''

He watched the black face, mobile and lined, the warm brown eyes, slightly bloodshot. They registered shock, disappointment, and finally despair. Emotionally all women were the same: color, age, shape added individual difference, but the basic clay, the soft ooze was common to all of them. She shook her head stoically, and went back to the kitchen. He listened to her heavy breathing. He'd see his lawyer in the morning, stop by the office to check over any new developments with Marty, then catch the five o'clock plane to Boston.

The room at the Cottage Inn in Peekskill was small, narrow, and had an antiseptic odor that lingered on the blankets: something sour and faintly astringent. The distempered walls were painted an anonymous gray; the eggshell ceiling might have possessed some significance if any of the women who had stared at it over the years could commit themselves to paper. The scratched metal bedstead made a bleating noise as though despondent about the awful labors it had been called upon to perform over the years. Rhoda had spent a fruitless day waiting for an interview with Myrna's doctor, who had been able to spare her only ten minutes, but had agreed to meet her for a drink in the evening. She put on a black wool dress, brushed her hair back off her face, and waited for seven o'clock, the appointed time. She still had a half hour. The Benzedrine she had taken three hours earlier had worn off, and she swallowed another one, a larger one, of ten grains—the kind they called *truck-drivers*.

The week that Jay had been away took on a strange, unreal quality of a living daydream. It had started with an accidental meeting. She had gone into the drugstore opposite Radio City Music Hall to buy a lipstick, and her past, in the person of Barney Green, had emerged from a telephone booth, clapped her by the wrist, led her to the lunch counter and said:

"Lady, I saved you from rape."

She was too startled to react. His face had aged grace-
lessly—a small pocket of crows-feet were graven like children's tattoos under his beady brown eyes, and his face was
puffy with small white crusts of dry skin behind the ears.

"I changed my mind." He guffawed in a leathery, automatic way. He removed his hat and revealed naked patches of
scalp which he could only just cover with what hair was still
available. He had a gravy stain on a dark blue tie, and a wide
striped blue suit which was too tight for his bulging waistline.

"To think, only to think that Whelan's brought us together.
Hey, Rhoda, don't tell me you forgot your best man?"

"No, Barney . . . it was just . . . that I was surprised . . .
's'all."

"How's the murderer? Haven't seen 'im in decades. Hear
he's got millions."

"Dollars and women. He's got more whores than a dog has
fleas."

"Jay? Oh, you're kidding me, Rho. Say it ain't so."

"Why should I, when it's true?"

"But with a wife that looks like you?" He touched her coat.
"Mink as well."

"A present for breaking up with his last girlfriend."

"I can't, I won't believe it." He handed her a menu. "Here,
have what you like. A ball: coffee, danish, an English muffin,
the sky's the limit. I can even go to an open hot roast beef
sandwich with french fries, if you insist. Only for you,
though."

"Barney, Barney, you haven't changed. How are things
with you?"

"I'm on top. Don't you read the papers? My picture was
all over the *Monticello Matzia* . . . a paper got out for blind
Jews who read Hebrew in Braille. I'm wanted dead or alive
from Kiamesha Lake to Fallsburgh. Every bartender and bookmaker has a warrant for my arrest. Next week, I have a grand
opening at the Hoomintosh Haven for Honeymooners. I get
two bills a week, amuse the guests playing Simple Simon, try
to get off with the rumba teacher but usually wind up teaching
French love to the chambermaids and women whose husbands

have let them off the leash for a week in the mountains and who should be doing important things with their lives, like having hysterectomies. It's a great life. Mussolini, the rat bastard, should have it."

Rhoda began to laugh, a great release of energy went into the laugh and she was grateful for it. He put his arm around her and pecked her on the cheek.

"Rhoda, *mein kind*, you bring back happy memories. What're you doin' here? Went to the moom pitchers? Where's Jake? At home counting his money?"

"In Florida, deciding if we ought to get a divorce."

"Hey, you're not serious?" He turned her chin to him. "Aw, Rho, I am sorry. I wonder what's got into Jay."

"Nothing, he just never changed. He makes up the rules as he goes along. Life with him is like playing cards with somebody who insists that you play until the winner drops dead. You can't win."

"You've got a kid, though."

"The one that got away. In Scranton. Remember?"

"I'll never forget. I never wanted no part of it, but Jay comes to me like a crazy man. Said he knocked up some whore who was going to take him to court. How did I know different? He was a friend. You help a pal out when he's in a jam. When I saw you, I didn't believe him, but there was nothin' I could do."

The counterman came up to them.

"You folks thinking of buying the place or watching to see that we wash the glasses?" he said.

"Nu, everybody's a comedian. That's why I can't get work. *Schmendrick* here thinks he's Milton Berle. You wearing rubber heels, friend?"

The counterman held up his shoes.

"Well, bounce up and kiss my ass."

He took Rhoda's arm and negotiated her past the cigar stand and out into the howling, bleak Sixth Avenue wind.

"My joint's only fifty steps. Come up and have a drink with an old friend." She accepted the offer and took his arm.

"It's so good to see a familiar face," she said.

"I got a face that's made for listening."

His hotel was a small, neon-lit, faceless building off Sixth Avenue, designed for men who want a quickie and sign the register "Jim Brown from Blow City," with "wife" written in as an afterthought. It was a hotel designed to provide obscurity for the obscure, the drifters, the junkies, the gin players who needed a room to clip some yokel, the married woman who didn't want to run into her sister-in-law while she went in for a little cradle-snatching, and the non-equity members of the profession who made home movies.

The room clerk looked up from his Western paperback, as Barney spat into an imaginary spittoon.

"Got 'em, Tennessee, daid center."

"Always with the jokes, Mr. Green, huh?"

"Testing your wits."

He handed Barney the key.

"If I had wits, I wouldn't have left school at twelve, and wound up here at twenty-six."

"You're one of the best, kid. Don't let nobody tell you different."

They went up to the sixth floor in a whining, creaking elevator in which some drunk had recently vomited.

"Thing I like about this place is the freedom. You can bring anyone in: man, woman, cat, dog, so long as they can walk. Hate landladies, and that's from a man that's had some of the best."

She followed him down the corridor which was surprisingly noisy. Somebody on the floor was trying to prove that he could knock a hole in the wall with only a woman's skull.

"It's lively," he said. "No deadheads here."

He opened the door of his room which had a low ceiling, truncated in the middle by a poorly plastered concrete slab which gave it a humped shape.

"Specially built for a wealthy camel, who decided to stay in Arabia at the last minute. I got it off him cheap."

"Oh Barney, you make me laugh. It feels so good. I don't think I've smiled twice in five years."

"Who's feeling sorry for herself? I'll get us a little booze."

He cupped his hand and spoke into it. "Room service, send up a bucket of ice, three bottles of champagne and caviar and bagels." He put down his hand. "Ritz crackers and a rather youthful scotch is all I can offer you."

"Stop apologizing, for God's sake."

He took his toothbrush out of a glass, and rinsed it and another empty one which he pulled from a drawer.

"This bureau's got a history that dates back before Christ. Every contraceptive known to men, from the ancient knight's sock to our own chewing gum variety has been housed here. It's a museum dedicated to the prevention of breeding."

She sat in a straight-back chair near the window, covered in baggy green velour which had been rubbed smooth.

"A view. All the advantages life can offer. You come home a little depressed, you got a choice"—he pointed to the gas pipe attached to the woodwork—"you take a sniff or give a little jump, and no more problems. Somebody else's got the problems, your old ones."

"Geez, Barney, it can't be so bad."

"Hey, I'm kiddin'. You don't think I ever"—he waved her down with his hand as though swatting a fly—"me? Never in a million Sundays. I like to suffer, it's all part of the racket. I picked this life. It's had some ups and downs, but I always make a few bucks, never starving. My mother didn't tell me to become a third-rate comedian, I just decided that that's what I wanted most in life." He sniffed his drink and pulled a face. "This stuff's great for massages." He handed her a glass, and chinked hers: "A little toddy for the body."

She downed the whiskey and pulled a face.

"I like my booze and women on the young side. Here's some water to chase it."

"It's not so bad—"

"Yeah, I know, but you're attached to the lining of your stomach."

The red shade of the one light in the center of the ceiling gave their faces an ochre glow. Rhoda was amused by Barney, who maintained a frantic buoyancy and lifted her up as well.

"I've never gone to a man's room—in a hotel."

"Well, let me assure you that if you decide to make a career of it, you won't starve. Now tell me, what's been happening with Jay? I hear about him from time to time. Successful in a big way. Hundreds of stores. Made it out of nothing. You gotta admire him."

"I don't have to."

"But look at him: five, six years ago, he didn't have what to eat. He used to hang around the poolroom with that *voxted*-a-bum-look on his face. Now you can't walk down a street between the Bronx and Staten Island that he ain't got a finger in. Maybe that's the trouble with him," Barney added.

"No, the trouble was long before that. I wish I knew what to do about it though."

"I tell a lie. I did see him, about four years ago. I was working the old Monte Carlo. Not as an act. Things were a bit slow so I took a job as a relief waiter, and he came in one night with—"

"—A redhead."

"Well, you know then. He didn't see me, but I spotted him. He flashed a roll to the mater-dee, and got a ringsider. I thought maybe I ought to go up and say hello. But I was in this uniform, see, with green and gold braid like a coachman, and I thought, leave it. He'll feel I'm out for a touch. But I ohmost did speak to him, then some guy, a drunk, sat down wid 'em, and it was too late. I was ashamed of myself." His head slipped to his shoulder and he appeared to be dreaming. After a moment he revived himself and went to the bureau and took something out which Rhoda thought was a handkerchief.

"S'cusie, minuto. I've got a sudden call to the john. Won't be a sec."

She sat in the room for almost ten minutes, forced herself to have another drink, this time from a bottle of bourbon, which went down more smoothly than the scotch, and she took out a pill, stared at it, then chewed it to give herself a lift. The faded daffodil wallpaper began slowly to move round in circles. Barney came back in, with a glowing, but somewhat fatuous smile.

"Christ, I'm an awful host, leaving you sit by yourself."

She tried her legs, but she couldn't stand. The room moved too rapidly, and the neon sign below them flashed into her eyes.

"You awright?"

"Yeah, fine," she said. "Maybe the drink. I'm a little heady."

"Lookit, you can stretch out on the bed for a quick forty if you like."

She ambled over and stared at the moth-eaten bedspread and fell on top of the bed. The furry nobbles of the spread tickled her nose and made her want to laugh. He eased off her high heels and pulled up the straight-back chair, and whispered conspiratorially in her ear.

"If you're blue, I got somethin'll perk you up."

She sat up abruptly, supporting herself on her elbow.

"Like what?"

He extracted from a scratched cigarette case a clumsily shaped cigarette with both ends twirled close, like the fuse on a firecracker. She held it up to the light and examined it.

"What is it?" she asked, although she knew.

"My private stock. Kept in the family cellars for generations at just the right temperature. Vintage Chicago light green, a sawbuck, an Oh-zee."

"It's a reefer, isn't it?"

"Lady, you've just won a kayak and a year's supply of mustache wax. Wanter give a try?"

She cackled like a hen in a chicken run. Tears collected in the corners of her eyes.

"It's funny?"

"No, but the joke is when you went out, I chewed a Bennie."

"Oh, don't tell me? Barney, where's your brains—a kindred spirit," he shouted. "Well, let us charge up ensemble."

"I never have . . . only pills."

"Oh, you're in for a treat." He showed her his handkerchief which contained a small filter. "*Schmeck*. I don't bang myself yet; I'm allergic to needles, they make holes in my skin."

He lit her up with the end of his cigarette.

"Take a long belt, swallow it, till you've got to exhale and then let it out through your nose." The smoke had a harsh abrasive taste, but she liked the sweet smell which reminded her of oregano. She passed the joint to him and he took a puff, held it for a long time and passed it back to her. When they finished, he emptied some tobacco out of a cigarette and carefully fitted the remainder into it with a matchstick.

"Cocktail?" he said.

She put the cigarette in her mouth and puffed until it was alight.

"Christmas, I feel out of this world."

"Good buzz, huh?"

She nodded.

In a strange Irish falsetto, he sang:

" 'All my cares and woes . . . Bye-bye blackbird . . .'

"I'm on top, Rho. You know that every comedian in the business steals my material . . . and people—whenever somebody tells a joke, it's one of my old ones. I been robbed. You can't copyright jokes though, like songs. Nothing to protect me."

She put an arm around his neck and pulled his face down to hers.

"I will, I'll protect you, Barney."

His mouth was wet and she ran her tongue along his lips, then closed her eyes as he unbuttoned her dress . . .

The bar in the Cottage Inn was crowded and Rhoda felt uncomfortable and exposed as men in the room smiled with their eyes at her. She lit a cigarette, and ordered a bourbon and coke. A thin, blond-haired man with a pug nose, a tired, drawn mouth, and small sharp brown eyes maundered through the bar, stretching his neck in search of somebody. Rhoda waved and he came over.

"Dr. Heller, I'm glad you were able to make it. Have a drink."

"No, I'll buy you one." He had a rough, leathery voice and

was about forty, and she thought well-dressed for a man who must have more on his mind than clothes.

"I've ordered one already. It's very nice of you to spare me the time."

The waiter served the drink and took Heller's order, looking surprised when she told him to put it on her tab.

"I was pretty busy this afternoon, but I'm glad you've come. She needs visitors from time to time, although it isn't as rewarding for them as one might hope. Did you come with your husband?"

"No . . . he couldn't make it."

"Pity."

"Why? He wasn't very close to Myrna. In fact they didn't like each other."

"That's why I would've thought a chat was in order. His name is one of the few she responds to. It's a stimulus. You see, I'm afraid that I can't offer much hope in terms of a recovery." He stared pensively at his fingers for a few moments. "We've had her four and a half years and tried any number of approaches. We've had some success, but it's been limited."

"What's really wrong with her? Is she insane?"

"Insane? No, of course not. Or at least not what I call insane, but it's such a difficult word to define, even in a legal sense. She has an illness which we're trying to cure. I don't want to throw a lot of psychiatric terms at you, but what she has can be classified as a compulsion neurosis. Baldly, this means that she has an idea about herself which terrifies her, so that she is forced to substitute another idea in its place and this in a sense becomes a symbol of what she wants to hide, rather than the secret itself."

Rhoda swallowed her drink and felt a wave of nausea come over her.

"Is it something to do with the abortion she had?"

"Partly. She seems to think that your husband was the father of her child, but we know this can't be the case because she met your husband a good two years after she had it."

Rhoda became increasingly disconcerted and upset by the

mention of Jay. She stretched her mind to piece together all of her recollections of the meetings they had had.

"Ridiculous," she said. "The truth, and I tell you this in confidence, is that my husband wanted me to have an abortion at one time. I told Myrna about it and she brought things to a head, so that in the end we got married and I had my child. She's confused."

"I wonder."

"What do you mean, 'you wonder,' " Rhoda said in a raised, indignant voice.

"If we're going to be absolutely honest with each other then I may have to ask you a few things that hurt, so don't think I'm merely prying. I have a very sick patient on my hands, and anything I can learn which might help her . . ." He broke off and motioned with his index finger to the waiter who brought them another round. "You did, after all, make the effort to come up here, so no doubt you still care about your sister."

"I do, terribly. We were very close when we were younger. She's had a lot of disappointments. First with a married man, and then by not having a musical career."

"Did she, to the best of your knowledge, have an affair with your husband?"

Rhoda felt her eyes burning from the smoke in the room and she wiped them with a handkerchief. She had a vision of Barney's tired face, and his hairy short body, and his wonderful moon-shaped smile. She had come alive with him, her body had responded, as though coming out of some long fetal sleep.

At last she said, "No, she never had an affair with Jay. She was probably jealous of the fact that I got married and she didn't." She knew, or thought she knew, Myrna too well to believe this, but her denial carried no conviction, and Heller sensed this.

"You mentioned her musical career. Well, what made me ask the question is the fact that she believes he ruined it. She played the clarinet for a number of years, and she insists that your husband broke it, by dropping it out of a window, so that

it shattered when it hit the ground. Does that make any sense
to you?''

''None.''

''Well, she's reconstructed that instrument. She's become
it. It's a very fragile instrument and an extremely rare one. It
must never come into contact with a hard surface because it
might break. As a consequence she has to sit in a wheelchair
like an invalid. She'll stand on a soft surface, like the mattress
of a bed, but not on the floor. She admits that she can use her
legs, but she's obdurate about not coming into contact with
the floor. When I ask her why, she says: 'It's much too valuable to risk breaking. It's the only one of its kind in the
world.' ''

''I'd like to see her.''

''Tomorrow, you can. I think unless your husband's prepared to meet me and discuss what, if any, part he's played
in her life, that there's no point in keeping her on here. He
pays the bills, so you might call his attention to what I've said.
You can take her home, but she'll require a nurse, or a com-
panion of some kind to be with her constantly. One more
thing, Mrs. Blackman, why does your husband pay the bills?''

Rhoda pushed the table away angrily and Dr. Heller caught
it just as it was about to fall, but he could not prevent the
glasses from smashing.

''I know what you're implying with your slimy digs,'' she
said, ''but it just so happens that my husband is a generous,
open-hearted man, and he pays because he can afford to.
You're a very unpleasant man, Dr. Heller, and I'll suggest to
my husband that we take my sister elsewhere.''

''You do that, Mrs. Blackman. Somebody else might get
the truth, not the version I've been handed. As for my being
unpleasant, let me assure you that I'm not in the least interested in popularity contests, or hand-holding, of interested relatives. I'm trying to help a sick woman.''

The next morning Rhoda waited in a large room with green
baize tables and French windows, which was the recreation-
cum-visiting room. She gasped when she saw a woman

dressed in black wheeled in through the push door. It was Myrna, and somehow it wasn't Myrna.

Her skin had acquired the sallow grainy texture which the bodies of confined people develop as a protest against being removed from the sun, the wind, natural elements. Her movements—the sudden tremor of her facial muscles, a reflex neck jerk—had about them something of the arbitrary quality of a tropism. Her derangement had, for Rhoda, destroyed her humanity. What she looked at now was not the sister she had grown up with in Borough Park, the young dark-haired girl who reacted so quickly and with such terrifying awareness to every nuance of mood in the household, but an object without a function. She watched with distaste as Myrna cradled her arms and swayed in the chair.

"I'll leave you alone," a voice said, and a woman who smelled of starch strode briskly out of the room.

"Hello, Myrna," Rhoda said in a cracking voice.

Eyes moved, yellowish eyes that she could not associate with Myrna. They resembled impure marbles in the unutterable void that lay behind them. She waited for a response, but the eyes looked over her shoulder through the window at the green-gray sky which cloaked the landscape like some spinster's eiderdown.

"It's me, Rhoda!" She touched her sister's hand and her flesh was cold. Her lips moved slowly, then thickened into an idiotic smile.

"Do you remember anything? *Me?*" Rhoda said softly. "The other day I had a dream about you, about your sweet-sixteen party. You were wearing a yellow organza dress with a high neck that Poppa got from a man who owed him money. And all the boys at the party thought you were the prettiest sister, and you were. I sat in a corner most of the evening, eating the ice cream cake Momma had made. It had lots of raisins and nuts in it. I can still taste it. She didn't do any cooking after, 'cause that's when she got sick, about four or five months after. And when it was my turn to have a party, you bought a cake from the bakery. One with a lot of pink and blue icing, and those soft butter-cream roses. It tasted awful, and I always resented the fact that Momma made your cake and not mine. Isn't that silly? But it shows that I think about you and miss you.

"I've got a little boy now. I told you about him the last time I was here. He's five and his name's Neal and he looks a bit like you around the mouth. He's got a way of sucking in his cheeks that's you to a T. I've told him about you and he wants to meet you. He's really a sweet kid, very deep, the way you were when you were younger. Myrna?"

Rhoda lit a cigarette and Myrna's eyes circled the smoke like a hawk after prey. She held the cigarette under the arm of the chair so that it would not distract her.

"Don't you like talking to me? Would you want me to take you home? To my house. I can afford to . . . we've got a lot of money now. Not much else. Money enough to keep me in pills and other things for the rest of my life, and money enough to keep you out of institutions, and money enough for Poppa to hold up his head and for Howie to have a convertible, and for Momma to have doctors whenever she needs them without worrying about paying the bills."

Myrna extended her left arm, and with her right hand as the bow, began to pick at her arm as though it were a violin.

"There's something you gotta tell me. Please try to take in what I'm asking you, 'cause I feel in my heart you understand me, even though you're not talking. Will you? Please, it's important . . . maybe it'll help you . . . and me as well. I want you to tell me about Jay."

"Aiiii!" A piercing scream reverberated through the empty room and Rhoda jumped to her feet. Myrna had risen out of the chair, extended her arms in front of her, like a somnambulist, and taken a step towards her, and Rhoda began to run in terror to the door. Myrna remained frozen to the spot, shrieking; and the woman who had pushed her chair opened the swing door. She had a little bag in her hand, from which she took a hypodermic needle. She punctured the rubber top of a small bottle which contained colorless liquid, filled it, and then shot a bit into the air. Rhoda stared at the bottle for the hole, but it closed before her eyes. Like a woman's body, she thought. It opens and closes. A box that nature opens and closes, then one day the box is closed and you're dead, and people cry. After a while they forget, and your face loses its shape, its contours, the sound of your voice merges with a thousand other voices and your voice is silent. One night, somebody, somewhere, dreams about you, and you know for certain that you're dead . . . and that's it.

15

The wind from the Charles River cut into Jay's face as he walked past the saluting doorman at the Statler into the large black Cadillac waiting for him at the curb. He hadn't called Terry as he had promised before coming to Cambridge. Rhoda could wait. As he sat down in the back seat, he had a vague flicker of Myrna's face across his path of vision, and he told the chauffeur to stop at the first liquor store they passed. He'd bring Terry some champagne and buy a few bottles of scotch to keep in the hotel room.

He bought two bottles of Krug '29, not because he cared a whit, or knew anything about vintage champagne, but because they were the most expensive bottles in the shop. The chauffeur, a tall, strapping man with tobacco-stained teeth and the expression of a dead eel, took the package from the man. When they got back into the car Jay asked the chauffeur where they were.

"Turning on to Commonwealth Avenue."

"It's very nice. I'm going to one hundred and sixty. Do you know it?"

"I'll find it," the man said in a Back Bay twang that cut right to the marrow.

"Any good restaurants in town?"

"This is Cambridge," the man said contemptuously.

"Yeah, that's why I'm asking."

"New Yorker?"

"That's right."

"Well, if you like roast beef, there's Durgin Park. That's in Boston."

The car pulled up to a smallish apartment house, the kind they call apartment studios. It was modern and sleek, and somehow out of keeping with the Victorian architecture which composed the street.

"Know where Durgin Park is?"

The man shrugged his shoulders.

"I'll find it. You'd better reserve a table. They get crowded on Fridays."

Jay took out a wad of bills.

"They always have a table for Hamilton."

"Just as you say, sir."

Jay put a bottle of champagne under each arm and walked briskly into the lobby. A set of buzzers with a mouthpiece designed for a four-foot man was located on the stucco wall behind the door. He spotted her name: "Miss T. Fredericks," and his mouth was dry with nervousness. He decided not to announce himself and walked up the two flights to her apartment. He pressed the doorbell, and a small blonde, wearing a crew neck shetland sweater, brown and white saddle shoes, and a brown tweed skirt, appraised his face with the same attention a jeweler gives to a suspect diamond.

"Wrong apartment?" he said.

"Who'd you want?"

"Uh, Terry Fredericks."

"Well, enter our sanctum, oh, beautiful one."

Jay stared at her, then broke into a smile.

"Bring the champagne," she said, when she saw him hesitate.

"You on junk, or just being natural?"

"My high spirits, which my good breeding has done little to stifle."

"Oh, yeah, I see." He came into a small foyer which had

a bookcase with more books than he'd ever seen. "Going into business?"

"Required reading . . . You must be Jay."

"I'm wearing a sign on my back or something?"

"I've heard all about you. Ter," she shouted through a closed door. "A visitor."

"You live here with Terry?" he asked, wishing to get the bad news over with at once.

"Didn't she mention me at all?" the blonde said, screwing up her nose into what was supposed to pass for disappointment.

"Not a word."

"The rat! God, what a gorgeous color you are, and poor little me, all white and pale as a lily. I'm Caroline Reed, Terry's roommate."

"You see your folks lately?" Jay asked.

"No. That's a funny question to ask."

He put his hand in his pocket, fished out a bill.

"Here's a yard. Why don't you catch the next plane and see them for the weekend?"

"You want to get rid of me?"

"That's the general idea."

"But I'm so discreet, so utterly discreet. You can count on me!" She took the champagne from Jay. "I'll cool them a bit, shall I?"

"Florida, then? You get yourself a quick tan, have a wild weekend."

"Ugh, you rich people."

"I thought the same thing when I was on Relief."

"Don't kid me. You probably inherited a fortune."

"The only thing I inherited was flat feet, a small mole on my behind, and fifty-seven starving relatives."

"Would you like to take off your coat, I'll hang it up."

"You can sell it if you like and travel on the proceeds."

She rubbed the coat on her cheek.

"Ummm, cashmere. Where'd you get it?"

"I met this goat on Fifth Avenue who needed two hundred dollars. Where's Terry?"

"In the bath. Why, don't you like talking to me?"

"I could live without it."

"God, I can see why Terry's insane about you. So direct, so vital; up from the people. The blood and guts of democracy."

"I don't know what you're talking about. There's no insulting you, is there?"

"It's your defense mechanism speaking, not you."

"I think I like you," he said.

She kissed him on the cheek then hopped over to the davenport and did a few pirouettes.

"You're giving free samples?"

"I'm irresistible."

Terry came out of the bathroom with a towel wrapped round her head and blushed through her suntan when she caught sight of Jay.

"Just the way I pictured you," he said.

"Oh, Jay. Aren't you awful. No call or anything." She rushed up to him and kissed him.

"Your cold cream's delicious," he said.

"Ooooooooo, isn't it wonderful," Caroline moaned ecstatically. "Can I stay and watch?"

"Caroline's going to open the champagne, then she's flying to New York," Jay said.

"I am not. I'm going to be with you every minute of the day and night."

"We don't need a scorekeeper."

She roared with laughter and danced into the kitchen.

"She's really great," Terry said.

"Yeah, she seems a ball."

"Are you going to take me out to dinner, sir?"

"Durgin Park?"

"Oh, I'd love that. I'll be able to show you off to everyone I know. It'll get back to my father."

"I'm going to see him on Monday."

"Then you've told your wife?"

"No, she wasn't home. And I couldn't hang around waiting. I got so edgy that I had to shoot up here to see you."

"I'll just get dressed. Give me a few minutes."

From the kitchen Caroline called out in a high, trilling voice:

"Isn't it wonderful—two men fighting for you? Jay and Mitch. It's drama."

She brought in a tray with glasses, the champagne swaddled in a wooden cheese box with cubes around its base. She had some saltine biscuits on a plate and a tube of something, the label of which he could not read.

"Look what I found in my little nook."

"The suspense is killing . . ." Jay said.

"S. S. Pierce's very own mock caviar." She squeezed a bit out on a biscuit and offered it to him. He moved away with the champagne bottle. He was fighting a losing battle with the cork.

"What is it, shoe polish?"

"Is it shoe polish?" A guffaw from Caroline.

"I think they shot this cork on with a pistol. I better get the chauffeur to open it."

"The limit, the last word," Caroline exclaimed. "The noble savage in cashmere. What a find you are . . ." She pulled the bottle away and popped the cork.

"I've always had other people to do this sort of thing."

"Yes, I can tell, you're definitely to the manner born."

"In the old country when we found a champagne bottle, know what we did with it?"

"No, I'd love to hear."

"Peed in it."

"Peed?"

"That's right. Fill them with pee, and drop them off the tops of buildings on the police—the Russian police. They exploded like bombs."

"God, you must have been mad!"

"You've never seen a squad of Russian police operate in a small Polish town, a border town. It's a gap in your education. Fifteen or twenty of them would have taken turns with you in one night. Then they would've knocked your teeth out, so that you could be even more accommodating in the future. If you were Jewish, whatever they did to you was considered a public service by the rest of the town. Ask your history teacher about that. He'll probably tell you it wasn't very important to history and there aren't any dates to memorize.''

She poured the champagne, and Terry emerged from the bedroom wearing a black wool dress with a turtleneck collar. The dress was skin tight, and the contours of her body shaped it. She looked like a statue to Jay.

"You've lost him to me, Ter. It's love at first sight."

"I swear she's a nut case. Well, you going away for the weekend?"

"Oh Jay, she can't," Terry said with an edge in her voice.

"I could spend the weekend with June. Her roommate's gone home."

He detected a stiffening in Terry, and he wondered if he had gone too far. The mood of the girls, and the atmosphere of a college town—Cambridge was above all a college town—made him decidedly uncomfortable. He wasn't accustomed to the banter, the manners of students, and somehow whenever he spoke, it sounded like someone else talking, desperately acting a part that he was peculiarly unsuited to play. The easy familiarity of the girls and their private jokes reminded him of the fact that he was a coarse, ignorant, inferior being who had dragged himself out of a slum, the smell and the commonalty of the slum still clung, was a constituent element of his skin, which he sensed was very thin indeed. He had the moral sensitivity to be embarrassed by himself and the constructive awareness not to regard this membrane of ignorance as a protective shield which he could brandish complacently to those with less money. A projection of Neal's face danced across the screen of his mind, and he hoped that when Neal had absorbed all of the advantages that money could provide, he would not abandon Jay precisely for having provided the advantages. He felt better when he realized that the girls were not superior, merely different, and he was tempted to invite Caroline to join them for dinner, but he wanted to be alone with Terry on the first night.

"Hey, look, if you're not busy tomorrow night, why don't you come out with us?" he said.

"Oh, you are a sweetie," she said. "But I wouldn't think—"

"—Bullshit. Get yourself a date, and we'll tear a red streak through Boston."

"Please, Caroline. He wouldn't have asked if he didn't want you to come."

"Well, I suppose I could."

"Settled."

"See you, kid. You can polish off the other bottle of champagne if you can open it."

Terry rested her head on his shoulder in the back of the car as the strange lights of Boston flashed past Jay's line of vision. He kissed her affectionately on the cheek.

"Baby, it's so good to be close to you. I couldn't even concentrate on business when I was in New York. Spent four hours in the office then zoomed to the airport. Florida was like a dream: meeting you, a business offer from your old man. I've never been so on top of the world in my life. All this is happening to me, Jay Blackman."

"Darling, I love you so much. What a nice surprise for me."

"I didn't offend Caroline?"

"No, don't be an idiot. I'm glad you asked her to come tomorrow." She looked at his face and ran her fingers under his chin. "We can't go back to the apartment tonight though," she added reluctantly.

"I guessed as much."

"So it'll have to be your hotel."

"My hotel!" He was incredulous.

"You're not going to be a prig, Jay?"

"It looks so bad. You'll get a reputation—"

She laughed sardonically.

"You're my reputation. Frankly, I don't give a damn."

The car turned into the driveway and the chauffeur opened the door.

"I'll be a couple of hours, so if you want to get lost some-where, it's okay."

The chauffeur tipped his hat and smiled.

As Jay had predicted the headwaiter did have a nice corner table for Mr. Hamilton.

"You're very pleased with yourself," Terry said.

"Private joke. The chauffeur said I couldn't get a table. Whenever people say you can't do, or get something, what they mean is, *they* can't. I thought I was going to hate Bos-ton."

He examined the menu which the headwaiter had, with a flourish and practiced sycophancy, handed to him. He was about to make suggestions, but Jay cut him short as he did all headwaiters, assuming a naïveté that might have been touching if it hadn't been quite so bellicose that headwaiters always had these special suggestions on hand for people who didn't be-long and would be likely to order the wrong things. He hated to be patronized and often reacted violently when people were only trying to be helpful, for he was unable to distinguish between the two.

He ordered a martini for Terry and a triple scotch for him-self. She gave him that peculiarly intense and concerned stare that young girls in love and in heat develop. It is a look of pure candescence and innocence, a look belonging to one of the few moments in the span of a lifetime when the division between mind and heart disappears. At thirty-five it becomes nostalgia, and at forty sentimentality. At twenty it is one of the few virtues that even an ugly girl possesses. Terry could not keep her hands off him. Even when she held the menu in one hand, she managed with the other to touch him under the table.

"Why are you having a lot to drink? Something bothering you?"

"I told my little boy I was going to leave."

"You did what?"

His hand shook and he flipped the glass back and downed the drink in one gulp. The waiter waited and Jay ordered the same again.

"I couldn't let my wife get in first. This sort of thing can cripple a kid for life. I had to try to explain that I wasn't some kind of monster."

"And she would have said you were?"

"She'd have reason to. We've been incompatible from the beginning."

"Is that all that's bothering you?"

"Isn't that enough?" he said truculently.

"All right, you don't have to lose your temper with me."

"He's a sick child with a sad unhappy expression on his face all the time. Born that way, as though something is missing from his life. I've given him everything—not just money— love, affection. I'm mad about him. I can't explain about him, but he's in my guts. I never stop thinking about him. You wouldn't think I'm the kind of man who worries about a kid all the time, would you?"

"I like you better for it."

"I married his mother because she was pregnant, and we tried to get rid of him. It's on my back all the time. So when he opens his eyes and wants to say something that he can't find words for, I get the feeling that he knows what I've done, and won't or can't let me off the hook. I'm always trying to make it up to him. So when I told him—not about *us*—but that I'd have to move out, I almost lost heart in the middle. There he was caught in the middle of two people—two people who have nothing to give each other—in a trap. Helpless. He doesn't get along with his mother very well and there he was stretching out his hand to me and I ran. I ran like hell as fast as I could. And he had this look on his face . . . I can't describe the look, but I see it all the time. When someone you love picks up a knife and says he's going to cut your throat. I've got a crazy idea that he wanted to say: 'Don't go, not because of me, but for your own sake.' He couldn't have said anything like that, could he? He's only five."

"Jay, calm down, you're losing control."

"Sorry," he said. He waved his empty glass at the waiter, who asked if they were ready to order. "Don't rush me." The man retreated to the bar.

"He wasn't rushing you, Jay. Honey, take it easy."

"I'm depressing you."

"Of course you're not. If you've got problems, then I have them also."

"Nothing to do with you. Must keep you out."

"It's not possible. I'm committed to you."

"You're involved with me, not committed. There's a big difference."

"What difference? I'm going to marry you. Neal will be like my own child. I'll treat him just as I would our own children when we have them."

Something jarred Jay sharply in the way she described how she would treat Neal. The prospect of more children terrified him. For him Neal was enough; he couldn't imagine introducing him to strange children and complicating his life even more. Neal would be forced to occupy that ill-defined, soul-destroying, incomparably hopeless position of the child who belongs to no one and is finally opted into a family where he is treated "just as though he were their own." Jay refrained from assaulting the idealistic state of affairs Terry had constructed. She didn't understand how he felt, nor would she ever understand and he could not bring himself to explain why and how the child, seemingly passive, had established such a strong hold over him. He imagined he saw Neal's face at the bottom of the convex whiskey glass which was empty again. And he saw the look, a look so staggeringly malevolent and demoniac that he shrank back. Had Neal come between him and Terry, would he always come between Jay and every other woman?

"Honey, let's order something. You're glassy-eyed."

"You order," he said, at last.

"Trust me?"

"With my life."

She picked up his hand and kissed it.

"I'll make everything up to you. I've got so much love to give you."

"You should save it for someone who deserves it."

"Jay? Honestly, I don't know what I have to do to convince you—"

"Just convince Neal. I'm sold on you."

Her smile cracked just a bit, enough for him to notice and not to comment on.

They were both tipsy when they got back to his hotel suite. He had slipped the elevator man five dollars, just to be on the safe side. He threw his coat carelessly on a chair and opened a bottle of whiskey.

"All you seem to do is drink," she said, standing on the bed. She began to jump on it as though it were a trampoline, and her head narrowly missed the ceiling.

"You passing judgment?"

"No, commenting."

"I wish you'd stop that jumping. I'm getting dizzy watching you."

He took a long drink, then sat down on a chair and took his shoes off.

"Romantic beast, aren't you? God, I hate rooms painted green. All hotels have green rooms, the smell of carbolic acid on the bedspread, and maroon drapes with little hanging balls."

"It was your idea, not mine."

"That sounds suspiciously like a reproach."

"I'm tired. Everything aches."

"Are we going to—?"

"What?" he said.

She gave him a sharp little smile that had a hint of menace in it. Her eyes were bloodshot and the pupils dilated.

"Fuck, of course."

He lifted his head up from the floor.

"I don't think you should use language like that."

"You *are* joking."

"I'm not."

"You use it all the time."

"Never with you."

"I'm not honored. Don't people use words like that in a bedroom?"

"Occasionally . . . when they're nice women who want to be treated like whores. The way you could never treat a whore. Yeah, the nastier kind of woman likes that."

She took off her shoes and started to open the clasp of her suspender belt to release her stockings. "Treat me like a whore."

"It wouldn't work."

"How do you know?"

"Please stop this crap." She came over and sat on his lap, and pushed his hand under her dress. "It's a wonder to me that a nice girl should behave like a pig."

"I thought of you as though you were one enormous prick, fucking me to death. A machine, pushing in deeper and deeper and deeper until I'm dead."

He pushed her to the floor gently and without the suggestion of violence, but he had an instinctive urge to strike her. He picked up his drink and emptied it.

"If you drink much more of that, you won't be able to—"

"That could be the general idea. It's fantastic what you don't know about people. I think I might be in love with you, at least I was sure it couldn't be anything else when I was away from you, and now you're taking that feeling and tearing it to shreds, as though it was a filthy old rag that nobody gave a damn about. I come up to see you, when I should be home with my kid, and all you're interested in is smutty talk. Drop down to a poolroom and you'll get all you can stand for nothing."

"It's the dirt that excites me. Underneath the two-hundred-dollar suit and the alligator shoes, and the French aftershave lotion, is a dirty little Jew. That's what attracts me. And you dress it all up in a fancy slipcover because you're embarrassed by it. The part that's important to me is repulsive to you."

"You've got strange ideas of excitement. If you need some guy to give you a shove, Boston must be loaded with them."

"It's you, Jay. It's you."

"I don't know what you're talking about. I owe your father a favor or two so I'll forget the dirty Jew crack, but if you'd like me to kick your teeth down your throat, you could try saying it again.''

"Sensitive spot, isn't it?''

"I was just thinking about what a wonderful mother you'd make. I've got a few beefs about Rhoda but she's a saint by comparison.''

"My father said she was a drug addict.''

"Your father was misinformed.''

"And he said you were an absolute degenerate in your sex life.''

"Well, I'm sorry to disappoint you about that too. You've had a lot of disappointments in one night.''

"You can't keep your hands off women. Everyone who knows you . . .''

"Nobody knows me. I was hoping you might be the one . . . Neal and me . . .''

She did her stockings up and straightened the seams in the mirror behind her.

"You've got a thing about that kid. It's unhealthy. Morbid. You can't act like a man because he's in the room with us, isn't he? Watching . . .''

"I'll call a cab for you. I think you'd better go, while you can still walk.''

"Just threats . . . full of threats.''

He got up from the chair very slowly, like an old man suffering from arthritis, and in a voice that rang through the room he began to scream: "Get out, get out.'' Tears streamed down his face and he advanced towards her. She retreated to the door and he allowed her to escape. He picked the bottle of whiskey up and pulled from the bottle, then he fell on the bed and began to bang his head against the wooden bedpost.

"Ooooh, baby, that was sensational,'' Barney said as Rhoda turned her head to the wall. "Wanta get high again?''

"It's late.''

"Whaat, eight o'clock in the morning's late?''

"I've got to get home. Haven't seen Neal for three days.''

"We could make it all day in bed. C'mon. Send out for sandwiches, a little booze. What's a day?"

"It's breaking . . . all of it's breaking up and I can't do anything about it."

"Rhoda, what're you talking about? We're on a good time, aren't we? We laugh it up. In bed, it's dynamite. You're the greatest."

"Tomorrow, or the next day maybe, or next week."

"Well, if you havta."

In a trance she rose from the bed, threw some cold water on her face, and rinsed her mouth. The street below was empty, and gray like a bit of ash.

"My head's . . ." She dressed hurriedly, threw her crumpled clothes into the small alligator suitcase that Jay had bought her on Mother's Day.

"Rhoda, take it easy. Let's make a date . . ."

"I'll call you," she said, and rushed out. She ran down the flights of steps like someone panic-stricken, escaping from a conflagration . . . On Fiftieth Street she went into the subway and caught a train. Tired, lined faces hidden behind newspapers turned pages of blurred newsprint. She heard herself sob and she stuffed a handkerchief in her mouth. At Fourteenth Street she changed trains and caught a Brighton express, then she changed trains again, and again until the names of the stations whizzed past her face without registering. Finally she got off the train and walked through the turnstile into the cold street, past the fruit and vegetable stalls where men and women wearing gloves cut off at the fingers stood by small potbellied stoves which they fed with the street garbage. She crossed the street and stood for a full five minutes swaying on the corner, until a car horn blasted through her brain. It was still there: Modes Dress Shoppe with its tattered green striped awning flapping in the wind, its crowded window with hopelessly passé dresses, the window glass cracked as though it had been seized by a sharp and death-dealing embolism, and its mound of dirt in the ruts that had not been swept into the gutter. She dragged her suitcase into the store, and when she was inside it was so dark that she could barely see who was sitting behind the counter. Then she gave an agonized moan. She tried to speak but nothing would come out. A figure approached her.

"It's me, Rhoda. I've come back. Please, please, Mr. F, forgive me. I didn't mean it. It was Jay . . . he made me do it. I never stole from anybody. He made a thief out of me."

The figure came closer until its head was very close to hers, but all she saw was Finkelstein's torn and ravaged face.

"I'll pay it back. I can afford to now. Please, I'm sorry." She lurched against the edge of the counter and almost knocked it over and cradled her head in her arms, as though to ward off blows. "I'm a decent woman . . . I was a good worker until he . . . he made me . . ." She couldn't continue because the man's eyes looked through her as though she were a pane of glass.

"For God's sake, lady, what do you want?" an outraged voice said.

"It's Rhoda. I should have stayed on with you and forgotten about him."

"What're you talking about?"

"Say you forgive me, Mr. F."

"I'm not Finkelstein. He died four years ago."

She stretched out her hands as if to grab him and the man drew away.

"I'll call the police if you don't get out," he said angrily. "You pull yourself together or you'll wind up in a canary hatch. Now if you don't want to buy, cop a walk."

She edged towards the door, backing away from the man. Where was she? She wiped her eyes and the voice droned: "If you got somethin' to confess, go to the station but don't bother me. What a way to start the day!"

Rhoda wiped her face with her sleeve and walked out. She took a shortcut to her parents' house and sat down on a flight of steps opposite it. The stone was cold and damp and water had gathered in the cracks. She lit a cigarette and waited. At 9:30 she saw her father open the door, rub his hands like a surgeon in a Marx Brothers film, then Miriam came out swinging a briefcase and hopping down the steps.

"You'll brek the sandwiches," he said, and Miriam giggled mischievously.

Rhoda made a move to go to them, but suddenly her father was inside the maroon Chevrolet that Jay had given him, and Miriam had slammed her door and the car shot down the street and she stood in the roadway with her arms stretched out trying to grasp something that was beyond her reach, something so elusive and distant that she came to her senses because the effort of holding her arms out had tired her, and she realized with a chill that what she now wanted, she had once had and that she could never again recapture it. She and Jay had conspired to murder it, and they had been successful. She walked down the street and turned onto Fourteenth Avenue. She stared aimlessly and blankly at the murky shop windows with their tired, out-of-date displays, the people who worked in the stores idling behind counters, sipping coffees, slaves to the useless and despairing commerce that she had once been a part of. On Forty-eighth Street she went into the Royal Music Shop where Myrna had worked. She pointed to a clarinet in a glass showcase and told the salesgirl that she would have it. She wrote out a check for ninety-one dollars, and the manager, who Rhoda recognized but who did not recognize her, approached her with that desperate servility and suspicion that people who are on commission assume whenever an easy, unexpected sale comes their way. She wrote the address to which it was to be sent, and the manager, who spent most of his time demonstrating sheet music on an out-of-tune Steinway located in the middle of the shop on a platform, hummed something vague and tuneless.

"It'll have to clear the bank before we can send it." He studied the name as though calligraphy were one of his hobbies. "Hey, isn't that . . . aren't you . . . ?" But Rhoda was out of the door before he could get an answer.

In the street she hailed a taxi and gave her address. She waited a few minutes to see if the driver was using his mirror to spy on her, and when she was satisfied that he wasn't, she took out a bottle of pills and swallowed two.

Jay was having breakfast when she arrived, looking very

tanned, fit, and sad. She sat down at the table, poured herself a cup of black coffee. He stared at her, exerting the terrible fascination of a mongoose, sleek, canny, and fast enough to anticipate any sudden move; an expert in the coarse art of survival.

"Funny time to get home," he said, cautiously. He was on dangerous ground and he didn't want to sink into a mire. "Your sister any better?"

"Fine . . . she's a cabbage. Very good soil up there for growing vegetables."

"Maybe we ought to put her in a different place."

"Maybe you shouldn't worry about it too much."

"You've been crying," he said, as she rubbed her eyes with the back of her hand. Her eyes were like red welts.

"From the minute I met you I started crying. Funny you should notice now."

Here it comes, he thought tremulously. He girded himself for the attack, but she held back . . .

"If it's going to be one of those—"

"—One of those what?"

"Mornings. Your eyes are popping out of your head again."

"Are they? Well, you won't have to worry about it much longer, will you?" She sipped her coffee meditatively. "Did you know that Finkelstein's dead?"

"What?"

"Dead."

"I don't know what you're talking about."

"Skip it. I thought when I saw you I'd rant and rave and have hysterics as usual."

"Yeah, I know the program . . . it's been running for five years."

"Jay, why don't you die? Wouldn't it be much better for everyone if you were dead?"

"Rhoda, if you're going to be unpleasant the minute we see each other, then I think we ought to talk seriously."

" 'We should talk seriously.' "

"Don't mimic me, I don't like it. You must've met a guy

if you're acting this strong. Frankly, I don't mind. Best thing that could happen to you.''

"I'm glad you approve. You see your lawyer and I'll see mine and they can arrange things between them.''

"So long as I can see Neal whenever I want . . . that's all I give a damn about.''

"It'll have to be discussed, won't it?''

He got very hot under the collar, but he managed to maintain a hold on his temper.

"Sore spot with you, isn't it?'' she said. "Nice to see you at a disadvantage for a change.''

"You'll poison his mind against me.''

"Why should I? Typical of you, Jay. Imputing your own motives to other people. Now if the shoe was on the other foot, I'd have plenty to worry about. Actually, it's your moral character that worries me. You've got a lot of influence on him, and he doesn't know right from wrong, so too much time with you might be damaging in the long run.''

The conversation made him uncomfortable, as did all conversations dwelling on his character, and he lost that sure-footed instinct which had enabled him to transcend, with a hawk's guile and rapacity, all of the positive and glaring deficiencies which disguised a lack of feeling for the responses of other people, and which he had diverted, so that they assumed the plumed wings of strength. She had seen that he was vulnerable and she dug her nails into the tender belly of his weakness—his love for Neal.

"What do you want, Rhoda?''

"To see you suffer.''

"The harder you make it for me, the harder it'll be for Neal. So before you make a decision, give that some thought. Even though we get a divorce, I'd like to try to give him a normal life.''

"With you as a father? That's a joke.''

"And you as a mother!'' he shouted, pointing an accusing finger at her.

"Keep your voice down, Maggie'll hear us.''

"It's Myrna,'' he said, losing his restraint.

"Myrna?" she peered quizzically over her cup at him, and tears formed in the pockets of her eyes. "Myrna . . ."

"You heard some crazy story. That doctor wrote to me about a year ago . . ."

"Myrna. I suppose that rounds out the picture."

"It's a goddamned filthy lie."

"Myrna."

"For Christ's sake, stop saying her name."

"The village idiot appears on your list of conquests."

"That's not true."

She knocked her cup over and the coffee ran down the side of the table onto the cream-colored carpet. She didn't make a move to stop the drip and let it soak into the carpet, fascinated by the regular movement.

"Myrna—"

"—Stop it. I can't stand it." He got up from the table and rushed into the bedroom to get his jacket and coat. She followed him.

"You should've jerked yourself off if you needed a woman so bad. Or why didn't you call one of the whores in your book? You knew enough of them. Or was this too exciting to resist? Sleeping with your wife's sister. A girl who was absolutely defenseless, who'd had a mental breakdown, and was living on her nerves. In our bed, with *my* sister." He tried to push past her, but she stood with her arms out, pressed against the door. "Haven't you got any shame, any decency?"

"I'll get my stuff moved this afternoon. I want to see Neal when he comes home from school and I'd appreciate it if you weren't here."

"Whenever you got into our bed, you always had a funny smell. The smell of other women, cheap perfume and powder and their sweat. It was such an ugly smell that it used to keep me awake all night. I couldn't ever get used to it. Their bodies. And you, like a pig rolling over in his own shit."

"I don't have to—"

"You should die, and if there's a God or any justice you should spend the time after you're dead frying in hell. But I suppose you won't . . . people like you get away with murder

and then get congratulated for it, but someday somebody'll cut
your throat when you least expect it.''

He lifted her arms which were still pinioned against the door
and forced his way past her. Their faces were almost touching,
and as she looked into his eyes, she could see that for the first
time since she had known him, he was hurt and pleading for
help. His mouth moved perilously close to her, and she
thought he was going to kiss her. She pressed the heel of her
palm under his chin, eased him away and spit in his face. He
stood for a moment, as though paralyzed, with the bubbly
saliva dripping down his face, then with a movement as swift
as a flash of lightning, he lifted his hand to strike her, and she
screeched: ''Neal, Neal, Neal,'' as though the incantation of
his name would dispel the terrible vengeance of an enraged
god. His hand, suspended in the air, the fingers brown like the
leather thongs of a whip, froze in motion, like a film which
had suddenly been jerked and was running in slow motion.

''I won't forget this,'' he said.

''I hope you won't. I hope it's carved on your headstone.''

Six months of dreamlike apathy passed before Rhoda saw Jay
again; six months in which her emotional life resembled the
frozen streets and snowcaps of a Taiga Brooklyn winter . . .
She would sometimes see his face in the glassy ice of the
pavements, or emerging from the frozen breaths of people
standing in line waiting for a bus. She constantly had the sensation that he was stalking her, and she would slink into obscure ill-lit little neighborhood bars where drunken eyes, and
mouths reeking of pizza and overcooked spaghetti, pursued
her. From time to time she went out with Barney, or sat, sloe-
eyed and ''charged'' in some small lurid club like a tongueless
hoplite, listening to him tell jokes to bored and grizzled small-
time businessmen whose assignations with mousy, heavily
mascaraed women seemed to her affairs of petty and mutual
despair. Barney clung to her, and she couldn't bear the responsibility that failure conferred on him. Once or twice she
paid his hotel bill when he couldn't get work, and this made
him impotent in bed with her.

With a Prussian's respect for punctilio and ceremony, Jay visited Neal every Sunday at noon, and she would leave the apartment a good hour before, to avoid a chance encounter, sit in the candy store at the corner, sipping black coffee and trying in a totally automatic way to find her bearings in the confused geography of her life. At twelve-thirty she would return to the apartment, stare out into the street through the opaque misted windows without a thought in her head. The impending divorce represented a caesura in the action of her life, and she could not see beyond it to make plans. Her relations with almost everyone she had known in the past took on the static quality of her own lethargy. Even Neal lost his reality for her, and she avoided questioning him about his afternoons with Jay—how wrong Jay had been, she thought. She lost the power of communicating anything but a simple imperative to the child. She saw Neal only in a formal concrete sense, the rest of him was hidden behind two translucent cataracts which had imposed themselves over her eyes. He always seemed to her to be performing, living, with a thin gossamer veil over him that teased the eye. He was no more than an optical illusion, a *trompe-l'oeil* which moved from the foreground into her path, then receded across some amorphous horizon, so that what he did, what he said, what he was feeling, was only something vague and putative which her brain carried to her senses. Occasionally, she realized, in the same unreflective way one recalls a useless fact—that the Amazon is the longest river in the world—that she loved Jay more than she ever had. Love would never become hate, as black can never become white, but her love had lost its knifelike edge, and had become unalterably passive. It was like a malignancy whose growth had been arrested—but if she decided to cut it out, it might grow back, larger and more virulent.

At the beginning of April, after the divorce settlement had been agreed upon and the hearing in court announced, she was startled one morning to hear his voice on the telephone. It was like a voice disembodied and eerie, coming from the back of an empty theater and she wanted to ask to whom it belonged.

"I thought I should call you . . ." he said in a halting,

strained manner, ". . . my mother died yesterday. I thought you'd want to know."

"Oh, Jay. I'm so sorry. It's so sudden."

"I loved her, you know."

"I know you did. I did too, in my own way. She wanted us to be happy."

"She loved you and Neal very much. It was a coronary . . . one, two, three. They couldn't do a thing. Funeral's today."

"I'd like to go, if—"

"I'd appreciate it if you would. I mean you're still my wife, and oh, God, Rhoda, I'm so unhappy I don't know what to do. I'm falling apart."

"It's terrible, I know."

He gave her the address of the chapel, and then said: "I'd pick you up, but I'm not allowed to drive."

"I'll go to the cemetery. It's maybe better that I don't come to the chapel."

There was a long silence, and she wondered if he had hung up, and she felt stupid and dazed because she had forgotten to ask the name of the cemetery.

"It's Beth David," he said. "Twelve o'clock . . . and thanks."

The cemetery ground had not thawed, except in isolated spots, and made a crunching sound underfoot. The wind howled through the treeless open space, and Rhoda walked carefully across the frozen scrubs of crabgrass, trying to avoid the pasty red loam. She wondered how Jay had reacted when the lawyer had asked him to sign over his King's Highway store to her, for she had been surprised when he had acceded to the demand without ever raising it with her. The cash settlement had been agreed to at once, but the store was like one of his limbs. She didn't know why she had asked for it except perhaps to hurt him; then she remembered that the suggestion had come from Howard, who had insisted that she would be better off usefully occupied in business than moping around the house. She had told this to her lawyer, not caring how things turned out, and now she realized that the store would indeed give her something to do, and she was anxious to resume working again.

She stood behind a gray mausoleum, which was adjacent to an open hole which, the guide had said, was the plot that Celia Blackman would be buried in. She made an effort to reconstruct Celia's face, but it would not take form. All that manifested itself was her angular figure, the thin reedy voice, the knotted veins on her hands, the halting walk as though she was perpetually carrying a burden, and the gold teeth like gates across her mouth.

A string of black cars followed an embowered hearse down the small road. The cars stopped, and a covey of black-veiled women extricated themselves from them. Some distance behind the others another car drew up, and a woman with red hair got out and stood by the front fender observing the procession. Rhoda recognized Eva, and couldn't understand how she had learned of the arrangements—unless she and Jay . . . She pondered the idea for a moment, concluding finally that Jay had gone back to her.

Behind a crowd of pallbearers tiptoeing like ravens after prey, she caught sight of Jay, trudging slowly forward over the hard muddy ground, his head lowered. At the graveside the casket was set down, and Jay, white-faced and trembling, peered down at the hole and shuddered. A small, gray-bearded figure stepped out of the crowd and said a prayer in Hebrew, then the casket was lowered. She came out from behind the gray wall and walked towards Jay. Before she reached him she heard a terrible moan over the staccato of the prayer which made her flesh crawl, and she recognized that its point of origin was Jay. His mouth was open and he was howling like some wild bereft animal. Dumbfounded, she halted about five feet from him, but the howl, the groan, the unutterable agony of the cry continued until his father leaped forward and slammed him across the mouth with the back of his hand.

"You dirty bestid," he squalled. "You crying for why? You kilt her!"

He continued to lash out with his fists and Jay covered himself up with his elbows.

"Oh, Mommmmmmmmma . . . Aieeeeeeee," he groaned, sinking to his knees.

Rhoda rushed up to him and seized the old man's flailing arms.

"Stop it, stop it," she shouted.

"You, Rhoda?" the old man said softly. "What you doink?"

"It's a cemetery . . . have respect for her," she said.

"Respect? He kilt her. Filtee bestid. With his own Momma he slept. She couldn't forget it and it kilt her."

Jay rose slowly from the ground, his trousers streaked with mud, and his fists clenched. In a quiet mournful voice he said:

"Liar," and walked through the throng of shocked faces to the road. Rhoda trailed after him and caught up with him. He turned to look at the crowd at the graveside. Only a few people still watched him.

"Tell me," she said. "It's not true, what he says."

"He's a liar. Never, and I swear on her, did I ever . . ."

"And that's the truth?"

"What's ruined me is not what I did, but what I wanted to do one afternoon a long time ago, and I've never forgiven myself for it, but she did. She forgave me, thank God."

She watched him get into the car with Eva. The car drove slowly down the rutted muddy road and she stared after it until it disappeared. He had needed her, for a moment, and now it was over.

IV

WINTER
PHLEGM
AIR

16

The divorce relieved Neal's tensions and simplified matters, for it settled the question of divided loyalties. What before had been a tyrannical struggle between two hostile factions, with his affection as the prize, degenerated into sporadic skirmishes between them over the years, and Neal felt neither loyalty nor disloyalty towards his parents: he tolerated them, and lived his life within the eye of a hurricane, so that they could not touch him. He had unconsciously slipped into the solipsist position, and at the age of twelve had developed the defenses of the practiced pessimist. What he wanted most was to be rid of Rhoda and Jay, as well as of Eva, whom he despised with an intensity which enraged him when he so much as thought of her. He accepted his mother's frequent and casual affairs with strange men who from time to time showed up at the apartment, then vanished as though they had fallen off the earth. He forgot about them and so did Rhoda. He was dark and thin like Jay, with Rhoda's green eyes; and the brooding manner of a man who has had a disastrous love affair, so that nothing could ever again be the same. In many ways, he had inherited Rhoda's capacity and penchant for suffering, but this was tempered by an equal ability to inflict pain both on himself and others. Because he was clever and an astute judge of the weaknesses of other people, there was something menacing about him, which Rhoda recognized and feared. It wasn't merely the way he said: "You can stay out all night if you like," when she informed him that she was going out on a date, or playing cards with friends, but the detached manner in which he said it—never insisting, or pointing out that, he had a prior claim on her time—and his total lack of involvement. They had a tacit understanding which neither of them transgressed. It amounted to *laissez faire* and made them companionable.

On a Friday, at about seven in the morning—Neal remembered the day clearly because it was the fourth weekend and he always spent it with Eva and his father—he was surprised to find a man sleeping on the sofa in the living room. He went into his mother's room and discovered her in a deep sleep, then he returned to the living room where the man had shifted on his side so that Neal could get a good look at his face without standing over him. He saw a square face with lank mottled brown hair, a long hooked nose with hairs dancing in the nostrils from the snores, and skin that was sallow and pocked like a piece of pigskin. The man had a small jaw and his beard was patchy. His clothes had been folded neatly across a chair in the dining room and his socks were pushed into a pair of navy blue suede shoes. Neal dressed quietly; for his mother always slept till ten, getting into the store at eleven, and they had an arrangement between them based on mutual respect for the sleeping—and apathy. Fully dressed, the scraped brown leather strap tied round his books, Neal prepared to leave. He studied the man who had now rolled over on his stomach, then went back into the dining room. He took all of the man's clothes, except the shoes and socks, and left the apartment, shutting the front door with the stealth of a professional thief. He tiptoed down the stippled concrete hallway, and decided to walk down the stairs instead of waiting for the elevator. On the third floor he stopped on the half-landing to see if he was being followed. Then he approached the incinerator and stuffed the clothing down it. He picked up a bag of garbage that had been left in the incinerator room and pushed it in to make certain that the clothes would not be trapped.

Bernard Zimmerman was waiting for him at the candy store.

"You're early," Neal said. "I haven't had any breakfast yet."

"I had to see you, so I rushed out," Bernard said, with a note of excitement. He was a short plump boy with a square-shaped face, irregular teeth, kinky red hair, and an assortment of blackheads on the bridge of his nose.

Neal ordered his breakfast; it never varied: orange juice, a chocolate malted, and toast with cream cheese. He had all his meals in the candy store because Rhoda never finished at the store till well after nine, and she had arranged for him to charge all his meals there. He hated the man who ran it, a balding, greasy individual with a mustache and watery gray eyes, by the name of Levy. Levy was a thief: everyone in the neighborhood knew Levy was a thief, except Rhoda, and Neal never bothered to tell her.

"My mother says she saw a man come up with your mother, and that the man didn't leave," Bernard said with sympathetic concern. "Did he sleep over?"

Neal bit into his toast and decided to tell Bernie what he had done: Bernie was his best friend, and Bea Zimmerman was the only pleasant adult woman he had ever met.

. "I fixed his wagon," Neal said.

Levy stared at the two boys, and edged closer.

"Whadyuh do?" Bernie exclaimed.

"Shush, he's listening. Levy, why don't you jerk off?"

"Dirty-mouthed little bastard."

"Don't curse, or I'll take my business across the street and you won't be able to pad any more bills."

Levy gave him a murderous stare, then commenced chopping the tuna fish salad.

"So? I'm busting to hear."

"I never saw the guy before. Found him sleeping in the living room. He had one of those shiny suits . . . a silk job, and I stuffed it down the incinerator."

Zimmerman inflated his cheeks, then slammed them with the palms of his hands and made a small exploding sound which indicated shock. A gob of saliva dribbled down his lower lip.

"Neal, you're crazy! Your mother'll kill you."

"She won't say a word . . . she'll be shitting in her pants about me telling my father."

"But the guy'll beat your head in."

"I fuck him where he breathes. If he sleeps in strange people's houses then he must be used to this sort of thing."

"Jeez, you've got nerve. He could be a tough guy or somethin' who ain't afraid. Maybe your mother likes him and wants
ta marry him."

"She can marry a black guy for all I care. One shitheeler's
the same as the next." He pushed his plate out of the way
and said: "Levy, mark it up. Thirty-five cents, not sixty-five,
gonif."

"Awright, Neal," he said with a snigger. "Pretty cute kid,
aren'tcha?"

"Smarter than you. C'mon, Bernie, or we'll be late. One
more 'late' and my mother'll have to come to see the teacher."

"Were you warned?"

"Yeah, warned, but they won't do anything 'cause my
marks are good."

"The second highest in the school," Zimmerman said ad-
miringly.

At 3:30 the two of them returned to Zimmerman's apartment,
as they did every day for milk and chocolate Mallowmars
which Bea provided. She was a warm friendly woman, incredibly obese, short-tempered, sloppy, with an obsessional
passion for crossword puzzles, which she solved with an
adeptness only a poorly educated person can develop. Neal
liked her—her evil-smelling kitchen with its grease marks on
the ceiling, her ragged dressing gowns, her slovenly habit of
picking the wax out of her ears with a hairpin and then rolling
it up into a ball and surreptitiously dropping it on the floor—
and he respected her for never sentimentalizing and not treating him with the treacly emotionalism which most adults displayed and which he realized was not concern but the capacity
for enjoying the troubles of others. He knew that Bea disap-
proved of his parents, but she never allowed it to cloud her
judgment.

"We're going to the schoolyard, Mom," Bernie said.

"Be back at five on the dot 'cause Neal's got to pack his suitcase."

"Oh, I forgot . . ."

"Fourth weekend of the month," Neal said. "That's the sentence the judge passed."

"Oh, it's not so bad, Neal. Wahme to help you pack?"

"No, I can manage, but can Bernie wait with me till my father comes?"

"Sure." As they were about to leave, she called out: "Bernie, don't forget to bring me the three evening papers." They also had crossword puzzles. Twice before, Bernie had not brought them, and she had beaten him.

"We only got an hour," said Bernie. "You wanta play stickball or should we go on the roof for a smoke?"

"The roof. I got three Camels left." He winked at Bernie. "Bit early for Lady Farberman."

"You never know," he said hopefully. "Remember, last Thursday when we cut assembly we caught her tickling her titties in the bathtub?"

They took the elevator up to the sixth floor and steathily crept up the side flight of stairs which led to the roof. Bernie peeked through the door.

He whispered: "Mrs. Klein's hanging her washing."

"Can we sneak past?"

"Yeah, I think maybe. Clock this, Neal. She's got her ass to the wind and her bloomers are waving hello."

"She's got varicose veins, ugh."

"Not in her ass."

"Oh, Bernie, she's awful. An old douchebag."

"What's a douchebag?"

"Dunno. I heard my father call some woman it."

"C'mon, tipsy-toe past."

They turned sharply around when they were outside and climbed up the metal ladder which brought them to a smallish house with an apex-shaped roof which had an enormous angular skylight. This was the top of the elevator shaft, and they could hide behind the jutting skylight if anyone came. Neal took out two crumpled cigarettes, cupped his hands to light a match, and on the third try managed to light his own. Bernie got a light from his cigarette, and Neal's almost went out. He puffed hard on Neal's cigarette to save the light, and Neal said testily:

"Don't wet it for shit's sake."

"Sorry. Here, I didn't wet it."

The view of Brooklyn was panoramic and they could see as far as King's Highway, the cars and people like ants under a rock.

"My father says Brooklyn's the asshole of the world."

"Funny thing to say."

"He wants me to move out to Great Neck with him and Eva."

"Ahhh, Neal, you won't, willya?" Bernie asked him with desperation. "We're best friends and we'd never see each other."

"I tell him I'd like to, so that when I want something he gets it for me. Can't do any harm."

"But he could tell your mother that you want to go and then you'd be up shit's creek."

"The judge gave her custody of me . . . my father's only got visiting rights, so he can't have me even if I wanted to go. I just string him along, like he strings me along. Hey, Kleinhorse's picking up her clothespins and going," Neal said.

"Should we have some fun?"

"Like what?"

"Throw ink on her clothes?"

"Don't be a *schmuck!* They'd send the super up to find out who did it, and the first stop he'd make would be my house."

"I hate him . . . the Nazi bastard," Bernie said, spitting at the skylight.

"Just 'cause he's German doesn't make him a Nazi."

"I hate his guts," Bernie said bitterly.

"So, he pushed you once. But he was right, wasn't he? After all you did stop the elevator between the floors for an hour."

Bernie screwed up his face and did his imitation of the

Hunchback of Notre Dame—his tongue twisted to the side, his nose tilted up, the pink of his eye hanging open like a gash.

"That's what I'd like to do to him, and if he ever touches me again, he'll get his good and proper. I'll get him fired," he threatened.

"What're you talking about?"

"I got something on him, don't you worry!"

"The truth?"

Bernie nodded.

"What is it?"

"I don't know if I should say."

"But we're best friends. Aw, c'mon, I tell you everything, don't be a rat."

"Tuesday night I came up to the roof."

"Without me!" Neal was incredulous.

"You were playing basketball at the community center. I brought my father's binoculars up with me—the ones he uses when he goes to the track. And I saw him with Lady Farberman."

"You didn't?"

"I swear to God I did. I couldn't believe it, but there he was, giving her the old Roy Rogers treatment. Giddyap, Trigger . . . 'I'm back in the saddle again,' " Bernie sang in a screeching falsetto. "What a cock he's got, long like a torpedo. He ain't circumcised like us. None of the Nazis get circumcised. If the owner and the Nazi's wife found out about it, plus Lord Farberman, he'd get his balls cut off."

"Why didn't you tell me?" Neal protested.

"Aw, I dunno. Gee, Neal, I'm sorry. I was gonna tell you."

Neal took out his last cigarette, lit it, and passed it to Bernie.

"We'll smoke this one together."

"Neal, wouldn't it be great to get laid? Wish we knew somebody."

"Moony laid Margie and you know what happened to him. He got the Crimean crutch rot, with scabs on his balls. They had to send him away to Riker's Island where the leper colony is. What about Lady Farberman?"

"I wouldn't touch her with a ten-foot pole. She's such a dirty pig. I'll bet she's got worms up her from the Nazi."

Neal shot the cigarette out with his index finger.

"It's the asshole of the world, all right."

"Would you rather live with your father and Eva?"

"I couldn't stand it."

"They still fight?"

"They never stopped. He cuts out when he feels like it, and when he gets home she screams, and screams, and screams, till she's blue in the face and her veins and eyeballs are popping out. I hate her guts. She's got this daughter about two years older than me, and she sees her only once a year. That's the kind of rat she is. I met her once, the daughter, a skinny, sadfaced titless scarecrow with freckles on her face and hair under her arms. Eva's very mean, and when my father and her make up, they sit around and drink, or they go out to bars and drink. And they get drunk and cry and talk in a slurry way like drunks talk, and then they argue some more and he hits her. They're pretty terrible people really."

"Yeah, but your father's swimming in dough."

"He can stick his dough up his ass and shit dollar bills. Aw, but sometimes he's nice and he tries, he really does try. But I dunno. It all makes me sick. I'd like to join the army and kiss them all good-bye."

"Why didn't your father go in the army?" Bernie asked. "You told me once but I forgot."

"Something wrong with his heart. He didn't have a heart attack but when my grandma died, something happened to it and made it weak. Something like that."

The clock by the church up the street tolled five o'clock and Bernie jumped up anxiously, while Neal sat pensively staring at the street below.

"C'mon, you gotta pack."

"Yeah, okay."

"Aren't you shitting green?"

"Why should I?"

"In case the guy who slept over's still there."

Neal climbed down the metal rungs and wiped his hands
on the clean sheets that Mrs. Klein had hung up.

"What can he do to me?" Neal said. "I'm only twelve
years old and I'm not scared, not any more."

"Gee." Bernie blew his cheeks out and slammed them.

There was a light on in the apartment, but Neal thought
nothing of it, as he and Rhoda always left the hall light on in
an attempt to discourage burglars. The radio was on, and he
knew that the man and possibly his mother were there. An
announcer was giving the racing results in a twangy voice,
and the man had his ear glued to the speaker. When he saw
Neal and Bernie he turned the radio off and smiled. They
stared at the man, for he wore camel-colored jodhpurs, blue
suede shoes, a loafer jacket which moths had riddled with their
own unique pattern, and a silk undershirt. The jodhpurs and
jacket Neal recognized as ancient and discarded possessions
of his father. Rhoda came out of the kitchen, but they didn't
notice her.

"You in the right apartment, Mister?" Neal asked.

"Neal?" the man said, crumpling a sheet of paper with
numbers on it and tossing it into the wastepaper basket. "I'm
Sol Pudnick." His voice had the quality of a toad croak, and
Neal was surprised by it. "Everyone calls me Sports."

"Hiya, Sports," Bernie said. "You come here to listen to
the radio?"

"I was waiting for Neal. To meet him."

"You met me. Now what?"

"I ought to beat your head in, Neal," Rhoda said angrily.

"Mom? You home?"

"You're goddamned right I'm home. Now what'd you do
with Mr. Pudnick's clothes?"

"Sports, please, Rho," Sports said, protesting against for-
mality.

"Where the hell are his clothes?"

"It was two C's worth of shantung, not to mention a very
special white-on-white job that come from Madison Avenue
at a double sawbuck."

"I don't know what you're talking about," Neal said quietly. "I've got to pack, 'cause Dad's coming to get me in a half-hour and he hates to be kept waiting."

"Bernie, maybe you'd better go home," Rhoda said.

"Sure, Mrs. Blackman."

"Bernie stays," Neal said with authority. "He's gonna help me pack. Mom, is this man bothering you? Should I call the cops?"

Rhoda came up to Neal, grasped his collar in her fist, and shook him. He gave a dull, fish-eyed look expressing total incomprehension.

"Leave the kid alone, Rho," Sports said.

"Sports stayed here last night."

Bernie edged towards the door anxiously.

"Did he? Where? I didn't see him."

"In the living room, he slept."

"I didn't go into the living room. I never do, do I? You always tell me not to."

"Then what'd you do this morning . . . from the moment you got up?"

"I washed, brushed my teeth, got dressed. Went into your room and kissed you on the cheek like I do every morning."

"You're not gonna hit him, are you, Mrs. Blackman?" Bernie whined.

"You never went into the living room?"

Neal outstared her, and her first impression of his lying gave way to doubt.

"Did you leave the door open when you left?"

"Don't think I did."

"Could be you did this time," Sports volunteered. But Neal shook his head definitely. He didn't want anyone's help, least of all the victim's, to get him off the hook.

"I'm sure the door was locked."

"Maybe the Nazi stole them," Bernie said.

"Who's the Nazi?" Sports said.

"The superintendent. No, I don't think he'd do a thing like that."

"Oh, wouldn't he?" Bernie pressed on.

"Yeah, I guess the door was open," Sports said helplessly. "Your kid wouldn't steal my clothes, and he didn't even know I was here." He put his arm round Neal. "You can't win 'em all, can you? Still two C's worth of precious cloth that come by plane from Hong Kong. Crying shame."

"Why did *he*"—Neal pointed to the gaily attired Sports— "stay here last night?"

There was an embarrassed silence and some heavy breathing from Bernie.

"I'm going now. See you, Neal. See you, everybody: Mrs. Blackman, Sports. See you."

Rhoda pursed her lips and sucked in her breath. She avoided Neal's serious, unrelenting eyes. Whenever she thought she had the upper hand, he always managed to reverse the situation, put her on the defensive, and sit in judgment on her without seeming to do so. He was like a wolf, sly, dangerous, and completely in control, never yielding, patient, stalking, capitalizing on the slightest mistake she made. What made it even more frustrating from her point of view was that Neal never appeared to be wielding the knife; he had a way of forcing her to turn the knife on herself. He was unattackable and he lived in a fortress which by some magic of personality he had rendered impregnable.

"I was at the Gin Rummy Club on Eastern Parkway and I couldn't get a taxi."

"It was very late," Sports added.

"Oh, the Gin Club. You showed me it once. Right across the street from Dubrow's Cafeteria."

"Yeah, that's right," Sports said.

"Don't they have a taxi station in front of Dubrow's? About thirty of them waiting in a line all the time?"

"Well, there weren't any last night," Rhoda said angrily.

"Oh, okay."

"There weren't any. And when I dropped your mother off, my car conked out. Couldn't start it and all the garages were closed, so your mom kindly offered me the davenport in the living room."

"My dad belongs to the AAA."

"So? What's that got to do with—?"

"Well, the good thing about them is that they come and start your car day or night, no matter where you are. They're very good like that, that's why my dad's a member." The information came forth from Neal's lips without a hint of irony and without a smile. Simply information which Sports might find useful in the future.

"I've got to pack now. 'S'cuse me, Mom." As he was about to leave the dining room he turned and said:

"I'd call the police about your clothes. Whoever stole them, well . . . it was a pretty horrible and nasty thing to do."

"Impossible," Rhoda moaned to Sports when he was gone. "Impossible little bastard. He was laughing at us all the time."

"I'm not sure, Rho. Let's give him the benefit of the doubt. Is he a liar?"

"No, not a liar. He just never tells the truth."

Neal came out of his room carrying a small leather weekend case. He paused on the threshold, then went up to his mother and kissed her on the cheek. He held out his hand and said:

"Glad to meet you, Sports."

"Same here."

Rhoda's exterior crumbled slightly when she realized that Neal had made the effort to be pleasant and outgoing.

"Have a good time and look after yourself."

"I'll try."

"I'm happy you and Sports met. You'll be seeing a lot of each other in the future."

"That's nice," Neal said.

Not until Neal had settled in his room in Jay's house did he consider the implications of Sports' sudden appearance as a house guest. All day at school he had given his mind to his studies, and even after the interview with his mother, the thought of Sports as a permanent fixture in the household merely occupied that place in his mind reserved for the other disembodied phantoms who had crossed his social perimeter and then evaporated like a cloud of smoke into some nebulous expanse of sky. On the surface the man was pleasant enough,

even likeable, but Neal did not like him: personable men with
what he called the "pals act" revolted him. He didn't want a
pal, nor did he wish to exchange confidences. If his mother
chose to marry again he would not stand in her way, or protest,
so long as new and more insidious restraints were not placed
on him. As it was, too many people told him what to do: the
prospect of yet another sympathetic, solicitous demi-relation
advising him was intolerable. He knew that Sports had known
he was guilty, and this made Neal uneasily suspicious of his
motives for concealing his knowledge. Why hadn't he pressed
his claim, or forced Neal to tell the truth? Why had he been
so quick to believe him, or seem to believe him? For Neal,
everyone operated in a shabby, dark world of motives: find
out the man's motives and you can beat him at his own game.
It was obvious: Sports planned to marry Rhoda; but why?
Could he possibly love Rhoda? That might be a possibility if
the man was less shifty, if the man was, in short, a man. But
he had detected that Sports' façade was as substantial as a
piece of tissue paper and as convincing as a Superman comic.
Rhoda had money, for Jay had not only given her a store
which was successful, but also a large cash settlement.

The divorce itself, what Neal remembered of it, had been a
masterpiece of good taste and *sotto voce* diplomacy. No
screaming, arguments, fights, name-calling—nothing like what
their marriage had been. It was all settled well and finally: two
cold-blooded and dissimilar people sitting around a table with
a few lawyers had signed a pact of dissolution and peace—
like the Indians and cavalry in a Western. Neal had come into
a room in a large official-looking building, after walking down
a long, gray, spotlessly clean corridor, the clicking of his
leather heels punctuated the tomblike silence. The room had
smelled like stale bread, and everyone smiled at him—open,
smiling, false faces and Jay had kissed him, then Rhoda kissed
him, and there was an acrid cigarette odor on her breath which
bothered him a bit, even though it was as familiar as her face.
He had nodded yes to several questions without fully understanding them, his back had been patted by a man who he had
learned was the judge, and it had all ended in an hour. He had

wanted to cry, to scream, to throw himself on the floor, writhing in an agony that he barely comprehended but which had torn a hole in him, but he was unable to cry, and he regretted not crying because he had never succeeded in crying afterwards, and he recognized that this represented an irreparable loss, and had *made* him, as much as anything else, what he was: a child waiting to become a man, so that he could break away from Rhoda and Jay. His only emotion when it was over was relief.

He decided that Sports wanted Rhoda's money and that he would have to tell his father, and Jay would do something about it. Neal would stand back from the action with an admiring sense of pride in Jay's firmness, and his power of decision. What he loved most about Jay was the way he could alter circumstances, and he knew his father was susceptible to his influence. He manipulated Jay like a set of trains. Jay loved Neal and never stopped telling him that he did and Neal loved Jay for loving him.

Eva was sitting in the den with a half-filled glass in her hand.

"You all settled in?"

"Uh-huh. Where's my father?"

"Talking to somebody on the phone . . ." She held up her glass to Neal and he took it. "Would you be a good boy and fix me another drink? Not too heavy on the water, we don't want to kill good scotch."

"Could you tell the difference?"

"What'd you mean by that? Of course I can tell good from crap."

"No, I mean if there's too much water in it?"

She thought about his question for a moment and said:

"Yeah, it tastes all watery and flat." Neal always seemed to upset her, and she lost her temper too easily with him. Why did she always look for hidden meanings in harmless things he said?

"Thanks, Neal. You've got a terrific future as a bartender. It's just right."

Jay walked in with blazing eyes.

"You got the kid mixing drinks for you? It's only five feet away. If that's too far, you can sit on top of it."

"Aw, Dad, don't argue. I like doing it."

"Really?" He brightened. "Sorry, Eva. I'm just annoyed that I got let down for some fight tickets. I told the broker to take his tickets and stick 'em."

"Aren't we going?" Neal asked.

"Twenty-fifth row?"

"I wanted to go."

"Well, I'll call him back if you do."

"No, don't, you're probably right."

"Tell you what, there's a new steak house opened up last week and I hear it's terrific. What do you say, Neal? Shrimp cocktail and a nice big charcoal-broiled steak?"

"Sure, great."

"I want to eat Chinese food," Eva said.

"Well, you go and eat Chinese food. Neal and me are gonna have steak."

"Never anything I want to do. Always Neal, Neal, Neal."

"You're ridiculous."

"Eva, don't you remember the last time we ate Chinese food you were sick all night, and said you'd never eat it again," Neal said with concern.

She gave him a quizzical stare, then broke into a smile.

"Always got the right thing up your sleeve, haven't you?"

"Finish your drink and we'll go. They sell booze in bars too, and you like bars better, don't you?"

"I'll just do my face."

"That's a lifetime's work. C'mon."

On the drive, they passed the Lee Chi Tea Garden and Neal shouted to his father to stop.

"Let's do what Eva wants to."

"Why? You were right about it never agreeing with her."

"Neal," she droned sourly, "you must be the only kid in the world who always gets his own way by giving in to other people."

"That's uncalled for," Jay said, pushing his foot hard on the accelerator so that they passed the restaurant in a flash.

"He's just a smart little bastard . . . too smart."

Jay hit her in the stomach with his elbow, without taking his eyes off the road.

"Daddy, don't!" Neal screamed.

"You watch your mouth with the child."

Eva did not react; she merely rubbed her stomach and slumped back in the seat.

"If you can't hold your liquor, then stay home!"

"One of these days . . . you and that kid," she threatened.

"Don't make threats unless you intend to carry them out."

They drove in silence, and Neal wondered, wondered for the thousandth time, why his father had married someone he so obviously despised. What had the reason been, the compulsion? Their marriage was a series of humiliations for both of them. Was it possible to make the same mistake twice? His father still had women—Neal had met a few of them in the showroom. They had all offered to take him to the circus. Nothing seemed to make sense when one became an adult. Didn't people have clear-cut choices which even a child could understand? Although he admired his father, he could not respect him: he didn't approve of hitting women.

"What's gonna happen?"

"Happen?" Jay repeated.

"To all of us," Neal said.

"See"—he prodded Eva—"you've upset him. Why we can't have a quiet family dinner once in a while is a mystery to me."

"No mystery at all," Eva shrugged apathetically. "It's simply that you love Neal more than me and you never stop reminding me that you do. If I did the same thing with Lorna, you'd go off your nut. That is if you gave a good goddamn about me or her."

"You're very warped," Jay said. "Now let's change the subject."

They changed the subject, or at least Jay did.

"How're you doing in school?"

"All right."

"All right, he says, when everybody tells me that he's the smartest kid in the whole school."

"I've heard this routine before."

"A genius. That's what his teacher told me. Tops on his I.Q. test."

"You should've warned me and I would have brought ear-plugs."

"Don't you take any pride in him?"

"Why should I? He only stands between us. Once I thought it was Herb who was our personal ghost. Now I know it's not, never has been."

"Who's Herb?" Neal asked.

"An old friend of Eva's."

"What happened?"

"Just deal you into the conversation? That what we're sup-posed to do?" Eva said.

"I just wanted to know."

"None of your business."

"Herb died a long time ago," Jay explained.

"We killed him. Me and your father."

"If you open your trap I'll dump you right out of the car."

Jay pulled into the Little Neck Steak House, and the parking attendant took the car. He and Neal walked ahead, and Eva trailed them in. A rustic wood-panelled bar led into the res-taurant. It was crowded and people were talking loudly and burning holes in each other's clothes with their cigarettes. Everyone seemed to be high in one way or another.

"Can I have a horse's neck?" Neal asked.

"Course you can."

Jay pushed his way into the bar, and the bartender, a tall, blond man with a tired hangdog expression, a walking ency-clopaedia of other people's troubles, suddenly became ani-mated.

"Well, as I live and breathe, Mr. Blackman."

"Hiya, Charlie. Since when've you been working here?"

"A month tomorrow. From the opening. It must be a good few years since I seen you last. You stopped coming into the St. Moritz with Mr. Fredericks."

"A lifetime ago."

Eva shoved her head through.

"Hello, hello, hello. Still the most beautiful redhead in New York."

Eva blinked.

"Charlie?"

"Right, Miss Meyers."

"Blackman."

"Congrats."

"Still double scotches on the rocks?"

"She'll drink anything. Sneaky Pete, if you sell it here."

"Always with the jokes, Mr. B, huh?"

"Junior'll have a horse's neck."

"That's ginger ale with grenadine, a slice of orange and a cherry," Neal said.

"Done," Charlie said. "It's good to see a few familiar faces."

"What kinda crowd they get here?"

"A few hookers. Amateurs. Cheaters and players mostly doing the circuit. Husbands can't afford the prices."

"I might come by during the week," Jay whispered.

Eva found herself a barstool, a few drunks away.

"Meet my boy Neal."

Charlie extended a wet paw and shook Neal's hand.

"If you're anything like your father, you'll go places, Neal."

Neal sulked against the bar. He found comparisons with his father distasteful. He didn't want to be like Jay, and everyone he met told him he ought to be. He couldn't understand adults. He would have preferred to spend the weekend with Zimmerman watching Lady Farberman, who operated nonstop on weekends. She had had more pricks in her than a porcupine, Zimmerman said, and Neal thought the joke was terribly funny and repeated it to everyone. Eva was ready for another drink before Jay had even bent his elbow.

"Things okay by you, Mr. B?" Charlie said, nodding his head in Eva's direction.

"Oh, marvelous. I'd like her to drive home now. Right now."

"In her condition?"

"Exactly."

"Oh, I'm sorry. You useta be so happy together."

"Yeah, well . . ." Jay finished his drink and went over to Eva. "Ready to eat?"

"I am eating."

"Yeah? Well, don't embarrass me."

He slipped Charlie two five-dollar bills.

"One's for you . . . and she can drink the other. If she starts getting loud or falls on her ass, send me a telegram."

"Thanks Mr. B."

"I'll have one more at the table. No bar scotch, though, Charlie. Black Label."

A crowd of people waited behind a cord where a slim-hipped man in a tight-fitting suit flapped a pack of menus against his wrist. Jay walked up to him.

"Blackman, table for three."

"Yes sir, Mr. Blackman. I took the reservation myself. Got a nice booth for you facing the fireplace."

Neal picked up the menu while the waiter stood punctiliously waiting for their order . . .

"I got a drink at the bar," Jay said. "Ask Charlie."

Charlie brought the drink to the table and gave Jay a perplexed look.

"I don't know what to say, Mr. Blackman. With the kid here, I don't like to . . ."

"Don't worry about him. Just spit it out."

"She left." He shrugged his shoulders awkwardly and leaned on the table, avoiding Neal's stare of amazement. "With some guy . . . a greaseball mambo teacher that hangs out here. A sort of specialist in married women."

"Thanks, Charlie."

"You want me to call the parking lot and have them stop his car?"

"Don't bother. Maybe I'll get lucky and she'll have an accident."

Jay's mood was buoyant throughout dinner. Like one of those "magic" blackboards with a thin sheet of translucent paper on it that could erase automatically when you lifted it up, he succeeded in extirpating Eva from his mind. She existed in some kind of vague peripheral relationship to him and he could shut her out whenever he chose to do so. It was a facility he was grateful to possess. From the moment he had resumed his affair with her, after leaving Rhoda, he had known that not only were they doomed people, but they were also out of love. He neither desired her nor affected desire: it was all as dead, as insubstantial as cigarette ash. He had been motivated by a lack of feeling, a tired insouciance, a hollow sensation and the urge to fill it in some way, and he had married her, although he realized that she no longer wanted or needed marriage. They lived on an emotional continent of old wounds and forgotten passion. The ingredients for a fire were there but they had become useless, partly, Jay knew, because he had become inaccessible. He could not even conjure up the ghosts of his dead loves: spectres also turn to dust. Only with Neal he came alive and he perceived with one of the few important insights he had ever had about himself that his all-embracing love for the boy was the result of love diverted, which did not render it any less potent. Neal came to possess him and he created an aura around him that people reserve for objects of piety, and rightly so, for when they are invested with flesh, made incarnate, they destroy and are destroyed.

"You're not happy, are you, Dad?"

"When we're together I am. I only wish that could be more often. Once a week and every fourth weekend isn't enough. I live for seeing you . . . I build my life around it. Doesn't matter if I'm busy or have to go out of town. Nothing's as important to me as being with you."

"I can't live with you."

"I know that. Maybe it's good that you can't. Eva's not the sort of person that you should live with."

"Is she always as bad as tonight?"

"It's mostly when you come that she goes off the rails. And the crazy thing is that deep down she cares for you. Eva buys all the presents I give you. I mean sometimes she'll pop into the showroom and say: 'Jay, I just saw the most terrific sweater for Neal.' And I say: 'Buy it then.' And she'll hold up a bag. 'That's just what I did, Jay. I bought it.' There's a lot of good in her. Mostly, I guess, it's my fault, because I'm always talking about you to everybody and she feels left out. Especially as she's got a kid who she never sees and can't stand."

"Why's that?"

"Reminds her of things she'd like to forget. Oh, Neal, it's such a mishmash. You think you're doing something because you want to, and you find out too late that you never wanted it in the first place. And you're lumbered. Make sure you learn from my mistakes and when you're old enough to get married be certain that there's no bad blood between you and the girl and you're not doing it to make up for something you did wrong. An apology shouldn't last a lifetime."

"Dad, if I tell you something, will you promise not to go back and tell Rhoda?"

Jay smiled at him and nodded.

Neal always called his mother by her first name when he spoke of her with Jay. The division had been made for him, and he could not reunite them, either in his mind or in conversation, because this created an illusion of unanimity which altered the balance of reality, and Neal was forced to avoid this myth in order to survive. He hated confusion. There were carefully defined borders, artificial ones, and they must be observed.

"Rhoda's got a man."

"A man? I thought men."

"A special one."

Jay made a gurgling sound as he swallowed his brandy.

"Since when?"

"Dunno. I found him asleep this morning."

"What'd you do?"

"I burned his clothes—in the incinerator."

"Whaaat? Burned them? Just like that?"

"Uh-huh."

"That's pretty funny. Practical joke, huh? I'll bet Rhoda and him were tee'd off."

"It wasn't really a joke. He might've been a thief or something and he could have tried to escape. But not without his clothes." He looked at Jay for support, and Jay touched him affectionately on the shoulder. "I mean he was a stranger . . . and I was a stranger and anything could've happened. He could've attacked Rhoda."

"A gorilla couldn't attack Rhoda."

"I thought of something even worse to do: pour boiling water on his face, so he couldn't move until I got the police."

"I'm glad you didn't do that," Jay said uneasily.

"He tried to be nice when I got home from school."

"He was still there? Without his clothes . . . ?"

"He was wearing some of the old stuff you left."

"What'd Rhoda have to say?"

"Angry. She was very angry, and she screamed, but I didn't tell her the truth. I couldn't. I can't tell her the truth about anything."

"I couldn't either."

"I always lie to her, and tell you the truth," Neal lied.

"The man try to hit you or something?"

"He didn't have the guts to. He wants Rhoda's money."

Jay seemed perplexed and leaned conspiratorially close to Neal.

"What makes you think that?"

"He would have beat the hell out of me if he was a man. If he didn't *want* something from her . . . She should've introduced me, don't you think? It would've been different then, don't you see?" he said with feverish animation.

"Of course, Neal. She should've introduced you. Making a flop-house outa your home. The woman's got more nerve than brains. She doesn't think about anybody but herself."

Neal nodded gravely.

"I'm glad I told you."

"You can always tell me everything, like I do you. We're not just father and son, we're buddies. You're my best friend."

"I'd trust you with my life," Neal said.
"You are."

Jay was disturbed by Neal's predicament and they drove home
unusually silent. Huntingdon Close was a treelined cul-de-sac
and Great Neck's most fashionable road. It represented for Jay
the embodiment of all the synthetic ideals he had picked up
from the movies: the penniless provincial foreigner who eventually winds up his jaded existence on millionaire's row—
self-made, country-club set, hunting lodge in Vermont, winter
villa in Florida, a boat on the Sound—in short his new life
was a sharp reproach to the society that created both him and
the illusionary vision he sustained in symbolic counterpoint.
Jay, however, had broken the mold. Except for the house,
which he had built at Eva's insistence, he enjoyed none of the
privileges that money entitled him to. He had undergone a
profound change, so profound that he could not gauge the
extent of it and he never regarded it as anything but a sudden
and inexplicable loss of faith in his old ideals. His business
no longer had any fascination; through sheer energy and ability
it had become largely autonomous: it was too big for any man,
and he and Marty had delegated most of the responsibility to
half a dozen young creative people who injected a new dynamism into a giant grown unwieldy. They had three hundred
shops from coast to coast and a dozen factories operating
round the clock, and although the reins of the business were
still held firmly in Jay's hands, he no longer had the drive and
initiative which had created a multimillion-dollar business out
of a small shop and a marginal wholesaler's loft.

The center of his universe was Neal; only Neal could re-
create the terrible agonizing love that he had felt towards
Terry. It was primarily an uncreative relationship in that it
ripped out his heart and guts, for he realized that the child was
suffering, that his loyalties were still divided, that he had developed a shell of armor as obvious as that of a turtle, and
that he was too old for his years. His manner and attitude Jay
found inscrutable. The divorce was a fact of life which Neal

had accepted calmly but it had driven him underground, and Jay always had the sensation of pursuing an elusive and wily animal with an innate sense of survival and all the destructive weapons of the beast in retreat.

Of all things, Jay had developed a conscience about Rhoda. He recognized the wisdom of activating the dead battery her life had become. The store he gave her in the divorce settlement provided her with a purpose and an interest. She was an excellent saleswoman, but she had been too deeply schooled in Finkelstein's business methods, and this very nearly destroyed the store. Two years earlier she had got into a terrible muddle with her accounts, bills were overdue, manufacturers were screaming about injunctions and subpoenas, and the staff was stealing with impunity. Jay had heard through trade gossip about this state of affairs, and at nine o'clock on a Monday morning, after almost two years of freedom, he had presented himself at the shop with two of his accountants, a batch of signs that proclaimed "Sale! Sale! Sale!" even though it was only November, and he had in ten minutes fired every sales assistant—eleven of them—given them two weeks' severance pay, and had closed the shop for the day.

When Rhoda had arrived she was astonished to find the store closed and had pounded on the door for a good ten minutes.

One of Jay's minions let her in.

"What's going on?" she had protested. "Did we have a fire?"

"No, Mr. Blackman's taken over."

"Taken over? He can't do that. It's not his to take."

She rushed into the small office in the back where the accountants were wrestling with double-entry books six months out of date which seemed to have been kept by someone using the continental form of seven and who had then decided that seven and four made eight.

"Jay, what d'you think you're doing? Where's all the girls?"

"I threw them out. I'm trying to straighten out this shithouse."

"Who asked—?"

"I can't let you go under . . . It makes me look bad."

"What about my staff?"

"I hired six girls, Saturday morning."

"Six? I had eleven."

"You had six girls. The other five sat on their asses when they weren't robbing you blind."

"You don't have any authority here. It's mine."

"I've got the authority of the bankruptcy courts. 'Cause if I don't take the bull by the horns, you'll be sitting there next month and tears won't do a bit of good. They'll chop you up like you were a piece of liver."

She pointed to a bespectacled little man with exquisitely shaped hands, using three different colored inks.

"Who's that?"

"That, Rhoda, is an accountant. He sees to it that if any stealing's going on, you're doing it. You're getting rooked, left, right, and center." He held up a sheaf of papers. "Bills, most of them ninety days overdue. They can put you in the hands of a receiver for something like this. It's a miracle you're not on the street already."

"What do you mean by that?" she said angrily.

"Look, Rhoda, what you don't know about business could fill the *Encyclopaedia Britannica*. When you got the store, the articles of incorporation were dissolved. I told you to become a limited company for fifty dollars. Any neighborhood shyster with a notary public stamp could've done it for you. Limited company, limited liability. They can't touch your personal assets. You wouldn't listen to me. They can put a lien on your bank account, take all your personal possessions at home . . . furniture, clothes, Neal's things, goddamnit! Do you understand now?"

The little man triggered some figures on an adding machine.

"Eleven thousand, two hundred and forty-six dollars, and sixty-one cents," he said. "Could be worse."

"Which means a loss of thirty thousand dollars on top of that, at the old net-profit figures. Added to a five percent loss in potential turnover figures. Forty-eight thousand."

The man turned some pages, did a few quick sums, and turned to Jay.

"How do you remember figures like that with so many stores and factory production figures as well? You're five hundred dollars off. How do you do it?"

"If you knew the answer to that, I'd be the accountant and you'd be running the business. You make out the checks and I'll sign them."

"Do you want to establish any cash balance with any of the people she owes money to? They might not want to give her credit in future."

"When they see my signature on the checks, they'll know the business is solvent and they'll give her all the credit she needs."

All the checks were signed in fifteen minutes.

"Willie," he said to the other man at the desk, "call a messenger service. I don't want any of these checks mailed. All delivered by hand and put one of my personal compliment slips in every envelope."

"Yes, Mr. Blackman."

Jay walked through to the front of the store and looked at the dresses on the racks. He picked up a dress every now and then and threw it to the floor in disgust.

"What're you doing, selling to funeral parlors? I can't believe that you bought all this *dreck*. Must be a blind man who's picking out this garbage."

"I haven't had time to cover the market and the store, so I only get to the city once a month."

"Then who's been giving you this crap?" He examined a dress, and recoiled when he saw it was priced at fifteen dollars. "This is a copy of one of my dresses. Blunt knocked it off. Mine sold at sixty dollars a dozen. So how in hell's name can you charge fifteen for a dress that isn't worth four?"

"I paid a hundred and twenty a dozen for it."

"Not possible. You know too much about dresses to be taken in."

"Jean, my manageress, bought it. I okayed the invoice. She

bought it from one of the salesmen who represents about six manufacturers.''

''Oh, my God,'' Jay moaned. ''Willie,'' he screamed. ''Get out here.''

Willie appeared, rubbing ink stains off his cuff.

''Check every one of Blunt's invoices and find the dress that goes with it. She's being overcharged.''

''The salesman usually gets here on Mondays. I wonder what he'll think when he sees the store closed.''

''What's his name?''

''Freddie Stevens.''

A face peered into the darkened grimy window, and a hand rapped against it. Jay opened the door. The man was wearing a camel's hair coat, a porkpie hat, and a slimline mustache.

''Good morning,'' Jay said.

''Wha' happened?''

''Who are you?''

''Freddie Stevens.''

''Come in, Freddie.''

''I know you?''

''You will. How are the horses treating you?''

Freddie smiled a whole set of capped teeth.

''Not bad. I hit the double at Hialeah on Friday. Been balling it up all weekend.''

''I like a man who knows his horses.''

''Thanks, friend. Where's Jean?''

''Jean took the day off.''

''Rhoda still running the joint?''

''In a manner of speaking.''

''Well, I've got some terrific numbers to show her. Immediate delivery.''

Jay switched the light on.

''Rhoda, Mr. Stevens is here to see you.''

Rhoda picked her way through a rail of dresses.

''Hiya, Rho, how're things? Where's Jean?''

''Off,'' she said, glaring at him.

''Somethin' wrong?'' he asked uneasily.

"No, what've you got?"

He opened his sample case, pulled out eight dresses.

"All colors and sizes except black and brown. And I can get you delivery no later than tomorrow afternoon. What do you say? They're runners everywhere."

"I've got something to tell you, you little mother-fucker," Jay broke in. "These dresses are last year's, and Blunt's got a factory full of them. They only sold in brown and black and you're out of stock on them."

"Now hold on, friend."

"I'm not your friend, I'm your enemy. And you're out of a job."

"Who the hell do you think you are? I work for Blunt."

"And Blunt does what I tell him to do, or he's up shit's creek. Now come into the office or do you want me to get tough and call the cops. You'll get three years for fraud and embezzling."

"You don't scare me."

"I will, don't worry."

They walked into the office in silence like pallbearers at a funeral.

"All done, Mr. Blackman. The messenger service'll be here in half an hour. And the goods should come by three. I just rang the office."

"You Jay Blackman?" Stevens asked, white-faced.

Jay dialed a number and waited.

"Mr. Blunt in? Tell him it's Jay Blackman."

"Jay? Hiya. How's the boy?" Blunt said affably.

"Not bad, not good, Milty. I'm afraid I've got some unpleasant news for you."

"Oh, Jay?"

"You know that five-oh-six number that you copied from me last season?"

"Yeah, sure."

"How much was it?"

"Hang on? Hey, you're not sore, are you?"

"Why should I be? It helped my own sales. They took one look at your *schmata* and bought me for two bucks more."

"It was thirty-six dollars a dozen."

"Not a hundred and twenty?"

"A hundred and twenty! Stop kidding. We're not making for Saks."

"Well you got a character who's been giving invoices for a hundred and twenty a dozen. A *putz* called Stevens. He's been peddling them to my wife's manageress and they've been splitting the difference."

"Your wife?"

"Rhoda's of King's Highway."

"I thought you sold that store."

"I gave it to her. Now, Milty, please, tell me you're not involved, because if you are you'll be making mailsacks in Ossining."

"Jay, I swear on my mother, on my kids, that I don't know anything about it."

"I sent out a check to you for fifteen hundred dollars on an overdue bill. It's a phony bill. Now either you wipe it off the slate or I take action. Somebody's got to make up the discrepancy. Either you or Stevens?"

"Stevens been robbing her? I don't know a thing about it."

"I'll find out. But make sure you're not lying to me." He slammed the phone down and turned to Stevens who gave him a glassy-eyed stare. He touched his mustache nervously and lit a cigarette.

"You know what happens to people who try to fuck me in business. They wind up on a bread line. Now you got a choice: either you come across with the dough or I ring the Brooklyn D.A. who's a pal of mine."

"How much do you want?"

"Every penny you and that broad stole. You got till one o'clock to bring the money . . . in cash. You been lucky with the ponies so you must have some stashed away."

Stevens' mouth trembled and he began to stammer.

"If only I'd known it was your—"

"It doesn't matter whose business it is. When you decide to steal, you make sure that you're smarter than the people you're screwing."

"I've got twelve hundred in the bank."

"Okay, Willie will go with you, just to see that nobody knocks you on the head carrying such a large sum. And even though you're not worth my time and trouble, I'm personally going to shit-list you with every dress house in the country. I think you'd better find a new trade."

Willie and Stevens left the room and Jay and Rhoda stood staring at each other.

"You finished?" Jay asked the man at the desk.

"I'll go back to the office," he said.

"Take the day off. You've done a good morning's work."

Jay slipped a hip flask out of his pocket and took a long pull.

"You never liked booze, or I'd offer you one," he said to Rhoda.

"I never remember you walking around with a bar."

"You take pills and I drink a little too much. There's not much to choose between the two."

"You told Blunt I was your wife. Shouldn't you have said ex-wife?"

"It didn't cross my mind."

"Eva'd take offense."

"Eva?" Jay shrugged his shoulders indifferently.

"You're going to marry her, aren't you?"

"Who knows?"

"Jay, I'm very grateful for what you've done. There's still some feeling left, isn't there?"

"You're a good person, Rhoda. And I've hurt you. If I can make it up . . ." He put on his hat and coat and started for the door. "A few of my people will be down this afternoon to unpack the merchandise I've given you. They'll set up the sale as well. Every rag, five bucks. Take it or leave it. Don't fight success, Rhoda, and you'll do all right. You're peddling rags to Brooklyn housewives, they don't want to know from Paris fashions. Give Neal a kiss from me, and tell him I'll see him on Sunday as usual."

*   *   *

A week after that, on an icy Monday, Jay and Eva were married in Syracuse. He could see out of the window, over the judge's shoulder, the snow-blanketed streets and people in galoshes and boots trudging through the slush. As he stood there listening to the judge intoning the words of the marriage ceremony, he had a vision of Terry and himself lying on the sand—the timbre of her voice a bit high-pitched with a broad "a" sound. Beneath the exterior of gentility and gracious living she had been just as dirty as him—something that had crawled out of a fetid and contaminated cloaca—with the same emotional needs. As with most philanderers, a strong puritan reaction to smut was submerged in the muddy waters of Jay's life fluids; he could accept wallowing in the mud with Eva, because he knew they were cut from the same piece of material, but he had imagined Terry belonged to some illusory high caste which he had dreamed of joining. The real estate venture with Fredericks had fallen through shortly afterwards. He had received an amicable letter with his check enclosed, stressing the fact that his investment would not be secure. Property was a gamble and Doug didn't like to endanger funds given by friends. "Friends" was a nice touch which was not wasted on Jay.

The judge had a powdery belt of dandruff on the shoulder of his navy blue serge suit, which gave it the appearance of a carefully crocheted lace shawl, and Jay had a nagging desire to brush it off.

"Do you take this woman . . . ?"

A man slipped on the icy pavement and a little boy helped him up and took his hand. How would Neal feel about Eva?

"To have and to hold . . ."

He had been able to help Rhoda and he was pleased with himself. What had been impossible in marriage had proved expedient in dissolution. Neal had eyes . . . such terribly deep eyes that swallowed Jay up whenever he looked at him. The eyes didn't look, they peered through the layers of defenses which Jay had erected. The hero's armor weighed him down. The eyes probed, and Jay was stripped naked. How could he get to Neal? Which button should he press? He couldn't buy him off, because he had an innate contempt for money that was almost patrician. He belonged to the caste that Jay had failed to get into.

"From this day forward . . . ?"

And Immie, what had become of Immie? Was he still serving greasy hamburgers and heartburn coffee in the same all-night dive on Delancey Street. And Barney Green? Could he make you laugh! Once he thought he had seen Barney in a nightclub. But it couldn't have been Barney because the man was wearing a waiter's uniform.

"I do," he heard his voice carry in the high-ceilinged chamber, with its rows of books in a glass case. A man living in a glass cage. Eva lifted her white veil. Rose-colored lipstick didn't suit her—too much blue in it.

He pressed his mouth against hers and tasted treacly chemicals. A nauseating taste. He'd have to tell her to take it off. The judge shook his head excitedly and dandruff floated through the air. Outside it had begun to snow heavily, and an Ontario wind yelped like a banshee as figures now dim through the frosted window struggled to cross the street, and cars stalled.

"Ten dollars a bottle, I've never had champagne that cost so much," the judge's wife, an old lady dressed in a Gibson Girl blouse and a tweed skirt two sizes too small, intoned to the gods.

"You want to get away from this weather," the judge said. "What say? Ah, Cuba. Havana? Well, well, well, I always smoke their cigars. A friendly race? Of course they are, Mother. All brown-skinned people are friendly. I remember reading . . ."

The chauffeur-driven car took them to the airport, and Blake, the factory manager, handed Jay a bottle of scotch to see them through the flight. Change at La Guardia Airport for a direct flight to Havana. Brown-skinned people, he thought, opening the bottle of scotch, are friendly. The stewardess brought them a setup of ice and glasses and Jay offered her a ten-dollar tip which she declined. Company rules. Eva held the bottle firmly in her hands; her nails were painted silver. She looked like a whore, he thought.

"No more of this," she said, "once we get settled. Have a new place of our own. A proper home. Only to be social." She tipped the bottle and gave them triples. "I'm so happy, Jay darling. It's been worth all the heartache."

"The heartache?"

"We love each other, so we've made each other suffer."

"Of course. Here's looking at you." Chivas Regal, trust Blake. A good guy.

The engines revved up and the plane started to move like a snowbird leaving the arctic or coming home to it.

"After your mother died—"

"Let's not talk about her."

"Sorry, hon. It reminds you—"

"Of good things. Of old smells, good smells."

"Funny memory."

"I always remember with my nose. That way I don't forget."

"I only remember camphor. Our house stank of it. I sent my mother a telegram."

"You're a good girl," he closed his hand around hers.

"We're off. A new beginning."

With the same ending, he thought bitterly.

The room at the Nacional overlooked the sea. A calm emerald and blue sea with palm fronds flickering gently in the distance.

"Jay, the bathroom's all tiled. Mosaic. I think we'll have something similar when we build the house. And for God's sake will you look at this. It looks like . . . but it's not."

"A bidet."

"I want one."

"Why get a small one? I'll get you the giant size."

"Oh, Jay, you're kidding. They only make one size."

"I'll be in the bar when you've finished unpacking."

"Now, Jay—"

"About an hour?"

"Not too much."

"I know when to stop. I've been well trained."

The barman asked him if he wanted to go to a whorehouse and Jay said yes. A taxi driver approached him as he left the bar.

"Usted el señor?"

Jay nodded. A road that snaked around the harbor eventually found its way to a small cobbled street on a hill. There was a smell of bread coming from a shop opposite the bar he entered. He followed the driver up a flight of stairs and a woman of about fifty flashed a welcoming smile at him. The taxi driver said to the woman: "Un señor . . . Un caballero. Americano."

She shook her head and her smile broadened into an expanse of ivory-colored teeth. The girls were all pretty and young. The oldest was about eighteen, and he went with her. He smoked a cigarette in the room, tossed her ten dollars and as she was about to remove her suspender belt, he changed his mind and left. The driver came after him, volatile and upset. Jay handed him five dollars and he was soothed. Jay went into the bakery and bought a loaf of bread, still hot from the oven, and ate it in the back of the taxi on the way back to the hotel.

Eva was wearing a black, sequined, low-necked dress. She had changed her lipstick and Jay felt happier. Two couples were talking loudly at her, and Jay watched her holding court while the barman rattled a jug of martinis with a long metal spoon.

"The man himself," she said, and the four of them turned to look at him.

"Worth waiting for," one of the women said.

"Where've you been, darling?"

"Buying myself bread."

"Oh, he's always kidding. Never know when to take him seriously. Jay, these lovely people have asked us to join them for dinner. I wouldn't make a decision until I asked you."

"Sure. Why not?"

"Party, party," a man in a seersucker suit and crew cut

said. He forced his hand on Jay. "Mah name's Hiram Gilbert and this is my wife Florence. We from Atlanta. Where you folks from?"

"New York."

"Yankees," his wife cackled.

The other couple were also from Atlanta and they were called Langford.

"You call me Lang and him Gil, heah?" Langford guffawed.

It was like that for ten days. Jay even got to like Southern Comfort and he liked the women so much that he slept with both of them, separately, but on the same afternoon, while Eva soaked her stockings in the bidet. He smiled to himself when he overheard Gil and Lang talking heatedly about how much they'd give for a peep inside Eva's drawers. They only had to buy her a drink.

He pulled the big Caddy convertible into Huntingdon Close. The engine purred softly down the new macadam. The road was lined with Oregon spruce, pine, and fir. Huge trees bought fully grown by the householders of the road; they got shade, the illusion of privacy in an area where even what a man ate for dinner was public knowledge, and they represented a tacit cognition of not to say a communion with nature. Man cannot live by mortar alone, but most of the people on the road did. Neal had drifted into a doze on the ride home, and Jay was reluctant to wake him. He slid the big car into the driveway circling the house and turned off the ignition. He opened Neal's door with care, arched his arm under his back and lifted him up. Thin for his age, needs fattening up. Needs care, Jay thought. He pressed the buzzer and the maid came immediately. She was about to speak, but Jay put his finger to his lips, and indicated Neal, sleeping in his arms. She walked quickly up the stairs and opened the door of Neal's room. A bedside lamp was switched on, and Jay began to undress Neal. Neal stirred and Jay shushed him.

"It's late," he said. "And you've had a big dinner."

"All right," Neal said, closing his eyes, as Jay and the maid put his pajamas on. Jay opened the windows and then kissed Neal on the forehead.

The maid was waiting outside on the landing for him.

"Whatsa matter, Ruby?"

"Dunno what to say. Mrs. Blackman—"

"Well, what about her?"

"I'd like to give you notice."

"Notice? What for?"

"She's downstairs . . . that's all. I'll go in the morning. You get yourself another girl from the agency."

"Now what's this all about? We like you."

"And I like *you.*" She pointed a finger at Jay to make her meaning clear.

He hurried down the stairs, taking them two at a time, and rushed into the study, but she wasn't there. He saw a light from under the living room door, and heard the sound of music, something low and romantic, coming from the room. He pushed open the door slowly, until it was flush against the wall and he could take in the full room. Eva was stripped down to her brassiere and panties and a man was sitting on the sofa applauding softly, like an opera lover at the end of an aria.

"Just in time for the late show," Eva said.

Jay pointed to the door and told the man to get out.

"Just a minute, pal. I was invited in here."

"Get out before I throw you out and then run you down with my car."

"A tough guy, huh?"

"Look, this is my house, and my wife."

"Oh, so you remembered who I was?" Eva piped in.

"Sorry, I didn't know this lady was married," the man said, starting for the door. "I got a totally wrong impression."

"Yeah, well it's been corrected for you."

"He's my guest," Eva shouted.

"Get dressed and go to a motel with him if you like, or go to bed."

"Alone again?"

"Didn't your mother ever teach you a little proverb? You don't shit where you eat. There's a child in the house. My child, and I don't want him to be upset."

"But I'm upset, doesn't that matter?"

"See you folks," the man said.

"You upset?" Jay said contemptuously. "Nothing can upset you."

"The minute I met you my life was over. Only I didn't realize it."

"What do you want?"

"Love. I want you to love me. You did at one time. When Rhoda threw you out, it was me who picked up the pieces."

"You could've said no. I wouldn't have minded."

"Then why did you come back and why did we live together for five years as man and wife, and why did you marry me?"

"Because I didn't care any longer."

"It was because of Marty, wasn't it?"

"Marty? Why Marty?"

"You were sore, weren't you, that Marty should be interested in me?"

"He was welcome to you."

"I wasn't going to sit around waiting for you to come back whenever you goddamn pleased, or when you got tired of your college girl. And Marty was very sympathetic."

"I'm not interested in the details. I wasn't at the time, and I'm not now."

"He was going to divorce his wife and marry me, did you know that?"

"I saved him the trouble."

"And he stepped out like a gentleman. Because he was more concerned about you than himself."

"I'll thank him tomorrow at the office. Let's forget ancient history. It proves nothing. Except that instead of one mistake I made two."

"More than two. There'll be Neal as well. You're ruining him."

"Let me be the judge of that," he said calmly. He was tired, and his heart palpitated. Irregular beats. He was getting dizzy. He moved the palm of his hand under his jacket, and she looked anxiously at him..

"Jay, what's wrong? Aren't you feeling well?"

"Just treat Neal with kindness and I'll give you anything you want."

"I want it to be for my sake, not his."

"It's too late. Too late for romance."

"It's crazy. I'm still young and you too. You'll live a long time if you take care of yourself . . . if you let me. We've got everything to live for. To be happy."

He moved his hand away from his heart and lit a cigarette with a shaking hand.

"Eva, why don't you get a divorce? This time it'll be painless."

She glared at him and came across the room, her face beet red, and said venomously:

"Never . . . I'm not going to be easy like Rhoda. I'll never divorce you. I'll see you dead first."

17

S he's got a thing with him, huh?" Zimmerman asked as they sat in the schoolyard after classes had ended. "Your mom, and Sports. I think he's a pretty nice guy."

"Your mother can marry him then."

"Aw, c'mon, she's married to my father. They can't . . ."

"He's a phony. You can tell a mile away."

"A nice one though."

"There's no such thing as a nice phony. Either you're real, like my father, or you're nothing."

Moony joined them. He was taller and altogether larger than Neal and Zimmerman. He had slanting peanut-colored eyes,

not quite brown, not quite yellow, a large bulbous nose, hair
stiff as cardboard which was held in place by something called
hair trainer. His hair was pushed forward in a three-inch pom-
padour, which he combed and recombed four or five hundred
times a day. An eleven-inch comb jutted out of the back
pocket of his electric blue, ten-inch pegged trousers, which
had dark blue pistol pockets in the back. He always felt a bit
inferior to the other boys because his father was a mechanic
and didn't make as much money; consequently he was the
toughest, most aggressive boy in the school, feared by everyone and the scourge of the teachers. He was the only boy in
school who had got laid, and Neal respected him.

"What're you crumbs doing?" Moony asked. He affected
tough-guy talk with anyone smaller than himself.

"Wanta play stickball?" Zimmerman said.

"It's too hot."

"Here"—Neal handed him a cigarette. "Have a Camel.
Puts hair on your balls."

Moony took it greedily.

"You always got some, don't you?"

"I say they're for my mother when anyone asks."

"I didn't mean that. I mean you got money for 'em."

"So? Big deal. I've got the money."

"Know how I get mine?"

Both boys looked at him inquisitively.

"I go on jobs." He took something out of his pocket,
pressed a small button the size of a pinhead and there was a
zang sound, and they stood staring raptly at the steel blade,
six inches long, which glinted in the sun, and reminded Neal
of the silver scaly back of a sunfish he had once caught.

"Wow, wow. A pushbutton."

"I saw one that the guineas use. It's called a stiletto. Comes
out of the top. You hold it against a guy's back and press the
button and the knife goes into him."

"This one comes outa the side."

"Where'd you get it?" said Zimmerman, awestruck.

"That *schmuck* that runs the army-navy store on Utica Avenue. Know the one?"

"Uh-huh."

"Well, I went into the store and asked him to get something from the back. A tent. By the time he got it out, I'd opened the showcase and robbed this. My big beautiful Betsy, that's what I call her."

"What if someone catches you with it?" Neal asked.

"You're not chicken shit are you, Neal?"

"No, I'm not."

"So why ask?"

"What do you do with it? Play Territory?" Zimmerman interposed, sticking out his hand to take the knife which Moony let him hold.

"On Friday nights when the movies are emptying out I pick me a girl and follow her. Or maybe two girls. I wait till they're alone and then I take out my knife and tell 'em to give me their money or I'll stick 'em."

Zimmerman could hardly believe his ears.

"You don't?"

"I got four dollars last week. Pulled two jobs. And on one of them when the girl handed over her dough, I felt her up too. She had real big soft tits. Then I jerked off in the bushes. Funny girl. She gave me her name and address. Didn't mind about the money. Said I should come over her house whenever I wanted to, but to bring my prick along."

"Bullshit," Neal said.

"Want to come with me? She's fourteen years old. Goes to Tilden. Seymour from Carrol Street says she likes line-ups, and he ought to know, 'cause they had a gang-bang in his club-room and she was one of the girls. Her and another broad from St. John's Place. Fourteen guys screwed them."

"Gee, I'd like to have been there," Zimmerman said.

"Get a little hair on your *petzel* first. I'm going tonight, so if you don't believe me, you can come too. It'll cost you a buck. They may have a hooker to give blow jobs. Wanta come? Nice big lips on your skinny little winkie. She pulled one guy's off a Chinaman—and now they call him One Ball Hung Low."

"I'll come," Neal said.

The challenge was irresistible, and as he studied Moony's long, horsey face, with its prescience, its overwhelming knowledge and insistence on evil, he felt himself being swallowed up, drawn into fellowship with the older boy.

"I'll meet you at nine o'clock in front of your house," he said.

"Who'll have the bags?" Zimmerman asked.

"You coming too?"

"Yeah, please let me."

"Okay, but it'll cost you a buck even if you don't screw her."

Both the television set and the radio were turned on full blast when Neal entered the apartment. Sports had moved the kitchen table into the small den, and sat with a bottle of rye and a mass of squiggled paper checking the results of the day's baseball games and horse races, and deciding his bets for the three night games.

"Hiya, Neal," he said amiably. "How was school?"

"Okay."

"Your mom's gone to the butcher and the grocery to do some shopping."

"Why?"

"For supper."

"She isn't cooking, is she?"

"Sure."

"She doesn't know how," Neal said contemptuously. "That's why we always eat out."

"No, it's because she's so busy at her store. But she can cook."

"You staying for supper?"

"If you don't mind."

"And if I do?"

"I'll go. I'd like to be friends."

"I've got friends."

Sports poured himself a shot of rye and eased it back calmly. He was wearing another mohair suit which looked exactly like the one Neal had burned.

"We'll get along fine. You'll see," Sports said.

"Are you going to marry my mother?"

"I'd like to."

"You only know each other three weeks."

"Time doesn't matter in these things. You can know a person five years and not know anything about them. And you can meet somebody and in two, three weeks you know all about each other."

Neal pondered for a moment the significance of Sports' declaration of faith.

"Do you work?" he asked.

"I am working."

"At what?"

"Well, if you can keep a secret I'll tell you." He paused and smiled at Neal. "I'll tell you because I'm sure I can trust you. See, if the police found out what I do, they'd come and arrest me."

"No kidding?"

Neal was shaking with excitement.

"Because what I do isn't strictly legal. In some places it's legal but not here in New York."

"Honest?"

"So if I trust you, you've got to keep it to yourself. Promise?"

"I swear to God."

"I'm a bookmaker."

"You bet on games and horses and things."

"No, other people bet with me. There's no reason why it shouldn't be legal. The church kicks up a stink though, so the cops have no choice. I mean I could be a grocer, couldn't I? There's no law against selling milk and butter. It's a service for people, and the grocer is entitled to make a profit. So I give a service to people. If they want to bet on the Yankees over Detroit, they can get off with me."

"What happens if they win?"

"I pay them, like a bank would, whatever they've bet."

"And if they lose?"

"I made a profit. Nothing wrong with that, is there? I'm taking a chance."

"Sure you are. Do you know how to cheat at cards, and things like that?"

Sports' sallow skin turned a bright cherry red, and he eased the large windsor knot of his white silk tie and opened the top button of his shirt. He poured himself another shot of rye and added an ice cube and some ginger ale.

"I never cheat," he said primly. "But I know how it's done. I've got to in my business or else I'm sucker bait, aren't I? Every now and then when I'm playing gin with a heavy and I need a little edge, I make a little *peckel* and it helps me over the hurdle. But it's legit."

"Will you teach me how to cheat?"

"I'll show you how it's done. What you do is your business, but it's not a good idea to cheat, 'cause if you get caught, it can be a little difficult healthwise. You can get an arm, a leg, both arms and legs maybe, broken and you can do four or five months in the hospital. Or some night you're crossing a street and wham"—he slammed his palms together and Neal jumped back—"a car bangs you. Hit-and-run accident. Better to be legit and try to get an edge."

"Gee, it must be exciting!" Neal said. Neal sensed that he was an obsessive gambler, and therefore weak.

"Listen, Neal. After supper, I promised to take your mom out. Will it be okay?"

"Sure."

"You don't need a baby-sitter or nothin'?"

He threw out his chest like a Nazi on parade.

"I'm twelve years old."

"Yeah, I forgot. You're a big boy."

Sports stuck out his hand and Neal shook it. He wasn't afraid of Sports.

"We'll be friends, you and me. We just don't crowd each other and everything's hunky dorey."

"I won't say a word to anybody about you being a book-maker," he said, but he was dying to tell Zimmerman, and

Moony, just to boast about a real underworld connection. "Does Mom know about it? I wouldn't even tell her, if you didn't want me to."

"I've let her in on the secret. We'll have fun, Neal. I'll take you to ball games and to the track. Even though you're underage, I'll get you in. A guy at the gate's a pal of mine."

"Boy-oh-boy," he shouted, with false enthusiasm.

The doorbell rang and he answered it. Rhoda, with a load of packages, her face flushed and exultant, leaned against the door and Neal took a bag from her.

"You two . . . been talking?"

"Yeah, Mom. He's really a swell guy."

She put down the packages on the floor and gave Neal a hug.

"I'm so glad you hit it off. It's the real thing, Neal. I think I'm going to marry him. For years I've been wandering around like a drunken sailor, wondering where I could put my head down, and then when I met Sports I knew that I'd found a man who would put me first . . . above everything."

"You're happy?" he asked timorously.

"The way I hoped I would be with Jay."

Surprisingly, Sports ignored them when they walked into the room. He was industriously writing figures on a large piece of drawing paper which had ruled lines on it, and the names of teams and horses and racetracks. He wrote in an exquisitely neat hand as the results, from a team of announcers, came in.

"We mustn't talk to him when he's working," Rhoda said, taking Neal into the kitchen. "He's got to concentrate. One wrong score can cost him thousands of dollars, so it's better to leave him alone."

"Does Jay know?"

"Jay? Why should he? What I do is my business. He didn't tell me he was going to marry that slut of his. He just did, and I found out later. The least he could've done . . ." She sounded like a woman with an old and painful grievance which her new happiness had not dispelled. "I mean to say . . . I was entitled to know, wasn't I?" She turned to Neal who stared out of the window at a game of stickball in progress in

the schoolyard. He couldn't make out the faces of the boys.
"Answer me."

"He says you're going out tonight."

"It's all right by you? You can look after yourself."

"Sure, I'll be okay." He had an image of the clubroom in
his mind: dark, with old camphor-smelling furniture, squalid,
dank, with a laundry sink in it and clothes drying.

After dinner, which was barely edible—burned steak—Neal
found himself alone again with Sports while Rhoda dressed.
She had proved incontestably that she possessed none of the
domestic virtues, but Sports thought otherwise, for Neal
learned that she had prepared the chopped eggs and onion and
steak exactly as he liked it. Neal would go back to the candy
store and Levy's homely cuisine with new enthusiasm. Loung-
ing in the club chair that had formerly been Jay's, his long
legs drooping over the ottoman as though it was his by some
divine right, Sports casually said:

"I had a good day. Need a few . . . ?"

"I don't getcha."

"Moola . . . money?"

"I get an allowance from Jay."

"How much?"

"Three dollars a week."

He handed Neal a five-dollar bill.

"Well, maybe there's somethin' special you wanta buy
yourself? A few extra always comes in handy."

Neal took the money even though he was uncomfortable
about accepting it, for it put him in Sports' camp. When he
held it in his hand, he realized that he had made a mistake,
but it was too late to hand it back. He also felt that he had
compromised Jay's position in his life, for Jay was the giver
of bread, the granter of favors, the all-powerful lawgiver who
decided right and wrong. But now he was joined by another
man, and Neal's confusion and guilt verged on panic. He had
been a traitor to his father's cause—he had allowed a pretender
to usurp his rightful position—but hadn't his parents been trai-
tors as well? Hadn't they in effect created him out of a climate
of hostility, suspicion, lying, deceit, ruthlessly and unfeel-

ingly? Weren't they still groping in the dark for something, a person perhaps, to give their lives a new direction? Wasn't treason the responsibility of the first begetter? Why did he owe them loyalty when they had disclaimed responsibility for him?

It had just begun to get dark when he met Moony in the alley behind the apartment house. He didn't see him at first, because Moony was sitting on top of an ash can, and not by the side of the back entrance where they had agreed to meet. He was chewing a toothpick and it moved rhythmically back and forth. "Hey, what're you doing over there?" Neal asked, a bit fearfully. The older boy had a curiously disquieting effect on him at night.

"Sometimes people throw out money by mistake. I found a fifty-cent piece a week ago."

"Are we going?"

"Yeah, sure we're going."

"Where's Zimmie?"

"He just left."

"Without us?" Neal moaned.

"Naw, he chickened out. I knew he had chicken shit for blood. Talks a good game, but when it comes to doing something he punks out. I could've beat his head in."

"You didn't, did you?" Neal was frightened for his friend. He didn't think that he and Zimmerman combined could take Moony in a fight.

"Know what he said to me? Just 'cause you smell from apeshit, don't think you're Tarzan. I could've slit his balls off for that. Who needs him anyway? He couldn't do anything, 'cause he don't have lead in his pencil."

Neal took out his five-dollar bill and showed it to Moony.

"The treat's on me, Moony."

"A fin! Neal, you're really a friend. I think I'd like you to be my best friend."

Neal was agreeably flattered, but he already had Zimmerman as a best friend. However he was reluctant to offend Moony. You didn't turn people down who offered themselves so openly, and he could use Moony's friendship for terror

value with anyone in the neighborhood he couldn't beat in a
fight.

"You, me, and Zimmie. The three Musketeers."

"Whaaat, Zimmie? After what he said to me! Not if he shit
wooden nickels."

"He's a good guy," Neal affirmed.

Moony's eyes were transfixed on the money.

"Waaal," he drawled, "if he's such a buddy of yours . . .
he must have sompin'."

"We can be buckers," Neal generously offered. "We'll
split the money."

"Aw, Neal, that's crazy."

"I want to."

They walked up the Utica Avenue Hill and stood by the
movie theater. The lights of the marquee were blacked out and
a man on a ladder was hanging the letters on top for the new
feature which began the following day. Neal was restive and
anxious.

"What're we waiting for?"

"We'll do a job first," Moony blandly replied.

"What for? We've got enough money. More than enough."

"That don't matter. I like to do jobs. If I miss a week, I
get rusty. Lookit, if you don't wanta go wid me why don'tcha
wait in the drugstore?" he added diplomatically, not to put
Neal's courage to the test. "You have an ice cream soda, and
I'll meetcha at ten."

"Isn't that late for . . . ?"

"Naw, it never starts before then. She works in Wool-
worth's or somewhere and she doesn't get finished till late."

The theater began to empty and people crowded into the
lobby. Moony peered at the photographs advertising the coming attraction, but out of the corner of his eye he hungrily
sought a victim for his assault. Two girls, one chubby and
about thirteen and the other tall and angular, chewing bubble
gum, passed them.

"C'mon," Moony said out of the side of his mouth.

"Where?"

"Them. We'll get them. They both got pocketbooks."

"Do we grab them and run?"

"Just follow 'em, till they go down a dark street."

"Maybe they live close," Neal said hopefully.

"Like a hunter in the jungle after a lion. We track. You Sabu, me great white hunter with gun. Then bam! We scare their tits off."

"If they recognize us . . . ?"

Moony took out two black handkerchiefs, and gave one to Neal.

"Before we attack, we put these on."

They followed the girls for about ten minutes. They were headed in the direction of a large park called Lincoln Terrace which covered about two square miles, and had innumerable exits which led to narrow winding streets.

"They don't want to walk up the hill, so they're taking a short cut," Moony whispered breathlessly. Neal could not understand his accomplice's mounting nervous excitement, for he felt only terror and apprehension. What if they were caught? The park was patrolled by policemen at night. Moony took his hand and they rushed through a narrow, muddied path, overgrown with bracken and low-hanging trees.

". . . Cut them off before they get to Eastern Parkway. We jump out of the bushes, and they're too scared to do anything."

Moony stuck his head out furtively over the bushes.

"Put your hankie on," he ordered.

Neal did as he was told. The handkerchief had a stale, rank odor of sweat and Neal gasped when he had tied it around his face. He couldn't control his breathing and he thought that he would have an asthma attack before they did anything. He heard a mechanical flicking sound and watched Moony rubbing the blade of his knife across the palm of his hand with the same indifferent manner as a barber about to shave somebody. After a second he closed it.

"You're not going to use it . . . ?" Neal protested. His voice squeaked ridiculously.

"Just scare 'em, so they won't try anything."

"Couldn't we scare them without the knife?"

The girls were giggling stupidly as they approached, now only a few yards away. Neal's eyes began to tear and his knees shook uncontrollably.

"Why am I doing this?" he asked himself, but before he could answer, his sleeve was tugged, and he and Moony jumped in front of the girls who stood stockstill staring at the masked figures.

"Gimme the bags!" Moony demanded in a high falsetto.

"Whatcha doin'?" one of the girls asked.

"I'll stick this into your tits," he said harshly, moving up against the short dumpy one whose eyes opened wide with shock. The knife made a loud noise in the quiet darkness as it flicked open, and the girl pressed her hand against her mouth.

"You scream, and I'll kill her. Now gimme the bags."

The tall girl was just as frightened as her friend but she maintained a show of composure and said:

"Give 'im what he wants, Shirley."

Shirley handed over her bag and started to cry.

"My mother gave me a ten-dollar bill for the movies. I gotta bring change . . ."

Moony threw one bag over to Neal and then started to run into the bushes.

"C'mon, go, go."

Neal ran as fast as he could. The two ran out of the park, cut down the long hill and slowed up when they reached Montgomery Street, two blocks from Neal's home. They went into the basement of an apartment house and caught their breath by the boiler room.

"I ohways come here. Nobody bothers yer."

Moony rifled open his bag and found a lipstick, two jacks, a packet of rubber bands, a wallet which contained no money but innumerable school cards, and thirty-seven cents. He pulled Neal's bag away and tore it open, breaking the lock in his excitement and there as the girl said was nine dollars and change. He crumpled the money greedily in his fist, then he flattened out the bills and began to count.

"Four seventy apiece," he said, thrusting Neal's share on him.

"I don't want . . ."

"Shit, you don't."

"I've got enough."

"You take your share."

"But why?"

"Why? Because we're Indian Braves and we share and share alike. You did it with me and whatever happens, we gotta stick together."

Moony picked up both handbags and thrust them into the boiler.

"The super shoves some coal in and the bags burn wid it, and they can't prove nuttin'. Now I got my own dough. After we finish at the clubroom we go out and have ourselves some pizza. I know a place where the waiter lets you drink beer wid it, so we'll get ourselves stinko."

The clubroom was the basement of a two-family house on President Street and it belonged to a boy called Rudy Feld whom Neal vaguely knew from the schoolyard where all the boys played baseball. Feld was fourteen and the captain of his club team, and his mother had allowed the boys to use the basement for meetings. Most of the faces were familiar to him, but none of them were Neal's friends or were in any of his classes.

Feld was standing at the door like a ticket-taker and when Neal entered said:

"Wall, wall, lookit who we got here! You ain't a member."

"Aw let 'im in, Rudy," Moony pleaded. "He's okay."

"Yeah, why?"

"You let me in, an' I'm not in the club."

"I like you, but I don't know this creep. How do I know he won't go home and tell his momma that he gets fucked in my clubroom?"

"Because I won't," Neal said sharply. "I never speak to my mother."

"You know Neal Blackman. His mother and father are divorced."

"Oh, yeah? Is your father the guy with three Cadillacs?"

"No, one," Neal said.

"Money dripping from his asshole like dingleberries. Well, maybe I'll give you a trial tonight. But 'cause you're not a member, the price is a buck fifty. Take it or leave it. We draw to see what order we fuck her in."

Neal paid his money and walked into the large basement room where eight boys stood talking loudly and drinking Cokes.

"Hey, Neal, hello," a boy called Patsy said. "Your momma know you're out so late?"

"She doesn't give a shit," Neal said sharply, hoping to silence the others.

"Have a Coke," Patsy said. "Unless you want some wine."

"I'll have wine," Moony said.

"You sure? It's the Sneaky Pete poison for the whores. They'll drink piss."

"Nuttin' wrong wid it, it's just strong."

"At sixty cents a bottle it must be lighter fluid."

The radio was turned on and the boys listened to the final scores of the night baseball games. Neal had a vision of Sports with his ear glued to the speaker of a radio somewhere, writing furiously and totaling up his winnings at the end. It never occurred to him that Sports might lose more than he won. He wanted to boast to the boys that the man who was to be his new stepfather was a bookmaker and bet thousands of dollars each day and that he knew all the important mobsters and killers in New York. Sports could probably get all their parents murdered if he decided to. That would give them all something to think about. Yes, his parents were divorced, and he was different from all of them. He couldn't alter the legal status of his parents, but one day he'd show them what it had meant to be different. He would *be* different because they had forced him to be different.

A dark-eyed girl with a nest of black hair piled high on her head walked in. She sniggered silently to herself as she walked up to the bar where Patsy, who played bartender, stood with silent, admiring eyes. She opened the bottle of wine, seized a glass which had some Coke in it and spilled it on the floor. Then she proceeded to fill the glass up with wine and she swigged half of it down in one gulp. Patsy took the bottle, filled the glass again and she winked at him. The other boys muttered quietly to each other.

She polished off another glass of wine, then turned to a small sandy-haired boy, who kept adjusting his glasses as she moved towards him. He stepped back.

"Wha's yer name, huh?"

"Irwin," he said cautiously, conscious of all the eyes in the room on him.

"Well, Irwin, you gonna volunteer. Huh? A nickel a *schtickel*."

Rudy Feld led the room in a hiccupy nervous laughter which grew to a hysterical crescendo, then stopped abruptly.

"So, Irwin, I'm waitin'."

"What's your name?" Irwin asked timidly.

"Wha's my name?" she said, playing to the older boys. "You tell him."

"Margie, Margie, Margie," they chanted.

"Hey, Marge, he ain't first," Feld interjected when the boys had come to order. "We draw lots." He started counting heads around the room. "Eight." He wrote numbers one to eight on small bits of brown paper, then tossed them in a baseball cap, mixed them up, and said with the studied air of a professional organizer, "Lowest number last, highest first."

"Fifty cents to watch," Margie added.

"Yeah, that's right. If you wanta see anybody in action it's an extra half a buck."

The boys giggled nervously and went towards the hat, sticking out anxious, shaking, hairless hands, dreading the thought of going first.

A tall pimpled boy, destined to be a rabbinical scholar, with a scholarly stoop and a large wine-colored carbuncle on the tip of his nose, declared himself.

"Me first."

"Sloppy seconds," Patsy said, looking at his number.

Neal had drawn number five and Moony number eight.

"Know what I do, Neal?" Moony said quietly. "I come two, three times without losing my hard-on and the broad never knows it."

"How old is she?"

"About fourteen. She used to go to Lincoln Park until the principal caught her fucking the gym teacher in the locker room. Everybody heard about that. She got expelled and he's doing time. They said he raped her, but how could he? The poor *schlemiel* just got caught with his pants down. You can't rape that girl, 'cause she'd be undressed before you could. Tough on him."

Margie stood on top of the bar and Feld put the phonograph on. The record was "Deep Purple" and Margie made a vague attempt to strip to the music, but she had no sense of rhythm and she was completely naked before the record was halfway through.

"See what I mean? Anxious. Can't get enough."

"You do it to her before?"

"To her and ten like her. You nervous or somethink, Neal? Just watch . . . it's simple."

Margie had large pendulous breasts which drooped down to her stomach, and a roll of fat around the abdomen which wobbled when she moved. She was wide-hipped, and Neal's blood boiled in his veins. He had never been so excited by a female before. He longed for his turn to come. He had wondered if he were ready, but he knew now that he was, and he counted silently as one boy after another jumped onto the couch with her. The longest took five minutes: number four was with her, and having difficulty.

At last, Neal's turn came and he approached Margie with dread and desperation. She opened his trousers matter-of-factly without moving from her position on the sofa, played with him, and said softly:

"Mount me, little boy. Like a pony."

He felt himself slide into a greasy wet abyss and the girl said:

"Pump me, c'mon. I ain't got all night."

He slipped in deeper and deeper and spots danced wildly across his eyes. Margie blew some smoke into his face and he began to cough. He was blinded and choking. The semen oozed out of him, and his member went soft with astonishing rapidity.

"Okay, Junior. Do your buttons up walking. Next," she called out.

Moony reluctantly acceded to Neal's demand that they leave before the next girl arrived. It was well past midnight as they strolled down the hill. The night air was heavy, humid and oppressive, and Neal's underwear stuck to him.

"Let's cool off."

"Okay," Neal said.

"Drink some beer and have a pizza between us." He wrapped his arm around Neal's shoulder. "Well, how does it feel to get off the nut?"

"Awful . . . and marvelous. What a pig she is!"

"You gotta wait till you're older before you bag nice gash. The only-for-you kind."

"Have you?"

"Not yet. I come close. A few accidental elbows in elevators and in the wardrobe at school, but not yet with a girl I really like."

"Must be great."

"That's why people get married. They like making it so much, that they decide it's got to be forever."

"I wonder if they get divorced when they stop liking it," Neal said.

"Hey, pal, asshole buddy, you gotta stop worrying about things like that. They're finished altogether . . . your old man and your mother, so forget it. When you're older, screw 'em where they breathe. Lookit me? My folks are together, but I'll tell you what I'd like to do. Give 'em both a swift kick in the ass."

"Why? I don't understand."

"I got a gripe too. They don't give a damn about me. So they're together, it don't do me no good. Not many parents really care about their kids, so don't feel sorry for yourself.''

"I don't." Neal hated the accusation, but it stuck to him like glue. Zimmie and his mother always intimated the same thing when he said that he couldn't stand his parents and wished he were an orphan. "You know what's wrong?''

"No, tell me.''

"They got a divorce, right?''

"Yeah. So what?''

"Well, when they're divorced they make the same lousy mistake again with somebody else.''

"Your mom isn't married again . . . ?''

"She will be.''

"Oh, what the hell!''

"That's right, Moon, what the hell.''

At a quarter past two, he and Moony were singing as they approached the apartment house.

"You're drunk." Moony squealed with laughter. "Neal's drunk. What'll your momma say?''

"Probably still out.''

"Should we wake up the whole neighborhood?''

"Nah, g'night, Moon. See you tomorrow.''

Neal lurched against the rail in the elevator. The movement made him dizzy and he was afraid to close his eyes because he knew he would vomit if he did. He spent several minutes unsuccessfully fiddling with his key in the lock. It was slippery, or was it? The key didn't fit. He tried another key, and as he was about to turn it, the door was swiftly yanked open, and a hand pulled him inside. He blinked in the blaze of light, but he could not believe it was actually Jay who was there.

"Daddy!''

"I've been half outa my mind. Two-thirty in the morning! I've been calling all night. Where've you been? Where's Rhoda? Why are you out so late?''

The flurry of questions startled Neal and he stood before Jay, listlessly swinging from side to side.

"Hey, what's the matter with you, Neal? C'mere. Hey, Neal''—he shook him vigorously and Neal sank to his knees—"you sick?" Jay pulled him up. "Neal, goddamnit, you've been drinking."

"Beer."

"Beer? This is ridiculous. You're twelve years old. A baby. Drinking beer? Where's Rhoda for God's sake at this time of night? Leaving you alone. What else have you been doing? I want to know."

"Just had a pizza and some beer with a boy."

"Where? I'll see that dirty bastard loses his licence. Selling beer to a minor. Where?"

"Can't say. Somebody took me. Daddy, I'm not feeling so well. Got to go to the bathroom."

Neal rushed past his father down the corridor and Jay followed him. He was already retching. Jay put a towel under the cold water and made a compress of it. He held it against Neal's forehead.

"You didn't vomit any food. Just a few bits of pizza. You didn't have anything in your stomach. Why didn't you eat? I don't understand what's happening here. Your mother gets plenty of money from me for your upkeep. You could eat steak four times a day. And you come in drunk at this time of night! What in God's name's happening to you? Doesn't she give a damn about you? Where is she?"

"I dunno," Neal said weakly. "She went out with this man Sports who's gonna marry her."

"Feeling any better?"

"Yes, thanks, Daddy."

Jay washed Neal's hands and face and helped him on with his pajamas. Neal appeared to be better although shaky and chalk-faced. Jay made some strong lemon tea and brought it in to him.

"Drink it. It'll settle your stomach."

Neal forced the hot tea down, but before he could finish it, he fell off to sleep. Jay sat on his bed for what seemed to be hours. It was 3:30 when he looked at his watch. He went into the kitchen and made himself a cup of coffee. The apartment had become tatty and squalid since he had left it. The sofa in the living room needed to be resprung, a corner of the wall-paper above the sink had been ripped off, there was dust under Neal's bed, dirty clothing hanging out of the hamper, soap scum on the bathroom faucets, dirty dishes in the sink, an empty pantry, grease stains on the stove, the carpet had loose threads; the apartment was beginning to take on that skeletal threadbare quality which neglect rather than poverty creates. It had about it the look and smell of a temporary headquarters for people in flight who had grown indifferent to their sur-roundings. He sat at the kitchen table which he had bought and said aloud:

"And to think this was a home."

Voices drifted in from the foyer and laughter. He got up from the table.

"Ooooooooh, there's somebody here . . ." Rhoda said ner-vously when she heard his footfalls on the wooden floor. Sports darted in front of her and said:

"Keep calm. I'm with you."

Jay stopped short when he reached them.

"What do you want, buddy?" Sports said, flicking a wooden hanger in Jay's face.

"I'm Neal's father."

Rhoda opened her eyes and came out from behind Sports' protective wing.

"Jay? What're you doing here? Neal, something's happened to Neal?"

"A lot you care."

"What are you talking about?"

"You don't give a shit about him."

"Now just a minute," Sports interjected.

"Shaddup you. This doesn't concern you. We're talking about *our* child. What the two of you do is your own affair. But the kid is my concern."

"Jay, I don't want to argue. It's late and—"

"Late! Why should that worry you now? You leave him alone all day . . . all night. Do you know or care if he gets into trouble? Did you know he got home at two-thirty, drunk! And that he vomited and I put him to bed. He went out with some kid and had pizza and beer. Beer! He's twelve years old. What's gonna happen to him?''

''I'll beat him till he's black and blue,'' Rhoda said, outraged.

''If you were home, he couldn't do that.''

''Don't tell me what to do with my life. I had enough of you for years.''

''I'll have Neal if he's getting in your way. With pleasure.''

''I'll never give you the satisfaction of having him.''

''I'll apply to the courts.''

''You can apply till doomsday. I divorced you, remember, and it was for adultery, and the courts don't reverse their decision. You signed him away in any case.''

''I've still got my rights.''

''For one month in every calendar year, and every fourth weekend.''

''But you don't want him.''

''That doesn't matter. You're not gonna have him. Do I make myself clear?''

''Rhoda, for God's sake. You're not hurting me, but Neal. He's the one who's suffering.''

Jay turned to Sports, his hands outstretched, and said: ''Who's he?''

Rhoda sneered: ''He's not a stranger, but my fiancé.''

''Do you want money?'' Jay asked. ''I'll give you money, and we'll get the decision reversed if you sign him over.''

''Amazing,'' she said to Sports, who was skimming through the sporting events in the newspapers. ''Now he wants his son. When I was carrying him, he knocked me down, and paid for an abortion I never went through with.''

''Oh, God. Old dirt. You have to drag it in.''

''Your wife is such a terrific influence?''

''She does what I tell her to do.''

''Yeah, I'll bet. Why don't you go home, Jay? This isn't your house anymore.''

''It's a disgrace. A filthy pig sty. The way you've let everything fall apart, neglected it. Dirty. And horrible that my child has to live here when I can give him everything. So you're paying me back through him. You're not a fit mother.''

"The apartment ain't so bad," Sports said. "I've seen worse. A couple of coats of paint and some new paper.''

"A fit mother? You can afford to talk—"

"Not bad at all. A few new pieces and—''

"You're moving in?" Jay demanded.

"Yeah, if it's awright with you?''

"In a place that another man paid for. Sleeping in a bed I slept in with—''

"I ain't squeamish. So lookit, Jay. If you said your piece, why don'tcha call it a night and let us all get some sleep, huh?''

"Rhoda, I'll make you sorry you were born.''

"You've done that already, so save your threats. Stick 'em up your ass or write me a lawyer's letter.''

He went to strike Rhoda and stopped in his tracks when he saw Neal staring at him.

"I woke up. Why're you screaming at Daddy, Mom? Why's everybody always screaming?'' He covered his ears with his hands when they started to shout again. They stopped when they saw him rush back to the bedroom. Jay went after him, and Rhoda screamed, "Get out, scum.''

Jay rushed to Neal's bedroom. Neal had crawled under the blankets and was squirming underneath.

"Neal," Jay said softly. "I'm sorry.''

The child's head came out of the blanket and he looked from Jay to Rhoda with an expression of long-suppressed rage, of frustration, and such loathing that Jay shrank back.

"I wish you were dead,'' he said.

Jay backed out of the room like a hyena in retreat, discovering that the carrion is still alive. "I'll get you for this, Rhoda. You'll go down on your knees to me before I finish with you,'' he said.

18

I want him, more than anything," Jay said, pacing in the long living room, which was a tribute to all the antique shops on Third Avenue: Meissen, Louis Quinze, Directoire, Chippendale, and Dresden—about eighty thousand dollars' worth of bric-a-brac, none of which Jay admired, appreciated, or understood—populated the room in the form of tables, vases, lamp bases, chairs, sofas, and figurines. "He's so goddamned unhappy."

"And you can make him happy, I suppose?" Eva asked.

"I can try. At least he won't be neglected. The conditions he's living in make me sick."

"But Rhoda says no, so that finishes it." She was relieved to end the discussion on that final note. Jay had returned at four in the morning. She had suspected that he had been on the town with a woman, but he hadn't been drinking and he had woken her to explain the condition in which he had discovered Neal. She had been grateful to Neal for keeping Jay off the streets for the night. The child was all that prevented Jay from falling apart. Neal had made Jay respectable. It was a sickening truth that she had difficulty facing at ten o'clock in the morning.

"I've got to get him back."

"You can't," she said sullenly.

"I can make life pretty tough for Rhoda."

"Neal won't thank you for it. And anyway it's against your nature to force little people out of business. You wouldn't get any pleasure from it."

"I'd get my son back."

"For a smart man, you're acting foolish. Have patience. If she marries this character, she'll want to get rid of Neal. He doesn't sound like the kind of guy who needs a kid around his neck. She'll be grateful for your offer."

"So I keep quiet and sweat it out."

"I'll help you. Don't forget I'm an expert in patience and sweating, and jumping through hoops of fire. I could do a circus act."

He swallowed his coffee and embraced her with affection. There was still something left of the old feeling—it hadn't all been left in other people's beds. He let her go. She smiled wistfully at him as though reading his mind.

"If you decide to let Lorna come and live with us, it could be great. You and Lorna, me and Neal. It would be a family for once. I want a family."

She turned sulky at the mention of Lorna's name and she poured herself another cup of coffee. She raised the cup to her lips, then put it down absentmindedly on the drum table. Her hair hung down to her waist, a red flame which was reflected against the black satin quilt of her robe.

"Think it over, Eva."

"I don't like reproaches walking on two feet in my house."

"Well . . ."

He forced her down on his lap. She had a bed smell commingled with the faint faded odor of Sortilege.

"It's dangerous doing business with you," she said. "I should take a lesson from all the others who've had their throats cut while you were helping them on with their coats."

"I'm not so bad, am I?" He slipped his hand inside her robe, and her breasts were warm and soft. The nipples hardened under his hand, but she got up abruptly.

"It's not fair to make a pass at me before I've been to the hairdresser." She laughed to herself bitterly. "I look a wreck. . . . I would, when you decide to . . ."

"I didn't think a husband could make a 'pass' at his own wife."

"Well, that's what makes you different from all other husbands. You make passes. And I'll tell you something, you bastard, that's part of the reason I'm still in love with you."

"Go to the hairdresser."

"And what're you going to do, sit around and mope?"

"Dunno. Thought maybe I'd see Harry."

"He plays golf every Saturday at Park Knoll."

"Yeah, I know. He keeps asking me to have lunch with him there. Maybe I will. Who knows, it might be fun to join."

"Join?" She put her hands over her eyes and cackled. "You join a country club? Christ, what next? Become a joiner, Jay Blackman. And be like everyone else? Enjoy life. Meet new people, go to parties, be part of society."

"Okay, I'll join, if that's what you want."

"I've only been asking you to do it for ages. Doesn't it strike you as peculiar that we've been out here for almost two years and we don't even know our next-door neighbor? I've given up hope."

"Well, things'll change. Look, I'll ring Harry and you drive out when you're finished at the hairdresser. We'll all have lunch."

"Yes, sir." She came over and kissed him on the cheek. "You need a shave, baby." She rubbed her hand through the bristles of his beard. "It's getting a little gray. The boy wonder grows old and gray."

"I'm not through living yet."

"God, I hope not. Who knows, I may be able to stop taking my medicine."

"Wouldn't that be nice? To have you sober for a full day."

"I can stop whenever I like," she said adamantly. "I've only been waiting for a chance to prove it." She was about to leave when she added in a quiet voice: "Jay, I've been faithful to you."

"Yeah, sure, don't worry about it."

"You do though. When I was with Marty, nothing happened."

"I don't want to hear any more," he said, rising angrily.

"Please listen, nothing happened. We lived together as brother and sister. He can't! But he made me swear that I'd never tell you. I guess I must love you more than I ever realized, 'cause I never expected to break my promise." She closed the door softly and he fell back into the settee. It was uncomfortable, made for a museum, not for a man to sit in. He'd have to get a comfortable chair. They'd start to live in the house.

Neal! Neal! Neal! The name, the child, haunted him like a vision of paradise. The luminous green eyes, the snubbed nose, the dark wavy hair, the agony of a child torn apart, remained with him. He admitted no judges but himself, and by his own standards his life had been a failure and could only ascend to success if Neal were happy. In some strange, illogical way, every action, beneficent and despicable, every experience, could be justified if Neal turned out all right. He realized as he drove up the winding country road to Park Knoll that his life depended on Neal, that he was the captive of his own eidetic image. Neal, the new self, must supersede the old one. He had a wild, buoyant sense of hope when he thought of Eva. He could redeem the overdue pledge he had given her. It still might be possible. His existence resembled a pawnbroker's attic in which little bits of himself lay strewn on the ground, dusty and dessicated, tarnished, visions, images, actions, experience, flung into a pervasive desuetude, so that he had nothing more to give, no more credit to demand—the only remaining course was to claim what had formerly been his and use it, use it well this time.

Jay had a foreigner's contempt for the large, grandiose lobby. A composite of knotty pine walls, spineless furniture which looked like a gypsy's idea of arts and crafts, chichi bamboo room dividers, modern paintings which would have been sensational as wallpaper patterns for the toilet, and a pack of beslacked tweed-dripping matrons done up in Fifth Avenue's idea of English gentry. Jay wondered if these women knew that the tweeds they flaunted had been soaked in prime Scottish urine in order to give them the right texture. About six of them gave him frantic stares. A tall blonde standing by a leather-topped desk which had a small illegible sign in some kind of script and which he gathered was a reception gave him a fine clinical smile. She looked like a failed air hostess, or perhaps a successful one.

"You're not a member?" The question was couched in a shrill reproachful tone.

"Nothing to be ashamed of, is it?"

She looked up from her hornrims and decided that he was a gate crasher.

"I'm sorry, this is for members only."

"I'm a guest."

"Oooh!"—entirely different tone—"some confusion?"

"My fault," he said gallantly. "I have no manners."

"You must have to say that."

He gave her Harry's name and she did a few "oh-ahs" and said: "Is he on the links?"

"On the balls of his ass most likely."

"Pardon?"

"Try the bar."

She had Harry paged by a superannuated bellhop who shuffled through the lobby carrying a black board with Harry's name printed on it, groaning *sotto voce*: "Mr. Harry Lee."

Harry emerged from a glazed door which had "Venetian Bar" written on it. He got a bit tangled in his tattersall plus fours as he strode up to Jay. Now that he had touched seventy, a melodramatic sanguinity peeped through the stiff-as-leather bronze which had become his natural color; little armies of crisscrossing capillaries ran like squirming worms under his skin.

"So, I've got you here at last," he said, tapping Jay on the shoulder.

"Would you sign, please?" the blonde demanded.

Jay made an x on the book, and she glared after him.

Roughly a hundred people were jammed into the Venetian Bar. Gondolas on the wall in which fat ladies with too much rouge on their cheeks were sitting idly back to admire the azure sky of Venice.

"Well, what do you think of the place, Jay?"

"It's like a *mikvah*, and you look like the lifeguard in your costume. Why not a dress?"

"You wear these for golf. Plus fours are traditional."

"Give me a jockstrap with luminous nailheads any day."

"You're still impossible. I guess you'll never get used to the better things in life. Have a drink."

"Okay, you twisted my arm. Eva's gonna meet us here at one."

"Terrific. You two straightened yourselves out?"

"Maybe."

"Aren't you sure?" He sounded aggrieved. Jay knew that he was particularly fond of Eva, and disturbed by the course their marriage had taken. It was as though he had a personal stake in their lives.

"Yeah. It'll probably be all right. It's my kid who's worrying me to death."

"Since when?"

"Since the day I split up with Rhoda. She's got herself some zombie now who's planning to marry her bank account, and the kid's all upset. He's neglected and pushed around and it kills me that I can't do anything to stop it. I mean to say"— he spoke in a loud voice, and the bartender wondered if he had too much after only one drink—"my kid, getting the short end of the stick. I could give him everything."

"What about Eva? How does she feel?"

"She wants to have him, if we can get him."

"What's the guy do?"

"I think he's a gambler or half-assed bookie or both."

"Then you sit back and wait. They'll run out of money and she'll want to make a touch, then you've got them by the balls."

"That's what Eva thinks. But in the meantime, Neal's running wild and getting drunk."

"Drunk?"

"I went by at two o'clock last night and the kid wasn't home. Came home at two-thirty loaded on beer and sicked his guts out. Rhoda went clubbing with the sportsman. And we had an argument which the kid heard. What am I supposed to do? Tell me."

"Keep after her. Hound her, and if she runs out of money, you step in."

"I thought of asking all the manufacturers in the market to

cut her credit, but I can't in my heart do it, even though I want him. If she found out that I was behind it—and she'd know—she'd never let him go.''

''Well, worrying about it isn't going to help. How're things at the office?''

''We finished with the underwriters last week. I've sent you a full account of it. We go on the market in two weeks and they think we'll be oversubscribed at least six times, so that we'll open with maybe a two-dollar premium. The traders'll get in and out with a quick profit and she'll settle down at about a dollar higher than the underwriting price.''

''How did you manage to beat them down on the percentage they wanted?''

Jay laughed contemptuously.

''They sent three or four college boys to deal with a crook. They're crooks too, but they like to think they're gentlemen or rather they want you to think they're gentlemen. I'm honest about it. I admit that I'm a thief. Hey, this'll kill you: one of them wanted to fix me up with a call girl to soften me up.''

''You're kidding.''

''So I said: 'Schmuck O'Brien, it's my invention. Call girls. I was fixing people up with call girls when the best part of you was running down your father's leg.' So I gave them two and a half percent. Which they didn't like, but they took it, and no stock options either. I told them they could get stock options with a company that needed them, not with an organization that's a blue chip the minute it goes on the Board. While I was fighting with them, I kept wondering to myself: 'Who am I doing this for?' You, Marty, myself, our eighteen thousand employees, but in my heart I knew that it was for Neal, so that when he's old enough he won't have to kill himself. It'll all be there for him and he'll be the gentleman, the human being, the college graduate. And then I go back to Brooklyn and find him laying in the apartment alone, with nobody, like a little gutter rat.''

Through the crowd of early drinkers a woman's arm emerged and thrust itself between Jay and Harry. She was caught in the crush at the bar and Jay nudged a man by his side who was gargling an old-fashioned and said:

"This lady's going to be minus an arm if you don't move."

The man shifted his weight uneasily and the woman came into view.

"I saw you from across the room."

"I don't believe it," Jay said.

"I'm still fighting to get near you."

"Terry . . . This is Harry Lee."

"Lawson's my married name. God, Jay, it's been years and years and years."

"An old friend," Jay explained to Harry.

She ignored Harry and pushed up close to Jay.

"I'm having lunch here with my partner and my *wife*," Jay said.

"Are you back with Rhoda?"

He flushed, unaccustomed to the question, and the memory of his short furtive experience with her.

"No, I've remarried."

"Really? When, for heaven's sake?"

She sounded a bit too interested, Jay thought.

Harry finished his drink quickly and said:

"Nice to have met you, Mrs. Lawson. I'll just see about our table."

She had filled out, Jay thought. Her body had lost its lanky, girlish shape; and a suppleness, a firmness of limb, had removed that high nascent pubescence which had first attracted him. She was a young woman, with limpid uneasy eyes that flicked from one face to another in the room. Too many late nights and too much booze, he surmised. She was the only woman wearing a dress, a khaki green paisley print with a high neck, and open-toed leather sandals—Cape Cod vintage. Her voice had altered slightly, it was a bit deeper and the harsh absonant Boston twang had a mixture of New York in it—not normally an improvement, but it was in her case. Her nails were chewed down to the skin, and she reminded him of about ten thousand other mixed-up women whose lives he had fleetingly entered and left, not unlike a bee who pollinates, then moves on, instinctively. He had a predilection, or was it a weakness, for unhappy dissatisfied women. He wished they'd leave him alone.

". . . It was about a year ago, on a Sunday morning with the papers in bed. We thought he was reading, and Mother screamed. Mitch and I were spending the weekend with them. Mitch rushed in. Too late. Nothing worked. Digitalis. Well, a chapter ends. Or maybe a book."

"You're happy . . . ?"

"Happy?"

"Ask a stupid question—"

"—You get a stupid answer. I've got two little girls now."

"It happens to everybody."

"Louise and Pamela. I'm not much of a mother though. I mean I like buying them frilly underwear and pretty dresses, but it's all surface affection. I don't worry about them unless they're sick in bed. I guess I take them for granted." She pointed to her chest. "I've got a hole in here."

"Not T.B."

"Could be T.B., but it's not. Just a hole. A cavity."

"And Mitch is the doctor you once told me about?"

She hummed something to herself under her breath.

"The same. He's got an appointment at the Presbyterian Hospital. We left Boston a year ago. Been in Great Neck now for about nine months. It's the same wherever you go. Hungry people looking for somebody to eat. You join a country club and you dine in company. Are you a member?"

"No, don't really want to join, but my wife insists, so I'll give in."

"Tell me about your wife?"

"I'll tell you myself," Eva said, taking Jay's arm, as though it were a trophy brought back from a safari. "Short and sweet."

"This is my wife Eva," Jay said stiffly, "Terry Lawson."

"One thing about Jay: if there's an attractive woman in the room, I know where she'll be. Holding Jay's elbow. Did you know, Miss Lawson—"

"Mrs. Lawson. Terry . . ."

"Terry, if I must. Jay sleeps with more women accidentally than most men do on purpose."

"Oh, shut up," Jay said, slamming his drink down.

"Good-bye, Mrs. Blackman," Terry said, moving away ... "Jay ..." she waved.

"Wherever we go you have to open your goddamn mouth."

"Am I wrong? Just tell me!"

"She's married to a doctor. They have two kids and we knew each other a long time ago, and there's nothing between us, never has been. She was a kid when I met her, sixteen or something."

A blush of embarrassment broke through the milk-white powder on Eva's face. She never knew when to believe Jay. She had accused him unjustly in the past and been proven wrong, but there were other times when she had not remotely suspected him, only to learn later that he had betrayed her. The petty infidelities were not important, meaningless in the long run; it was the chain of muted half-truths, impossible to verify or disprove, which represented the ultimate in subtle treachery. She remembered meeting Hiram Gilbert at the Plaza, where she had gone to have lunch with a friend. Gil had strode across the lobby, with great gawping steps and taken her hand. His face had been familiar, but she could not place him until he said: "Havana, your honeymoon." And then she had recalled. Suddenly in the lobby he began pawing her familiarly, and she had tried to escape and he kept up a flurry of half-hearted, half-understood words that bounced off her brain. "Poetic justice. You an' me. That'd teach him a lesson he wouldn't forget in a hurry. You still with the son-ovabitch? Mah wife, she run off with a lifeguard, but afore she left, she tole me that yoh husbin slep with her in Havana, on yoh honeymoon. You get shot of that bastard, then you give ole Gil a ring, heah." She had run from the lobby in a panic. Down Fifth Avenue. Knocking into people. Into Radio City Music Hall, where she watched the stage show in the empty balcony for an hour. Then home. The slow, deadening journey on the L.I.R.R. through the symmetrical suburbs and the slums of Brooklyn. A man on the train had bought her a drink. What was his name? In advertising or public relations. In Garden City she got off the train with him and they drove to a motel but the man got too drunk and passed out and she took a taxi back to Great Neck alone and waited for Jay to come home. And when he did, she could not bring herself to mention the incident because she was too drunk to say a word.

"Harry's got a table for us," Jay said.

"I don't want to join unless you really do."

"Aw, Christ, Eva, make up your mind. What's the Hollywood production for? What's the big deal? Be an executive, make a fast decision. Yes, or no. I couldn't care less. If you're having such a problem, it must be because you think it's important. So let's join and end the discussion, which is one goddamn bore."

He telephoned Terry two days later, ostensibly to apologize for Eva's insulting behavior. She sounded distracted and far away, and he was almost sorry that he had called when she said:

"I probably would've reacted in the same way, if I'd've been her. It might've been," she added regretfully.

On the strength of this he invited her to dinner. She accepted.

"God, you're brave, with *that* wife."

"What about the doctor?"

"He's gone to Baltimore for the week. Johns Hopkins has a lecture course in his field. I won't tell you about it because you're probably not interested."

"Are you?"

"Touché."

"What?"

"You've scored a point."

"Good, I'll see you at six."

She lived in a large gabled house about a mile from him. It was the sort of house that no one lived in for very long, and had changed hands a dozen times in twenty years. It rambled and had a weather-beaten appearance which, with the ivy which undulated like a pack of snakes on the façade, made it like one of those overgrown residences universities convert into library annexes. It was well-furnished though, by Eva's standards. A lot of antique crap that she would've swooned over. Terry seemed ill at ease in the house. The studio apartment in Boston had been more in keeping with her character. Marriage had made her taste drearily respectable. She mixed the drinks competently, Jay thought. It was difficult to find a woman who did not know how to mix drinks competently. The times, he reflected. Everybody's grown up, with too much time, too much money that they hadn't earned, and life becomes something they hope to escape from, using good scotch and eighteenth-century beds. He was grateful to have Neal, for Neal gave his existence a meaning that none of the people he knew either wanted or needed.

"Did you know my father was very disappointed that nothing came of our meeting?"

The information staggered him, particularly the flippant manner in which she tossed it off as if it were mere cocktail party small talk.

"I don't believe you."

"Here's your drink. Test it." He sipped it. It was cold and tasteless: a vodka martini. "It leaves gin standing still."

"There's that to say for it."

"Why would I lie? It's over and done with. And I couldn't lie about the dead."

"I can't think why you would."

"It's the truth. He admired you, and when he learned that your marriage was breaking up, he wanted to give me first crack."

"But I remember him insisting that I should go back to my wife. A lot of bull about divorces holding men back."

"The test."

Jay sank back into the soft cushions of the club chair she had forced him to sit in.

"The business partnership was a gambit to get you there. To involve you two in something binding."

"I'll have another drink. Make it scotch."

"Bad idea to mix your liquors."

"You sound like an expert. I've been playing this game a little longer than you."

She poured him a large scotch on the rocks. He let the ice chill it for a minute, then took a long drink, and as she was standing with the bottle by his side, he reached out for her arm.

"C'mon, hit me again. Fine," he said when she had filled it up. "What I can't understand is why he didn't come right out with it. Everybody would've been a lot happier."

"You would've run for your life."

"I suppose I would've. Did you ever tell him about us?"

"I gave him an edited version."

"I'd love to hear it." The drink had gone to his head and he felt a bit woozy. It was a momentary sensation of being high that he experienced from time to time when he was excited, and which hit a plateau after he had half a dozen drinks. A leveling off followed which invariably gave him the illusion that people were nicer and cleverer than they usually were, and women inevitably assumed a grace and desirability which made his infidelities seem natural fulfilments, adorned with romantic accoutrements, instead of drunken sex with strangers.

"Have another drink," she said anxiously. They were on their fifth.

"Well . . . ?"

"I had to protect myself."

"I wouldn't expect you to do less."

"I said that you were only interested in having an affair with me."

"So he wrote me off like a bum check."

"I'm afraid he did."

"And our Boston adventure. Did you leave that out?"

"No, I put it in a different light."

"This is marvelous, please go on. I feel like the good guy for once."

"He knew you were in Boston. I called to say that you'd come up. And after our disagreement—"

"—That's nice: 'disagreement.' What was that all about?"

"That I refused to go to bed with you and you walked out."

"Now I know what an edited version is. Thanks." He rose from the armchair.

"You're not going?" she said, alarmed.

"My foot's fallen asleep. Just shaking it."

"So what're we going to do?"

"That sounds like big drama. We're gonna eat a steak at the Little Neck, and then we're gonna do what we intended to do."

"Which is . . . ?"

"Cheat."

"Uh-huh," she said with a leering smile. "You always buy your girls a steak?"

"It depends on how much I care."

"I'm flattered." She had begun to drag her consonants and slur.

"After I've had a few drinks and a steak, if I'm still interested in knocking the broad off, I figure I'm interested. And if I'm not, I give her cab fare."

"Jay." She threw her arms around him and kissed him with such urgency that he was almost touched. "Jay, I'm sorry. Genuinely. I've messed up my life."

"We all have, so don't feel bad. I'm president of the organization. We've got chapters from coast to coast."

She threaded her hands through the hollow of his arm and leaned her head on his shoulder. "It should've been you and me. We loved each other."

"For a while."

"I've never loved anybody but you, Jay," she intoned his name mournfully, and his heart began to palpitate.

"What, Terry?"

"It's a tragedy. I've had two children by a man I never cared for. Maybe that's why I'm a lousy mother."

"The kids shouldn't have taken the rap."

"It's awful. I wanted your children."

"What about Neal?"

"I would've loved him. I said some stupid things. I was very young."

"And I was too old."

"You still as crazy about him?"

"It'll always be Neal. You see, he's me, and I'm him, and there aren't divorces in that kind of marriage."

At the Little Neck, Charlie fawned on them as though they were royalty. He set out a fresh platter of hors d'oeuvres, and wiped the bar as they sat down.

"You straighten out that little matter, Mr. Blackman?"

Other bars, other places, but the same faces, Jay thought. The same bored restless little people in search of excitement, change, new circumstances, and old experiences.

"Yeah, I straightened it out. Say hello to Mrs. Lawson." Charlie said hello. "If she comes in on her own, you look after her and keep the dancing teachers away."

"Sure will," Charlie replied. He'd do anything for money.

"We're old friends, Mr. Blackman and I. He used to squire me about when I was a child."

"Yeah, squire her about, hear that, Charlie? A lady!"

She couldn't explain why she had bothered to mention the fact that she and Jay had known each other before, and of all people, to a bartender she had only just met. There was no making it respectable, so why should she try? She had thought about Jay incessantly over the years, at first with anguish and then with a sense of loss so profound that she had reached a state of indifference about what happened to her. What she particularly regretted was the fact that she had acted totally out of character. She had tried to bring herself down to his level, only to learn—too late for it to help—that he was above her. He was decent and she indecent. He had principles, she had none; he cared about other people, she only about herself. His roughness and lack of education she had assumed was commensurate with a lack of character. If anything he had too much character and too much innate decency to put up with her behavior. Perhaps her father had understood this, and perhaps that was why he had singled Jay out as the son-in-law he would have preferred.

"Jay, would you marry me?"

He scooped up some lettuce with his fork and chewed it.

"The salad's terrific. I love roquefort cheese dressing."

"Your breath will smell from it."

"Don't let it worry you. Why don't you eat something? I promised to buy you a steak, and I'm a man of my word. They won't run out of booze. You can drink more on a full stomach."

She pecked at her steak glumly and he studied her long fingers out of the corner of his eye. She attracted him and he wanted her to repulse him. She hadn't aged much, her type never did. They had a permanent youthful freshness and vivacity that took them right up to fifty. Eva would turn old overnight. He should have married Terry. Perhaps that would have prevented him from making one mistake after another. But now the situation was impossible, or was it? He mustn't hope for too much. When she put down her knife and fork and stared listlessly through space, he picked up her hand and kissed it.

"That was sweet," she said. "I like to have you touch me. It means something."

"What does it mean?"

"That what I've made of things . . . me . . . it's not completely hopeless. To have *the* man you love . . . well, it's different. Nothing else matters. I love you and I always will."

"That's nice."

"A lot of women have been in love with you."

"Too many. One would've been enough."

"I'd like to cry."

"Don't bother. It doesn't mean a thing any more. C'mon," he patted her hand, "we're old friends having a drink and some dinner together, so let's keep it light and pleasant. You've got a good husband, two little girls, security, so what's the point of getting depressed? No good at all."

"What about afterwards?"

Afterwards took place in her bedroom. He sat in a soft-backed chair with a drink in his hand gazing at little figurines on her dresser. She had rolled down the bedspread and there was a mauve satin quilt under it. All that was missing were the dolls. Other men's beds, other bodies. The room was warm and she opened the window, and then when she pulled the curtains they drooled listlessly in the faint breeze. She lit a cigarette, then brushed her hair without enthusiasm. The bedstead was brass and when she lay down her hair was reflected in the metal ball at the corner. He finished his drink, and took her cigarette from her and puffed it.

"If you want another drink, there's a bottle on the dresser."

"Separate rooms, you and the doctor?"

"He reads late every night."

"A good excuse."

She rose from the bed angrily and went for the bottle of scotch but he got there first and took her wrist.

"Jay, don't play games with me. If you're not interested . . . well, I've had to live with it long enough, so I'll die with it."

"What's brought this on?" he asked with surprise.

"For God's sake, I've been through it. Shall I tell you about Mitch? Would you like to hear?"

"No, I don't think I would."

"Well, I'll tell you whether you care to hear or not. He has something wrong with him. Psychological, physical, who knows what? Whenever he comes near me, he has his, you know what, so we've never properly consummated our marriage vows. Do you understand? And it's a mercy I'm grateful for."

He wanted to ask her about the children, but she said: "We've had two children. And if you only knew the sickening things I've had to go through to have them, how it was achieved, maybe you won't get all hypocritical about the kind of mother and wife I am."

"I'm sorry," he said ruefully. He had been toying with her and he realized that she had regained her moral ascendancy over him; it was like a delicate watchmaker's scale, and he had gambled with her and lost. He knew why he had gambled: to confirm and justify his decision to abandon her, but he was wrong and he went towards her with a new sympathy which overwhelmed him by its fullness.

"I love you, Jay. Can you understand that? I'm not a housewife on the loose desperate for a man, any man. I've overcome that feeling years ago. So don't think you have to go to bed with me because it's expected of you. Nothing's expected of you, and don't treat me like a piece you can walk all over just because I was stupid one night a long time ago with you. In fact, if you believe I'm really like that, like I acted then, I'd prefer you to carry that memory around with you instead of the way I really am, the real one. I'd like you to be able to vindicate your judgment of me, and that way you can.''

He stared at his face in the mirror and he wondered if he was as dissolute as he appeared. His eyes were bloodshot and small, but he was sober.

"I love you," he said. "I wasn't going to admit I did because I was let down, and I didn't want you to have the satisfaction of knowing that I still do love you. But it's silly really. The trouble is too much time's passed and it's not possible to start again."

She put her arms around his neck and pressed his face against hers.

"Don't leave me again, Jay."

Later the knowledge hit him like a thunderbolt. His blood insisted that he had done the right thing—he loved Terry. Somehow he would have to come to terms with Eva, for he sensed that the ruined mansion of his life might be restored, and not with plaster and mortar, but with love. He had to love, it was more important than being loved.

19

Neal was shipped to summer camp with the same dispatch as a soldier in wartime, to be trained, disciplined, toughened and taught how to survive in a forest. The camp had militaristic leanings and was under the charge of a maniacal

spartan, a P.T. instructor in a Bronx high school whose wife's
inheritance provided the initial capital for the camp. It was
called the Moscalero, after a degenerate and now extinct
Apache band whose anarchy and vindictiveness were legendary. Carl Holtz, the commandant of Camp Moscalero, saw
no contradictions, either moral or social, in the name or the
training program he had devised for his initiates. "I want them
to be braves. Like the Spartans of yore," he told anxiety-
ridden parents who wanted to get rid of their children for the
summer. He usually genuflected when he provided his sales
talk, then did twenty-five push-ups and twenty-five sit-ups in
the middle of the living room to demonstrate that he practiced
what he preached. The camp accommodated one hundred and
ten boys and that meant Carl did a lot of push-ups every year.
"Not bad for a man of fifty-six?" he would demand with that
peculiar hunger for praise that was at the back of every rhe-
torical question he asked—and he only asked this type of
question.

On sight Neal detested him. And when the bull-necked,
squatly built, hawk-nosed, simian-shuffling man asked him to
call him "Uncle Carl," he could have killed his parents. What
irked him was the knowledge that the camp represented a solution to both his parents' problems. At the meeting which had
been held in Jay's office and was attended by both Rhoda and
Sports, her minister without portfolio and without, as Jay
learned, a pot to piss in, only Evá had come to Neal's defense.

"I don't see why he shouldn't come to the beachhouse with
us," she said.

Jay could only think that he would be tied to Neal whenever
he might be with Terry. He didn't love Neal less than before,
but he very definitely loved Terry more than he thought he
could love any woman. So he rationalized: what he was offering Neal was supervision, the very opposite of neglect.

"He'd get bored in a week at the beach and there aren't
many kids to play with."

Holtz had walked around the office on his hands to show
just what a well-conditioned fifty-six-year-old man could do
when he was a student of gymnastics.

"Don'tcha get tired?" Sports asked, out of breath watching him.

"Tired? I do this to relax. Well, Neal, wouldn't you like to learn how to do this?"

"Not particularly," Neal had replied flatly. He had developed the ironist's tool of laconicism.

"You could show your friends, and boy'd they be jealous," Holtz continued, his face the color of an overripe tomato, split-skinned and on the way to going rotten.

"They'd stop talking to me if I walked around on my hands."

"Don't be rude," Rhoda ordered. She couldn't afford to let Neal upset her summer plans.

"Yah, go on, Neal. What d'you wanta sweat yer head off in the city for? Go to public swimming pools and get athlete's foot for?" Sports observed with what Neal had discovered to be a positive genius for irrelevancy.

Holtz had righted himself and he took up Sports' theme agilely.

"No athlete's foot at Moscalero, I can tell you. We've got a lake, our own. Lake Crow. Exclusively ours"—he flapped the brochure in Sports' face—"and it's two miles across. Every boy over thirteen is required to swim it to pass his Junior Life-Saving Test, and then he can wear his Red Cross badge on his swimming trunks."

"Neal loves to swim," Rhoda said.

A document was brought out from the inside pocket of Holtz's sweat-stained seersucker jacket which released the camp from its responsibility for the boys' health and safety. This safeguard was interwoven among clauses dealing with camp uniforms, and snaked out as "Untoward, unforeseeable accidents . . . Camp Moscalero . . . accepts no legal responsibility and no claims thereof will be entertained."

Jay examined the document. It was six hundred dollars plus fifty dollars for spending money on trips, and seemed exceedingly reasonable to someone in his income bracket. He picked up his pen and was poised to sign when Neal shouted out:

"Don't, Daddy, it's a concentration camp."

"Oh, dear me, it's not. The only things we concentrate on are sports, self-reliance, swimming, and making men. No, no, you're very wrong, Neal. You'll change your opinion, you'll see."

Neal recognized the implicit menace in Holtz's manner, and he reversed his tactics. His parents and Sports were insistent and diligent in their desire to be rid of him. Why Eva wanted him around was a mystery, but she no doubt had a motive, so he accepted the fait accompli, for there was nothing he could do. He dissolved the antagonism that had been built up in Holtz, by saying:

"I'm probably wrong . . . Uncle Carl."

Approval. A sinister smile which developed into a guffaw, a pat on the back, spiritual bonhomie. The pen did its work, the deed was done, and Uncle Carl got his check for $650 without a whimper and not on the special installment plan available to economically pressed parents. Jay, with an insight which shocked Neal, made a valiant effort to smooth over the terrain that Neal had disturbed.

"He comes from a divorced home, and he's a little over-sensitive."

"Of course. I understand," Holtz said, and he did, a bit.

"Don't hang it around his neck like a dead albatross," Eva said sharply. Defeat might be made to work for her. "You wouldn't like Neal to use that as an excuse or hide behind it."

Thoroughly perplexed but ruminating on the wisdom of this remark, Holtz rambled something vague about taking the middle ground. His casuistry was discernible to Neal.

One hundred and ten braves of varying sizes, ages, and dispositions, some with pimples, some not yet old enough to have them, met at the beginning of July on an incredibly muggy morning at the bus terminal on Forty-second Street. Parents forced their protesting charges into the buses, decorated with the green and red pennants of Camp Moscalero. A species of being Neal had never before seen entered his life; the camp counsellor. Most of them were on the short side of twenty and all went to colleges of some description. Uncle Don, Neal's

counsellor, was nineteen, squinty-eyed, with toothpick-thin
arms swarming in hair and a crew cut. He had a red whistle
on a lariat which he blew every five seconds to the conster-
nation of everyone in the perspiring crowd. He didn't seem
very intelligent and Neal sensed that he would be susceptible
to flattery and brownnosing. Neal's bunk was made up of four
other boys who looked as disconsolate as he felt. One of the
boys, wearing a name tag the size of a hamburger, blubbered
into a snot-filled handkerchief. His name was Artie Kahn. Uncle Don made several vain efforts to quiet him down by
blowing the whistle in his ear, but nothing stopped Artie. He
had been delivered, and left, by two fat parents who didn't
want to miss any sun on the beach.

Like some prophet announcing doomsday, Uncle Carl
emerged from the center of the crowd, shouting through a
large megaphone: "We're off, folks. All parents off the buses.
Leaving in one minute." He slipped into a station wagon and
the buses started up and turned in small circles around the
platforms to form a convoy. The trip took five hours to Mil-
haven, Connecticut. The buses made one stop at a roadside
rest during which Artie vomited huge slabs of salami, and
Bobby Fish, another bunkmate, made a break for freedom, but
was caught by Uncle Don as he tripped down a steep gradient.

"Say you're sorry," Uncle Don demanded in a high-pitched
adenoidal voice.

"Fuck yourself," Bobby replied.

There were too many people watching Uncle Don for him
to attempt to swat Bobby, but he did say that he was putting
him down on his shit list.

"And when somebody's on that list, they gotta work their
asses off to get off."

Neal was sure that he and Bobby would be allies if not
friends.

Camp Moscalero rested on an acclivity just outside Mil-
haven. It was well laid-out and the facilities reflected Uncle
Carl's cast of mind. High hurdles on a cinder track, a bar for
high jumping, another bar for pole vaulting, tennis courts
which were chapleted with weeds, a baseball diamond with

eight inches of grass, a wooden basketball court, archery targets, and an enormous pit filled with sawdust to train Olympic long-jumpers. The bunks were a series of raw timbered, functional cabins, situated in a quadrangle, and the mess hall and Uncle Carl's manse were on the top of the hill. It took a good five minutes to walk up the hill from the bunks to the camp proper, and Neal supposed that Uncle Carl wanted his braves to work up an appetite before they got to the dining hall. There was a shower house behind the bunks which served thirty boys, and each bunk contained a can and two sinks.

Half a dozen trunks were lying on the porch of Neal's bunk, and Uncle Don announced that they'd have a swim after unpacking. The beds were laid out in a daisy chain, and Neal took the one next to Bobby's.

"My name's Neal Blackman," he said. "And if that scumbag puts a hand to you, I'll jump him."

"Thanks," Fish said, surprised. "Maybe they aren't all fairies here. Where you from?"

"Brooklyn. And you?"

"The Bronx. Tremont Avenue. Know it?"

"No, I only know the Grand Concourse."

"Been to camp before?" Fish asked.

"No, I didn't want to come. But Uncle Fat Ass started walking around on his hands in front of my parents, so they signed me on."

"Shake"—he extended his hand—"me too. My folks are going to Europe so they had to park me. Boy, was I mad. Who needs all this crap? I coulda stayed with my grandma but they wouldn't let me go. My mother says she might die. Isn't that a rotten thing to say?"

"Both mine're dead," Neal said.

"Well, maybe they were telling me the truth."

"Your parents fight a lot?"

"Sometimes. Not very often. They're not bad really. But this place stinks. Know any of the udder guys before?"

"No, never saw them."

"Do you smoke?"

"Yeah. I got three packs of Old Golds hidden in my duffel bag."

"Great. Let's go to the showerhouse after swimming."

"Any girls' camps around?"

"Holtz told my parents they had dances once a week with some camp." He gave Neal a lascivious stare and his blue eyes opened wide. "You got plans, or somethin'?"

"Well, I don't want to spend the summer jerking off."

Fish scratched his long legs and then unbuttoned his shirt. His sandy hair fell into his eyes and he pushed it back.

"How old're you?"

"Thirteen."

"And you been laid awready?"

"Sure."

"No bullshit."

"When you get to know me, you'll see that I don't tell stories," Neal said haughtily, seizing the upper hand that was being offered him.

Uncle Don, stripped to his undershorts and tee shirt, came over to them.

"Want any help?"

"No, I'm okay," Neal said.

"Well, you two share the third and fourth cubbies. Make it snappy and we'll get down to the lake." He glared at Fish through his thick befogged lenses. "And you, none of that kinda language to me and I'll forget what you said on the road."

"You need a pair of windshield wipers for your specs, Uncle Don."

"Oh, boy, you're gonna get your ass in a sling before this summer's over."

"Lay a hand on me and you'll wind up in court," Fish snapped.

"Okay by me if that's the way you wanna play it, Fishcake."

"My name's Fish, foureyes."

Uncle Don scratched his funky armpits and sneered.

They unpacked their clothes and placed them along the dusty shelves adjacent to the toilet. Trousers, jackets, and coats were hung in a community closet, and the boys at last, to their great relief, were allowed to put on bathing suits. They were told to sit on their beds and Uncle Don sat on his, trying to look like a sage and a military leader, in a tartan swimsuit.

"I wanner have a talk with everybody, but I'll save it till after the swim. But a few things I gotta say, so's we know where we stand. We're gonna live together for a whole summer and we might as well be friends,'cause if we're not friends, you guys are gonna have a rotten time."

Fish interrupted.

"I thought you were gonna save the speeches for lata."

"No more lip from you, Fish."

"What about freedom of speech?" Neal said.

"Sure there's freedom of speech, but there's got to be respect. Now we'll adjourn this chat,'cause it's pretty hot. You boys form a line on the porch, and when I inspect it I want to see it straight as a ruler."

On the porch, Fish murmured: "He's a dick. I don't know from respect, except for my parents."

"Don't talk too much," Neal advised. "Let him shoot off his mouth, then we'll bury him in his own bullshit."

The three other bunkmates hardly spoke. They were too intimidated by their new environment either to pledge friendship or risk making enemies, and they stood rigidly, waiting for approval.

"Size places," Uncle Don shouted.

Fish moved to the back of the line and Neal changed with the boy in front of him who was a bit taller. The path down to the lake was muddy, strewn with rocks, and along the sides of its meandering course, ferns, thick gorse, and miles of trees hedged them in. Uncle Don pointed out the poison ivy and the poison sumac.

"Any of you guys get lost, make sure you don't touch that stuff,'cause it'll give you a rash you won't get rid of for years."

Lake Crow was spectacularly beautiful. It was much larger

than Neal had thought. It lay in the hollow of a valley and in the distance he could see the rolling Berkshire hills surrounding them like an emerald umbrella. Half a dozen counsellors stood on a wooden pier which was divided into three sections by ropes.

"All nonswimmers in the crib," a man with a megaphone called out. "Junior life-savers and intermediates into five-foot water. The raft for deep water swimmers only."

Uncle Don marched them into the bathhouse and gave them all numbers for their bathrobes and towels, formed them into a line, and when he was satisfied that it was as straight as it could be, inasmuch as none of them had yet had Moscalero training, he led them out to the pier.

"Since I don't know how any of you swim, you'll have to be in the crib, till the waterfront counsellors decide where you can go."

"It's only about three feet deep," Artie Kahn protested. "And I passed my J.L.S. test in school last winter."

"The crib, Artie," Uncle Don said.

There were about thirty other boys paddling in the shallows of the crib, most of them much smaller than Bunk 11.

Neal turned to Bobby and said: "You and me stick together no matter what."

They shook hands under water because Uncle Don was glaring at Fish.

"It might not be so bad," Fish said. "It's just that it's all so strange. One minute you're running around in the streets, and nobody telling you what to do. Then all of a sudden they put you in the army."

"I'm glad I've come," Neal remarked. His forehead became ruckled and pensive, and he stared down at the clear water. He could see his feet, and there were only small pebbles on the bottom.

"I thought you didn't like it," Fish asked with some confusion.

"Anything's better than being with my parents. They're divorced."

* * *

In the summer, Jay and Eva usually went to Southampton. They had a large, rambling beachhouse which Jay had bought from an architect, and he liked the timbered atmosphere, and the enormous copper fireplace which fluted up to the chimney. It was conveniently situated; he could drive from his office in Manhattan to the house in about two hours.

He and Terry met whenever they could, but the time they had together possessed a fugitive quality which unnerved them, and created an air of charged desperation when they resumed the respectable functions of their lives. But midway through the summer fortune smiled on them, for Eva suggested that a "getting-to-know-each-other" period with Lorna might relieve the tension and anxiety that overwhelmed her whenever she and her daughter were together. Jay graciously offered the beachhouse and Eva accepted. She had been scared when confronted with the prospect of being on her own with Lorna, but Jay had saved the situation by saying: "We'll ask your mother to come with you. She's on her own, and it'll give the three of you a chance to get acquainted"—which went to prove that improvisation was the handmaiden of love. Eva had flung her arms round Jay and murmured: "Oh, God, Jay you've saved the day. You're wonderful." Which might have confirmed for cynical people the efficacy and value of having enough money to get rid of one's wife.

Jay telephoned Terry as soon as he was out of the house. She shared his excitement, but told him that it was impossible for them to meet because Mitch was coming home for dinner.

"Impossible?" He was astounded. "I've got to see you."

"What's the point if we can't be alone?"

"I don't give a damn."

"Jay, you're being unreasonable."

"Don't tell me what I'm being." The ground had been cut from under him, and a sleepless night, a hangover, and the airless phone booth conspired to make him irritable.

"How do you think I feel, knowing you're free?"

"I wonder . . ."

"Well, you can stop wondering."

"I'll come to dinner."

"How can you?"

"Easy. I'll just show up. You tell him that you invited me. That you met me and Eva at Park Knoll."

"It can't be done out of the blue."

"It'll have to be. See you at six." He hung up as she started to protest. He was becoming desperate, and the sensation both terrified and exalted him. For a man who prided himself on carefully planning most of the moves of his life, he perceived a quirkish change of character in his technique. He was behaving stupidly and carelessly, exposing himself to a position from which no retreat could be made. Any unconsidered action could break up two marriages, but he was prepared for it, and indeed hoped that he would emerge with the prize he sought: marital happiness with Terry.

Dr. Lawson wore one of those badly cut navy-blue doctor's suits, complete with baggy trousers and ironing sheen on the tail of the jacket. He was more hospitable than Jay expected in view of the fact that he was entertaining a stranger who had crashed in on a quiet family dinner, and with whom he had nothing in common save the fact that unknown to him this stranger performed with complete success certain duties which the doctor attempted energetically but disastrously at a cost of incalculable anguish. Neither of them appreciated the irony of the situation: they were both ignorant of French farce, and epigrams did not come easily to either of them. Terry behaved with the cold and distant manner of a surgical nurse; she did everything perfectly, so perfectly in fact, that it was evident to Jay, although not to her husband, that she might begin to scream at any moment during the laborious hour of small talk and lethal highballs which preceded dinner. She could not make up her mind about Jay's action. Perhaps it would be best to come out in the open and risk hurting Mitch, very suddenly, and so sharply that the shock would be violent and almost painless? A ruthless solution to an impossible situation. The other course would involve deceit and slyness and inevitably force him into the position of witness and abettor of his own cuckolding. This seemed to her ignoble and disgusting, but she could not act until Jay made the decision. The two men sat on the sofa, facing each other, like cocks in wooden cages, each with his morsel of cornmeal, affable, both the same generic breed, until they were armed with spikes and shoved into the sawdust pit. One would be the killer, the other the victim, and she watched with that peculiar horrified fascination which transcends all human decency, and centuries of civilization, when one is a spectator at any form of combat.

"I don't think my speciality would be of interest to you," Mitch said. "It bores the hell out of everybody, including Terry."

"I wouldn't say that. Give me some credit."

"Oh, you're a marvelous wife. The best I could have hoped for." He turned to Jay and added with a hint of passing on confidential information: "She always knocks herself. Thinks she doesn't put out enough, but that's because she gives so much."

Jay polished off his drink rapidly and waited, she thought, for a lead from her, but she was unable to provide it.

"I wish I could say the same thing about my wife."

"Oh, come on, you're kidding. Everybody at the country club's been talking about nothing else since you had lunch with her. Even the headwaiter thinks she's a knockout. He dropped his menus when she walked in," Mitch said, giggling like an errant schoolboy.

"Well, if he can support her, he can have her with my compliments."

"Don't make that offer around Park Knoll; somebody might take you up on it. A few of them might even be prepared to bid. When's she coming back?"

"In about two weeks."

"So you're a lone wolf on the loose."

"You're not suggesting that Jay ought to fool around," Terry said.

"Of course I am," Mitch replied. "Only not here."

He laughed and Terry and Jay joined him uncomfortably. If it went on much longer she'd have to tell him. Perhaps that's what Jay intended. You shoot a lame horse to put it out of its agony.

"It's healthy for a man to have a fling now and then."

"Does that apply to a woman as well?" Jay asked.

"In some cases."

"Which ones?" he continued, unable to prevent himself from being drawn in.

"I'm not sure. I'm afraid I'd relate that to a woman's physical condition. If she wasn't able to have children for instance. Then there'd be no danger. It would only boil down to such nonmedical factors as loyalty and love. Abstractions. With a man it's all so simple, so superficial. He doesn't have to feel very much, except a biological need. With a woman it's a total commitment—"

"Must you go on and on . . ." Terry interjected.

"Sorry," said Mitch, and from the sad empty look in his gray eyes, Jay thought he was sorry. He seemed older than thirty-five. Perhaps it was the way he parted his hair, unevenly on the left side so that the crown stood up in the back, or the understanding bedside manner he had to assume. In a way he was nice-looking, but he had a weak pliable mouth which gave him the appearance of someone docile and house-trained. His eyes watered a bit behind his tortoiseshell glasses, and Jay realized that Terry had embarrassed him.

"My fault," he said almost in defense of Mitch. "I asked the question."

"Don't be silly," Mitch responded quickly, unwilling to accept Jay as a defender.

"Maybe we're all hungry," Terry said to relieve the tension which had begun to hang on the warm summer air. She would've liked to say to Jay: either do it, or keep quiet, but don't play around. She didn't want to be left to put out a fire he had started.

Dinner was uneventful. They gossiped about a number of people Jay didn't know, discussed golf handicaps, whether Florida tans were better than Cape Cod's, and Jay's business success, which Mitch found even more fascinating than the orange soufflé which he had allowed to get cold. Terry was calmer over coffee, for whatever she had expected to happen seemed to have died as suddenly and as quixotically as a sum-

mer storm. They were over the hump—in limbo—she thought.
Jay would go, and Mitch would forget about him until they
ran into each other at Park Knoll. A superficial bonhomie
might emerge over a drink, but the status quo would not be
disturbed.

Mitch poured Jay a large Rémy Martin with his coffee and
then settled back in his armchair which faced the stone fireplace, the only new feature in the room. Jay allowed himself
to relax; he had achieved his purpose and seen Terry. Mitch
wouldn't give him any more uncomfortable nights. He'd work
out some kind of arrangement with Eva, and nature would take
its course. Jay swallowed his brandy and tried to move his
glass away when Mitch came over with the bottle, but Mitch
poured him another snifter.

"I've overstayed my welcome," Jay said. "And you've
probably got a busy day tomorrow, right, Mitch?"

"Not that busy. You don't have to run, do you? My father
was a lot like you. He came over from Ireland at the turn of
the century. Settled in Boston with the rest of the Micks, even
though he was from Northern Ireland and hated the church.
In some way or another he managed to get into a bank as a
messenger and by the time he died he was vice-president.
Funny, the way he was so insistent on education. Sent me to
the best schools—Andover, Harvard, forced me to become a
doctor."

"You did like studying medicine," Terry said.

"I would've preferred doing what Jay did. I'm just a trained
technician. He's the pirate, the romantic figure, the man who
has had none of the important advantages and who carries off
the booty. I mean, if we were both young and Terry had to
pick one of us, which one would she choose? I'm sure it'd be
you."

"You're jumping to conclusions, Mitch," Jay said awkwardly. He couldn't believe that Mitch knew about them.

"Well, she did pick a man over me once. I wonder what
happened . . ."

"Don't be such an idiot! You've had too much to drink—"
Terry was on her feet, her face drawn and cherry red.

"Maybe you'll pay me the compliment of being honest?"

"About what?" Jay said, even though Mitch had spoken to Terry.

"Well, for Christ's sake, this little evening wasn't supposed to wind up in a game of charades. You came over to say something to me, so let's get it over."

"You seem to be pretty well-informed," Terry said, sinking into the sofa next to Jay.

"Private affairs are public knowledge in a small community, and the two of you haven't exactly been discreet."

"You're wrong," Terry said.

"Let's try to work out a compromise . . . I'm prepared to allow Terry to have her little love life with you, provided she continues as my wife and looks after the children. Because that's it, isn't it? All that's between you . . . going to bed!"

"Not entirely," Jay said. His face was contorted in anger.

"You seem shocked by the suggestion. I thought you might react that way because basically philanderers are hypocrites—cheap, phony, sentimental, gutless puritans—who want to believe they've got some decency."

Jay made a lunge for Mitch, but Mitch turned his back.

"I'm not going to risk an injury in a fight with somebody like you over a woman like Terry. Take her, she's yours. You can pack your bags tonight and shack up in some motel. And when you're together try to tell each other that it isn't sex that draws you together."

"It's not!" Terry shouted.

"You don't have to convince me," Mitch replied. "Convince yourself. Or better still, him!"

Rhoda stood by the rail as the horses lined up at the starting gate. The wind from the track blew her hair, but the day was warm and the field behind the tote board seemed unreal. She had never seen grass quite so green. Sports handed her a hot dog, and she wolfed it down in two bites.

"I don't like the clubhouse much."

"It's better standing up here where you can see everything. Who'd you bet on?"

"The light bay: number nine."

She looked it up on the program. "Regis. It's six to one on the tote. Did you bet much?"

"A grand. The jockey plays poker with a friend of mine, and said they were going to give the pony a bang!"

"A thousand dollars!" She couldn't conceive of anyone betting such a huge sum on the outcome of a horse race. "That means if you win it'll be six thousand dollars."

"Yeah, six dimes . . . big dimes." He nibbled his hot dog abstractedly, his eyes darted from number to number as he studied the changing odds on the tote, and his body tensed like a greyhound's when the starting bell rang and the automatic gates clanged.

"C'mon baby," he chanted. "Don't break yet."

"How long is the race?"

"Seven furlongs. I want her to break at the five-furlong post, because the front runner'll die by then."

The horse broke at the fourth furlong post and tore out in front of the two horses vying for the lead. By the sixth furlong Regis was five lengths ahead, and increasing her lead.

"Go, go, go, go, Regis," Rhoda screamed, caught in a frenzy of excitement. She seized hold of Sports' hand and squeezed it with all her strength until he forced her to release it. "We've won, we've won."

"Take it easy, Rho. They gotta make an official announcement and the judge has to look at the photo."

A voice over the loudspeaker said: "The judges have examined the photograph and the Winner is Regis; second, Kelly Green; third, My Baby; fourth, Heaven Sent."

Numbers on the tote changed magically and Rhoda pointed to it: "It's seven dollars and fifty cents for *win*."

"That's better than I thought. Seventy-five hundred. Thank God they didn't do a saliva test."

"How do you do it so fast?"

"It's my business, Rhoda. Percentages. I'm an engineer: angles and curves."

She guffawed delightedly and threw her arms around him. He pecked her on the cheek, studied his program over her shoulder, and patted her behind with his free hand.

"You bring me luck."

"Do I?" She was desperate for compliments, and she repeated: "I really do?"

"Sure you do. I broke the jinx with you. A few more of these and I'm on my way to the top. Latkin gets his two grand and then . . ."

"What then?"

"We'll see, huh?"

"Who's Latkin?"

"A furrier who does some shylocking. Got a great business. When I've got maybe twenty big ones, I go into the same business. No headaches. Loan some other fall guys bread at a hundred percent interest per week and we're on easy street."

By the end of the afternoon Sports was jubilant and Rhoda in a state of bemused shock. He had won twelve thousand dollars and on the strength of it he proposed marriage. As they walked back to the car, a canary yellow Chevrolet convertible, she had a queasy feeling in her stomach.

"But what about Neal? Shouldn't we wait till he comes back from camp?"

"That's another seven weeks and means I can't move into the apartment, 'cause you want everything should be nice and respectable. And when he comes back, it's liable to embarrass him. You wouldn't like him to be at the ceremony?"

"No, not really. It's just that—"

"If you don't care for me, that's another matter!"

"You know I do. I wouldn't be sleeping with you if I didn't care."

"Then what's stopping us? Tell me that, huh?"

"It'll take a few days for the license and blood tests."

"Why wait? Listen, we jump into the car and shoot down to Maryland, grab a judge and he marries us on the spot. Pronto. And on the way, we catch the Phillies in Philadelphia for the night game with Chicago and we stay overnight. And Baltimore in the morning."

"God, Sports, it's so exciting, so quick."

"Well, you knew I was serious. I mean you interduced me

to your ex as the fiancé. Look, you're free, white, and twenty-one.''

''Yes, yes.'' She felt exalted as the wind blew into her face and the car moved out of the traffic and onto the open highway. ''We'll stop by the apartment and I'll pick up a few things and a suitcase.''

''Haven't got time, if we want to get to Philly for the night game. I'll buy yuh everything new. So stop worrying about incidentals. You're terrific, Rho, a terrific item. We're gonna have ourselves a marriage that'll be fun from morning till night.''

''I need to have fun. I do. I get so blue at times when I think of what I've been through with Jay that I think I ought to end it all—''

''Nothing but laughs—''

''And Neal tying me down. Somebody who'll put me first. I'll be the most important thing in his life—''

''In the winter we got football and basketball. We'll travel around the country with all the teams. Maybe I can make a connection and we can do some business with the players. They can win the game, but we get 'em to shave a few points off—''

''—Neal will just have to get used to the idea. I can't live on my own forever. I mean what's he expect of me? I'm still a young woman. Flesh and blood. I've got feelings and I can't ignore them just 'cause I've got a son from another marriage. He can't expect me to lay down my life for him, can he?''

''Who're you talking about?''

''Neal,'' she said anxiously. ''You'll make an effort to get along with him.''

''I got him in my pocket awready. Just give him a few bucks and he's happy.''

''He ought to respect you. It's important. He doesn't respect anybody or anything. He's got to learn respect.''

''He won't butt in. Take my word for it, Rho. I'll charm him and we'll be friends. He's not a bad kid, but he better not burn any more suits. I won't be so forgiving next time. After all, what can he do? He's only a kid. You don't have to account to him.''

She got very angry and heatedly agreed:

''Why should I account to him? I'm his mother. It should be the other way around. He owes me explanations. Why should I justify myself to him? Didn't I go through hell with Jay for his sake. Living with a man I didn't love, who mistreated me for no reason. I mean it was his fault that I started taking my pills. He brought on my condition. I was perfectly all right when I was younger.''

''If the pills help, then who am I to say no?'' Sports averred, as he pressed down on the accelerator. ''I don't mind a pill myself, now and again, when I'm feeling a little tired or depressed. Peps you up and you're winging.''

''So what if I get a little high? It's my business, isn't it? Who can judge me? It's certainly healthier than drinking myself into the ground like Jay. He polishes off a bottle a day. I'd call that alcoholic, wouldn't you, Sports?''

''High intake of booze, most definitely. Although on occasions I indulge, myself.''

''Well, with you it's different . . . jolly and laughs. At least you're not a hypocrite.''

''Sure, live and let live. What I say is the other guy goes to his church and I go to mine.''

''And with us it's love. We accept each other as we are. Angels live in heaven.''

''Where they belong. In life there's good and bad.''

''Exactly. Maybe in a few days we can drive up to camp and surprise Neal. Tell him the good news and give him time to get used to the idea.''

''Fine by me. Never been to Connecticut. It's a state without a team. Not at all athletic-minded till you hit Boston.''

Sports pulled into a service station and told the pump man to fill it up. He got some change and informed Rhoda that he had to make a telephone call to his bookmaker, so that he could have a bit of action on the baseball game. In the car, she fished in her handbag, and found her bottle of pills. She chewed a Benzedrine and when Sports hopped back into the car, she had a satisfied beam on her face.

"The color of the car suits you," she said.

"You really think so?"

"It does. It's a happy color."

"That's what I thought when I got it. A lucky color too. A man driving a car like this can't be a loser, that's what I said to myself."

"I'm so happy . . . so very, very happy."

"We'll follow the sun. That's the way to live." He leaned over and kissed her on the mouth and she put her arms around his neck with a passion she had long ago forgotten. It had been born and died over the course of a single winter with Jay, and a woman deserved more than a single winter of passion to carry her through a lifetime. She wanted to ask Sports to stop at a motel along the Jersey Turnpike, so that they could have a quiet hour in bed, but he was determined to get to Philadelphia in case the game was a sellout.

"Well, it's happened at last," Terry said with a mixture of relief and despair. They had driven down to Southampton the following day. "I'm out of my cage, or are we both in a cage together? It's hard to be sure."

"Does it matter?" Jay was still in a state of shock. "I always seem to be in strange hotel rooms. It's the story of my life."

"You can back out if you like."

He shrugged his shoulders apathetically and took a pull from the bottle of scotch he had picked up on the way up. "Don't be a fool. It's only that I want to know when it's all gonna end. Living like a bum and behaving like a pig. I'm not, you know."

"Oh, Jay darling, of course you're not. I am! After all I'm the one who walked out on her husband and children. People will make excuses for a man, but I'd hate to hear what they'll say about me. And they'll be right. But life's too short to waste on a guilty conscience. You do what you have to, and if it works out then you've done the right thing."

"And if it doesn't work out?"

"Well, you've got the satisfaction of knowing that *you* made the decision and you didn't just drift along."

"You'll miss your children, the way I do Neal."

"This will probably upset you, but the truth of the matter is that you're more important to me than they are."

She seemed incredibly lovely to him. He reached out, pulled her on his lap, and fondled her face. The nape of her neck was white and soft, and her skin had the texture of velvet. The swell of her breasts rested on the arm he had wrapped around her, and she turned to him with a sad distrait expression in her eyes, which made him uncomfortable and guilt-ridden, for he realized that there was something mercenary and almost depressing in achieving what he had wanted. He had wanted love, and he had gotten it from her, he had wanted to love her, and he did, and his disgust for himself stemmed from the consciousness of having achieved his ends.

"You've got a sense of responsibility," she said.

"Is that what I've got?"

"Enough for the two of us. If we both had it, I'm sure it would be sudden death."

"That's a funny thing to say. How can I have any sense of responsibility?"

"You're living your life and that's everything. You're bothered and worried by the way you're living your life and you've got a tremendous amount of contempt for yourself because of it, but you shouldn't have. There's nothing to believe in, Jay, except another human being. I believe in you. I know that essentially you're good and that I exist when I'm with you. We're supposed to be immoral people, but we're not. We may have done things that other people consider to be immoral, but we've been moral with each other."

"You sound like you're apologizing to someone who isn't here."

"I'm not," she was insistent, "because I don't exist with other people. A woman who looks like me, who wears my clothes, who talks like me, and uses my name—a woman who impersonates me—gives people the impression that they know me. It's a kind of confusion which I'm responsible for."

"Who is the other woman?"

"Nobody. She never lived and she never died. She just wasn't there."

"Will Mitch give you a divorce?"

"Does it matter? If you'd like me to try, I will."

"Wouldn't you like to marry me?"

"I am married to you."

It began to rain, a thin, summer drizzle, and Jay got up to close the window. He looked out of the window at the jagged-shaped harbor, and the boats moored to the pier. He liked the aspect and the sound of the wind which was canalized by other buildings close to the hotel, forming an alleyway which led to the bay. It was late and except for a party breaking up on one of the boats, the square in front of the harbor was deserted. For a moment he expected a squad of Russian officers to come out of a tavern and begin to catwhistle at the closed darkened shutters, but he smiled to himself. He knew that it was a dream, a silly old dream, which he should have forgotten. But he supposed it would come back to him from time to time, just as his fuzzy memories of Vienna sometimes did.

He turned from the window and she was under the covers; two bare white arms were stretched out over the blue blankets.

"I've got a thing about water and boats," he said. "I thought I came out to Southampton to see Eva, but she doesn't seem very important now. I suppose I hoped I was going to explain things to her. We ought to have a boat."

"Not an ocean liner like my father had. Something private that sleeps only two."

"I don't know the first thing about boats, but I like them."

He got under the covers with her and he lit a cigarette.

"I didn't pull the curtains, do you mind?"

"No, I don't mind." She moved up closer to him and rested her head on his shoulder. "It's a good sound, rain. The way it taps on the window. I always liked it."

"I've never noticed it. But I think I like it too."

She turned over on her side and held him. He didn't move

for a minute, but continued to smoke and look at the window over her shoulder.

"This is the way it was meant to be," she said. "Warm and safe."

He put his cigarette out in the ashtray on the bedside table.

"We're in a cage together," he said. "The difference is that we've built it."

"Our own cage. Warm and safe."

The summons from Uncle Carl sounded ominous to Neal. He wondered what the old fool had heard. He was certain that he hadn't been caught smoking in the showerhouse, because if he had been, Uncle Don would have dealt with him. Uncle Don had a variety of unpleasant punishments which Neal had discovered in his first week. The least injurious of them was to be docked from swimming—the sentence for boys who were heard swearing. Anyone who goldbricked during bunk cleanup had his desserts taken away for a day, and as desserts were the only reasonably edible courses in the insipid diet, the loss of them was regarded as serious. Talking after lights-out brought a more subtle and painful castigation: a boy would be told to hold out his arms and was swatted on the backside with a broom whenever he dropped them. Neal had held out for three minutes, which was a bunk record. Uncle Don had narrowed down his antagonists to Neal and Bobby Fish. Bobby presented a solid but not impenetrable façade of tough-guy talk degenerating into total passivity when physical retaliation was threatened. So, Neal realized the combat was really between him and Uncle Don. Uncle Don's authority depended on the boys' acceptance of it, and he was merciless in securing this end. Neal had lost two days' desserts, had his mouth washed with soap once, been swatted with a broom a dozen times, been docked from swimming three times, had lost his canteen (which meant no ice cream or candy), and had finally been beaten with the pride of Uncle Don's small arsenal of corporal instruments—a fraternity paddle which had broken better and older boys than Neal.

"You're gonna get your ass beaten every day until you start listening," Uncle Don said, scratching his crinkly hair which made the same sound as water hitting a plastic shower curtain. Neal would smirk and nod, and Uncle Don, his pallid, freckled skin assuming a brightness which came close to fuchsia, would swat away. Artie Kahn would cry as he watched the punishment, and Neal, after four or five swipes, would say out of twisted white lips: "Shut your hole, shitbag"; and Uncle Don with the diligence of a professional martinet would bash him harder than before. It had been a full first week for Neal, and as he walked up the sloping grass bank to Uncle Carl's headquarters, he decided to change his tactics because he knew that Uncle Don could not change his. Uncle Carl, wearing white tennis shorts, a green sunvisor, and a powerful sweat smell, patted his head and said: "Everything going fine, Neal? Yes, I can tell that you're destined to become one of the group leaders. Fine boy." Neal wondered whom he was talking about. "Taking part in all the activities . . . yes, I can see, a natural athlete. Good coordination. Well, that's that. Surprise for you. Your mother's come up."

Rhoda came out on the porch.

"I'll leave you to have your chat. Keep fit." He turned to Rhoda. "I play a great game of tennis for a fifty-six-year-old man. Perhaps you'd like to watch me."

"Thanks," said Rhoda.

Uncle Carl dashed off the porch with his racket and headed for bunk inspection. He used the racket on the boys rather than the court. But the parents were impressed. Out of the screen door a strange figure emerged, which Neal could not at once identify. He saw a man's chest in one of those hideous print shirts of elongated insects painted a rainbow of pastels, which he associated with captive Indians on reservations after the cavalry rode off. Rhoda put her arms around Neal and hugged him. He wanted to pull away. She had on one of those sweet cheap scents which made him sick to his stomach.

"Hello," he said.

"Say hello to Sports."

"Hello, Sports."

"Hello yourself. How you keeping, Neal? It's not so bad as stir, is it?"

"No, I like it." He had a terror-stricken moment in which it occurred to him that they might take him out of camp.

"How're they treating you, son?"

"Swell."

"Need any dough?" Sports inquired, fondling a bankroll.

"Don't be ashamed to ask if you need some," Rhoda said proudly. "You can ask Sports for anything you want now. He's your stepfather. It's an awful word. He'll be your second father. Pretty lucky to have two fathers. None of the other boys do."

"No, they don't," Neal agreed.

"It's wonderful, Neal. Sports and I got married in Baltimore yesterday morning, and we decided that it would be best to tell you the good news before anybody else heard."

"Why Baltimore?"

"It was easier there," Sports explained, without explaining a thing, Neal thought.

"Are you happy?" Rhoda asked.

"If you are."

"Well, I'm thrilled. It's wonderful. I'm a new person, Neal. We'll be a family now, not like when Jay was with us. We'll go everywhere together."

"You're not upset you missed the wedding, Neal, are yuh?"

"No, why should I be? I'm glad I did."

"See, Rhoda. I told yuh."

"Sports, you're such a smart man. He's a very good judge of people, isn't he, Neal?"

The bunks had grouped around the flagpole where they assembled every morning after cleanup to be told of the day's activities. Neal decided that peace with Uncle Don was mandatory if he were to survive the summer. His mother's lips were moving, the slimy, greasy, scarlet lipstick made her mouth seem unreal.

"Mom, I've got to get back to my bunk. I'll miss the activities if I don't."

"You haven't wished us good luck."

"Good luck," he stammered, then added, "to both of you."

"Well, shake Sports' hand and say: 'Welcome to the family, Dad.' "

Neal peered at him. Sports' mouth curved upwards and his nose twitched apprehensively as he waited for Neal to react.

Neal took his hand lamely and said: "Welcome to the family." Then he faltered. "I don't think it would be right to call you 'Dad,' do you?"

"Naw, never mind, Neal."

Rhoda restrained herself from shouting at Neal. She forced a smile to her mouth and tried to kiss Neal but he moved out of the way with agility.

"We're off on our honeymoon, Neal."

"Write me all about it. Have a good time. I've got to get to my bunk or they'll think something funny happened to me."

He didn't look back as he walked off the porch, but he could hear their voices in the background, and he knew they were waving, but he couldn't look back, not then, or ever again.

Terry opened the door to let the room-service waiter in with the breakfast tray. She called out to Jay who was shaving in the bathroom. He came out wiping the lather off his ear; in his vest, he looked slim and muscular.

"You don't look a day over thirty," she said.

"I've got a special tonic."

"Have you?"

"Women."

"Woman, my dear, woman. From now on, you're doing a single."

"Well, yes. Yes, I think I am."

"I own the means of production and distribution."

"Sounds like a good business."

"It's terrific. A monopoly."

He had a clear head even though he had had a great deal to drink. The shave and shower had refreshed him, but mostly he thought it was Terry who had made waking up such a pleasurable experience. She possessed an ineffable charm and style. What the style was comprised of he could not venture to guess, because the woman was the style, and she was incomparably more than the poised manner, the graceful movements, the brittle wit might indicate. There existed between them a sensuous intimacy which bordered on delirium. He had to touch her, and she had to touch him, and the discovery of this need tore through the layers of resistance which Jay had grown when he had found out that sleeping with a woman had virtually no effect on him. Familiarity did not breed contempt, only boredom.

"I guess I better get the dirty work over with," he said.

"Yes, it's a good day for laundry."

"You make a joke out of everything."

"You don't expect me to become despondent, do you?" She brushed her hair in bed and began to trill like a soprano practicing her exercises. "Ah, Jay, it's that middle-European sadness of yours, that quite touching love of melodrama. Why get all worked up? I'm going shopping for a bathing suit. I think we ought to go swimming, then drive over to Gil Clark's for lobsters, a cup of clam chowder. Oysters, large ones? We'll get plane tickets tomorrow and fly to the South of France. My father used to take me to a lovely little hotel in Antibes."

"I've got a business to look after, and don't forget Neal's at camp. I can't just up and go."

"Why not? I'll lend you the money."

"Very funny."

"Well, the business won't fall apart without you. Your partner can look after it."

"Harry's retired. Marty's just the salesman."

"So for a couple of weeks American women will walk around in the nude. It'll save thousands of marriages."

"You're crazy."

"I am. I agree. Now if you have to get your little Viennese operetta over with, get started. Tears, strife, a scene of monstrous proportions, completely devoid of emotional content. Your wife will curse me, both of us, and I'll get us fifteen thousand dollars' worth of traveler's checks in the meanwhile and buy a knockout of a white bathing suit—something that

covers the least amount of me." She hopped off the bed and
lifted up her nightgown. "Would you like a little encouragement to bolster your courage? A short turn on a wide bed . . .
forget me not, tra-la-la-la-la-la, tiddly-dee-dee."

"It's sex, like your husband said."

"Of course it is, you silly fool. Sex and a million and one
other things. Any complaints"—she picked up a butter knife
and flourished it—"because if there are, you will most certainly be a man around town but in chunks." He sat her on
his lap and kissed her, and she laughed when she drew away.
"Ah, is it madness, yes midsummer madness?"

"Last night, did you . . . ?"

"Did I what?"

"Well, I wasn't very careful."

"I thought you were not only careful, but magnificent into
the bargain."

"Precautions."

"I threw them to the wind when I left my husband, or did
you forget?"

"Seriously?"

"Most seriously."

"What if . . . ?"

She laughed so violently that her whole body shook with
the pure joy of it.

"This is my own unique form of planned parenthood. Both
the man and the woman avoid the use of anything but skin,
and if they're lucky, first shot, they are delivered of a little
bundle nine months hence."

"You must be kidding."

"Darling, it'll be *our* child. A bastard or bastardess because
we shan't have had the benefit of matrimony. So, there. Alas
and alack, and all that crap. Now off you go, and tell your
wife the good news and then meet me at Saks."

Eva concealed her surprise when he appeared unannounced at
the house. She was sitting on the sun terrace alone, reading a
magazine, but her face tightened when he sat down on the
white bench opposite her, and her uneven breathing sent out

a nervous, apprehensive emotional code which he detected at once.

"You've just missed Lorna and my mother."

"That's a shame," he replied without conviction.

"Why didn't you give me a ring? Everything okay at business?"

"Of course," he said with curious violence.

"You don't have to jump down my throat. I only asked a civil question."

He reached out and picked up a glass of fresh orange juice which was on the wooden table and drank it.

"I haven't even asked you if you've had breakfast."

"Yes, I have. Thanks just the same. I'm only thirsty."

She lit a cigarette and her hand trembled as she held the match to it. She saw that he was watching her and she tried to control her nervousness.

"Did you bring your clothes?"

"No, I don't plan to stay."

"Oh, I wish you'd change your mind. It's been pleasant with Lorna and my mother but you being here would give us all a lift. Couldn't I persuade you? Please." He put down the empty glass. "I'll squeeze some more, would you like that?"

"No, I'm fine."

"You were just passing by and you decided to stop by to say hello?"

"Not exactly."

"We ought to talk about having a vacation. Anywhere particular you want to go, or should we stay down here for the summer? I've met a few people who've asked me to get you down here. Everyone's so anxious to meet you . . . a lot of Wall Street people who know all about you and they say that the stock is going to be a blue chip when it's on the market."

Jay turned his head slightly and closed his eyes. The sun was hotter than he expected for eleven o'clock in the morning. A few beads of sweat appeared on his forehead and he wiped them off with his handkerchief.

"I saw one of your suits in the bureau so you can change and have a swim."

He opened his eyes and turned his head slowly so that his eyes were in a line with hers, but then quickly she averted her face. He could see how frightened and nervous she was, and he had a sinking, doomed feeling inside.

"I'm going to go," he said.

She was working desperately to control herself, but her mouth twitched and she started to blink, so she put on the sunglasses that were hooked over the edge of the chaise longue.

"I have to, Eva."

"I knew it was coming. Oh God, Jay, I feel too awful to say anything. For days I've been walking around with this terrible tense feeling in the pit of my stomach. Nerves, I told myself. On edge. But all the time I was sinking and I couldn't hold onto anything. It's coming. My body knew. I'm almost relieved that I've heard. I used to get the same nervous tension when I was a kid and I waited for my school report card. I used to dream of failing all my subjects."

"I'll get my stuff out today."

"Whenever you like. Will you go to a hotel or what?"

"I think so. It's your house. In your name."

"Oh, boy. Compensation."

"No, not compensation. Money isn't involved. I'm sure you're not thinking of money."

"You're right. I always wondered how I'd react when this finally came. And the day we got married I was sure that you'd leave me and not the other way around. A big emotional scene. Screaming. Abuse. I can't, though—I'm not built that way." She took out a cigarette and this time he lit it for her. "Your hands are shaking too. Which must mean that you feel something and it's not just cold-blooded murder."

"Sure I feel something."

"We tried to build a marriage on the bones of a dead man and what's dead doesn't live again. But you did care for me, didn't you? Once?"

"Very much."

"But not enough. Is it the girl you never mentioned?"

"Yes, it is."

"The college girl who threw you over."

"I threw her over."

"That doesn't make sense."

"I don't suppose it does."

"The one who came over to you at the country club bar?"

He nodded. The futility implicit in her quest for information disturbed him. It was like watching someone with a rash scratch uncontrollably until the skin was a mass of bleeding sores.

"I knew it was her. Don't ask me how I knew. But in my bones, I sensed that we were dead together."

"I'd better go," he said, unwilling to prolong her agony, but as he got up to leave he turned and in a voice that came as close to entreaty as he was capable of, he said: "Would you consider a divorce?"

She pursed her lips tightly and the long cigarette ash fell on her bare stomach, but she did not appear to notice it.

"I've acted like a lady, and you like a gentleman, very unusual for us." She paused as though remembering his question. "I can't divorce you, Jay. I just couldn't do it."

"I didn't think—"

"Remember me to Neal, will you? He's really a nice kid. I'm sorry he didn't like me, but I guess he had his reasons."

Jay drove from the house in a daze. He was out of Southampton on the road back to New York when he realized where he was. He pulled into a driveway and turned his car around. In Southampton he parked his car in front of Saks and walked in. The lights made him feel a bit giddy. He circled most of the counters in the front of the store, then somebody took his arm.

"Jay, Jay, darling," Terry said, "you're crying."

"Am I?"

She wiped his face with her handkerchief.

"Was it so terrible?"

"No, that's the point, it was almost painless."

"You feel something for her and you're sad. But it's sentiment."

"You're probably right."

"You've found me, Jay. You're my man. The best man in the world."

"Let's have a drink somewhere."

"Yes, let's have a drink. Only one."

"Why only one?"

"Well, there's nothing to forget now, is there?"

V

THE
HUMAN
ELEMENT

20

The severity of the winter seemed almost supernatural to Sports. He regarded the snow as a nemesis which fate had designed to torment and test him. He had been on a losing streak for two months; it had begun on Christmas Eve with a fixed basketball game in Madison Square Garden, a game he was so confident of winning that he broke his longstanding habit, and started to count his money before it ended. The team he bet on lost by two points in the last eleven seconds, and he recalled the sinking, recoiling sensation which turned his stomach upside down as he stood in the exit with Rhoda by his side as the ball sailed through the hoop. Two quick losses on football games followed and he knew with that instinctive helpless sixth sense that gamblers possess that he was on a losing streak. The difficulty, as he explained to Rhoda, who had begun to deplete her savings in an effort to save him, centered on making the right move: "Do I just sit on the sidelines with no action, hoping that my luck changes, or do I stick my head into a meatgrinder?"

Perplexed and with growing desperation, she had replied:

"I dunno what to advise you . . . I trust you."

"I'm in a hole, and I gotta fight back," he protested.

"Then fight! I'll stick with you no matter what."

And she was as good as her word. She would study the television screen with as much concentration as she could muster, while he twisted his hands, bit his fingernails, picked sores on his face, his complexion a composite of sallowish green, his eyes red from loss of sleep as he listened, listened, interminably to sports commentaries which, by the end of January, sounded as though they were the product of the same voice describing the same game she had heard hundreds of times.

"I need money. I gotta pay off, or they come for me," he threatened. "And when they come, they break everything. They wreck the house completely and put me in the hospital."

She gave him the store's receipts which she was to deposit in the bank on Monday.

"Business is bad, Sports. It's the slow season. All the sales are on, and I'm stuck with loads of dresses I can't move, and bills I can't pay."

"I need money," was the plaintive cry, and she gave it to him. "Go to the bank. They'll give you a loan."

"You don't see a customer all day. Nobody walks out of the house in this weather. Eighteen inches of snow last night. The Saturday is a write-off."

"Go to the bank, Rhoda!" he said in a menacing voice, slamming his fist down on the cash register and breaking the glass.

"Sports, I'm in hock up to my neck. I'm afraid to go to the bank because I haven't made last month's repayment on the car."

"Who the hell needs a canary yellow convertible in the Arctic? What do we need it for? Let's get rid of it."

"But how can we? It's not ours to sell. The bank manager won't give me the right time. If I ask him for another loan, he'll get worried and he'll send somebody down to the store and they'll see that we're losing money."

"Get a personal loan."

"What do you think I got?" she shrieked, helplessly.

"Well, Latkin's coming this afternoon and he'll want his money. Ten thousand dollars."

"I'll go home with you. We'll plead for more time."

"He knows from pleadings? Are you crazy or something? Who do you think goes to him? Pleaders, people who can't get nowhere else? Do you understand, Rhoda?"

She looked at the empty store, and the dust on the floor which had not been cleaned for weeks: the dirty marks made by galoshes and boots.

"It's a pigsty, this store. That's what Jay would say. It was a business principle with him to have a clean store. He said people leave dirty filthy homes, they want to shop in a clean store. We've got rats in the basement, and I'm afraid to go down to put the rat poison on the bread." She flourished the stale bread in his face. "Would you do it for me?"

"Please, don't bother me. I'm not a businessman. This ain't my business."

"No? Well, you spend the money that comes out of it pretty good."

"I don't ask you to decide on teams and you don't ask me to sell dresses."

"I wasn't asking you to sell dresses, but to act like a man, a husband."

He scratched his ear violently, picked some wax out of it, and flicked it on the floor.

"A husband!" he jeered. "Listen, Rhoda, I been a pretty goddamned good husband, by anybody's standards."

"You've never worked since I met you."

"I perform my other duties all right by you. Frankly, sleeping with you ain't no picnic. With the kind of appetite you got. I done my share."

"I was starved for a long time. Didn't have any real affection."

"So that makes you a glutton? You got no complaints."

"No, I got what I deserved."

"I've got to have the money."

"What should I do, manufacture it out of thin air? Tell me what I should do, and I will."

"You got any jewelry you haven't told me about?"

"It's all been hocked. Sell the car and we'll both wind up in jail."

"Can you get anything for the furniture?"

"Maybe three or four hundred dollars. It's eight years old. And Jay bought it!"

"So Jay bought it, but it's yours."

"Doesn't it bother you, selling another man's furniture?"

"Oh, you're getting self-righteous with me? C'mon, let's

go home and wait for Latkin. He said he'd be there at twelve
o'clock.''

"What happens if you're not there?"

"Simple. You become a widow."

The synagogue was a large, square building on Eastern Parkway which had been built in the early twenties. It stood on a
dark corner and its gray façade had been recently cleaned.
Young Rabbi Davidson who was in charge of it took a special
pleasure in welcoming those who came to Saturday morning
services. He was a pink-cheeked man, with a strong sense of
decorum and he enjoyed the feeling of older, wealthier men
seeking his counsel; sometimes they came away after a discussion with him convinced that he was a sage. Latkin was
his favorite, for Latkin consulted him frequently on fine points
of theology, and made himself readily available when the synagogue was one short of a *minyan*. They had a mutual interest
in trivial pedantries—the rabbi scholastic, and Latkin purely
pragmatic, for he was determined at all costs to get into heaven
which he regarded as an exclusively Jewish club—its physical
characteristics he imagined were similar to a good *frim* Catskill mountain hotel where the men sat on the lawn at card
tables playing pinochle and the women sweated in the kitchens
cooking food, and elderly infidels (all those who were not
members of the tribe) ran back and forth bringing cigarettes
and ice water to the players. He never got around to revealing
this celestial vision to Rabbi Davidson because he was sure
that the rabbi had his own "particala idear of da place: some-
tink more *heim*, as befitted a man still lean in years."

"It's a sad anniversary," Davidson said, as he stood on the
steps, the wind blowing his long black coat.

"Fifteen years," Latkin admitted, "an' I still feel like it
was yesteryear." Western films had given his broken English
a contemporary flavor.

Davidson blew hot breath on his white frostbitten hands.

"She was a good woman," he said.

"A good woman?" Incredulously, Latkin clapped his hands

together, for he was not sympathetic to understatement. "Da best. A heart made from gold, she had."

"How old was she when you had your loss?"

Latkin did some hasty logarithms on his tobacco-stained fingers.

"Seventy-four. A young woman. Kerried herself like sixty."

"You were a good son."

"I nevah married," he said, rolling his r's with the same enthusiasm he reserved for sweet Passover wine. "My life— I geve it up for her, but who's complainink. Did you hear me complainink? I should live so long if I ever . . ."

The rabbi began rubbing his arms, engaging in something close to a self-embrace as he attempted to restore the circulation in his flaccid muscles. Latkin could keep him standing there for an hour and a half, and he knew he couldn't move because Latkin had just given him a check for a thousand dollars—his annual contribution. Latkin sucked in his cheeks, made a popping sound, and sighed in Davidson's face. Davidson waited for him to continue. He himself had no intention of providing the conversation with any additional fuel. Latkin nodded to him and Davidson nodded back. The week before they had nodded to each other for a good fifteen minutes, and Davidson's neck had hurt all week. Latkin walked down a single step and repositioned himself, and Davidson, assuming that the interview was concluded, hastened to walk up two steps, but Latkin seized his sleeve and pulled him close, so that the younger man had to stoop awkwardly. He whispered through his frosty breath:

"You a wise man. Full of wisdom. When you get a little older you will be wiser still."

Davidson thanked him wordlessly. Where the devil was the sexton, he wondered, for he had arranged for the man to call him to the phone when Latkin and he got outside.

"I'll see you next Friday evening."

"See me? Of course you'll see me. Is there ever bin a Friday night when you didn't see me?" Davidson's wisdom-wall had been breached.

"I didn't mean to imply that I wouldn't see you."

"I have to make *Kaddish*, no?"

"Certainly you do."

"Then why not next Friday?"

The sexton, an elderly forgetful man with a monklike bald pate and saliva running down his chin appeared at the doorway, a man in the full flower of his dotage. He waved at Davidson and called out:

"On the phone, they want you."

"Just coming . . ." He wheeled around and extended his hand to Latkin. "*Git Shabbos*, Mr. Latkin."

Latkin squeezed his hand till it hurt and the rabbi tried to extricate himself but without success. It was like a bear-trap. "The phone," he said in a thin whine.

"Where's the phone?"

"Someone's waiting to speak to me."

"I got news for you. The world is waitink to speak to you . . . the whole world. A man so young in years and wise in wisdom."

"Thank you." Davidson pulled his hand away when Latkin's defenses were lulled.

"*Git Shabbos*, Rabbi Davidson. And don't forget, the world is waitink for a message."

"I won't." He rushed up the steps and was about to close the door when he saw Latkin following him, but Latkin paused and bent down and picked up a coin.

"You were standing on a penny. Gold, it falls from your mouth. This penny is my blessing. A sign from God."

He turned and began to walk towards his car. The Sabbath was not over, but he had to see Sports. He had a new Packard and he puffed as he drove the car like an engineer operating a steam engine, manually. The traffic was straggly as he negotiated the hill down to Sports' apartment. He was surprised and delighted when he saw there was furniture and a doorman in the lobby and he asked the man to buzz Sports on the house phone. Sports' distorted voice came over the minuscule speaker and Latkin was shown to the elevator. He rubbed his hands affectionately because the omens were favorable to his collecting the debt.

Neal opened the door for him and Latkin massaged his scalp. Neal pushed his hand off, and glared at him suspiciously. He didn't like Latkin's dark, bituminous eyes, or the swaying fleshy chins which hung pendulously from his jaw. Latkin tried to fondle him again and Neal skirted out of the way. Latkin removed his hat and handed it to Neal; the hat was too tight or Latkin's head was too large, for there was an uneven saucerlike ring bisecting the tufts of hair on his head which appeared to spring out of the most unlikely places like cactus in a desert.

"You Sports' son?" He removed his coat and draped it on Neal's arm.

"No, I'm not. I don't run the checkroom either," he said, handing Latkin's coat back to him. He disliked the strange, aggressive visitors who wandered through the apartment, treating him like a bellhop. Two days earlier he had returned from school and had found a man sleeping in his bed, and when he asked Rhoda where he could do his homework he was told to do it on the kitchen table so that he wouldn't disturb the sleeping visitor. It didn't seem real to Neal—the constant talk about games, horses, track conditions, radios blaring all night long, the stream of furtive men and women who played cards in the living room till three or four in the morning, and whose names were repeated to him time and time again, but he could never remember them. His mother had grown increasingly listless and apathetic, allowing him total freedom, never asking where he had gone, who he had been with. And she avoided looking at him. The change had taken place since she had married Sports. Neal would find her lying on her bed smoking cigarettes which had a peculiar odor and then she would begin to giggle stupidly or fall into morose silence, while Sports energetically shouted numbers on the telephone to ghostlike voices. Neal decided to run away from home when the weather got warmer—possibly some time in March—and hitchhike down to Florida or Texas and find a job on a farm that employed young boys. He had seen a film about a ranch where boys worked for their room and board and three dollars a week, and he believed he could do the same thing.

Latkin shuffled into the living room where Sports and Rhoda stood disconsolately by the imitation fireplace. The red light which was supposed to suggest fire revolved around a small wheel.

"Varra nice," Latkin observed. "You livin' like a king, no, Sports?"

"It ain't bad."

"A cup of tea I wouldn't mind."

"Rhoda, make him some tea."

"I don't have any tea."

"It's cold like anything outside," Latkin said. "Schnapps you got?"

Sports went over to the liquor cabinet and poured him a large drink.

"We've got rye, okay?"

"Nutting wrong mit rye. It warms."

"Want some water or soda with it?" Rhoda asked. She was too nervous to stand around.

"No, nevah. 'S'like putting water in hot soup. Nobody does. So why in Schnapps, I esk you?"

He held the glass tightly in his chubby fist, sniffed the bouquet, and downed about two fingers, ejaculated a long resounding "Aaah," then squinted at the two of them. He had often been in similar situations, and he knew the people were uncomfortable and fearful when they couldn't pay up. He divided the world into those who could pay, and those who couldn't. The latter always displayed an obsequious, dissembling attitude which skidded into belligerence, hollow unconvincing defiance which he could rend with a wave of his hand. He was an astute judge of human nature, and he specialized in lending money to gamblers because he knew most of them were incapable of violence, cowardly, and they all told the same lies.

"It's a sad day. Today I say *Kaddish* for my Mamma."

"It's a sad day for a lot of other people," Sports replied.

If Sports had had the money he would have flashed it by this time, Latkin thought; the inevitable excuses, apologies, explanations, would now follow. He swallowed the rest of the whiskey and belched into his fist. Sports took his glass and filled it again. Latkin looked at Neal standing in a corner and he felt a great wave of sadness for the child who might now find himself on the street. He played with an alternative idea which might enable Sports to pay him off without forcing him to break up his home.

"Business is very bad, Mr. Latkin," Rhoda said.

"Terrible. I know for myself. I can't move a silver fox or even a Persian lamb. Stock I got like corns." He removed a grubby well-thumbed notebook from his vest pocket and turned to a page which contained Sports' account. His lips moved as he did some rapid sums. "It comes to ten tousan' dollars. You make it the same?"

"That's right. Ten grand." Sports gazed out of the window at a car waiting for a green light. The license plate of the car ended with three. He would've bet that the next car to pass the light also ended in an odd number. A seven came past and he squeezed his hands excitedly. It was an even money bet. Why couldn't he have bet Latkin on it, or the next car, or the one after that? He turned back to Latkin, who sipped his drink pensively. He had to stop making mind bets. One of his friends had started to lose his mind making bets like this. According to the friend, various people, unknown to themselves, owed him sixty-two million dollars. That was the kind of streak he was on.

"Maybe you should stop gembling?" Latkin suggested.

"And do what?"

"Gemblers don't win, but the bookmakers live in two-family houses and their wives wear mink coats."

"That's true," Rhoda said. "When Sports was booking he was making three, four thousand dollars a week."

"Then why stop? That's a good living."

"He's smarter than the bookmakers. He would make three and bet five," she explained.

"I never liked booking. There's no skill in it. You're like a banker. You have to take the teams that other people don't want."

"But the odds help a bookmaker, no?"

"That's not the point. It's having the action that's exciting. It's pitting your brains against other people's and fate."

"Fate," Latkin spat the word out contemptuously. "Fate is one ting: you're born and you die. Gembling is a sickness."

Sports shifted his weight from one foot to the other uneasily. The discussion was tiring him, and he was getting nowhere with Latkin. How could he explain the excitement, the thrill of betting on a winner? The money was unimportant—it was the action.

"I haven't got it," he said finally. The admission relaxed him.

"Don't you think I know you don't got it?"

"What's gonna happen?" asked Rhoda, on the edge of panic.

"What should happen?"

"The apartment, the furniture . . . it's worth something? Maybe three thousand. We could sell it by the end of next week!"

"Where would the boy live?"

"He'll live where I decide. He's my son."

"To move out of such a nice apartment. It's a pity."

"That's not our fault, is it?" Sports said captiously. "You want your money."

"I'm entitled . . . no? I didn't esk to lend you. You esked me."

"Aw, Christ, what's the point?"

"Maybe I can help."

"Give me more time!" Sports was jubilant.

"No, that I can't do. Enough time you've had." He looked around the room. "Nice apartment. How many rooms you got?"

"Six. Neal has a bedroom and we have one."

"The living room's fine. A good-sized room."

"For what?" Rhoda said.

"I run a little game, and the people don't have where to play."

"What kind of game?" Rhoda said.

"Creps."

"A floater?"

"Whadelse? Nice respectable men in the game. No rough-necks."

"How big is the game?" Sports inquired; he saw an opportunity to get even.

"The biggest. But you won't play."

"Why not?"

"They don't play for credit and nobody borrows money. A man goes bad, he leaves the game, like a gentleman. He's always welcome to play when he's got enough."

"What's enough?"

"No one without twenty thousand. Pikers can look for an-oder game."

"So what's in it for me?"

"A thousand a night. Ten nights, they play here . . . we're even. Longer is up to you."

"A thousand a night. For a game like that, the house takes ten percent off every winning roll."

"I know. The ten percent is me."

"Will you be here every night?"

"Me? You crazy? I go to bed ten o'clock ever night. The game starts at twelve till five. What do I want to stay up all night? I don't know anytink about gembling."

"If the cops break it up I can do three years. The guys on the bunko squad don't do business. They make a pinch and the D.A. gets busy."

Latkin's dark eyes roamed Sports' face for a sign of strength, for resistance.

"You a gembler, right? Well, this is a gemble. You win or lose. If you lose before the ten nights is out, then I write off what you owe me."

"While I'm in the *keister*. Raymond Street, or the Tombs."

"At five o'clock on the dot I call on the telephone. The phone rings four times, so you can think about it. You pick up the phone, that means you don't want to cooperate. You let it ring four times and you don't owe me no more.'' He extended his hand to Rhoda, then to Sports, patted Neal's head, and walked out of the room. As he made to open the door, Sports rushed up to him.

"Latkin, if you're not at the game collecting your ten percent, then who is?''

Latkin smiled with some embarrassment and shrugged his shoulders.

"Sports, you don't hev to worry your head. I got somebody what looks after my interests. A good reliable man who don't cheat, and don't gemble. So, denks for thinking of me. But don't worry. No, you don't need to worry for mine sake.''

The phone rang promptly at five o'clock and Sports stared at it helplessly. Rhoda came over to him on the second ring and put her arm around his neck, but he forced her to remove it. It rang a third time. The sweat from the pocket above his lip began to drip and he wiped it with the back of his hand. On the fourth ring he lifted his hand, but Rhoda pulled it away from the phone.

"We've got no choice.''

"I'm sorry, Rhoda. What can I say?''

"If the police come, what then?''

"We're both in it. The lease is in your name, and that makes you just as guilty.''

Rhoda poured herself a drink, and swallowed a pill with it. She went over to the window and stared out at the gray buildings and the empty playing field which lay in the distance. She almost never looked out of the living-room window, even though the view was a good one. Sleet was falling and it made a sharp ricocheting sound as it caromed off the sides of cars.

"It doesn't matter any more," she said. "It really doesn't . . .''

"We're being victimized.''

"Hah, victimized! It's gonna snow.''

Terry had her hair in an upsweep and she had her feet up on the settee pillow. The snow was falling and she thought it looked like wads of cotton sprinkled from the roof of the hotel. In the months that she and Jay had lived at the Waldorf Astoria's prime suite, she had added some homely touches, and the sitting room was, to her eye, agreeable because of the hi-fi and the television which Jay had bought. The liquor cabinet was also new—a low-slung, angular one which gave the room an ambience of home. The Vlaminck painting of a farmhouse which she had bought as a surprise for Jay made her feel that the room had a greater permanence. She heard the door in the anteway open and Jay burst in. He had snow on his hair and his shoes were wet.

"Hey, if you come into my place with wet shoes, I'll brain you."

"How do you feel?"

"Fine. Will I ever housebreak you?"

"That depends on what you're prepared to offer."

"Oh, take your pick. It could be twins."

"Does the doctor think—?"

"The doctor does not think, he just doctors, and he says I'm a perfectly wonderful specimen of a specimen."

"Do you want to go to a movie?"

"No, not really, unless you do."

"Then we'll stay in. Have dinner sent up and watch television."

"Sounds exciting."

"It's snowing outside."

"So I've noticed."

He put his hand on her stomach and rubbed it then kissed her behind the ear.

"I feel so big today. Just like an enormous animal. A hippo."

"You're gorgeous."

"I think that the last six weeks are longer than the other months put together."

"It's your imagination."

"I've been talking to it all afternoon. Unlike me. But I wasn't being sentimental. Very Master Sergeantish and ordering it to emerge from its dark, warm valley and give me my figure back. I don't think it heard me. What are you going to do about it, Jay? I won't have a disobedient child.''

"I could get room service to send out for Chinese food.''

"You're not paying attention.''

"I have to see it to belt it. I can't hit a man smaller than me. It's unfair.''

"Yes, I'd like Chinese food. How'd your meeting go?''

"No problems. We're increasing the dividend.''

"I'll ring my broker to buy fifty thousand shares.''

"Hey, you're kidding . . . that's privileged information.''

"Well, then, I won't buy any of your lousy shares.''

He smiled and sat down beside her, lifted her head and rested it on his lap. She closed her eyes and he kissed her eyelids.

"Wake up.''

"Why? You won't let me make any money.''

"Surprise. I bought a hundred thousand last month through my broker . . . in your name.''

"You aren't serious, are you?''

"Sure I am.''

"We need the money. You can't pay our hotel bill?''

"No, but I can manage to buy the hotel and throw all the guests out if you like. That would give us about eight hundred rooms, and you could have a friend stay with us.''

"Ah, you're an impossible man, a quite impossible man.''

At about eight o'clock the room-service waiter wheeled in a steaming hot trolley. He uncovered it and Terry lifted the small silver tops of the dishes. Jay had ordered the chicken and almonds which she had once said she liked. She broke open a fortune cookie and read aloud: " 'He who sleeps heavily will father few.' ''

"Oh, c'mon, I don't believe it,'' he said, yanking the piece of paper from her, while she squealed with laughter. He read it: " 'On solemn occasions a man walks softly: women cry and men go to war.' What's that supposed to mean?''

"The Chinese have great dignity and many children.''

"No, seriously. I don't get it . . .''

"It means that unless we eat the spareribs they'll get cold."
She took a rib and began to munch it. "Hey, I just had a
lovely idea. Wouldn't it be nice to get Neal early tomorrow
and all have breakfast together. We can't go for a drive because of the snow; but we could catch the early show at Radio
City."

He blinked with surprise. He could not fathom what was
behind this new interest in Neal, and yet it seemed genuine.
The weekend he had broken with Eva, Terry had insisted on
writing a long explanatory letter to Neal. He had been against
it, but after considerable persuasion he had relented. "No one
tells the kid anything. He's always being knocked off balance.
For example: Rhoda and Sports coming up to camp—
completely out of the blue—and informing him that they got
married. How do you think he felt? And even though he didn't
much like Eva, he still thinks that you're together. If we try
to spring it on him—that you're finished—he won't have
much regard for me. He's got to respect us and he's got to be
persuaded that what we've done is best for us—and him in
the long run—because it's built on love. If he learns that one
single human lesson he won't go wrong." Jay had read and
reread the letter half a dozen times before she had sent it. "I
don't care about what anybody says about us, but as far as
Neal is concerned, the letter will be our passport to respectability and it's essential that he back us up because when Mitch
gets through with us we'll be knee-deep in filth and Neal won't
know what to believe unless we've laid a foundation." After
posting the letter, he realized that her logic was irrefutable,
and he wondered if she was using Neal for a sounding board
for the time when she had to face her own child. It had worked
miraculously, for when the three of them did meet at the end
of the summer, Neal was thoroughly captivated by Terry. Jay
had expected their first meeting to be unrelievedly awkward
and embarrassing and before starting out he had needed a
drink, but she had forced him to put the bottle down. "If he
smells liquor on your breath, he'll think you didn't have the
courage to face him on his own terms. He's probably more
nervous than you are, and if anybody needs a drink it's him,

but he's only a kid and that makes him ineligible." She had kissed Jay affectionately on the cheek. "Therefore be bold, my sweet."

In the middle of the night, Neal got out of bed to go to the bathroom. The scene he had witnessed between Latkin and Sports earlier in the day had floated out of his mind. Apart from the fact that Sports owed Latkin a debt which he could not pay, Neal had not listened to or been particularly interested in the terms of the treaty dictated by Latkin. What had impressed him most about the scene was that Latkin had confirmed his own suspicions about Sports: namely, that he was a gutless weakling, who had married Rhoda for a number of reasons, none of them remotely connected with the ideal of love which sustained Terry and his father. He had made a desperate effort to discover some positive virtues in his mother's relationship with Sports, but he could not imagine what had first drawn them to each other nor what kept them together. Sports was a dull, thoughtless man, not physically attractive, passively ignorant, with a neutral personality, a total lack of interest in every human activity except gambling, and an active contempt towards Rhoda which he did not disguise. There had been times when Neal had wanted to go to his mother and ask: "Why, why him?" But he had been convinced beforehand that the question would only serve further to complicate their domestic life, so he slipped into the apathetic, backsliding atmosphere that prevailed in the apartment. He asked no questions and sought no counsel. On one point only could he muster any passion, and this came about when he saw with his own eyes that Rhoda was giving Sports money. He resented having guessed Sports' motive before he married Rhoda. If he was capable of this induction why couldn't Rhoda see it? What prevented her from seeing what was so evident? How was it that he had been cleverer than his own mother? He couldn't understand why she had walked into a bear trap, and what was worse, remained there of her own free will. The complexity of their relationship was beyond him, but he felt certain that even when he was older and more experienced it would still seem to him an act of gratuitous destruction.

Someone was running the water in the bathroom and there were voices coming from the living room. He tiptoed down the long dark corridor and peeked into the room. He saw about fifteen men on their knees chanting and whispering to each other as a man rubbed a pair of dice together and then flung them against the corner of the woodwork. The man who rolled the dice scooped up a pile of money which was placed in the center of the floor and another man was busy counting money which he held tightly in his fist. Sports ambled around the circle dropping ash from his cigarette on the carpet, and Rhoda walked in carrying a tray of glasses and ice in a pitcher. The men called out "scotch" or "rye" and Sports, acting as bartender, poured out the drinks. Rhoda appeared to be dazed as she stood in a corner of the room watching the men skirmishing around the pile of money. Neal stifled a scream when somebody took his arm and shook him.

"You lost or somethin', sonny?"

It was the man who had been in the bathroom.

"I wanted to go to the toilet."

"Yeah? Well, it's free now. You can go, then hit the sack."

"And if I don't . . . ?" he started to ask defiantly.

"Just do as you're told," the man said, increasing his pressure on Neal's arm, so that his muscle began to throb.

"It's my house and if you don't let me go I'll call the cops," Neal said.

He was shocked when the man released his pressure and then suddenly smacked him. The sound of the slap frightened him more than the actual pain and he bit his lip angrily, refusing to cry.

"You better learn some manners, sonny. When you make threats, back them up."

"Hey, what the hell do you think you're doing?" Rhoda demanded as she came towards them. Neal was rubbing his face.

"This your kid, lady?"

"That's right. What've you done to him?"

"He threatened to call the cops. You better have a talk with him. I'm not gonna have a kid louse up the whole setup."

"Just leave him alone."

Sports heard their voices over the din and switched on the light in the corridor.

"What's up?"

"A little trouble with the brat," the man said.

"Neal, you go back to bed," Sports ordered.

Neal glared at him angrily and Sports turned away.

"I'll go back to bed, but not because you say I should." He turned to his mother who had the flat of her hand pressed against the wall as though for support. "He's a worm, Mom. A worm!" Neal said, and strode down the corridor back to his room.

"He'll tell Jay," Rhoda whined as Neal closed his bedroom door.

"Who's Jay?" the man asked.

"Never mind. I'll straighten it all out," Sports said soothingly.

Jay now never came up to the apartment when he had to meet Neal. He pressed the house phone buzzer twice promptly at ten o'clock every Sunday morning and Neal would shoot out of the apartment and see him in the lobby five minutes later. This time Neal had not answered Jay's signal as he usually did, by pressing the buzzer back twice, but had asked him over the phone to come up. Jay was disquieted by this change in their routine. Neal opened the door of the elevator for him.

"Hi, Neal, aren't you ready yet?" he asked. He held his watch up to the light. "I'm not early."

"I need you, Daddy."

"What do you mean?"

"The suitcase is too heavy for me."

"Suitcase? What suitcase?"

"I'm coming to live with you."

Jay was taken aback and walked with Neal down the darkened hallway to the apartment door which was held open by a door stopper.

"I don't like to go inside," he said. "Your mother's still probably sleeping."

"The valise is in the foyer. I dragged it in myself, but I can't lift it."

"What's all this about, Neal? You know you just can't come and live with me without your mother's permission."

He studied Neal's anxious face and grew increasingly distressed when he switched on the light.

"What's happened to your face?"

Neal struggled to lift the case, but Jay pulled his hand away.

"I asked what happened. Your eye's bruised. Did anybody . . . ?" his voice rose on the tail of the unfinished question.

"Please, please, Dad. I'll tell you what happened in the car."

They pulled into a diner on the East Side for breakfast. Although Terry was waiting for them, Jay thought it would be better to get the whole story from Neal first so that he could devise a plan by the time he got back to the hotel.

"We'll just have orange juice and coffee now. Terry wants to take you to a place in Westchester that specializes in pancakes."

Neal sipped his juice and his face lost that long doleful expression which had alarmed Jay during the course of their drive.

"I don't think it's a very good idea for you to live in a hotel. Maybe we'll go househunting when Terry's feeling better."

"I'm not going back there," Neal said with finality.

"You won't have to. If your mother wants to get tough, I'll take her to court. It could last a couple of years, and she hasn't got the kind of money to do that. I better ring my lawyer."

"Will I be able to stay with you?"

"Of course you will," he said, but he wasn't at all certain that he could keep his word. He telephoned Nathan Clay and arranged a meeting at his hotel for two o'clock that afternoon.

When they got to Jay's hotel, Terry was waiting for them in the lobby. She wore a fully cut mink coat which concealed the fact that she was in her eighth month. Neal rushed up to her and embraced her and she rubbed her hands through his hair. Her eyes were bright and she kissed Jay on the cheek.

"I thought my two men were standing me up. Did you oversleep, Neal?"

"No, we stopped off for a quick coffee and I had to phone my lawyer," Jay said.

"Why, what's wrong?"

"Neal's going to come and live with us . . . I hope."

Her eyes opened wide with surprise and Jay's mouth trembled. As he stood between them he had a shrinking, constricting sensation in his throat, for he had not prepared her for the news, and he wondered how she would react. He closed his eyes for a second and when he opened them he saw her holding Neal's hands and dancing round him in a circle.

"That's marvelous!" she exclaimed, and he sensed that her pleasure was as genuine as his. He didn't know what he would have done if she had shown any reluctance, but he could see from the expression of open joy on Neal's face and her warm acceptance of him that a real bond of affection existed between them.

"Well, are you going to tell me all about it, or not?"

"Let's have some breakfast," Neal said.

"Sure, if we can persuade this elderly gentleman to drive us up to Larchmont."

Neal sat in the back of the car and stared out of the window at the mountainous snowdrifts in Central Park. Sunday morning in New York was quiet, and the empty park had a whiteness and peace which made him feel secure. Every now and then, Terry would turn around to him, smile, and squeeze his hand as she listened to Jay's account of the life Neal had been coerced into, and had submitted to, as a consequence of Rhoda's remarriage. When he had finished, she kissed Neal on the forehead and said:

"Don't you worry, baby. Not any more. It's all going to be okay."

After a large breakfast of Southern-style buckwheat pancakes and sausages, during which Jay frequently left the table to make telephone calls, they started back to the city. Neal felt much more confident and he tried to remember bits of Terry's letter which he had not understood entirely. He now realized that he was seeing for himself with his own two eyes what she meant. They had never discussed the letter, since Neal had accepted her at their first meeting which took place at the hotel after he had debarked from the train. He had grown three inches over the summer, his posture was better, and he had acquired a firmer grip on his circumstances or so he thought. After his initial period of rebellion, he submitted to the rigorous training at the camp, and he learned an important lesson: in order to combat a system you have to succeed within the system because then you know its weaknesses. He won the award for the most outstanding camper in his age group, and when he got the medal back to his bunk he had crumpled up the bit of soft copper in his fist and flushed it down the toilet. He had a new strength, which he hoped would carry him over the winter with his mother, but Sports was the imponderable. He could not prevent Rhoda from pandering to his sickness—and gambling was a sickness—because Sports was Rhoda's sickness, and her ministrations for him worked in reverse. She had been trying to save herself, and Neal had been left stranded like an alien at the border without a passport. He barely spoke to either of them, for they were seldom around, and he preferred solitude to their company. It occurred to him that despite Terry's remark: "Morality isn't a question of what other people think but what I do myself," that her situation was in a sense similar to his mother's. And yet there was a basic difference which he could not puzzle out. There was something right about what she had done, and something incontestably wrong about his mother's relationship with Sports. Was it in the quality of the man or was it the very nature of love?

"Jay, pull up, will you?" Terry said.

"I'll drop you at Radio City." He seemed surprised.

"Neal and I'll have a walk. A pregnant woman's got to get her quota of exercise. We can do some window shopping."

He stopped at the corner of Fifty-fifth Street and Fifth Avenue and said:

"I'll see you when?"—he looked at his watch—"Four-thirty?'' She leaned over and kissed him and he rubbed his hand affectionately across her cheek. "It's better if I see them on my own. Look after her for me, Neal, will you?''

"He's my squire. I like them young.''

She took Neal's gloved hand and interwove it with hers.

At two o'clock promptly the doorbell rang and Clay's assistant, a youngish man called Brewster, answered it.

Rhoda entered first. She had on too much pancake makeup and the flesh of her neck and throat had a chalk-like texture which made her face unreal, as though she could peel it off. She was wearing the mink coat that Jay had given her years before and it hung on her, as shapeless as a gunnysack. She might have just dashed out of a restaurant and grabbed someone else's coat. Sports slunk in behind her wearing a tweed coat with raglan sleeves which were too short for him. He stared at the carpets and when he moved his eyes, he concentrated on the blank wall over Jay's shoulder, then his eyes roved to the bedroom, as though he were doing a quick plan of the layout.

"Now what's all this about?'' Rhoda's voice was loud and harsh. She always shouted, Jay remembered, when she was frightened.

"I think you remember Mr. Clay who handled things for me when we drew up the settlement. And this is Mr. Brewster who deals with the divorce actions.'' Brewster nodded his head.

"Don't tell me it's not legal?'' Sports said.

"It's legal all right,'' Clay said, rubbing a hand over his paunch and making a face to indicate that he suffered from dyspepsia.

"So you got your ambulance chasers,'' Sports said. "If you give me warning, I would've had a few boys over. They don't know from legal stuff, but they got other things they use to win arguments.''

"Are you threatening us?'' Brewster asked politely.

"Take it as you like, pal.''

"Shut up, Sports,'' Rhoda said. "Now what's this crap about Neal coming to live with you?'' She flourished a document in Jay's face. "I've got this signed by the judge and I brought it along in case you forgot."

"It's meaningless," Clay said.

She flushed and was about to shout something, when Jay pointed to a chair, and said: "Keep calm, Rhoda. Take a seat and we'll talk about it."

"What's to talk about?"

Clay rubbed his hands together and sat down at a table in the center of the room and opened his briefcase. "I've got a copy of the custody order."

"That and a dime gets you a ride on the subway," Sports said out of the side of his mouth.

"Maybe you ought to hear what I have to say before you waste all your wisecracks?" Clay said sullenly.

"Let's hear," Rhoda said.

"Well, there are two possibilities: either we notify the police that you're operating a gambling house; and the debt you're attempting to repay and the people who are forcing you to repay it are indicted by the grand jury, or we settle the matter amicably."

"Now just a minute, who told you that?" Rhoda protested.

"Neal," Jay replied.

"Well, he's a liar. He always tells lies about me. I'll tell you something for nothing, Jay. He loves you because you've got the money and for no other reason."

"We're digressing," Clay said.

"What do you mean, 'digressing'?" Sports asked.

"Moving from the point."

"He's told you a pack of lies," Rhoda insisted. "Is there a law against having a few friends over for a quiet card evening?"

"You're a liar, Rhoda." Jay paused. "Why's his eye black?"

"Simple," Sports retorted. "When I walked into the bathroom, the door hit him in the face because he was leaving at that moment."

"You mean to say you believe the story he cooked up?" insisted Rhoda.

"He had no reason to lie. Did he make up Latkin, or does he exist? It's a simple matter for us to check," Jay replied hotly. "Rhoda, use your head. If we tell the police, and you're arrested, you'll lose every right to legal custody. And I suppose you've got to think of your husband as well, not that he deserves it. A shylock always has people working for him, and they'll put you both in the hospital, or even worse."

She began to cry, and the streaks of makeup on her face cracked like soft earth in a heavy storm. In a moment her face was unrecognizable and all the men in the room, except for Jay, turned away. He poured her a drink and gave her a handkerchief. She continued to sob, and when she tried to force the drink down her throat, she made a rasping gurgling sound.

"You can't look?" she shrieked. "Turn around, Sports, and see what I look like! You bastard. It's for you that I called my own kid a liar." She threw Jay's handkerchief at him as he moved to take the glass from her. "And you, it's all on account of you, that I am what I am. Dirt you've made out . . . my sister . . . we're all dead . . . we're just waiting to be buried. All the time you win, why you? What makes you a winner?"

"What have I won, Rhoda? Two broken homes, a child that's dangling in thin air, who can't fall because there's no one to catch him? I'm trying to catch him, Rhoda. You can see that?"

She cleared her voice and swallowed the remaining whiskey.

"I'm sorry, Jay. I had no reason to say . . . You've tried to be fair."

"I'll give you ten thousand dollars in cash so that you can get out of this."

"And in return?"

"In return I want the same custodian privileges that you had. He can visit you, you can take him on vacations—"

"—But you have to approve, right?"

"It's the best thing for him, honestly. He's been paying for our mistakes for too many years now."

"Will he live with you?"

"I think a private school's the best thing for him. Until he's got a solid home to come to."

She held out her hand, and Jay held it and shook it. Brewster brought over a sheaf of papers and an open fountain pen.

"You'll have to sign all three copies."

"That's the story of my life—signing things in three places. Won't the judge have to approve?"

"We'll deal with that," Clay said.

"I got into this hole, and I'll have to dig my way out."

"I'll help you any way I can," Jay said.

She took the money and walked over to Sports, who opened the door for her. She shoved the money in his face, and it fell to the floor.

"Here, take it and get out of my home." He stopped to pick up the money and paused at the door, his mouth twisted in a grimace, his lips moving soundlessly and then he left.

The weeks that followed were the happiest Neal had ever known. Terry and he discussed his schoolwork, and for the first time he had the satisfaction of knowing that someone took an interest in what he did and what he would make of his future. The only difficulty he encountered was in getting to and from school, for he was unable to transfer in midterm without losing half a year. Jay dropped him at school in the mornings, but in the afternoon he was forced to take a long subway ride across Manhattan.

On a bitingly cold crisp afternoon towards the end of February, he was surprised to find Terry waiting for him in the lobby of the hotel. Her eyes bulged and she seemed tired and pale.

"Shouldn't you be in bed?"

"I'm not an invalid, just because—" she broke off in mid-sentence as though distracted by some thought which she could not express, and she shifted uneasily against the marble column she had been leaning against. "Let's go to Schrafft's for a hot chocolate," she said, taking him by the arm. "I remember when I was a kid I used to nag my father till he thought he'd go mad to take me there."

They walked down Lexington Avenue and the late afternoon sun fed out slivers of light which brightened up the ice-covered pavements.

"Bracing walks, ta-da, and all that," she trilled. "Hey, you're going too fast."

"Sorry." He hated to displease her, and he realized that he had acted thoughtlessly, for it was slippery. "We could've had it sent up."

"You're not adventurous today."

"I got ninety-five on my algebra exam."

"The only thing I can remember about algebra is that rate times time equals distance. How's that?"

"Very good," he said, smiling broadly, for he liked the way she always implied that he was cleverer than she.

"I'm afraid your father wouldn't know one end of an equation from another, but he can add, boy, can he add."

He pushed open the revolving door and about a hundred old ladies in strange, furry hats, and woolly dresses and long silk scarves, stared at them. Neal felt himself flush as he followed Terry to a corner table.

"What were they looking at?" he said.

"Us. We don't look like brother and sister, and you're too big to be my son, so they must have thought—Well, she's got a lover. A good-looking little boy friend. And that gives them enough conversation for another party."

"Aw Terry, you're kidding?"

She held his hand tightly in her fist and squeezed it.

"You're sweet, Neal." She opened her handbag and fished out something that appeared at first glance to be an advertisement, and passed it to Neal who looked at it cursorily.

"What's this? A school or something?"

"A school or something? Dear boy, it's Carlisle ... *the* school. There are a handful of them in the country: Groton, Andover, Horace Mann, Lawrenceville, and Carlisle."

"What's it got to do with me?"

"Wouldn't you like to be able to go there?"

He picked up the menu and glanced at it for a moment, as the waitress hovered over them.

"I'd like a hot chocolate and a grilled-cheese sandwich," he said.

"Twice," Terry said. "Well, Neal, tell me what you think?

Your term's over in ten days and they've accepted you for their spring term.''

"They have? How?"

"I wrote to the principal about a month ago, explained our situation, and he got in touch with your high school and they forwarded your record.''

"Why there? It's in''—he picked up the prospectus— "Burlington, Vermont. I'll have to live there.''

"But you'll have about four and a half months for vacation and we'll spend the time together.''

His throat tightened and he handed the buff-colored pages back to her.

"Do you want to get rid of me?"

"Oh, boy, of all the silliest. . . . The only reason I thought of it was that my father went there as a boy, and any boy who graduates from Carlisle can have his pick of colleges. You're a bright boy, and they'll give you the best education you could possibly get.''

He considered her point, but remained unconvinced and suspicious. She peered straight at him, and he knew she was being honest, and that her interest and concern were genuine. But again he felt isolated, unwanted.

"We're going to have a particularly nasty court case in about a month and I want you well out of the way.'' She sipped her hot chocolate and he rubbed his hand along the rough-cast wall, his chin dropped into his fur jacket. "Neal, I care . . . I care about what happens to you. When this is all over, we'll buy a house and you can choose between going to Carlisle or living with us. Try it for a term.''

"Does my father know?"

"No, not yet. But the judge suggested that you go to a private school. You can build a new life, and meet new friends.''

"I have friends.''

Her face eased into a smile and she pointed to his untouched sandwich. He lifted it to his mouth reluctantly.

"You're not being forced to do anything. I leave it entirely to you. If you want to go, you can. If not, then we'll have to work something else out. I only want to save you from facing a lot of unpleasantness.''

''Is it your husband?''

She threw her hands in the air with faint irritation and pursed her bloodless lips. He stared at her face as the color drained from it. Her skin was shiny and her green eyes became larger. Her hand shot to her stomach and she gasped.

''Neal, I've got to get to the hospital ... money in my bag ... just leave it.'' Her voice was barely audible and she rose as though drunk, and staggered against her chair, knocking it over into the aisle. Neal rushed over to her, and supported her back because he was afraid she might fall. He threw a dollar on the table and led her to the door.

''I'll get a taxi. Sit down.'' He pointed to a chair by the cashier's desk.

''Can't sit,'' she murmured. ''Fast, Neal.''

He rushed through the revolving door and dashed for a taxi which was cruising along, but just as he gained speed, he felt himself slipping. His legs shot out ahead of him and he crashed to the ground. He lay there for a moment, dazed and rigid, while the high buildings whirled round his half-open eyes; the taxi driver had caught his signal and came over to him and lifted him off his back.

''Boy, that was a beaut. You okay?''

Neal was speechless, then he remembered Terry waiting in the restaurant.

''Wait, you've got to take us to the hospital.''

He ran past the man and brought Terry out. Her face had turned ashen and she could hardly keep her eyes open. The driver helped her into the taxi, and waited to be told where to take them.

''Terry, Terry, which hospital?'' Neal asked with a screeching urgency.

Her forehead was wet and when she opened her eyes they were glassy and her lids flicked over them.

''Sutton Clinic,'' she said breathlessly.

The taxi cut across Lexington Avenue through the mainstream of rush hour traffic. Every few seconds the driver slammed his hand on the horn, and the blaring sound gave the ride an eerie quality which increased Neal's helplessness.

"What should I do, Terry? Tell me," he pleaded.

"It'll be awright, kid. Have her there in five minutes." The car shot through a red light and a great caterwauling whine of horns echoed through the streets. He pulled over at a small nondescript building on Sutton Place and helped Terry out of the car. Neal rushed after them, but a nurse barred his way.

"All right, young man, I'll look after her now." She lifted Terry's arm and put her large white starched arm under her back and limped with her to a room. Neal crept along the corridor and Terry opened her eyes and her mouth contorted into the suggestion of a smile.

"Terry, I'll go to the school, I will."

"Goo' boy," she said through twisted dry lips. "Call your fath—"

Jay and Neal ate a hurried dinner at a small drugstore near the hospital, and Neal was driven back to the Waldorf by Jay's chauffeur. They had been asked to leave the hospital as Terry's labor pains were irregular, and the intervals between them instead of decreasing had lengthened; the obstetrician had assured Jay that his alarm was touching and expected, but that neither Terry nor the baby were in any danger. All this information, delivered in a dry, clinical, patrician voice by Dr. Mill, instead of calming and reassuring him, served only to increase his sense of guilt and anxiety. Legally he had no rights whatever to the child, as Terry was still married to Mitch and she was listed on the register as Mrs. Mitchell Lawson. It was a peculiarly uncomfortable position. To kill time and fortify himself Jay wandered into a small, dank, foul, little bar, off Sutton Place. Half a dozen bar flies too far gone and too apathetic to turn their heads stood at the scratched mahogany bar. A single woman in her thirties with mascara stains riven in her hollow cheeks asked him for a match. She asked him to buy her a drink and he did, then she informed him that her apartment was "a stone's throw away," and he said in a grim, nervous voice:

"Be a lady and don't push your luck."

She mumbled something indistinct—he wasn't even sure that he understood—about being a lady. He moved away from her and waved to the barman for a refill. His temples pulsated irregularly, as though his skull had hiccups, and he studied the movement in the grimy mirror behind the bar. His face was drawn and his eyes had that bloodshot haze which two drinks always gave to them. He realized with some irritation that he had begun to look his age. In the mornings he seemed older, for even though his hair hadn't thinned it was flecked with gray, and the lines on his face had set like stone. He lifted the whiskey and threw his head back. The woman accosted him again as he was about to leave and he had to walk around her.

"You got the concession here? Well, ten or twelve years ago, I would've thought 'maybe,' but I'm getting too old for this sort of thing."

Outside it was snowing. A thin, razorish flurry of white snow drifted through the dark night, whirling eddies which slashed at his face and eyes like small glass splinters. He held up his hand to shield his face, and walked the long block, keeping close to the darkened stores where grimly sculptured stalactites jutted out from above the rolled sun awnings. It was cold and the street was deserted. It had that peculiar hollow silence which he thought must be similar to the death state. His shoes made a scrunching sound over the powdery snow covering the tegument of ice. He shook his collar when he got into the warm anteroom of the hospital, and stomped his feet on the perforated black rubber mat. The nurse had her head down over a magazine as he approached.

"You're not the same one as before," he said.

"It's the night shift," she explained. "Visiting hours are over."

"My—" he stammered. "There's a Mrs. Lawson who's going to have a baby."

"You the father?"

"That's right." She got up off her haunches, and put a long cardboard strip which said YOUR PLACE in the magazine and closed it. "It's down the corridor. Dr. Mill's waiting to see you."

The nurse knocked on Terry's door and the doctor opened it. His angular face was pinched and rubicund, as though nature had deprived him of his rightful physiognomy. He had a long thin nose over which a pair of tortoiseshell glasses slipped whenever he moved his head.

"I'll come into the corridor with you," he said.

Jay twisted his head to look over the doctor's shoulder at Terry, but his view was blocked. The doctor closed the door and lit a cigarette.

"Is she all right?"

"Not very well, I'm afraid."

"You don't mean to say—"

"No, but there were complications, and she's in a delicate condition."

"She won't die?"

"She shouldn't. We've given her medication. I think she's picked up a virus of some kind."

"Don't you know?"

"If we did we wouldn't call them viruses."

"She's given birth, hasn't she?" He felt his muscles tense as Dr. Mill avoided his gaze. His lips were dry. His eyes blinked uncontrollably. The walls of the whitewashed corridor appeared alive with strange moving animals. "Well, tell me," he said in a hoarse voice.

"The baby had cyanosis."

"Is it dead?"

"I'm very sorry to tell you that *she* is."

Jay slumped against the wall, and his shoulder made a dull thud. He pushed himself off the wall with his left hand, and the doctor pointed to a wooden bench a few feet away.

"Let's sit down."

"Does Terry know?"

"No, she was given an anaesthetic, and when she wakes we'll give her a sedative. She won't know till tomorrow."

An overhead light with a green metal band around lit the area by the bench.

"Died, just like that?"

"It was a combination of circumstances. A malformation of

the heart which wasn't detectable in prenatal examination, and when we attempted to do something, an obstruction was also discovered.''

"Did she live at all?"

"For about five minutes."

"Can I see her?"

"I don't think it's a very good idea."

"But one of us should, and she can't."

The doctor nodded his long thin face, and the nurse came up to them.

"I'm just going to take Mr. Blackman along . . ."

In a small room on the second floor adjacent to the operating theater Jay saw the child. The room had no tables and no chairs, only a scratched metal dolly which was used to wheel patients. It was the emptiest room he had ever seen. The child was wrapped in a white sheet, only its head exposed. The face was a sickly bluish color and it hardly seemed human. He lifted the sheet and looked at the body which was slightly lighter in color than the face. It resembled a small rubberized mummy. He lifted the hand and the doctor said:

"We should go now."

Jay dropped the hand and the doctor ushered him out of the room. They walked down the stairs in silence and their clapping footfalls made the quiet almost unbearable to Jay.

"Does a baby have a name in a case like this?"

"If you'd like to give her a name you can."

"Celia. Can you put down Celia?"

"Yes, I will, but as I explained to you when Mrs. Lawson first came to me, the baby's surname must be the mother's because she is still married."

"I guess it doesn't matter now. A girl . . . I wanted a girl."

They stood awkwardly by Terry's door and Jay turned the doorknob.

"I'd rather you didn't go in. Until we're absolutely certain we know exactly what she's got, she shouldn't be disturbed."

"Can I stay all night?"

"You can, but there's really no point. If there's any change in her condition they'll phone me and we've got two doctors on duty all night. You ought to go home and try to sleep. If you come at about ten in the morning, I'll be in a better position to give you more information.''

The city was encrusted with another layer of snow in the morning. A gelid, snarling wind lashed across the high buildings, and the sky color was a strange medley of slaty lead and magenta above the low-moving clouds. Jay sat in the back of the car, silent; his mind suspended in an eerie void. He had canceled all his appointments for the week, and although Marty had been sympathetic when Jay phoned him he couldn't remember what he had said or why he had hung up on him. The car headed over the Williamsburg Bridge down Delancey Street, but all Jay saw was the glass partition and the back of the chauffeur's head. He and Neal had hardly spoken to each other on the ride to Brooklyn, and he was grateful for the boy's tact and restraint. The car turned down Second Avenue and Jay recognized the small catering hall and restaurant where he and Rhoda had met. The name had been changed and a small banner proclaimed: UNDER NEW MANAGEMENT and COMPLETELY AIR CONDITIONED. He lifted a letter which he had not opened out of his briefcase. The return address—J. Parker and Associates—told him that it was from Mitch's lawyers. They were probably demanding a meeting: ''sit around a table and discuss this matter sensibly and informally.'' The car turned into Sutton Place, and the chauffeur opened the door for Jay.

''The flowers are in the front,'' the chauffeur said. ''Shall I take them in?''

''No, I'll do it. You can pick Neal up at four o'clock. I won't need the car.'' Jay took the flowers, three dozen roses, all yellow, her favorite color. He recognized the day nurse at the reception desk and he forced himself to smile at her.

''Good morning, Mr. Blackman,'' she said jauntily, and he felt a bit better. The corridor was just as austere and forbidding in daylight as it had been the previous night. As he followed her white uniform, he had a desperately shrinking sensation which made him cringe. He saw her white back and the walls, which he could not take in except in peripheral vision, were so white that they dazed him. The absence of color shocked him. Three men, one of them Dr. Mill, stood by the door talking in low conspiratorial voices and he strained his ears to hear them. Like butchers waiting for the meat to come in, Jay thought. They stopped talking when they realized he was there. A short, balding man fingered his stethoscope in a nervous, revealing way and stared at him rigidly. No one was talking.

"I'm Dr. Crane," the short, bald man said.

"I phoned you at nine this morning, but your hotel said you'd already left," Mill said. "So there was no way—"

"It's nine forty-five"—Jay brandished his watch—"and you told me to be here at ten. Nothing's happened?"

Nobody answered for a moment, then the three talked at once. Crane's low bass voice cut the others off.

"At eight-thirty this morning Mrs. Lawson became considerably weaker and I was called. She was having trouble breathing so we placed her in an oxygen tent, and although she responded to it for a few minutes—"

"Oh no," Jay gasped. "No, no."

"She died at ten minutes to nine," he continued while the other two nodded their heads and made clucking sounds with their tongues. "No one suspected that she might have a blood clot."

"Suspected?"

"An embolism. A blockage of the blood supply in the lungs. It's very unusual in a case like this, but it does sometimes occur."

"It has—!" Jay heard his voice, but he couldn't believe that it belonged to him. His head reeled and the doctors' white coats had blood stains on them. He pushed through them and opened the door to the room. They stood in the doorway and Mill said:

"I've never had a case like this."

"You've got to inform her husband," Crane replied.

"But surely . . ." the other doctor said.

"The husband has to claim the body."

"Blackman has no legal rights."

"He's a doctor as well," Mill said.

Jay closed the door of the room and went over to the bed. Her features were distorted by the translucent tent-covering and her head hung to one side. He lifted the tent off and it crackled as it slipped to the floor. He shifted her head and brought it to the center of the pillow, then he kissed her on the lips. Her hands were still warm but her lips, dry and cracked, were cold. Her forehead shone and he rubbed his hand over it. Her skin had that niveous slightly bluish cast which he had seen before when his mother was dead. He got up and went to the window and his breath fogged it. There were frozen crystals on the panes and on the small, faded stone ledge icicles hung precariously. He turned back to the bed, blinked, and noticed that when he opened and closed his eyes rapidly, she appeared to move. He knew that it was useless. She was dead. He picked up her hand and slipped his gold marriage band on her finger, for she had stopped wearing one when she left Mitch. The door of the room was pushed open, and the doctors stared at him.

". . . The child last night," one of them said.

He started to walk through them and they moved out of the way.

"We're all deeply sorry, Mr. Blackman. But there's the legal position to consider," Mill said. "We've got to contact Dr. Lawson."

Jay took the lawyer's letter out of his pocket and handed it to him and then walked down the corridor. He was conscious of hunching his shoulders; with a great effort he straightened up. At the front door he paused and looked into the street. It was snowing again. He stood watching a little boy pulling his sled across the street. The metal runners cut furrows in the soft snow and the boy stopped on the corner, looked both ways for cars, then crossed over. The road was empty.

Rhoda wiped her eye with the corner of her handkerchief, and Jay lit a cigarette then crumpled up the pack and dropped it on the platform. The train pulling out of the station unleashed a sharp gust of wind which almost blew her hat off.

"Jay," she said nervously, "Neal doesn't hold anything against me?" She waited for an answer. "He kissed me good-bye and I felt that he had his heart in it."

"You're his mother, he loves you," Jay said tonelessly.

"I've done my best. More, nobody can ask. He'll understand when he's older, won't he? And he'll get a good education at Carlisle. It's the best thing for him . . . to be away," she said, unable to take the thought any further. Jay started for the staircase, and she trailed him. When he reached the top, he waited for her to catch up. The enormous groined vault of Pennsylvania Station encased them like a tomb. The bustling people rushing up and down escalators and the loud clear train announcements disoriented him. She came alongside him; his arms flailed the air and she was overcome by panic. "What's the matter? You okay?"

"For years I've been moving. Years." She looked at him uncomprehendingly. "Moving so fast that I never knew where I was. And now I've stopped. I can't believe it." He gesticulated wildly. "Is this where I am? I mean, has everything I've done and tried to do with my life . . . brought me to this spot and this situation? Because to tell you the truth, Rhoda, I don't know where I am or for that matter what I've done. What's it all about? Do you know? Have I got what I deserved?" He began to walk away, taking long rapid strides, and she chased after him.

In a breathless voice she said:

"You're a survivor, Jay. We both are."

She watched his shape recede in the milling throng of rushing people. They were survivors, but what had happened to their lives? She couldn't answer the question.